ESCAPE

Also by James Clavell

The Asian Saga

Shōgun 1600
Tai-Pan 1841
Gai-Jin 1862
King-Rat 1945
Noble House 1962
Whirlwind 1979

The Children's Story
Thrump-O-Moto
The Art of War by Sun Tzu
(edited by James Clavell)

JAMES CLAVELL

ESCAPE

Hodder & Stoughton

10 9 8 7 6 5 4 3 2 1

A CIP catalogue record for this title is available from the British Library

ISBN 0 340 65415 5

Typeset by Hewer Text Composition Services, Edinburgh
Printed and bound in Great Britain by Mackays of Chatham PLC

Hodder and Stoughton
A division of Hodder Headline PLC
338 Euston Road
London NW1 3BH

For
Shigatsu

BOOK ONE

Friday
FEBUARY 9th, 1979

Tehran – McIver's Apartment: 8:30 P.M. *The three of them were huddled around the big shortwave battery radio, the broadcast signal faint and heterodyning badly. 'This is the BBC World Service, the time is 1700 hours Greenwich Mean Time . . .' 5 p.m. GMT was 8.30 p.m. local time.*

The two men automatically checked their watches. The woman just sipped her vodka martini. Outside the apartment the night was dark. There was a distant burst of gunfire. They took no notice. She sipped again, waiting. Inside the apartment it was cold, the central heating off weeks ago. Their only source of warmth now was a small electric fire that, like the dimmed electric lights, was down to half power.

'. . . at 1500 hours GMT there will be a special report on Persia, now called Iran "From Our Own Correspondent" . . .'

'Good,' she muttered and they all nodded. She was fifty-one, young for her age, attractive, blue-eyed and fair-haired, trim, and she wore dark-rimmed glasses. Genevere McIver, Genny for short.

'. . . but first a summary of the world news: The situation throughout Iran is still very fluid with well-armed, rival factions vying for power: Prime Minister Callaghan announced the Queen will fly to Kuwait on Monday to begin a three-week visit of the Persian Gulf states: in Washington, Pres – '

The transmission faded completely. The taller man cursed.

'Be patient, Charlie,' she said gently. 'It'll come back.'

'Yes, Genny, you're right,' Charlie Pettikin answered. He was forty-six, ex-RAF, originally from South Africa, his hair dark and grey flecked, senior pilot and chief of their helicopter training programme for the Iranian air force. Another burst of machine-gun fire in the distance.

'A bit dicey sending the Queen to Kuwait now, isn't it?' Genny said. Kuwait was an immensely wealthy oil sheikdom just across the Gulf, flanking Saudi Arabia and Iraq. 'Pretty stupid at a time like this, isn't it?'

'Bloody stupid, bloody government's got its head all the way up,' Duncan McIver, her husband, said sourly. 'All the bloody way to Aberdeen.'

She laughed. 'That's a pretty long way, Duncan.'

'Not far enough for me, Gen!' McIver was head of S-G Helicopters in Iran, a British company that had been servicing Iran for many years, mostly the oil industry. He was a heavyset man of fifty-eight, built like a boxer, with grizzled grey hair. 'Callaghan's a bloody twit and th – ' He stopped, hearing faint rumbles of a heavy vehicle going past in the street below. The apartment was on the top

floor, the fifth, of the modern residential building in the northern suburbs of Tehran. Another vehicle passed.

'*Sounds like more tanks,*' *she said.*

'*They're tanks, Genny,*' *Charlie Pettikin said.*

'*Perhaps we're in for another bad one,*' *she said.*

For weeks now every day had been bad. First it was martial law in September when public gatherings had been banned and a 9.00 p.m. to 5.00 a.m. curfew imposed by the Shah that had only further inflamed the people. Particularly in the capital Tehran. There had been much killing, and more violence, the Shah vacillating, then abruptly cancelling martial law in the last days of December and appointing Bakhtiar, a moderate, prime minister, making concessions, and then, incredibly, on January 16 leaving Iran for 'a holiday'. Then Bakhtiar forming his government and Ayatollah Khomeini – still in exile in France – decrying it and anyone who supported it. Riots increasing, the death toll increasing. Bakhtiar trying to negotiate with the Ayatollah who refused to see him or talk to him, the people restive, the army restive, then closing all airports against him, then opening them to him. Then, equally incredibly, eight days ago on February 1, the Ayatollah returning. The revolution began in earnest.

'*I need another drink,*' *she said and got up to hide a shiver.* '*Can I fix yours, Duncan?*'

'*Thanks, Gen.*'

She went towards the kitchen for some ice. '*Charlie?*'

'*I'm fine, Genny, I'll get it.*'

She stopped as the radio came back strongly: '. . . *China reports that there have been serious border clashes with Vietnam and denounces . . .*' *Again the signal vanished, leaving only static. More machine-gun fire, closer this time.*

After a moment Pettikin said, '*I had a drink at the Press club on the way here. There's a rumour that Prime Minister Bakhtiar's preparing a showdown. Another was that there's heavy fighting in Meshed after a mob strung up the chief of police and half a dozen of his men.*'

'*Terrible,*' *she said.*

'*I wish to God they'd all settle down. Iran's a great place and I don't plan to move.*' *The radio came in for a second then went back to emitting static.* '*It must be sunspots.*'

'*Enough to make you want to spit blood,*' *McIver said. Like Pettikin, he was ex-RAF. He had been the first pilot to join S-G, and now as director of Iran operations, he was also managing director of IHC – Iran Helicopters Company – the fifty-fifty joint venture with the obligatory Iranian partners that S-G leased their helicopters to, the company that got their contracts, made their deals, held the money – without whom there would be no Iranian operations. He leaned forward to adjust the tuning, changed his mind.*

'*It'll come back, Duncan,*' *Genny said.* '*I agree Callaghan's a twit.*'

He smiled at her. They had been married thirty years. '*You're not bad, Gen. Not bad at all.*'

'*For that you can have another whisky.*'

'*Thanks, but this time put some in with the wat –* '

'. . . *deteriorating situation in Iran, a carrier force has been ordered to proceed from the Philip –* ' *The announcer's voice was drowned by another station, then both faded.*

In silence they waited, very tense. The two men glanced at each other, trying to hide their shock. Genny walked over to the almost empty whisky bottle that was on the sideboard. Also on the sideboard, taking up most of the space, was the HF, McIver's communicator with their helicopter bases all over Iran – conditions permitting. The apartment was big and comfortable, with three bedrooms and two sitting rooms. For the last few months, since martial law and the subsequent street violence, Pettikin had moved in with them – he was single now, divorced a year ago – and this arrangement pleased them all.

A slight wind rattled the windowpanes. Genny glanced outside. There were a few dim lights from the houses opposite, no streetlamps. The low rooftops of the city stretched away limitlessly. Snow on them, and on the ground. Most of the five to six million people who lived here lived in squalor. But this area, to the north of Tehran, the best area, where most foreigners and well-to-do Iranians lived, was well policed.

She made the drink light, mostly soda, and brought it back. 'There's going to be civil war. There's no way we can continue here.'

'We'll be all right, Carter can't let . . .' *Abruptly the lights died and the electric fire went out.*

'Bugger,' *Genny said.* 'Thank God we've the butane cooker.'

'Maybe the power cut'll be a short one.' *McIver helped her light the candles that were already in place. He glanced at the front door. Beside it was a five-gallon can of petrol – their emergency fuel. He hated the idea of having petrol in the apartment, particularly when they had to use candles most evenings. But for weeks now it had taken from five to twenty-four hours of lining up at a petrol station and even then the Iranian attendant would more than likely turn you away because you were a foreigner. Many times their car had had its tank drained – locks made no difference. They were luckier than most because they had access to airfield supplies, but for the normal person, particularly a foreigner, the queues made life miserable. Black-market petrol cost as much as 160 rials a litre – $2 a litre, $8 a gallon, if you could get it.*

'You were saying about Carter?'

'The trouble is if Carter panics and puts in even a few troops – or planes – to support a military coup, it will blow the top off everything. Everyone'll scream like a scalded cat, the Soviets most of all, and they'll have to react and Iran'll become the set piece for World War Three.'

McIver said, 'We've been fighting World War Three, Charlie, since forty-five. . . .'

A burst of static cut him off, then the announcer came back again. '. . . *for illicit intelligence work: It is reported from Kuwait by the chief of staff of the armed forces that Kuwait has received large shipments of arms from the Soviet Union. . . .*'

'Christ,' *both men muttered.*

'. . . *President Carter reiterated the U.S. support for Iran's Bakhtiar government and the "constitutional process". Throughout the British Isles exceptionally heavy snow, gales and floods have disrupted much of the country, closing Heathrow Airport and grounding all aircraft. And that ends the news summary. You're listening to the World Service of the BBC. And now a report from our farm correspondent, "Poultry and pigs". We begin . . .'*

McIver reached over and snapped it off. 'Bloody hell, the whole world's falling apart and the BBC gives us pigs.'

Genny laughed. 'What would you do without the BBC, the telly, and the football pools? Gales and floods.' She picked up the phone on the off chance. It was dead as usual. For months it had been completely unreliable, with no dial tone that would miraculously reappear for no apparent reason. 'Hope the kids are all right.' They had a son and a daughter, both married now and on their own and two grandchildren, one from each. 'Little Karen catches colds so badly and Sarah! Even at twenty-three she needs reminding to dress properly! Will that child never grow up?'

Pettikin said, 'It's rotten not being able to phone when you want.'

'Yes. Anyway, it's time to eat. The market was almost empty today for the third day on the trot. So it was a choice of roast ancient mutton again with rice, or a special. I chose the special and used the last two cans. I've corned beef pie, cauliflower au gratin, and treacle tart, and a surprise hors d'oeuvre.' She took a candle and went off to the kitchen and shut the door behind her.

'Wonder why we always get cauliflower au gratin?' McIver watched the candlelight flickering on the kitchen door. 'Hate the bloody stuff! I've told her fifty times . . .' The nightscape suddenly caught his attention. He walked over to the window. The city was empty of light because of the power cut. But southeastward now a red glow lit up the sky. 'Jaleh, again,' he said simply.

A few months ago, tens of thousands of people had taken to the streets of Tehran to protest the Shah's imposition of martial law, particularly in Jaleh – a poor, densely populated suburb – where bonfires were lit and barricades of burning tyres set up. When the security forces arrived, the raging, milling crowd shouting 'Death to the Shah' refused to disperse. Tear gas didn't work. Guns did. Estimates of the death toll ranged from an official 97 to 2,000 to 3,000 by the militant opposition groups.

Unexpectedly the telephone jangled, startling them.

'Five pounds it's a bill collector,' Pettikin said, smiling at Genny who came out of the kitchen, equally startled at hearing the bell.

'That's no bet, Charlie!' Banks had been on strike and closed for two months in response to Khomeini's call for a general strike, so no one – individuals, companies, or even the government – had been able to get any cash out and most Iranians used cash and not cheques.

McIver picked up the phone not knowing what to expect. Or who. 'Hello.'

'Good God, the bloody thing's working,' the voice said. 'Duncan, can you hear me?'

'Yes, yes, I can. Just. Who's this?'

'Talbot, George Talbot at the British embassy. Sorry, old boy, but the stuff is hitting the fan. Khomeini's named his own prime minister and called for Bakhtiar's resignation or else. About a million people are in the streets of Tehran right now *looking for trouble. We've just heard there's a revolt of airmen at Doshan Tappeh – and Bakhtiar's said if they don't quit he'll order in the Immortals.'* The Immortals were crack units of the fanatically pro-Shah Imperial Guards. *'Her Majesty's Government, along with the U.S., Canadian, et al., are advising all non-essential nationals to leave the country at once. . . .'*

McIver tried to keep the shock off his face and mouthed to the others, 'Talbot at the embassy.'

'. . . Yesterday an American of ExTex Oil and an Iranian oil official were ambushed and killed by "unidentified gunmen" in the southwest, near Ahwaz' – McIver's heart skipped another beat – *'. . . you're operating down there still, aren't you?'*

'Near there, at Bandar-e Delam on the coast,' McIver said, no change in his voice.

'How many British nationals do you have here, excluding dependents?'

McIver thought a moment. 'Forty-five, out of our present complement of sixty-seven, that's twenty-six pilots, thirty-six mechanic/engineers, five admin, which's pretty basic for us.'

'Who're the others?'

'Four Americans, three German, two French, and one Finn – all pilots. Two American mechanics. We'd treat all our lads as British if necessary.'

'Dependents?'

'Four, all wives, no children. We got the rest out three weeks ago. Genny's still here, one American at Kowiss and two Iranians.'

'You'd better get both the Iranian wives into their embassies tomorrow – with their marriage certificates. They're in Tehran?'

'One is, one's in Tabriz, Erikki's wife Azadeh.'

'You'd better get them new passports as fast as possible.'

By Iranian law all Iranian nationals coming back into the country had to surrender their passports to Immigration at the point of entry, to be held until they wished to leave again. To leave they had to apply in person to the correct government office for an exit permit for which they needed a valid identity card, a satisfactory reason for wanting to go abroad, and, if by air, a valid prepaid ticket for a specific flight. To get this exit permit might take days or weeks. Normally.

Talbot was saying *'Fortunately we don't have any squabbles with the Ayatollah, Bakhtiar, or the generals. Still, any foreigners are liable for a lot of flak so we're formally advising you to send dependents off, lickety-split, and cut the others down to basic – for the time being. The airport's going to be a mess from tomorrow on – we estimate there are still about five thousand expats, most of them American – but we've asked British Airways to cooperate and increase flights for us and our nationals. The bugger of it is that all civilian air traffic controllers are still totally out on strike, Bakhtiar's ordered in the military controllers and they're even more punctilious if that's possible. We're sure it's going to be the exodus over again.'*

Last month a rampaging mob went berserk in the industrial city of Isfahan, with its enormous steel complex, petrochemical refinery, ordnance and helicopter factories, and where a large proportion of the 50,000-odd American expats and their dependents worked and lived. The mobs burned banks – the Koran forbade lending *money for profit – liquor stores – the Koran forbade the drinking of alcohol – and two movie houses – places of 'pornography and Western propaganda', always particular targets for the fundamentalists – then attacked factory installations, peppered the four-storey Grumman Aircraft HQ with Molotov cocktails, and burned it to the ground. That precipitated the 'exodus'.*

Thousands converged on Tehran Airport, clogging it as would-be passengers scrambled for the few available seats, turning the airport and its lobbies into a disaster area. Men, women and children camping there, afraid to lose their places. No schedules, no priorities, each airplane overbooked twenty times, no computer ticketing, just slowly handwritten by a few sullen officials – most of whom were openly hostile and non-English-speaking. Quickly the airport became foul and the mood ugly.

Adding to the chaos were thousands of Iranians, all hoping to flee while there was still time to flee. The unscrupulous and the wealthy jumped the queues. Many an official became rich and then more greedy and richer still. Then the air traffic controllers struck, shutting down the airport completely.

At length most foreigners who wanted to leave left. The Ayatollah had said, 'If the foreigner wants to leave, let him leave; it is American materialism that is the Great Satan . . .' Those who stayed to keep the oil fields serviced, airplanes flying, nuclear plants abuilding, chemical plants working, tankers moving – and to protect their gigantic investments – kept a low profile.

McIver held the phone closer to his ear as the volume slipped a fraction, afraid that the connection would vanish. 'Yes, George, you were saying?'

Talbot continued: 'I was just saying, Duncan, we're quite sure everything's going to work out eventually. There's no way in the world the pot will completely blow up. An unofficial source says a deal's already in place for the Shah to abdicate in favour of his son Reza – the compromise HM Government advocates. The transition to constitutional government – helped by the long overdue military coup – may be a bit wobbly but nothing to worry about. Sorry, got to dash – let me know what you decide an – '

The phone went dead.

McIver cursed, jiggled the connectors to no avail, and told Genny and Charlie what Talbot had said. Genny smiled sweetly. 'Don't look at me, the answer's no. I agr – '

'But, Gen, Tal – '

'I agree the others should go but this one's staying. Food's almost ready.' She went back to the kitchen and closed the door, cutting off further argument.

'Well she's bloody going and that's it,' McIver said.

'My year's salary says she won't – until you leave. Why don't you go for God's sake? I can look after everything.'

'No. Thanks, but no.' Then McIver beamed in the semi-darkness. 'Actually it's like being back in the war, isn't it? Back in the bloody blackout. Nothing to worry about except get with it and look after the troops and obey orders.' He watched Pettikin for a while, trying to raise their base at Bandar-e Delam. 'Did you know the American who was killed, Stanson?'

'No. You?'

'Yes. Just an ordinary sort of fellow, an area manager for ExTex. I met him once. There was a story he was CIA but I think that was just a rumour.' McIver frowned at his glass. 'Talbot was right about one thing: we're bloody lucky to be British. Tough on the Yanks. Not fair.'

'Yes, but you've covered ours as best you can.'

'Hope so.' When the Shah had left and violence everywhere increased, McIver had issued British IDs to all Americans. 'They should be all right unless the Revolutionary Guards, police, or SAVAK check them against their licences.' By Iranian law all foreigners had to have a current visa, which had to be cancelled before they could leave the country, a current ID card giving their corporate affiliate – and all pilots a current annual Iran pilot's licence. For a further measure of safety McIver had had corporate IDs made and signed by the chief of their Iranian partners in Tehran. So far there had been no problems.

Pettikin was trying to call Bandar-e Delam on the HF with no success. 'We'll try later,' McIver said. 'All bases'll be listening out at 0830 – that'll give us time to decide what to do. Christ, it's going to be bloody difficult. What do you think? Status quo, except for dependents?'

Very concerned, Pettikin got up and took a candle and peered at the operations map pinned to the wall. It showed the status of their bases, crew, ground staff, and aircraft. Most were self-contained with transport, spares and repair facilities. The bases were scattered over Iran, from air force and army training bases at Tehran and Isfahan, to a logging operation in Tabriz in the northwest, a uranium survey team near the Afghan border, from a pipeline survey on the Caspian, to oil rig operations on or near the Gulf and the Strait of Hormuz. Of these only five were operational now: 'We've fifteen 212s, including two non-operational on their two-thousand-hour checks, seven 206s, and three Alouettes, all supposed to be working at the moment. . . .'

'And all leased on binding legal contracts, none of which have been rescinded, but none of which we're being paid for,' McIver said testily. 'We can't even legally remove any one of them without the approval of the contractor, or our dear partners' approval – not unless we could declare force majeure.'

'There isn't any yet. It has to be status quo, as long as we can. Talbot sounded confident. Status quo.'

'I wish it was status quo, Charlie. My God, this time last year we had almost forty 212s working and all the rest.' McIver poured himself another whisky.

'You'd better go easy,' Pettikin said quietly. 'Genny'll give you hell. You know your blood pressure's up and you're not to drink.'

'It's medicinal, for Christ's sweet sake.' A candle guttered and went out. McIver got up and lit another and went back to staring at the map. 'I think we'd better get Azadeh and Erikki, our Flying Finn back. His 212's on its fifteen-hundred-hour so he could be spared for a couple of days.' This was Captain Erikki Yokkonen and his Iranian wife, Azadeh, and their base was near Tabriz in East Azerbaijan Province, to the far northwest, near the Soviet border. 'Why not take a 206 and fetch them? That'd save him three hundred and fifty miles of lousy driving and we've got to take him some spares.'

Pettikin was beaming. 'Thanks, I could do with an outing. I'll file a flight *plan by HF tonight and leave at dawn, refuel at Bandar-e Pahlavi, and buy us some caviar.'*

'*Dreamer. But Gen'd like that. You know what I think of the stuff.*' McIver *turned away from the map. 'We're very exposed, Charlie, if things got dicey.'*

'*Only if it's in the cards.*'

Chapter 1

At Base Tabriz One: 11:05 P.M. Erikki Yokkonen was naked, lying in the sauna that he had constructed with his own hands, the temperature 107 degrees Fahrenheit, the sweat pouring off him, his wife Azadeh nearby, also lulled by the heat. He lay on one arm and looked at her. She was lying on a thick towel on the bench opposite. Her eyes were closed and he saw her breast rising and falling and the beauty of her – raven hair, chiselled Aryan features, lovely body, and milky skin – and as always he was filled with the wonder of her, so small against his six foot four. He was Finnish by birth, thirty-seven, American and British schooled and trained, and like most helicopter pilots, cosmopolitan.

Tonight had been grand with lots of food and two bottles of the best Russian vodka that he had purchased black market in Tabriz and had shared with his two English engineers, and their station manager, Ali Dayati. 'Now we'll have sauna,' he had said to them just before midnight. But they had declined, as usual, with hardly enough strength to reel off to their own cabins. 'Come on, Azadeh!'

'Not tonight, please, Erikki,' she had said, but he had just laughed, wrapped her fur coat around her clothes, and carried her through the front door of their cabin, out past the pine trees heavy with snow, the air just below freezing. She was easy to carry, and he went into the little hut that abutted the back of their cabin, into the warmth of the changing area and then, unclothed, into the sauna itself. And now they lay there, Erikki at ease, Azadeh, even after a year of marriage, still not quite used to the nightly ritual.

Gods of my ancestors, thank you for giving me such a woman, he thought. For a moment he could not remember which language he was thinking in. He was quadrilingual, Finnish, Swedish, Russian and English. What does it matter he told himself, giving himself back to the heat, letting his mind waft with the steam that rose from the stones he had laid so carefully. It satisfied him greatly that he had built his sauna himself – as a man should – hewing the logs as his ancestors had done for centuries.

This was the first thing he had done when he was posted here four years ago – to select and fell the trees. The others had thought him crazy. He had shrugged good-naturedly. 'Without a sauna life's nothing. First you build the sauna, then the house; without sauna a house is not a house; you English, you know nothing – not about life.' He had been tempted to tell them that he had been born in a sauna, like many Finns – and why not, how sensible when you think of it, the warmest place in the home, the cleanest, quietest, most revered. He had never told them, only Azadeh. She had understood. Ah, yes, he thought, greatly content, she understands everything.

Outside, the threshold of the forest was silent, the night sky cloudless, the stars very bright, snow deadening sound. Half a mile away was the only road through the mountains. The road meandered northwest to Tabriz, ten miles away, thence northwards to the Soviet border a few miles farther on. Southeast it curled away over the mountains, at length to Tehran, 350 miles away.

The base, Tabriz One, was home for two pilots – the other was on leave in England – two English engineers, the rest Iranians: two cooks, eight day labourers, the radio op, and the station manager. Over the hill was their village of Abu-Mard and, in the valley below, the wood-pulp factory belonging to the forestry monopoly, Iran-Timber, they serviced under contract. The 212 took loggers and equipment into the forests, helped build camps and plan the few roads that could be built, then serviced the camps with replacement crews and equipment and flew the injured out. For most of the landlocked camps the 212 was their only link with the outside, and the pilots were venerated. Erikki loved the life and the land, so much like Finland that sometimes he would dream he was home again.

His sauna made it perfect. The tiny, two-room hut at the back of their cabin was screened from the other cabins, and built traditionally with lichen between the logs for insulation, the wood fire that heated the stones well ventilated. Some of the stones, the top layer, he had brought from Finland. His grandfather had fished them from the bottom of a lake, where all the best sauna stones come from, and had given them to him on his last home leave eighteen months ago. 'Take them, my son, and with them surely there'll go a good Finnish sauna tonto' – the little brown elf that is the spirit of the sauna – 'though what you want to marry one of those foreigners for and not your own kind, I really don't know.'

'When you see her, Grandfather, you'll worship her also. She has blue-green eyes and dark-dark hair an – '

'If she gives you many sons – well, we'll see. It's certainly long past the time you should be married, a fine man like you, but a foreigner? You say she's a schoolteacher?'

'She's a member of Iran's Teaching Corps, they're young people, men and women, volunteers as a service to the state, who go to villages and teach villagers and children how to read and write, but mostly the children. The Shah and the Empress started the corps a few years ago, and Azadeh joined when she was twenty-one. She comes from Tabriz where I work, teaches in our village in a makeshift school and I met her seven months and three days ago. She was twenty-four then. . . .'

Erikki glowed, remembering the first time he ever saw her, neat in her uniform, her hair cascading, sitting in a forest glade surrounded by children, then her smiling up at him, seeing the wonder in her eyes at his size, knowing at once that this was the woman he had waited his life to find. He was thirty-six then. Ah, he thought, watching her lazily, once more blessing the forest tonto – spirit – that had guided him to that part of the forest. Only three more months then two whole months of leave. It will be good to be able to show her Suomi – Finland.

'It's time, Azadeh, darling,' he said.

'No, Erikki, not yet, not yet,' she said half asleep, drowsed by the heat but not by alcohol, for she did not drink. 'Please, Erikki, not y – '

'Too much heat isn't good for you,' he said firmly. They always spoke English together, though she was also fluent in Russian – her mother was half Georgian, coming from the border area where it was useful and wise to be bilingual. Also she spoke Turkish, the language most used in this part of Iran, Azerbaijan, and of course Farsi. Apart from a few words, he spoke no Farsi or Turkish. He sat up and wiped the sweat off, at peace with the world, then leaned over and kissed her. She kissed him back and trembled as his hands sought her and hers sought him back. 'You're a bad man, Erikki,' she said, then stretched gloriously.

'Ready?'

'Yes.' She clung to him as he lifted her so easily into his arms, then walked out of the sauna into the changing area, then opened the door and went outside into the freezing air. She gasped as the cold hit her and hung on as he scooped up some snow and rubbed it over her, making her flesh tingle and burn but not painfully. In seconds she was glowing within and without. It had taken her a whole winter to get used to the snow bath after the heat. Now, without it, the sauna was incomplete. Quickly she did the same for him, then rushed happily back into the warm again, leaving him to roll and thrash in the snow for a few seconds. He did not notice the group of men standing in a shocked group up the rise, half-hidden under the trees beside the path, fifty yards away. Just as he was closing the door he saw them. Fury rushed through him. He slammed the door.

'Some villagers are out there. They must have been watching us. Everyone knows this is off limits!' She was equally enraged and they dressed hurriedly. He pulled on his fur boots and heavy sweater and pants and grabbed the huge axe and rushed out. The men were still there and he charged them with a roar, his axe on high. They scattered as he whirled at them, then one of them raised the machine gun and let off a burst into the air that echoed off the mountainside. Erikki skidded to a halt, his rage obliterated. Never before had he been threatened with guns, or had one levelled at his stomach.

'Put axe down,' the man said in halting English, 'or I kill you.'

Erikki hesitated. At that moment Azadeh came charging between them and knocked the gun away and began shouting in Turkish: 'How dare you come here! How dare you have guns – what are you, bandits? This is our land – get off our land or I'll have you put in jail!' She had wrapped her heavy fur coat over her dress but was shaking with rage.

'This is the land of the people,' the man said sullenly, keeping out of range. 'Cover your hair, woman, cover y – '

'Who're you? You're not of my village! Who are you?'

'I'm Mahmud, a mullah in Tabriz.'

'Your accent isn't Tabrizi. What are you, a false mullah who tries to marry the Koran and Marx and serves foreign masters?'

'We serve God and the masses. I'm not one of your lackeys,' he said angrily and jumped aside as Erikki lunged at him. The man with the gun was off balance but another man, safely away, cocked his rifle: 'By God and the Prophet, stop the foreign pig or I'll blow you both to the hell you deserve!'

'Erikki, wait! Leave these dogs to me!' Azadeh called out in English, then shouted at them, 'What do you want here? This is our land, the land of my father Abdollah Khan, Khan of the Gorgons, kin to the Qajars who've ruled here for centuries.' Her eyes had adjusted to the darkness now and she peered at them. There were ten of them, all young men, all armed, all strangers, all except one, the kalandar – chief – of their village. 'Kalandar, how dare you come here!'

'I'm sorry, Highness,' he said apologetically, 'but the mullah said I was to lead him here by this trail and not by the main path and so – '

'What do you want, parasite?' she said, turning on the mullah.

'Show respect, woman,' the man said even more angrily. 'Soon we'll be in command. The Koran has laws for nakedness and loose living: stoning and the lash.'

'The Koran has laws for false mullahs and trespass and bandits and threatening peaceful people, and rebellion against their chiefs and liege lords. I'm not one of your frightened illiterates! I know you for what you are and what you've always been, the parasites of the villages and the people. *What do you want?*'

From the base, people were hurrying up with flashlights. At their head were the two bleary-eyed engineers, Dibble and Arberry, with Ali Dayati carefully in tow. All were sleep ruffled, hastily dressed, and anxious. 'What's going on?' Dayati demanded, thick glasses on his nose, peering at them. His family had been protected by and had served the Gorgon Khans for years. 'Who ar – '

'These dogs,' Azadeh began hotly, 'came out of the nigh – '

'Hold your tongue, woman,' the mullah said angrily, then turned on Dayati. 'Who're you?'

When Dayati saw the man was a mullah, his demeanour changed and at once he became deferential. 'I'm . . . I'm Iran-Timber's manager here, Excellency. What's the matter, please, what can I do for you?'

'The helicopter. At dawn I want it for a flight around the camps.'

'I'm sorry, Excellency, the machine is in pieces for an overhaul. It's the foreigner's policy an – '

Azadeh interrupted angrily, 'Mullah, by what right do you dare to come here in the middle of the night to – '

'Please, Highness,' Dayati said, pleading with her. 'Please leave this to me, please, I beg you.'

But she began to rage and the mullah to rage back, and the others joined in, the mood becoming ugly, until Erikki raised his axe and let out a bellow of rage, infuriated that he could not understand what was being said. The silence was sudden, then another man cocked his machine pistol.

'What's this bastard want, Azadeh?' Erikki said.

She told him.

'Dayati, tell him he can't have my 212 and to get off our land now or I'll send for the police.'

'Please, Captain, please allow me to deal with it, Captain,' Dayati said, sweating with anxiety, before Azadeh could interrupt. 'Please, Highness, please leave now.' Then turned to the two engineers, 'It's all right, you can go back to bed. I'll deal with it.'

It was then that Erikki noticed Azadeh was still barefoot. He scooped her up into his arms. 'Dayati, you tell that *matyeryebyets* and all of them if they come here again at night I'll break their necks – and if he or anyone touches one hair of my woman's head I'll crawl into hell after him if need be.' He went off, massive in his rage, the two engineers following.

A voice in Russian stopped him. 'Captain Yokkonen, perhaps I could have a word with you in a moment?'

Erikki looked back. Azadeh, still in his arms, was tense. The man stood at the back of the pack, difficult to see, seemingly not very different from the others, wearing a nondescript parka. 'Yes,' Erikki told him in Russian, 'but don't bring a gun into my house, or a knife.' He stalked off.

The mullah went closer to Dayati, his eyes stony. 'What did the foreign devil say, eh?'

'He was rude, all foreigners are rude, Her High – the woman was rude too.'

The mullah spat in the snow. 'The Prophet set laws and punishments against such conduct, the People have laws against hereditary wealth and stealing lands, the land belongs to the People. Soon correct laws and punishments will govern us all, at long last, and Iran will be at peace.' He turned to the others. 'Naked in the snow! Flaunting herself in the open against all the laws of modesty. Harlot! What are the Gorgons but lackeys of the traitor Shah and his dog Bakhtiar, eh?' His eyes went back to Dayati. 'What lies are you telling about the helicopter?'

Trying to hide his fear, Dayati said at once that the fifteen-hundred-hour check was according to foreign regulations imposed upon him and the aircraft and further ordered by the Shah and the government.

'Illegal government,' the mullah interrupted.

'Of course, of course illegal,' Dayati agreed at once and nervously led them into the hangar and lit the lights – the base had its own small generating system and was self-contained. The engines of the 212 were laid out neatly, piece by piece, in regimented lines. 'It's nothing to do with me, Excellency, the foreigners do what they like.' Then he added quickly, 'And although we all know Iran-Timber belongs to the People, the Shah took all the money. I've no authority over them, foreigner devils or their regulations. There's nothing I can do.'

'When will it be airworthy?' the Russian-speaking man asked in perfect Turkish.

'The engineers promise two days,' Dayati said and prayed silently, very afraid, though he tried hard not to show it. It was clear to him now that these men were leftist mujhadin believers in the Soviet-sponsored theory that Islam and Marx were compatible. 'It's in the hands of God. Two days; the foreign engineers are waiting for some spares that're overdue.'

'What are they?'

Nervously he told him. They were some minor parts and a tail rotor blade.

'How many hours do you have on the rotor blade?'

Dayati checked the log book, his fingers trembling. '1073.'

'God is with us,' the man said, then turned to the mullah. 'We could safely use the old one for fifty hours at least.'

'But the life of the blade . . . the airworthy certificate's invalidated,' Dayati said without thinking. 'The pilot wouldn't fly because air regulations requi – '

'Satan's regulations.'

'True,' the Russian speaker interrupted, 'some of them. But laws for safety are important to the People, and even more important, God laid down rules in the Koran for camels and horses and how to care for them, and these rules can apply equally to airplanes which also are the gift of God and also carry us to do God's work. We must, therefore, care for them correctly. Don't you agree, Mahmud?'

'Of course,' the mullah said impatiently and his eyes bore into Dayati who began to tremble. 'I will return in two days, at dawn. Let the helicopter be ready and the pilot ready to do God's work for the People. I will visit every camp in the mountains. Are there other women here?'

'Just . . . just two wives of the labourers and . . . my wife.'

'Do they wear chador and veil?'

'Of course,' Dayati lied instantly. To wear the veil was against the law of Iran. Reza Shah had outlawed the veil in 1936, made the chador a matter of choice and Mohammed Shah had further enfranchised women in '64.

'Good. Remind them God and the People watch, even in the foreigner's vile domain.' Mahmud turned on his heel and stomped off, the others going with him.

When he was alone, Dayati wiped his brow, thankful that he was one of the Faithful and that now his wife would again wear the chador, would be obedient, and act as his mother with modesty and not wear jeans like Her Highness.

In Erikki's Cabin: 11:23 P.M. The two men sat at the table opposite each other in the main room of the cabin. When the man had knocked on the door, Erikki had told Azadeh to go into the bedroom but he had left the inner door open so that she could hear. He had given her the rifle that he used for hunting. 'Use it without fear. If he comes into the bedroom, I am already dead,' he had said, his pukoh knife sheathed under his belt in the centre of his back. The pukoh knife was a haft knife and the weapon of all Finns. It was considered unlucky – and dangerous – for a man not to carry one. In Finland it was against the law to wear one openly – that might be considered a challenge. But everyone carried one, and always in the mountains. Erikki's matched his size.

'So, Captain, I apologise for the intrusion.' The man was dark-haired, a little under six feet, in his thirties, his face weather-beaten, his eyes dark and Slavic – Mongol blood somewhere in his heritage. 'My name is Fedor Rakoczy.'

'Rakoczy was a Hungarian revolutionary,' Erikki said curtly. 'And from your accent you're Georgian. Rakoczy's not Georgian. What's your real name – and KGB rank?'

The man laughed. 'It is true my accent is Georgian and that I am Russian from Georgia, from Tbilisi. My grandfather came from Hungary but he was no relation to the revolutionary who in ancient times became prince of Transylvania. Nor was he Muslim, like my father and me. There, you see, we both know a little of our history, thanks be to God,' he said pleasantly. 'I'm an engineer on the Iran-Soviet natural gas pipeline, based just over the border at Astara on the Caspian – and pro-Iran, pro-Khomeini, blessings be upon him, anti-Shah and anti-American.'

He was glad that he had been briefed about Erikki Yokkonen. Part of his cover story was true. He certainly came from Georgia, from Tbilisi, but he was not a Muslim, nor was his real name Rakoczy. His real name was Igor Mzytryk and he was a captain in the KGB, a specialist attached to the 116th Airborne Division that was deployed just across the border, north of Tabriz, one of the hundreds of undercover agents who had infiltrated northern Iran for months and now operated almost freely. He was thirty-four, a KGB career officer like his father and he had been in Azerbaijan for six months. His English was good, his Farsi and Turkish fluent, and although he could not fly he knew much about the piston-driven Soviet army close support helicopters of his division. 'As to my rank,' he added in his most gentle voice, 'it is friend. We Russians are good friends of Finns, aren't we?'

'Yes, yes that's true. Russians are, not communists – Soviets. Holy Russia was a friend in the past, yes when we were a Grand Duchy of Russia. Atheist Soviet Russia was friendly after 1917 when we became independent. Soviet Russia is now. Yes, now. But not in '39. Not in the Winter War. No, not then.'

'Nor were you in '41,' Rakoczy said sharply. 'In '41 you went to war against us with the stinking Nazis, you sided with them against us.'

'True, but only to take back our land, our Karelian, our province you'd stolen from us. We didn't walk on to Leningrad as we could have done.' Erikki could feel the knife in the centre of his back and he was very glad of it. 'Are you armed?'

'No. You said not to come armed. My gun is outside the door. I have no pukoh knife nor need to use one. By Allah, I'm a friend.'

'Good. A man has need of friends.' Erikki watched the man, loathing what he represented: the Soviet Russia that, unprovoked, had invaded Finland in '39 the moment Stalin had signed the Soviet-German non-aggression pact. Finland's little army had fought back alone. They had beaten off the Soviet hordes for one hundred days in the Winter War and then they had been overrun. Erikki's father had been killed defending Karelian, the southern and eastern province, where the Yokkonens had lived for centuries. At once Soviet Russia had annexed the province. At once all Finns left. All of them. Not one would stay under a Soviet flag so the land became barren of Finns. Erikki was just ten months old then and in that exodus thousands died. His mother had died. It was the worst winter in living memory.

And in '45, Erikki thought, bottling his rage, in '45 America and England betrayed us and gave our lands to the aggressor. But we've not forgotten. Nor have the Estonians, Latvians, Lithuanians, East Germans, Czechs, Hungarians, Bulgars, Slavs, Rumanians – the list endless. There will be a day of reckoning with the Soviets, oh yes, one day there will surely be a day of reckoning with the Soviets – most of all by Russians who suffer their lash most of all. 'For a Georgian you know a lot about Finland,' he said calmly.

'Finland is important to Russia. The détente between us works, is safe and a lesson to the world that anti-Soviet American Imperialistic propaganda is a myth.'

Erikki smiled. 'This is not the time for politics, eh? It's late. What do you want with me?'

'Friendship.'

'Ah, that's easily asked, but as you would know, for a Finn, given with difficulty.' Erikki reached over to the sideboard for an almost empty vodka bottle and two glasses. 'Are you Shi'ite?'

'Yes, but not a good one, God forgive me. I drink vodka sometimes if that's what you ask.'

Erikki poured two glasses. 'Health.' They drank. 'Now, please come to the point.'

'Soon Bakhtiar and his American lackeys will be thrown out of Iran. Soon Azerbaijan will be in turmoil, but you will have nothing to fear. You are well thought of here, so is your wife and her family, and we would like your. . . your cooperation in bringing peace to these mountains.'

'I'm just a helicopter pilot, working for a British company, contracted to Iran-Timber, and I'm without politics. We Finns have no politics, don't you remember?'

'We're friends, yes. Our interests of world peace are the same.'

Erikki's great right fist slammed down on the table, the sudden violence making the Russian flinch as the bottle skittered away and fell to the floor. 'I've asked you politely twice to come to the point,' he said in the same calm voice. 'You have ten seconds.'

'Very well,' the man said through his teeth. 'We require your services to ferry teams into the camps within the next few days. We . . .'

'What teams?'

'The mullahs of Tabriz and their followers. We requ – '

'I take my orders from the company, not mullahs or revolutionaries or men who come with guns in the night. Do you understand?'

'You will find it is better to understand us, Captain Yokkonen. So will the Gorgons. All of them,' Rakoczy said pointedly and Erikki felt the blood go into his face. 'Iran-Timber is already struck and on our side. They will provide you with the necessary orders.'

'Good. In that case I will wait and see what their orders are.' Erikki got up to his great height. 'Good night.'

The Russian got up too and stared at him angrily. 'You and your wife are much too intelligent not to understand that without the Americans and their fornicating CIA Bakhtiar's lost. That motherless mad-man Carter has ordered U.S. marines and helicopters into Turkey, an American war fleet into the Gulf, a task force with a nuclear carrier and support vessels, with marines and nuclear armed aircraft – a war fleet an – '

'I don't believe it!'

'You can. By God, of course they're trying to start a war, for of course we have to react, we have to match war game with war game for of course they'll use Iran against us. It's all madness – we don't want nuclear war . . .' Rakoczy meant it with all his heart, his mouth running away with him. Only a few hours ago his superior had warned him by code radio that all Soviet forces on the border were on Yel-low Alert – one step from Red – because of the approaching carrier fleet, all nuclear missiles on equal alert. Worst of all, vast Chinese troop movements had been reported all along the 5,000 miles of shared border with China. 'That motherfucker Carter with his motherfucking Friend-ship Pact with China's going to blow us all to hell if he gets half a chance.'

'If it happens it happens,' Erikki said.

'Insha'Allah, yes, but why become a running dog for the Americans, or their equally filthy British allies? The People are going to win, we are going to win. Help us and you won't regret it, Captain. We only need your skills for a few da – '

He stopped suddenly. Running footsteps were approaching. Instantly Erikki's knife was in his hand and he moved with catlike speed between the front door and the bedroom door as the front door burst open.

'SAVAK!' a half-seen man gasped, then took to his heels.

Rakoczy jumped for the doorway, scooped up his machine pistol. 'We require your help, Captain. Don't forget!' He vanished into the night.

Azadeh came out into the living room. With the gun ready, her face white. 'What was that about a carrier? I didn't understand him.'

Erikki told her. Her shock was clear. 'That means war, Erikki.'

'Yes, if it happens.' He put on his parka. 'Stay here.' He closed the door after him. Now he could see lights from approaching cars that were racing along the rough dirt road that joined the base to the main Tabriz-Tehran road. As his eyes adjusted to the darkness, he could make out two cars and an army truck. In a moment the lead vehicle stopped and police and soldiers fanned out into the night. The officer in charge saluted. 'Ah, Captain Yokkonen, good evening. We heard that some revolutionaries were here, or communist Tudeh – firing was reported,' he said, his English perfect. 'Her Highness is all right? There's no problem?'

'No, not now, thank you, Colonel Mazardi.' Erikki knew him quite well. The man was a cousin of Azadeh, and chief of police in this area of Tabriz. But SAVAK? That's something else, he thought uneasily. If he is, he is, and I don't want to know. 'Come in.'

Azadeh was pleased to see her cousin and thanked him for coming and they told him what had occurred.

'The Russian said his name was Rakoczy, Fedor Rakoczy?' he asked.

'Yes, but it was obviously a lie,' Erikki said. 'He had to be KGB.'

'And he never told you why they wanted to visit the camps?'

'No.'

The colonel thought a moment, then sighed. 'So the mullah Mahmud wishes to go flying, eh? Foolish for a so-called man of God to go flying. Very dangerous, particularly if he's an Islamic Marxist – that sacrilege! Flying helicopters, you can easily fall out, so I'm told. Perhaps we should accommodate him.' He was tall and very good-looking, in his forties, his uniform immaculate. 'Don't worry. These rabble-rousers will soon be back in their flea-bitten hovels. Soon Bakhtiar'll give the orders for us to contain these dogs. And that rabble-rouser Khomeini – we should muzzle that traitor quickly. The French should have muzzled him the moment he arrived there. Those weak fools. Stupid! But then they've always been weak, meddling, and against us. The French've always been jealous of Iran.' He got up. 'Let me know when your aircraft is airworthy. In any event we'll be back just before dawn in two days. Let's hope the mullah and his friends, particularly the Russian, return.'

He left them. Erikki put the kettle on to boil for coffee. Thoughtfully he said, 'Azadeh, pack an overnight bag.'

She stared at him. 'What?'

'We're going to take the car and drive to Tehran. We'll leave in a few minutes.'

'There's no need to leave, Erikki.'

'If the chopper was airworthy we'd use that but we can't.'

'There's no need to worry, my darling. Russians have always coveted Azerbaijan, always will, Tsarist, Soviet, it makes no difference. They've always wanted Iran and we've always kept them out and always will. No need to worry about a few fanatics and a lone Russian, Erikki.'

He looked at her. 'I'm worried about American marines in Turkey, the American task force and why the KGB think "you and your wife are much too intelligent", why that one was so nervous, why they know so much about me and about you and why they "require" my services. Go and pack a bag, my darling, while there's time.'

'Very well. But not to Tehran, not tonight. Too dangerous. First we must see the Khan, my father.'

Saturday

Chapter 2

Near Tabriz: 6:05 P.M. In the snow-covered mountains not far from the Soviet border, Pettikin's 206 came over the rise fast, continuing to climb up the pass, skimming the trees, following the road.

'Tabriz One, HFC from Tehran. Do you read?' he called again.

Still no answer. Light was closing in, the late afternoon sun hidden by deep cloud cover that was only a few hundred feet above him, grey and heavy with snow. Again he tried to raise the base, very tired now, his face badly bruised and still hurting from the beating he had taken. His gloves and the broken skin over his knuckles made it awkward for him to press the transmit button. 'Tabriz One. HFC from Tehran. Do you read?'

Again there was no answer but this did not worry him. Communication in the mountains was always bad, he was not expected, and there was no reason for Erikki or the base manager to have arranged a radio watch. As the road climbed, the cloud cover came down but he saw, thankfully, that the crest ahead was still clear, and once over it, the road fell away and there, half a mile farther on, was the base.

This morning it had taken him much longer than expected to drive to the small military air base at Galeg Morghi, not far from Tehran's international airport, and though he had left the apartment before dawn, he did not arrive there until a bleak sun was well into the polluted, smoke-filled sky. He had had to divert many times. Street battles were still going on with many roads blocked – some deliberately with barricades but more with burned-out wrecks of cars or buses. Many bodies sprawled on the snow-covered sidewalks and roadways, many wounded, and twice, angry police turned him back. But he persevered and took an even more circuitous route. When he arrived, to his surprise the gate to their section of the base where they operated a training school was open and unguarded. Normally air force sentries would be there. He drove in and parked his car in the safety of the S-G hangar but found none of the day skeleton crew of mechanics or ground personnel on duty.

It was a cold brisk day and he was bundled in winter flight gear. Snow covered the field and most of the runway. While he waited he ground-checked the 206 that he was going to take. Everything was fine. The spares that Tabriz needed, tail rotor and two hydraulic pumps, were in the baggage compartment. Tanks were full which gave it two and a half to three hours' range – two to three hundred miles depending on wind, altitude, and power

settings. He would still have to refuel en route. His flight plan called for
him to do this at Bandar-e Pahlavi, a port on the Caspian. Without effort he
wheeled the airplane on to the apron. Then all hell let loose and he was on
the edge of a battle.

Trucks filled with soldiers raced through the gate and headed across the
field to be greeted with a hail of bullets from the main part of the base with
its hangars, barracks and administration buildings. Other trucks raced down
the perimeter road, firing as they went, then a tracked armoured Bren carrier
joined the others, its machine guns blazing. Aghast, Pettikin recognised the
shoulder badges and helmet markings of the Immortals. In their wake came
armoured buses filled with paramilitary police and other men who spread out
over his side of the base, securing it. Before he knew what was happening,
four of them grabbed him and dragged him over to one of the buses, shouting
Farsi at him.

'For Christ's sake, I don't speak Farsi,' he shouted back, trying to fight
out of their grasp. Then one of them punched him in the stomach and he
retched, tore himself free, and smashed his attacker in the face. At once
another man pulled out a pistol and fired. The bullet went into the neck
of his parka, ricocheted violently off the bus, speckles of burning cordite
in its wake. He froze. Someone belted him hard across the mouth and the
others started punching and kicking him. At that moment a police officer
came over. 'American? You American?' he said angrily in bad English.

'I'm British,' Pettikin gasped, the blood in his mouth, trying to free himself
from the men who pinioned him against the hood of the bus. 'I'm from S-G
Helicopters and that's my – '

'American! Saboteur!' The man stuck his gun in Pettikin's face and Pettikin
saw the man's finger tighten on the trigger. 'We SAVAK know you Americans
cause all our troubles!'

Then through the haze of his terror he heard a voice shout in Farsi and he
felt the iron hands holding him loosen. With disbelief he saw the young British
paratroop captain, dressed in a camouflage jumpsuit and red beret, two small,
heavily armed soldiers with Oriental faces, grenades on their shoulder belts,
packs on their backs, standing in front of them. Nonchalantly the captain was
tossing a grenade up and down in his left hand as though it were an orange,
the pin secured. He wore a revolver at his belt and a curiously shaped knife
in a holster. Abruptly he stopped and pointed at Pettikin and then at the
206, angrily shouted at the police in Farsi, waved an imperious hand, and
saluted Pettikin.

'For Christ's sake, look important, Captain Pettikin,' he said quickly, his
Scots accent pleasing, then knocked a policeman's hand away from Pettikin's
arm. One of the others started to raise his gun but stopped as the captain
jerked the pin out of his grenade, still holding the lever tight. At the same
time his men cocked their automatic rifles, held them casually but very ready.
The older of the two beamed, loosened his knife in its holster. 'Is your chopper
ready to go?'

'Yes . . . yes it is,' Pettikin mumbled.

'Crank her up, fast as you can. Leave the doors open and when you're ready to leave, give me the thumbs-up and we'll all pile in. Plan to get out low and fast. Go on! Tenzing, go with him.' The officer jerked his thumb at the chopper fifty yards away and turned back, switched to Farsi again, cursed the Iranians, ordering them away to the other side where the battle had waned a little. The soldier called Tenzing went with Pettikin who was still dazed.

'Please hurry, sahib,' Tenzing said and leaned against one of the doors, his gun ready. Pettikin needed no encouragement.

More armoured cars raced past but paid no attention to them, nor did other groups of police and military who were desperately intent on securing the base against the mobs who could now be heard approaching. Behind them the police officer was angrily arguing with the paratrooper, the others nervously looking over their shoulders at the advancing sound of 'Allah-uuuu Akbarrrr!' Mixed with it was more gunfire now and a few explosions. Two hundred yards away on the perimeter road outside the fence, the vanguard of the mob set fire to a parked car and it exploded.

The helicopter's jet engines came to life and the sound enraged the police officer, but a phalanx of armed civilian youths came charging through the gate from the other direction. Someone shouted 'Mujhadin!' At once everyone this side of the base grouped to intercept them and began firing. Covered by the diversion, the captain and the other soldier rushed for the chopper, jumped in, Pettikin put on full power and fled a few inches above the grass, swerved to avoid a burning truck, then barrelled drunkenly into the sky. The captain lurched, almost dropped his grenade, couldn't put the pin back in because of Pettikin's violent evading action. He was in the front seat and hung on for his life, held the door open, tossed the grenade carefully overboard and watched it curve to the ground.

It exploded harmlessly. 'Jolly good,' he said, locked the door and his seat belt, checked that the two soldiers were okay, and gave a thumbs-up to Pettikin.

Pettikin hardly noticed. Once clear of Tehran he put her down in scrubland, well away from any roads or villages, and checked for bullet damage. When he saw there was none, he began to breathe. 'Christ, I can't thank you enough, Captain,' he said, putting out his hand, his head aching. 'I thought you were a bloody mirage at first. Captain . . .?'

'Ross. This's Sergeant Tenzing and Corporal Gueng.'

Pettikin shook hands and thanked both of them. They were short, happy men, hard and lithe. Tenzing was older, in his early fifties. 'You're heaven sent, all of you.'

Ross smiled, his teeth very white in his sunburned face. 'I didn't quite know how we were going to get out of that one. Wouldn't have been very good form to knock off police, anyone for that matter – even SAVAK.'

'I agree.' Pettikin had never seen such blue eyes in a man, judging him to be in his late twenties. 'What the hell was going on back there?'

'Some air force servicemen had mutinied, and some officers, and loyalists were there to put a stop to it. We heard Khomeini supporters and leftists were coming to the help of the mutineers.'

'What a mess! Can't thank you enough. How'd you know my name?'

'We'd, er, got wind of your approved flight plan to Tabriz via Bandar-e Pahlavi and wanted to hitch a ride. We were very late and thought we'd missed you – we were diverted to hell and gone. However, here we are.'

'Thank God for that. You're Gurkhas?'

'Just, er, odd bods, so to speak.'

Pettikin nodded thoughtfully. He had noticed that none of them had shoulder patches or insignias – except for Ross's captain's pips and their red berets. 'How do "odd bods" get wind of flight plans?'

'I really don't know,' Ross said airily. 'I just obey orders.' He glanced around. The land was flat and stony and open, and cold with snow on the ground. 'Don't you think we should move on? We're a bit exposed here.'

Pettikin got back into the cockpit. 'What's on in Tabriz?'

'Actually, we'd like to be dropped off just this side of Bandar-e Pahlavi, if you don't mind.'

'Sure.' Automatically Pettikin had begun start-up procedures. 'What's going on there?'

'Let's say we have to see a man about a dog.'

Pettikin laughed, liking him. 'There's lots of dogs all over! Bandar-e Pahlavi it is, then, and I'll stop asking questions.'

'Sorry, but you know how it is. I'd also appreciate it if you'd forget my name and that we were aboard.'

'And if I'm asked – by authority? Our departure was a little public.'

'I didn't give any name – just ordered you,' Ross grinned, 'with vile threats!'

'All right. But I won't forget your name.'

Pettikin set down a few miles outside the port of Bandar-e Pahlavi. Ross had picked the landing from a map that he carried. It was a duned beach, well away from any village, the blue waters of the Caspian Sea placid. Fishing boats dotted the sea, great cumulus clouds in the sunny sky. Here the land was tropical and the air humid with many insects and no sign of snow though the Elburz Mountains behind Tehran were heavily covered. It was highly irregular to land without permission, but twice Pettikin had called Bandar-e Pahlavi Airport where he was to refuel and had got no answer so he thought that he would be safe enough – he could always plead an emergency.

'Good luck, and thanks again,' he said and shook all their hands. 'If you ever need a favour – anything – you've got it.' They got out quickly, shouldered their packs, heading up the dunes. That was the last he had seen of them.

'Tabriz One, do you read?'

He was circling uneasily at the regulation seven hundred feet, then came lower. No sign of life – nor were any lights on. Strangely disquieted he landed close to the hangar. There he waited, ready for instant takeoff, not knowing what to expect – the news of servicemen mutinying in Tehran, particularly the supposedly elite air force, had disturbed him very much. But no one came. Nothing happened. Reluctantly, he locked the controls with great care and got out, leaving the engines running. It was very dangerous and against regulations – very dangerous because if the locks slipped it was possible for the chopper to ground-loop and get out of control.

But I don't want to get caught short, he thought grimly, rechecked the locks and quickly headed for the office through the snow. It was empty, the hangars empty except for the disembowelled 212, trailers empty, with no sign of anyone – or any form of a battle. A little more reassured, he went through the camp as quickly as he could. On the table in Erikki's cabin was an empty vodka bottle. A full one was in the refrigerator – he would dearly have loved a drink but flying and alcohol never mix. There was also bottled water, some Iranian bread, and dried ham. He drank the water gratefully. I'll eat only after I've gone over the whole place, he thought.

In the bedroom the bed was made but there was a shoe here and another there. Gradually his eyes found more signs of a hasty departure. The other trailers showed other clues. There was no transport on the base and Erikki's red Range Rover was gone too. Clearly the base had been abandoned somewhat hastily. But why?

His eyes gauged the sky. The wind had picked up and he heard it whine through the snow-laden forest over the muted growl of the idling jet engines. He felt the chill through his flying jacket and heavy pants and flying boots. His body ached for a hot shower – even better, one of Erikki's saunas – and food and bed and hot grog and eight hours' sleep. The wind's no problem yet, he thought, but I've got an hour of light at the most to refuel and get back through the pass and down into the plains. Or do I stay here tonight?

Pettikin was not a forest man, not a mountain man. He knew desert and bush, jungle, veld, and the Dead Country of Saudi. The vast reaches on the flat never fazed him. But cold did. And snow. First refuel, he thought.

But there was no fuel in the dump. None. Many forty-gallon drums but they were all empty. Never mind, he told himself, burying his panic, I've enough in my tanks for the hundred and fifty miles back to Bandar-e Pahlavi. I could go on to Tabriz Airport, or try to scrounge some from the ExTex depot at Ardabil, but that's too bloody near the Soviet border.

Again he measured the sky. Bloody hell! I can park here or somewhere en route. What's it to be?

Here. Safer.

He shut down and put the 206 into the hangar, locking the door. Now the silence was deafening. He hesitated, then went out, closing the hangar door after him. His feet crunched on the snow. The wind tugged at him as he walked to Erikki's trailer. Halfway there he stopped, his stomach twisting. He sensed someone watching him. He looked around, his eyes and ears searching the forest and the base. The wind sock danced in the eddies that trembled the treetops, creaking them, whining through the forest, and abruptly he remembered Tom Lochart, one of their chief pilots, sitting around a campfire in the Zagros on a skiing trip, telling the Canadian legend of the Wendigo, the evil demon of the forest, borne on the wild wind, that waits in the treetops, whining, waiting to catch you unawares, then suddenly swoops down and you're terrified and begin to run but you can't get away and you feel the icy breath behind you and you run and run with bigger and ever bigger steps until your feet are bloody stumps and then the Wendigo catches you up on to the treetops and you die.

He shuddered, hating to be alone here. Curious, I've never thought about it before but I'm almost never alone. There's always someone around, mechanic or pilot or friend or Genny or Mac or Claire in the old days.

He was still watching the forest intently. Somewhere in the distance dogs began to bark. The feeling that there was someone out there was still very strong. With an effort he dismissed his unease, went back to the chopper, and found the Verey Light pistol. He carried the huge-calibre, snub-nosed weapon openly as he went back to Erikki's cabin and felt happier having it with him. And even happier when he had bolted the door and closed the curtains.

Night came quickly. With darkness animals began to hunt.

Tehran: 7:05 P.M. McIver was walking along the deserted, tree-lined residential boulevard, tired and hungry. All streetlights were out and he picked his way carefully in the semi-darkness, snow banked against the walls of fine houses on both sides of the roadway. Sound of distant guns and, carried on the cold wind, 'Allahhh-u Akbarrr.' He turned the corner and almost stumbled into the Centurion tank that was parked half on the sidewalk. A flashlight momentarily blinded him. Soldiers moved out of ambush.

'Who're you, agha?' a young officer said in good English. 'What're you doing here?'

'I'm Captain . . . I'm Captain McIver, Duncan . . . Duncan McIver, I'm walking home from my office, and . . . and my flat's the other side of the park, around the next corner.'

'ID please.'

Gingerly McIver reached into his inner pocket. He felt the two small photos beside his ID, one of the Shah, the other of Khomeini, but with all the day's rumours of mutinies, he could not decide which would be correct so produced neither. The officer examined the ID under the flashlight. Now that McIver's eyes had adjusted to the darkness, he noticed the man's tiredness and stubble beard and crumpled uniform. Other soldiers watched silently. None were smoking which McIver found curious. The Centurion towered over them, malevolent, almost as though waiting to pounce.

'Thank you.' The officer handed the well-used card back to him. More firing, nearer this time. The soldiers waited, watching the night. 'Better not to be out after dark, agha. Good night.'

'Yes, thank you. Good night.' Thankfully McIver walked off, wondering if they were loyalist or mutineers – Christ, if some units mutiny and some don't there's going to be hell to pay. Another corner, this road and the park also dark and empty that, not so long ago, was always busy and brightly lit with more light streaming from windows, servants and people and children, all happy and lots of laughter among themselves, hurrying this way and that. That's what I miss most of all, he thought. The laughter. Wonder if we'll ever get those times back again.

His day had been frustrating, no phones, radio contact bad, and he had not been able to raise any of his bases. Once again none of his office staff had arrived which further irritated him. 'Tomorrow'll be better,' he said, then quickened his pace, the emptiness of the streets unpleasant.

Their apartment block was five storeys and they had one of the penthouses. The staircase was dimly lit, electricity down to half power again, the lift out of action for months. He went up the stairs wearily, the paucity of light making the climb more gloomy. But inside his apartment, candles were already lit and his spirits rose. 'Hi, Genny!' he called out, relocked the door, and hung up his old British warm. 'Whisky time!'

'Duncan! I'm in the dining room, come here for a minute.'

He strode down the corridor, stopped at the doorway, and gaped. The dining table was laden with a dozen Iranian dishes and bowls of fruit, candles everywhere. Genny beamed at him. And so did Sharazad. She was one of the pilot's wives, Tom Lochart. 'Bless my soul! Sharazad, this's your doing? How nice to see you wh – '

'Oh, it's nice to see you too, Mac, you get younger every day, both of you are, so sorry to intrude,' Sharazad said in a rush, her voice bubbling and joyous, 'but I remember that yesterday was your wedding anniversary because it's five days before my birthday, and I know how you like lamb horisht and polo and the other things, so we brought them, Hassan, Dewa and I, and candles.' She was barely five foot three, the kind of Persian beauty that Omar Khayyám had immortalised. 'Now that you're back, I'm off.'

'But wait a second, why don't you stay and eat with us an – '

'Oh but I can't, much as I'd like to, Father's having a party tonight and I have to attend. This is just a little gift and I've left Hassan to serve and to clean up and oh I do hope you have a lovely time! Hassan! Dewa!' she called out, then hugged Genny and hugged McIver and ran down to the door where her two servants were now waiting. One held her fur coat for her. She put it on, then wrapped the dark shroud of her chador around her, blew Genny another kiss, and, with the other servant, hurried away. Hassan, a tall man of thirty, wearing a white tunic and black trousers and a big smile, relocked the door. 'Shall I serve dinner, madam?' he asked Genny in Farsi.

'Yes, please, in ten minutes,' she replied happily. 'But first the master will have a whisky.' At once Hassan went to the sideboard and poured the drink and brought the water, bowed, and left them.

'By God, Gen, it's just like the old days,' McIver said with a beam.

'Yes. Silly, isn't it, that that's only a few months ago?' Up to then they had had a delightful live-in couple, the wife an exemplary cook of European and Iranian food who made up for the lighthearted malingering of her husband whom McIver had dubbed Ali Baba. Both had suddenly vanished, as had almost all expat servants. No explanation, no notice. 'Wonder if they're all right, Duncan?'

'Sure to be. Ali Baba was a grafter and had to have enough stashed away to keep them for a month of Sundays. Did Charlie check in?'

'Not yet. Paula's staying the night again – Nogger isn't. They went to dinner with some of her Alitalia crew.' Her eyebrows arched. Paula was an air hostess. 'Our Nogger's sure she's ripe for nogging, but I hope he's wrong. I like Paula.' They could hear Hassan in the kitchen. 'That's the sweetest sound in the world.'

McIver grinned back at her and raised his glass. 'Thank God for Sharazad and no washing up!'

'That's the best part.' Genny sighed. 'Such a nice girl, so thoughtful. Tom's so lucky. Sharazad says he's due tomorrow.'

'Hope so, he'll have mail for us.' McIver decided not to mention the tank. 'Do you think you could borrow Hassan or one of her other servants for a couple of days a week? It'd help you tremendously.'

'I wouldn't ask – you know how it is.'

'I suppose you're right, bloody annoying.' Now it was almost impossible for any expats to find help, whatever you were prepared to pay. Up to a few months ago it had been easy to get fine, caring servants and then, with a few words of Farsi and their help, running a happy home, shopping, was usually a breeze.

'That was one of the best things about Iran,' she said. 'Made such a difference – took all the agony out of living in such an alien country.'

'You still think of it as alien – after all this time?'

'More than ever. All the kindness, politeness, of the few Iranians we'd meet, I've always felt it was only on the surface – that their real feelings are the ones out in the open now – I don't mean everyone, of course, not our friends; Annoush, for instance, now she's one of the nicest, kindest people in the world.' Annoush was the wife of General Valik, the senior of the partners in Tehran. 'Most of the wives felt that, Duncan,' she added, lost in her musing. 'Perhaps that's why expats flock together, all the tennis parties and skiing parties, boating, weekends on the Caspian – and servants to carry the picnic baskets and clean up. I think we had the life of Riley, but not any more.'

'It'll come back – hope to God it does, for them as well as us. Walking home I suddenly realised what I missed most. It was all the laughter. No one seems to laugh any more, I mean on the streets, even the kids.' McIver was drinking his whisky sparingly.

'Yes, I miss the laughter very much. I miss the Shah too. Sorry he had to go – everything was well ordered, as far as we were concerned, up to such a short time ago. Poor man, what a rotten deal we've given him now, him and that lovely wife of his – after all the friendship he gave our side. I feel quite ashamed – he certainly did his best for his people.'

'Unfortunately, Genny, for most of them it seems it wasn't good enough!'

'I know. Sad. Life is very sad sometimes. Well, no point in crying over spilt milk. Hungry?'

'I'll say.'

Candles made the dining room warm and friendly and took the chill off the apartment. Curtains were drawn against the night. At once Hassan brought the steaming bowls of various horisht – literally meaning soup but more like a thick stew of lamb or chicken and vegetables, raisins and spices of all kinds – and polo, the delicious Iranian rice that is parboiled, then baked in a buttered dish until the crust is firm and golden brown, a favourite of both of them. 'Bless Sharazad, she's a sight for sore eyes.'

Genny smiled back at him. 'Yes, she is, so's Paula.'

'You're not so bad either, Gen.'

'Get on with you, but for that you can have a nightcap. As Jean-Luc would say, *Bon appétit!*' They ate hungrily, the food exquisite, reminding both of them of meals they had had in the houses of their friends.

'Gen, I ran into young Christian Tollonnen at lunch, you remember Erikki's friend from the Finnish embassy? He told me Azadeh's passport was all ready. That's good, but the thing that shook me was he said, in passing, about eight out of every ten of his Iranian friends or acquaintances are no longer in Iran and if it kept up in the new exodus, pretty soon there'd only be mullahs and their flocks left. Then I started counting and came up with about the same proportion – those in what we'd call the middle and upper class.'

'I don't blame them leaving. I'd do the same.' Then she added involuntarily, 'Don't think Sharazad will.'

McIver had heard an undercurrent and he studied her. 'Oh?'

Genny toyed with a little piece of the golden crust and changed her mind about not telling him. 'For the love of God don't say anything to Tom who'd have a fit – and I don't know how much is fact and how much a young girl's idealistic make-believe – but she happily whispered she'd spent most of the day at Doshan Tappeh where, she says, there's been a real insurrection, guns, grenades, the lot . . .'

'Christ!'

'. . . militantly on the side of what she called "our Glorious Freedom Fighters" who turn out to be mutinying air force servicemen, some officers, Green Bands supported by thousands of civilians – against police, loyalist troops, and the Immortals. . . .'

Monday

Chapter 3

At Tabriz One: 8:12 A.M. Charlie Pettikin was fitfully asleep, curled up on a mattress on the floor under a single blanket, his hands tied in front of him. It was just dawn and very cold. The guards had not allowed him a portable gas fire and he was locked into the section of Erikki's cabin that would normally be a storeroom. Ice glistened on the inside of the panes of glass in the small window. The window was barred on the outside. Snow covered the sill.

His eyes opened and he jerked upright, startled, not knowing where he was for the moment. Then his memory flooded back and he hunched against the wall, his whole body aching. 'What a damned mess!' he muttered, trying to ease his shoulders. With both hands he awkwardly wiped the sleep out of his eyes, and rubbed his face, feeling filthy. The stubble of his beard was flecked with grey. Hate being unshaved, he thought.

Today's Monday. I got here Saturday at sunset and they caught me yesterday. Bastards!

On Saturday evening there had been many noises around the cabin trailer that had added to his disquiet. Once he was sure he heard muffled voices. Quietly he doused the lights, slid the bolt back, and stood on the stoop, the Verey pistol in his hand. With great care he had searched the darkness. Then he saw, or thought he saw, a movement thirty yards away, then another farther off.

'Who are you?' he called out, his voice echoing strangely. 'What do you want?'

No one answered him. Another movement. Where? Thirty, forty yards away – difficult to judge distances at night. Look, there's another! Was it a man? Or just an animal or the shadow of a branch. Or perhaps – what was that? Over there by the big pine. 'You! Over there! What do you want?'

No answer. He could not make out if it was a man or not. Enraged and even a little frightened he aimed and pulled the trigger. The banggg seemed like a clap of thunder and echoed off the mountains and the red flare ripped towards the tree, ricocheted off it in a shower of sparks, sprayed into another to bury itself spluttering and spitting in a snowdrift. He waited.

Nothing happened. Noises in the forest, the roof of the hangar creaking, wind in the treetops, sometimes snow falling from an overladen tree branch that sprang back, free once more. Making a big show he angrily stamped his feet against the cold, switched on the light, loaded the pistol again, and rebolted the door. 'You're getting to be an old woman in your old age,' he said aloud, then added, 'Bullshit! I hate the quiet, hate being alone, hate snow, hate the cold, hate being scared and this morning at Galeg Morghi shook me, God curse it and that's a fact – but for young Ross I know that SAVAK bastard would've killed me!'

He checked that the door was barred and all the windows, closed the curtains against the night, then poured a large vodka and mixed it with some frozen orange juice that was in the freezer and sat in front of the fire and collected himself. There were eggs for breakfast and he was armed. The gas fire worked well. It was cosy. After a while he felt better, safer. Before he went to bed in the spare bedroom, he rechecked the locks. When he was satisfied he took off his flying boots and lay on the bed. Soon he was asleep.

In the morning the night fear had disappeared. After a breakfast of fried eggs on fried bread, just as he liked it, he tidied the room, put on his padded flying gear, unbolted the door and a submachine gun was shoved in his face, six of the revolutionaries crowded into the room and the questioning began. Hours of it.

'I'm not a spy, not American. I keep telling you I'm British,' over and over.

'Liar, your papers say you're South African. By Allah, are they false too?' The leader – the man who called himself Fedor Rakoczy – was tough-looking, taller, and older than the others, with hard brown eyes, his English accented. The same questions over and over: 'Where do you come from, why are you here, who is your CIA superior, who is your contact here, where is Erikki Yokkonen?'

'I don't know. I've told you fifty times I don't know – there was no one here when I landed at sunset last night. I was sent to pick him up, him and his wife. They had business in Tehran.'

'Liar! They ran away in the night, two nights ago. Why should they run away if you were coming to pick them up?'

'I've told you. I was not expected. Why should they run away? Where're Dibble and Arberry, our mechanics? Where's our manager Dayati and wh – '

'Who is your CIA contact in Tabriz?'

'I haven't one. We're a British company and I demand to see our consul in Tabriz. I dem – '

'Enemies of the people cannot demand anything! Even mercy. It is the Will of God that we are at war. In war people get shot!'

The questioning had gone on all morning. In spite of his protests they had taken all his papers, his passport with the vital exit and residence permits, and had bound and thrown him in here with dire threats if he attempted to run away.

Later, Rakoczy and two guards had returned. 'Why didn't you tell me you brought the spares for the 212?'

'You didn't ask me,' Pettikin had said angrily. 'Who the hell are you? Give me back my papers. I demand to see the British consul. Undo my hands, God dammit!'

'God will strike you if you blaspheme! Down on your knees and beg God's forgiveness.' They forced him to kneel. 'Beg forgiveness!'

He obeyed, hating them.

'You fly a 212 as well as a 206?'

'No,' he said, awkwardly getting to his feet.

'Liar! It's on your licence.' Rakoczy had thrown it on the table. 'Why do you lie?'

'What's the difference? You believe nothing I say. You won't believe the truth. Of course I know it's on my licence. Didn't I see you take it? Of course I fly a 212 if I'm rated.'

'The komiteh will judge you and sentence you,' Rakoczy had said with a finality that sent a shock wave up his spine. Then they had left him.

At sunset they had brought him some rice and soup and gone away again. He had slept hardly at all and now, in the dawn, he knew how helpless he was. His fear began to rise up. Once in Vietnam he had been shot down and caught and sentenced to death by Viet Cong but his squadron had come back for him with gunships and Green Berets and they had shot up the village and the Viet Cong with it. That was another time that he had escaped a certainty. 'Never bet on death until you're dead. Thataway, old buddy,' his young American commander had said, 'thataway you sleep nights.' The commander had been Conroe Starke. Their helicopter squadron had been mixed, American and British and some Canadian, based at Da-nang. What another bloody mess that was!

Wonder how he's doing now? he thought. Starke was in charge of their Kowiss base. Lucky bastard. Lucky to be safe at Kowiss and lucky to have Manuela. Now there's one smasher and built like a koala bear – cuddly, with those big brown eyes of hers, and just the right amount of curves.

He let his mind wander, wondering about her and Starke, about where were Erikki and Azadeh, about that Vietnam village – and about the young Captain Ross and his men. But for him! Ross was another saviour. In this life you have to have saviours to survive, those curious people who miraculously come into your life for no apparent reason just in time to give you the chance you desperately need, or to extract you from disaster or danger or evil. Do they appear because you prayed for help? At the very edge you always pray, somehow, even if it's not to God. But God has many names.

He remembered old Soames at the embassy with his, 'Don't forget, Charlie, Mohammed the Prophet proclaimed that Allah – God – has three thousand names. A thousand are known only to the angels, a thousand only to the prophets, three hundred are in the Torah, the Old Testament, another three hundred in the Zabur, that's the Psalms of David, another three hundred in the New Testament, and ninety-nine in the Koran. That makes two thousand nine hundred and ninety-nine. One name has been hidden by God. In Arabic it's called: Ism Allah ala'zam: the Greatest Name of God. Everyone who reads the Koran will have read it without knowing it. God is wise to hide His Greatest Name, eh?'

Yes, if there is a God, Pettikin thought, cold and aching.

The door opened. It was Rakoczy with his two men. Astonishingly, Rakoczy smiled, politely helped him to his feet and began undoing his bonds. 'Good morning, Captain Pettikin. So sorry for the mistake. Please follow me.' He led the way into the main room. Coffee was on the table. 'Do you drink coffee black or English style with milk and sugar?'

Pettikin was rubbing his chafed wrists, trying to get his mind working. 'What's this? The prisoner was offered a hearty breakfast?'

'Sorry, I don't understand.'

'Nothing.' Pettikin stared at him, still not sure. 'With milk and sugar.' The coffee tasted wonderful and revived him. He helped himself to more. 'So it's a mistake, all a mistake?'

'Yes. I, er, checked your story and it was correct, God be praised. You will leave immediately. To return to Tehran.'

Pettikin's throat felt tight at his sudden reprieve – apparent reprieve, he thought suspiciously. 'I need fuel. All our fuel's been stolen, there's no fuel in our dump.'

'Your aircraft has been refuelled. I supervised it myself.'

'You know about choppers?' Pettikin was wondering why the man appeared so nervous.

'A little.'

'Sorry, but I, er, I don't know your name.'

'Smith. Mr. Smith.' Fedor Rakoczy smiled 'You will leave now, please. At once.'

Pettikin found his flying boots and pulled them on. The other men watched him silently. He noted they were carrying Soviet machine pistols. On the table by the door was his overnight bag. Beside it were his documents. Passport, visa, work permit, and Iranian CAA-issued flying licence. Trying to keep the astonishment off his face, he made sure they were all there and stuck them in his pocket. When he went for the refrigerator, one of the men stood in his way and motioned him away. 'I'm hungry,' Pettikin said, still very suspicious.

'There's something to eat in your plane. Follow me, please.'

Outside, the air smelled very good to him, the day crisp and fine with a clean, very blue sky. To the west more snow clouds were building. Eastward, the way over the pass was clear. All around him the forest sparkled, the light refracted by the snow. In front of the hangar was the 206, windshield cleaned, all windows cleaned. Nothing had been touched inside though his map case was now in a side pocket, not beside his seat where he normally left it. Very carefully he began a preflight check.

'Please to hurry,' Rakoczy said.

'Of course.' Pettikin made a great show of hurrying but he didn't, missing nothing in his inspection, all his senses tuned to find a subtle sabotage, or even a crude one. Gas checked out, oil, everything. He could see and feel their growing nervousness. There was still no one else on the base. In the hangar he could see the 212 with its engine parts still neatly spread out. The spares that he had brought had been put on a bench nearby.

'Now you are ready.' Rakoczy said it as an order. 'Get in, you will refuel at

Bandar-e Pahlavi as before.' He turned to the others, embraced both of them hastily and got into the right seat. 'Start up and leave at once. I am coming to Tehran with you.' He gripped his machine gun with his knees, buckled himself in, locked the door neatly, then lifted the headset from its hook behind him and put it on, clearly accustomed to the inside of a cockpit.

Pettikin noticed that the other two had taken up defensive positions facing the road. He pressed the Engine Start. Soon the whine and the familiarity – and the fact that 'Smith' was aboard and therefore sabotage unlikely – made him light-headed. 'Here we go,' he said into the boom mike and took off in a scudding rush, banked sweetly and climbed for the pass.

'Good,' Rakoczy said, 'very good. You fly very well.' Casually he put the gun across his knees, muzzle pointing at Pettikin. 'Please don't fly too well.'

'Put the safety catch on – or I won't fly at all.'

Rakoczy hesitated. He clicked it in place. 'I agreed it is dangerous while flying.'

At six hundred feet Pettikin levelled off, then abruptly went into a steep bank and came back towards the field.

'What're you doing?'

'Just want to get my bearings.' He was relying on the fact that though Smith clearly knew his way around a cockpit, he couldn't fly a 206 or he would have taken her. His eyes were searching below for a clue to the man's nervousness and his haste to leave. The field seemed the same. Near the junction of the narrow base road with the main road that went northwest to Tabriz were two trucks. Both headed for the base. From this height he could easily see they were army trucks.

'I'm going to land to see what they want,' he said.

'If you do,' Rakoczy said without fear, 'it will cost you much pain and permanent mutilation. Please go to Tehran – but first to Bandar-e Pahlavi.'

'What's your real name?'

'Smith.'

Pettikin left it at that, circled once, then followed the Tehran road southeast, heading for the pass and biding his time – confident now that somewhere en route his time would come.

On the Outskirts of Tabriz: 9:30 A.M. The red Range Rover came out of the gates of the Khan's palace and headed down the rise towards Tabriz and the road for Tehran. Erikki was driving, Azadeh beside him. It had been her cousin, Colonel Mazardi, the chief of police, who had persuaded Erikki not to drive to Tehran on Friday: 'The road would be highly dangerous – it's bad enough during the day,' he said. 'The insurgents won't return now, you're quite safe. Much better to go and see His Highness the Khan and ask his advice. That would be much wiser.'

Azadeh had agreed. 'Erikki, of course we will do whatever you want but I would really feel happier if we went home for the night and saw Father.'

'My cousin's right, Captain; of course you may do as you wish, but I swear by the Prophet, God keep His words safe for ever, that her Highness's safety is just as important to me as to you. If you still feel so inclined, leave tomorrow. I can assure you there's no danger here. I'll post guards. If this so-called Rakoczy or any other foreigner or this mullah comes within half a mile of here or the Gorgon palace they'll regret it.'

'Oh, yes, Erikki, please,' Azadeh said enthusiastically. 'Of course, my darling, we'll do whatever you like but it might be you would want to consult His Highness, my father, about what you plan to do.'

Reluctantly Erikki had agreed. Arberry and the other mechanic Dibble had decided to go into Tabriz to the International Hotel and spend the weekend there. 'Spares're due Monday, Captain. Old Skinflint McIver knows our 212's got to be working by Wednesday or he'll have to send another one and he won't like that. We'll just sit tight and get the job done and get her airborne. Our apology for a base manager can come and fetch us. We're British, we've nothing to worry about – no one's going to touch us. And don't forget we're working for their guver'ment, whoever's the bleeding guver'ment and we've no quarrel with any of these bleeding wo – these bleeders, begging your pardon. Now don't you worry about us, you and the Missus. We'll just sit tight and expect you back by Wednesday. Have a fun time in Tehran.'

So Erikki had gone in convoy with Colonel Mazardi to the outskirts of Tabriz. The sprawling palace of the Gorgon Khans was set in mountain foothills, in acres of gardens and orchards behind high walls. When they arrived, the whole house awoke and congregated – stepmother, half sisters, nieces, nephews, servants, and children of servants, but not Abdollah Khan, her father. Azadeh was received with open arms and tears and happiness and more tears, and immediate plans were made for a luncheon feast the next day to celebrate their good fortune in having her home at long last – 'But, oh, how terrible! Bandits and a rogue mullah daring to come on your land? Hasn't His Highness, our revered father, donated barrels of rials and hundreds of acres of land to various mosques in and around Tabriz!'

Erikki was welcomed politely, and guardedly. All of them were afraid of him, the enormity of his size, his quickness with a knife, the violence of his temper, and could not understand his gentleness towards his friends and the vast love he radiated for Azadeh. She was the fifth of six half sisters, and an infant half brother. Her mother, dead now many years, had been Abdollah Khan's second, concurrent wife. Her own adored blood brother, Hakim, a year older than she, had been banished by Abdollah Khan and was still in disgrace at Khvoy to the northwest – banished for crimes against the Khan that both Hakim and Azadeh swore he was not guilty of.

'First a bath,' her half sisters said gaily, 'and you can tell us all that happened, every detail, *every detail*.' Happily, they dragged Azadeh away. In the privacy of their bathhouse, warm and intimate and luxurious and completely outside the domain of all men, they chatted and gossiped until the dawn. 'My Mahmud hasn't made love to me for a week,' Najoud, Azadeh's eldest half sister, said with a toss of her head.

'It has to be another woman, darling Najoud,' someone said.

'No, it's not that. His erection is giving him trouble.'

'Oh, you poor darling! Have you tried giving him oysters . . .'

'Or tried using oil of roses on your breasts . . .'

'Or rubbed him with extract of jacaranda, rhino horn, and musk . . .'

'Jacaranda, musk with rhino horn? I haven't heard of that one, Fazulia.'

'It's brand new from an ancient recipe from the time of Cyrus the Great. This is a secret but the Great King's penis was quite small as a young man, but after he conquered the Medes, miraculously it became the envy of the host! It seems that he obtained a magic potion from the Medes that if rubbed on over a period of a month . . . their high priest gave it to Cyrus in return for his life, providing the Great King swore to keep the secret in his family alone. It's come down from father to son over the centuries and now, dear sisters, the secret's in Tabriz!'

'Oh who, dearest darling Sister Fazulia, who? The Blessings of God be upon thee for ever, who? My rotten husband Abdullah, may his three remaining teeth fall out, he hasn't had an erection for years. Who?'

'Oh be quiet, Zadi, how can she talk if you talk! Go on, Fazulia.'

'Yes, be quiet, Zadi, and bless your good fortune – my Hussan is erect morning, noon and night and so filled with desire for me he gives me no time to even wash my teeth!'

'Well, the secret of the elixir was bought by the great-great-grandfather of the present owner at a huge cost, I was told for a fistful of diamonds . . .'

'Eeeeeeeeee . . .'

'. . . but now you can buy a small vial for fifty thousand rials!'

'Oh, that's too much! Where on earth can I get so much cash?'

'As always you'll find it in his pockets, and you can always bargain. Is anything too much for such a potion when we can't have other men?'

'If it works . . .'

'Of course it works, oh, where do we buy it, dearest dearest Fazulia?'

'In the bazaar, in the shop of Abu Bakra bin Hassan bin Saiidi. I know the way! We'll go tomorrow. Before lunch. You will come with us, darling Azadeh!'

'No thank you, dear sister.'

Then there was lots of laughter and one of the young ones said, 'Poor Azadeh doesn't need jacaranda and muck – she needs the opposite!'

'Jacaranda and *musk*, child, with rhino horn,' Fazulia said.

Azadeh laughed with them. They had all asked her, overtly or covertly, if her husband was equally proportioned and how did she, so skinny and so fragile, deal with it and bear his weight? 'By magic,' she had told the young ones, 'easily,' the serious ones, and 'with unbelievable ecstasy as it must be in the Garden of Paradise,' the jealous ones and those she hated and secretly wanted to taunt.

Not everyone had approved of her marriage to this foreign giant. Many had tried to influence her father against him and against her. But she had won and she knew who her enemies were: her sex-mad half sister, Zadi, lying Cousin Fazulia with her nonsense exaggerations, and, most of all, the honeyed viper of the pack, eldest sister Najoud and her vile husband Mahmud, may God punish them for their evil ways. 'Dearest Najoud, I'm so happy to be home, but now it's time for sleep.'

And so to bed. All of them. Some happily, some sadly, some angrily, some hating, some loving, some to their husbands and some alone. Husbands could have four wives, according to the Koran, at the same time, provided they treated each with equality in every way – Mohammed the Prophet, alone of all men, had been allowed as many wives as he wished. According to legend, the Prophet had had eleven wives in his lifetime though not all at the same time. Some died, some he divorced, and some outlived him. But all of them honoured him for ever.

Erikki awoke as Azadeh slipped into bed beside him. 'We should leave as early as possible, Azadeh, my darling.'

'Yes,' she said, almost asleep now, the bed so comfortable, him so comfortable. 'Yes, whenever you like, but please not until after lunch because dearest Stepmother will weep buckets. . . .'

'Azadeh!'

But she was asleep now. He sighed, also content, and went back to sleep.

They did not leave on Sunday as planned – her father had said it was inconvenient as he wished to talk to Erikki first. At dawn today, Monday, after prayers that her father had led, and after breakfast – coffee and bread and honey and yoghurt and eggs – they had been allowed to leave and now swung off the mountainside road on to the main Tehran road and there ahead was the roadblock.

'That's weird,' Erikki said. Colonel Mazardi had said he would meet them here but he was nowhere to be seen, nor was the roadblock manned.

'Police!' Azadeh said, with a yawn. 'They're never where you want them.'

The road climbed up to the pass. The sky was blue and clear and the tops of the mountains already washed with sunlight. Down here in the valley, it was still dark and chill and damp, the road slippery, snow banked, but this did not worry him as the Range Rover had four-wheel drive and he carried chains. Later, when he came to the base turnoff he passed it by. He knew the base was empty, the 212 safe and waiting for repairs. Before leaving the palace he had tried unsuccessfully to contact his manager, Dayati. But that did not matter. He settled back in his seat, he had full tanks, and six spare five-gallon cans that he had got from Abdollah's private pump.

I can get to Tehran easily today, he thought. And back by Wednesday – if I come back. That bastard Rakoczy's very bad news indeed.

'Would you like some coffee, darling?' Azadeh asked.

'Thanks. See if you can find the BBC or the VOA on the shortwave.' Gratefully he accepted the hot coffee from the Thermos, listening to the crackle of static and heterodyning and loud Soviet stations and little else. Iranian stations were still strikebound and closed down, except the ones worked by the military.

Over the weekend friends, relations, tradesmen, servants had brought rumours and counter-rumours of everything from imminent Soviet invasion to imminent U.S. invasion, from successful military coups in the capital to abject submission of all the generals to Khomeini and Bakhtiar's resignation.

'Asinine!' Abdollah Khan had said. He was a corpulent man in his sixties, bearded, with dark eyes and full mouth, bejewelled and richly dressed. 'Why should Bakhtiar resign? He gains nothing so there's no reason, yet.'

'And if Khomeini wins?' Erikki had asked.

'It is the Will of God.' The Khan was lounging on carpets in the Great Room, Erikki and Azadeh seated in front of him, his armed bodyguard standing behind him. 'But Khomeini's victory will be only temporary, if he achieves it. The armed forces will curb him and his mullahs, sooner or later. He's an old man. Soon he will die, the sooner the better, for though he has done God's Will and been the instrument to remove the Shah whose time had come, he's narrow-sighted, as megalomaniacal as the Shah, if not more so. He will surely murder more Iranians than the Shah ever did.'

'But isn't he a man of God, pious and everything an ayatollah should be?' Erikki asked warily, not knowing what to expect. 'Why should Khomeini do that?'

'It's the habit of tyrants.' The Khan laughed and took another of the halvah, the Turkish sweets he gorged on.

'And the Shah? What will happen now?' As much as Erikki disliked the Khan, he was glad for the opportunity to get his opinion. On him depended much of his and Azadeh's life in Iran and he had no wish to leave.

'As God wants. Mohammed Shah did incredibly well for Iran, like his father before him. But in the last few years he was totally curled up in himself and would listen to no one – not even the Shahbanu, Empress Farah, who was dedicated to him, and wise. If he had any sense he would abdicate at once in favour of his son Reza. The generals need a rallying point, they could train him until he's ready to take power – don't forget Iran's been a monarchy for almost three thousand years, always an absolute ruler, some might say tyrant, with absolute power and removed only by death.' He had smiled, his lips full and sensuous. 'Of the Qajar shahs, our legitimate dynasty who ruled for a hundred and fifty years, only one, the last of the line, my cousin, died of natural causes. We are an Oriental people, not Western, who understand violence and torture. Life and death are not judged by your standards.' His dark eyes had seemed to grow darker. 'Perhaps it is the Will of God that the Qajars will return – under their rule Iran prospered.'

That's not what I heard, Erikki had thought. But he held his peace. It's not up to me to judge what has been or what would be here.

All Sunday the BBC and the VOA had been jammed which was not unusual. Radio Moscow was loud and clear as usual, and Radio Free Iran that broadcast from Tbilisi north of the border also loud and clear as usual. Their reports in Iranian and English told of total insurrection against 'Bakhtiar's illegal government of the ousted Shah and his American masters, headed by the warmonger and liar President Carter. Today Bakhtiar tried to curry favour with the masses by cancelling a total of thirteen billion dollars of usurious military contracts forced on the country by the deposed Shah: eight billion dollars in the USA, British Centurion tank contracts worth two point three billion, plus two French nuclear reactors, and one from Germany worth another two point seven billion. This news has sent Western leaders into panic and will undoubtedly send capitalist stock markets into a well-deserved crash . . .'

'Excuse me for asking, Father, but will the West crash?' Azadeh had asked.

'Not this time,' the Khan had said and Erikki saw his face grow colder. 'Not unless the Soviets decide this is the time to renege on the eighty billion dollars they owe Western banks – and even some Oriental banks.' He had laughed sardonically, playing with the string of pearls he wore around his neck. 'Of course Oriental moneylenders are much cleverer; at least they're not so greedy. They lend judiciously and require collaterals and believe no one and certainly not in the myth of "Christian charity".' It was common knowledge that the Gorgons owned enormous tracts of land in Azerbaijan, good oil land, a large part of Iran Timber, seafront property on the Caspian, much of the bazaar in Tabriz, and most of the merchant banks there.

Erikki remembered the whispers he had heard about Abdollah Khan when he was trying to get permission to marry Azadeh, about his parsimony and ruthlessness in business: 'A quick way to Paradise or hell is to owe Abdollah the Cruel one rial, to not pay, pleading poverty, and to stay in Azerbaijan.'

'Father, please may I ask, cancellation of so many contracts will cause havoc, won't it?'

'No, you may not ask. You've asked enough questions for one day. A woman is supposed to hold her tongue and listen – now you can leave.'

At once she apologised for her error and left obediently. 'Please excuse me.'

Erikki got up to leave too, but the Khan stopped him: 'I have not dismissed you yet. Sit down. Now, why should you fear one Soviet?'

'I don't – just the system. That man has to be KGB.'

'Why didn't you just kill him then?'

'It would not have helped, it would have hurt. Us, the base, Iran Timber, Azadeh, perhaps even you. He was sent to me by others. He knows us – knows you.' Erikki had watched the old man carefully.

'I know lots of them. Russians, Soviet or Tsarist, have always coveted Azerbaijan, but have always been good customers of Azerbaijan – and helped us against the stinking British. I prefer them to British, I understand them.' His smile thinned even more. 'It would be easy to remove this Rakoczy.'

'Good, then do it, please.' Erikki had laughed full-throated. 'And all of them as well. That would really be doing God's work.'

'I don't agree,' the Khan said ill-temperedly. 'That would be doing Satan's work. Without the Soviets against them, the Americans and their dogs the British would dominate us and all the world. They'd certainly eat up

Iran – under Mohammed Shah they nearly did. Without Soviet Russia, whatever her failings, there'd be no check on America's foul policies, foul arrogance, foul manners, foul jeans, foul music, foul food and foul democracy, their disgusting attitudes to women, to law and order, their disgusting pornography, naive attitude to diplomacy, and their evil, yes, that's the correct word, their evil antagonism to Islam.'

The last thing Erikki wanted was another confrontation. In spite of his resolve, he felt his own rage gathering. 'We had an agreem – '

'It's true, by God!' the Khan shouted at him. 'It's true!'

'It's not, and we had an agreement before your God and my spirits that we'd not discuss politics – either of your world or mine.'

'It's true, admit it!' Abdollah Khan snarled, his face twisted with rage. One hand went to the ornamental knife at his belt, and at once the guard unslung his machine pistol and covered Erikki. 'By Allah, you call me a liar in my own house?' he bellowed.

Erikki said through his teeth, 'I only remind you, Highness, by your Allah, what we agreed!' The dark bloodshot eyes stared at him. He stared back, ready to go for his own knife and kill or be killed, the danger between them very great.

'Yes, yes, that's also true,' the Khan muttered, and the fit of rage passed as quickly as it had erupted. He looked at the guard, angrily waved him away. 'Get out!'

Now the room was very still. Erikki knew there were other guards nearby and spyholes in the walls. He felt the sweat on his forehead and the touch of his pukoh knife in the centre of his back.

Abdollah Khan knew the knife was there and that Erikki would use it without hesitation. But the Khan had given him perpetual permission to be armed with it in his presence. Two years ago Erikki had saved his life.

That was the day Erikki was petitioning him for permission to marry Azadeh and was imperiously turned down: 'No, by Allah, I want no Infidels in my family. Leave my house! For the last time!' Erikki had got up from the carpet, sick at heart. At that moment there had been a scuffle outside the door, then shots, the door had burst open and two men, assassins armed with machine guns, had rushed in, others fighting a gun battle in the corridor. The Khan's bodyguard had killed one, but the other sprayed him with bullets then turned his gun on Abdollah Khan who sat on the carpet in shock. Before the assassin could pull the trigger a second time, he died, Erikki's knife in his throat. At the same moment Erikki lunged for him, ripped the gun out of his hands and the knife out of his throat as another assassin rushed into the room firing. Erikki had smashed the machine gun into the man's face, killing him, almost tearing off his head with the strength of his blow, then charged into the corridor berserk. Three attackers and two of the bodyguards were dead or dying. The last of the attackers took to their heels but Erikki cut them both down and raced onward. And only when he had found Azadeh and saw that she was safe did the bloodlust go out of his head and he become calm again.

Erikki remembered how he had left her and had gone back to the same Great Room. Abdollah Khan still sat on the carpets. 'Who were those men?'

'Assassins – enemies, like the guards who let them in,' Abdollah Khan had said malevolently. 'It was the Will of God you were here to save my life, the Will of God that I am alive. You may marry Azadeh, yes, but because I do not like you, we will both swear before God and your – whatever you worship – not to discuss religion or politics, either of your world or mine, then perhaps I will not have to have you killed.'

And now the same cold black eyes were staring at him. Abdollah Khan clapped his hands. Instantly the door opened and a servant appeared. 'Bring coffee!' The man hurried away. 'I will drop the subject of your world and go to another we can discuss: my daughter, Azadeh.'

Erikki became even more on guard, not sure of the extent of her father's control over her, or his own rights as her husband while he was in Azerbaijan – very much the old man's fief. If Abdollah Khan really ordered Azadeh back to this house and to divorce him, would she? I think yes, I'm afraid yes – she certainly will never hear a word against him. She even defended his paranoic hatred of America by explaining what had caused it.

'He was ordered there, to university, by his father,' she had told him. 'He had a terrible time in America, Erikki, learning the language and trying to get a degree in economics which his father demanded before he was allowed home. My father hated the other students who sneered at him because he couldn't play their games, because he was heavier than they which in Iran is a sign of wealth but not in America, and was slow at learning. But most of all because of the hazing that he was forced to endure, forced, Erikki – to eat unclean things like pork that are against our religion, to drink beer and wine and spirits that are against our religion, to do unmentionable things and be called unmentionable names. I would be angry too if it had been me. Please be patient with him. Don't Soviets make a blood film come over your eyes and heart for what they did to your father and mother and country? Be patient with him, I beg you. Hasn't he agreed to our marriage? Be patient with him.'

I've been very patient, Erikki thought, more patient than with any man, wishing the interview was over. 'What about my wife, Highness?' It was custom to call him that and Erikki did so from time to time out of politeness.

Abdollah Khan smiled a thin smile at him. 'Naturally my daughter's future interests me. What is your plan when you go to Tehran?'

'I have no plan. I just think it is wise to get her out of Tabriz for a few days. Rakoczy said they "require" my services. When the KGB say that in Iran or Finland or even America, you'd better clear the decks and prepare for trouble. If they kidnapped her, I would be putty in their hands.'

'They could kidnap her in Tehran much more easily than here, *if* that is their scheme – you forget this is Azerbaijan' – his lips twisted with contempt – 'not Bakhtiar country.'

Erikki felt helpless under the scrutiny. 'I only know that's what I think is best for her. I said I would guard her with my life, and I will. Until the political future of Iran is settled – by you and other Iranians – I think it's the wise thing to do.'

'In that case, go,' her father had said with a suddenness that had almost frightened him. 'Should you need help send me the code words . . .' He thought a moment. Then his smile became sardonic: 'Send me the sentence: "All men are created equal." That's another truth, isn't it?'

'I don't know, Highness,' he had said carefully. 'If it is or if it isn't, it's surely the Will of God.'

Abdollah had laughed abruptly and got up and left him alone in the Great Room and Erikki had felt a chill on his soul, deeply unsettled by the man whose thoughts he could never read.

'Are you cold, Erikki?' Azadeh asked.

'Oh. No, no, not at all,' he said, coming out of his reverie, the sound of the engine good as they climbed up the mountain road towards the pass. Now they were just below the crest. There had been little traffic either way. Around the corner they came into sunshine and topped the rise; at once Erikki changed down smoothly and picked up speed as they began the long descent, the road – built at the order of Reza Shah, like the railway – a wonder of engineering with cuts and embankments and bridges and steep parts with no railings on the precipice side, the surface slippery, snowbanked. He changed down again, driving fast but prudently, very glad they had not driven by night. 'May I have some more coffee?'

Happily she gave it to him. 'I'll be glad to see Tehran. There's lots of shopping to be done, Sharazad's there, and I have a list of things for my sisters and some face cream for Stepmother . . .'

He hardly listened to her, his mind on Rakoczy, Tehran, McIver and the next step.

The road twisted and curled in its descent. He slowed and drove more cautiously, some traffic behind him. In the lead was a passenger car, typically overloaded, and the driver drove too close, too fast, and with his finger permanently on the horn even when it was clearly impossible to move out of the way. Erikki closed his ears to the impatience that he had never become used to, or to the reckless way Iranians drove, even Azadeh. He rounded the next blind corner, the gradient steepening, and there on the straight, not far ahead, was a heavily laden truck grinding upward with a car overtaking on the wrong side. He braked, hugging the mountainside. At that moment the car behind him accelerated, swerved around him, horn blaring, overtaking blindly, and hurtled down the wrong side of the curving road. The two cars smashed into each other and both careened over the precipice to fall five hundred feet and burst into flames. Erikki swung closer into the side and stopped. The oncoming truck did not stop, just lumbered past and continued up the hill as though nothing had happened – so did the other traffic.

He stood at the edge and looked down into the valley. Burning remains of the cars were spread over the mountainside down six or seven hundred feet, no possibility of survivors, and no chance to get down there without serious climbing gear. When he came back to the car he shook his head unhappily.

'Insha'Allah, my darling,' Azadeh said calmly. 'It was the Will of God.'

'No, it wasn't, it was blatant stupidity.'

'Of course you're right, Beloved, it certainly was blatant stupidity,' she said at once in her most calming voice, seeing his anger though not understanding it as she did not understand much that went on in the head of this strange man who was her husband. 'You're perfectly right, Erikki. It was blatant stupidity but the Will of God that those drivers' stupidity caused their deaths and the deaths of those who travelled with them. It was the Will of God or the road would have been clear. You were quite right.'

'Was I?' he said wearily.

'Oh, yes, of course, Erikki. You were perfectly right.'

They went on. The villages that lay beside the road or straddled it were poor or very poor with narrow dirt streets, crude huts and houses, high walls, a few drab mosques, street stores, goats and sheep and chickens, and flies not yet the plague they would become in summer. Always refuse in the streets and in the joub – the ditches – and the inevitable scavenging packs of scabrous despised dogs that frequently were rabid. But snow made the landscape and the mountains picturesque, and the day continued to be good though cold with blue skies and cumulus building.

Inside the Range Rover it was warm and comfortable. Azadeh wore padded, modern ski gear and a cashmere sweater underneath, matching blue, and short boots. Now she took off her jacket and her neat woollen ski cap, and her full-flowing, naturally wavy dark hair fell to her shoulders. Near noon they stopped for a picnic lunch beside a mountain stream. In the early afternoon they drove through orchards of apple, pear and cherry trees, now bleak and leafless and naked in the landscape, then came to the outskirts of Qazvin, a town of perhaps a hundred and fifty thousand inhabitants and many mosques.

'How many mosques are there in all Iran, Azadeh?' he asked.

'Once I was told twenty thousand,' she answered sleepily, opening her eyes and peering ahead. 'Ah, Qazvin! You've made good time, Erikki.' A yawn swamped her and she settled more comfortably and went back into half sleep. 'There're twenty thousand mosques and fifty thousand mullahs, so they say. At this rate we'll be in Tehran in a couple of hours . . .'

He smiled as her words petered out. He was feeling more secure now, glad that the back of the journey had been broken. The other side of Qazvin the road was good all the way to Tehran. In Tehran, Abdollah Khan owned many houses and apartments, most of them rented to foreigners. A few he kept for himself and his family, and he had said to Erikki that, this time, because of the troubles, they could stay in an apartment not far from McIver.

'Thanks, thanks very much,' Erikki had said and later Azadeh had said, 'I wonder why he was so kind. It's . . . it's not like him. He hates you and hates me, whatever I try to do to please him.'

'He doesn't hate you, Azadeh.'

'I apologise for disagreeing with you, but he does. I tell you again, my darling, it was my eldest sister, Najoud, who really poisoned him against me, and against my brother. She and her rotten husband. Don't forget my mother was Father's second wife and almost half Najoud's mother's age and twice as pretty and though my mother died when I was seven, Najoud still keeps up the poison – of course not to our face, she's much more clever than that. Erikki, you can never know how subtle and secretive and powerful Iranian ladies can be, or how vengeful behind their oh so sweet exterior. Najoud's worse than the snake in the Garden of Eden! She's the cause of all the enmity.' Her lovely blue-green eyes filled with tears. 'When I was little, my father truly loved us, my brother Hakim and me, and we were his favourites. He spent more time with us in our house than in the palace. Then, when Mother died, we went to live in the palace but none of my half brothers and sisters really liked us. When we went into the palace, everything changed, Erikki. It was Najoud.'

'Azadeh, you tear yourself apart with this hatred – you suffer, not her. Forget her. She's got no power over you now and I tell you again: you've no proof.'

'I don't need proof. I know. And I'll never forget.'

Erikki had left it there. There was no point in arguing, no point in rehashing what had been the source of much violence and many tears. Better it's in the open than buried, better to let her rave from time to time.

Ahead now the road left the fields and entered Qazvin, a city like most every other Iranian city, noisy, cramped, dirty, polluted and traffic-jammed. Beside the road were the joub that skirted most roads in Iran. Here the ditches were three feet deep, in parts concreted, with slush and ice and a little water trickling down them. Trees grew out of them, townsfolk washed their clothes in them, sometimes used them as a source of drinking water, or as a sewer. Beyond the ditches the walls began. Walls that hid houses or gardens, big or small, rich or eyesores. Usually the town and city houses were two floors, drab and boxlike, some brick, adobe, some plastered, and almost all of them hidden. Most had dirt floors, a few had running water, electricity, and some sanitation.

Traffic built up with startling suddenness. Bicycles, motorcycles, buses, lorries, cars of all sizes and makes and ages from ancient to very old, almost all dented and patched, some highly decorated with different coloured paints and small lights to suit the owners' fancy. Erikki had driven this way many times over the last few years and he knew the bottle-necks that could happen. But there was no other way, no detour around the city though one had been planned for years. He smiled scornfully, trying to shut his ears to the noise, and thought, There'll never be a detour, the Qazvinis couldn't stand the quiet. Qazvinis and Rashtians

– people from Rasht on the Caspian – were the butts of many Iranian
jokes.

He skirted a burned-out wreck, then put in a cassette of Beethoven and
turned the volume up to soothe the noise away. But it didn't help much.

'This traffic's worse than usual! Where are the police?' Azadeh said, wide
awake now. 'Are you thirsty?'

'No, no thanks.' He glanced across at her, the sweater and tumbling hair
enhancing her. He grinned. 'But I'm hungry – hungry for you!'

She laughed and took his arm. 'I'm not hungry – just ravenous!'

'Good.' They were content together.

As usual the road surface was bad. Here and there it was torn up – partially
because of wear, partially because of never-ending repairs and road works
though these rarely were signposted or had safety barriers. He skirted a deep
hole then eased past another wreck that had been shoved carelessly into the
side. As he did so a crumpled truck came from the other direction, its horn
blaring angrily. It was brightly decorated, the bumpers tied up with wire,
the cab open and glassless, a piece of cloth the tank cap. On the flatbed was
brushwood, piled high, with three passengers hanging on precariously. The
driver was huddled up and wrapped in a ragged sheepskin coat. Two other
men were beside him. As Erikki passed he was surprised to see them glaring
at him. A few yards further on a battered, overladen bus lumbered towards
him. With great care he went closer to the joub, hugging the side to give the
bus room, his wheels on the rim, and stopped. Again he saw the driver and
all the passengers stare at him as they passed, women in their chadors, young
men, bearded and clothed heavily against the cold. One of them shook his
fist at him. Another shouted a curse.

We've never had any trouble before, Erikki thought uneasily. Everywhere
he looked were the same angry glances. From the street and from the vehicles.
He had to go very slowly because of the swarms of rogue motorcycles,
bicycles, among the cars, buses and trucks in single lanes that fought for space
– obedient to no traffic laws other than those which pleased the individual –
and now a flock of sheep poured out of a side street to clutter the road, the
motorists screaming abuse at the herdsmen, the herdsmen screaming abuse
back and everyone angry and impatient, horns blaring.

'Damned traffic! Stupid sheep!' Azadeh said impatiently, wide awake now.
'Sound your horn, Erikki!'

'Be patient, go back to sleep. There's no way I can overtake anyone,' he
shouted over the tumult, conscious of the unfriendliness that surrounded
them. 'Be patient!'

Another three hundred yards took half an hour, other traffic coming from
both sides to join the stream that got slower and slower. Street vendors and
pedestrians and refuse. Now he was inching along behind a bus that took up
most of the roadway, almost scraping cars the other side, most times with
one wheel half over the lip of the joub. Motorcyclists shoved past carelessly,
banging the sides of the Range Rover and other vehicles, cursing each other
and everyone else, pushing and kicking the sheep out of the way, stampeding

them. From behind, a small car nudged him, then the driver jammed his hand
on his horn in a paroxysm of rage that sent a sudden shaft of anger into Erikki's
head. Close your ears, he ordered himself. Be calm! There's nothing you can
do! Be calm!

But he found it increasingly difficult. After half an hour the sheep turned
off into an alley, and traffic picked up a little. Then around the next corner
the whole roadway was dug up and an unmarked ten-foot ditch – some six
feet deep and half filled with water – barred the way. A group of insolent
workmen squatted nearby, hurling back abuse. And obscene gestures.

It was impossible to go forward or back, so all traffic had to detour into a
narrow side street, the bus ahead not making the turn, having to stop and
reverse to more screams of rage and more tumult, and when Erikki backed
to give it room, a battered blue car behind him swerved around him on
the opposite side of the road into the small opening ahead and forced the
oncoming car to brake suddenly and skid. One of its wheels sank into the
joub and the whole car tipped dangerously. Now traffic was totally snarled.

Enraged, Erikki put on his brake, tore his door open, and went over to
the car in the ditch and used his great strength to drag it back on the road.
No one else helped, just swore and added to the uproar. Then he strode for
the blue car. At that moment the bus made the corner and now there was
room to move, the driver of the blue car let in his clutch and roared off with
an obscene gesture.

With an effort Erikki unclenched his fists. Traffic on both sides of the
road honked at him. He got into the driver's seat and let in the clutch.

'Here,' Azadeh said uneasily. She gave him a cup of coffee.

'Thanks.' He drank it, driving with one hand, the traffic slowing again.
The blue car had vanished. When he could talk calmly, he said, 'If I'd got
my hands on him or his car I'd have torn it and him to pieces.'

'Yes. Yes, I know. Erikki, have you noticed how hostile everyone is to us?
So angry?'

'Yes, yes, I have.'

'But why? We've driven though Qazvin twenty tim – ' Azadeh ducked
involuntarily as refuse suddenly hit her window, then lurched across into his
protection, frightened. He cursed and rolled up the windows, then reached
across her and locked her door. Dung hit the windshield.

'What the hell's up with these *matyeryebyets*?' he muttered. 'It's as though
we've an American flag flying and we're waving pictures of the Shah.' A stone
came out of nowhere and ricocheted off the metal sides. Then, ahead, the bus
broke out of the narrow side street diversion into the wide square in front of a
mosque where there were market stalls and two lanes of traffic either side. To
Erikki's relief they picked up some speed. The traffic was still heavy but it
was moving and he got into second, heading for the Tehran exit the far side
of the square. Halfway around the square the two lanes began to tighten as
more vehicles joined those heading for the Tehran road.

'It's never been this bad,' he muttered. 'What the hell's the hold-up
for?'

'It must be another accident,' Azadeh said, very unsettled. 'Or road works. Should we turn back – the traffic's not so bad that way?'

'We've plenty of time,' he said, encouraging her. 'We'll be out of here in a minute. Once through the town we'll be fine.' Ahead everything was slowing again, the din picking up. The two lanes were clogging, gradually becoming one again with much hooting, swearing, stopping, starting again and grinding along at about ten miles an hour, street stores and barrows encroaching on the roadway and straddling the joub. They were almost at the exit when some youths ran alongside, began shouting insults, some foul. One of the youths banged on his side window. 'American dog . . .'

'Pig Amer'can . . .'

These men were joined by others and some women in chador, fists raised. Erikki was bottled in and could not get out of the traffic or speed up or slow down nor could he turn around and he felt rage growing at his helplessness. Some of the men were banging on the bonnet and sides of the Range Rover and on his window. Now there was a pack of them and those on Azadeh's side were taunting her, making obscene gestures, trying to open the door. One of the youths jumped on the hood but slipped and fell off and just managed to scramble out of the way before Erikki drove over him.

The bus ahead stopped. Immediately there was a frantic mêlée as would-be passengers fought to get on and others fought to get off. Then Erikki saw an opening, stamped on the accelerator throwing off another man, got around the bus, just missing pedestrians who carelessly flooded through the traffic, and swung into a side street that miraculously was clear, raced up it and cut into another, narrowly avoided a mass of motorcyclists, and continued on again. Soon he was quite lost, for there was no pattern to the city or town except refuse and stray dogs and traffic, but he took his bearings from the sun's shadows and at length came out on to a wider road, shoved his way into the traffic and around it and soon came on to a road that he recognised, one that took him into another square in front of another mosque and then back on the Tehran road. 'We're all right now, Azadeh, they were just hooligans.'

'Yes,' she said shakily. 'They should be whipped.'

Erikki had been studying the crowds near the mosque and on the streets and in the vehicles, trying to find a clue to the untoward hostility. Something's different, he thought. What is it? Then his stomach twisted. 'I haven't seen a soldier or an army truck ever since we left Tabriz – none. Have you?'

'No – no, not now that you mention it.'

'Something's happened, something serious.'

'War? The Soviets have come over the border?' Her face lost even more colour.

'I doubt it – there'd be troops going north, or planes.' He looked at her. 'Never mind,' he said, more to convince himself, 'we're going to have a fine time in Tehran, Sharazad's there and lots of your friends. It's about time you had a change. Maybe I'll take the leave I'm owed – we could go to Finland for a week or two . . .'

They were out of the downtown area and into the suburbs now. The suburbs were ramshackle, with the same walls and houses and the same potholes. Here the Tehran road widened to four lanes, two each side, and though traffic was still heavy and slow, barely fifteen miles an hour, he was not concerned. A little way ahead, the Abadan-Kermanshah road branched off southwest, and he knew that this would bleed off a lot of the congestion. Automatically his eyes scanned the gauges as he would his cockpit instruments and, not for the first time, he wished he was airborne, over and out of all this mess. The petrol gauge registered under a quarter full. Soon he would have to refuel but that would be no problem with plenty of spare fuel aboard.

They slowed to ease past another truck parked with careless arrogance near some street vendors, the air heavy with the smell of diesel. Then more refuse came out of nowhere to splatter their windshield. 'Perhaps we should turn around, Erikki, and go back to Tabriz. Perhaps we could skirt Qazvin.'

'No,' he said, finding it eerie to hear fear in her voice – normally she was fearless. 'No,' he repeated even more kindly. 'We'll go to Tehran and find out what the problem is, then we'll decide.'

She moved closer to him and put a hand on his knee. 'Those hooligans frightened me, God curse them,' she muttered, her other fingers toying nervously with the turquoise beads she wore around her neck. Most Iranian women wore turquoise or blue beads, or a single blue stone against the evil eye. 'Those sons of dogs! Why should they be like that? Devils. May God curse them for ever!' Just outside the city was a big army training camp and an adjoining air base. 'Why aren't soldiers here?'

'I'd like to know too,' he said.

The Abadan-Kermanshah turnoff came up on his right. Much of the traffic headed down it. Barbed-wire fences skirted both roads – as on most of the main roads and highways in Iran. The fences were needed to keep sheep and goats and cattle and dogs – and people – from straying across the roads. Accidents were very frequent and mortality high.

But that's normal for Iran, Erikki thought. Like those poor fools who went over the side in the mountains – no one to know, no one to report them or even to bury them. Except the buzzards and the wild animals and packs of rotten dogs.

With the city behind them, they felt better. The country opened up again, orchards once more beyond the joub and the barbed wire, the Elburz Mountains north and undulating country south. But instead of speeding up, his two lanes slowed even more and congested, then reluctantly became one again, with more jostling, hooting and rage. Wearily he cursed the inevitable roadworks that must be causing the bottleneck, shifted down, his hand and feet working smoothly of their own volition, hardly noticing the stopping and starting, stopping and starting, inching along again, engines grinding and overheating, noise and frustration building in every vehicle. Abruptly Azadeh pointed ahead. 'Look!'

A hundred yards ahead was a roadblock. Groups of men surrounded it. Some were armed, all were civilians and poorly dressed. The roadblock was just this side of a nondescript village with street stalls beside the road and in the meadow opposite. Villagers, women and children mingled with the men. All the women wore the black or grey chador. As each vehicle stopped, papers were checked and then it was allowed to pass. Several cars had been pulled off the road into the meadow where knots of men interrogated the occupants. Erikki saw more weapons among them.

'They're not Green Bands,' he said.

'There aren't any mullahs. Can you see any mullahs?'

'No.'

'Then they're Tudeh or mujhadin – or fedayeen.'

'Better get your identity card ready,' he said and smiled at her. 'Put on your parka so you won't catch cold when I open the windows, and your hat.' It wasn't the cold that worried him. It was the curve of her breasts, proud under the sweater, the delicacy of her waist and her free-flowing hair.

In the glove compartment was a small, sheathed pukoh knife. This he concealed in his right boot. The other one, his big knife, was under his parka, in the centre of his back.

When at last their turn came, the surly, bearded men surrounded the Range Rover. A few had U.S. rifles, one an AK47. Among them were some women, just faces in the chador. They peered up at her with beady eyes and grim disapproval. 'Papers,' one of the men said in Farsi, holding out his hand, his breath reeking, the pervading smell of unwashed clothes and bodies coming into the car. Azadeh stared ahead, trying to dismiss the leers and mutterings and closeness that were totally outside her experience.

Politely Erikki passed over his ID card and Azadeh's. The man accepted them, stared at them, and passed them to a youth who could read. All the others waited silently, staring, stamping their feet in the cold. At length the youth said, his Farsi coarse, 'He's a foreigner from somewhere called Finland. He comes from Tabriz. He's not American.'

'He looks American,' someone else said.

'The woman's called Gorgon, she's his wife . . . at least that's what the papers say.'

'I'm his wife,' Azadeh said curtly. 'Ca – '

'Who asked you?' the first man said rudely. 'Your family name's Gorgon which is a landowning name and your accent's high and mighty like your manner and more than likely you're an enemy of the people.'

'I'm an enemy of no one. Pl – '

'Shut up. Women are supposed to know manners and be chaste and cover themselves and be obedient even in a socialist state.' The man turned on Erikki. 'Where are you going?'

'What's he say, Azadeh?' Erikki asked.

She translated.

'Tehran,' he said quietly to the thug. 'Azadeh, tell him we go to Tehran.' He had counted six rifles and one automatic. Traffic hemmed him in, no way to break out. Yet.

She did so, adding, 'My husband does not speak Farsi.'

'How do we know that? And how do we know you're married? Where is your marriage certificate?'

'I don't have it with me. That I'm married is attested on my identity card.'

'But this is a Shah card. An illegal card. Where is your new card?'

'A card from whom? Signed by whom?' she said fiercely. 'Give us back our cards and allow us to pass!'

Her strength had an effect on him and the others. The man hesitated. 'You will understand, please, that there are many spies and enemies of the people that must be caught . . .'

Erikki could feel his heart pumping. Sullen faces, people out of the Dark Ages. Ugly. More men joined the group around them. One of them angrily and noisily waved the cars and trucks behind him ahead to be checked. No one was honking. Everyone waited their turn. And over the whole traffic jam was a silent brooding dread.

'What's going on here?' A squat man shouldered his way through the crowd. The others gave way to him deferentially. Over his shoulder was a Czechoslovakian machine gun. The other man explained and gave over the papers. The squat man's face was round and unshaven, his eyes dark, his clothes poor and filthy. A sudden shot rang out and all heads turned to look at the meadow.

A man was lying on the ground beside a small passenger car that had been pulled over by the hostiles. One of these men stood over him with an automatic. Another passenger was pressed against the side of the car with his hands over his head. Abruptly this man burst through the cordon and dashed away. The man with the gun raised it and fired, missed and fired again. This time the running man screamed and fell, writhing in agony, tried to scramble away, his legs useless now. Leisurely the man with the gun came up to him, emptied the magazine into him, killing him by stages.

'Ahmed!' the squat man shouted out. 'Why waste bullets when your boots would do just as well? Who are they?'

'SAVAK!' A murmur of satisfaction swept the crowd and villagers and someone cheered.

'Fool! Then why kill them so quickly, eh? Bring me their papers.'

'The sons of dogs had papers claiming they were Tehrani businessmen but I know a SAVAK man when I see one. Do you want the false papers?'

'No. Tear them up.' The squat man turned back to Erikki and Azadeh. 'So it is that enemies of the people will be smoked out and done with.'

She did not reply. Their own IDs were in the grubby hand. What if our papers are also considered false? Insha'Allah!

When the squat man finished scrutinising the IDs he stared at Erikki. Then at her. 'You claim you're Azadeh Gorgon Yok . . . Yokkonen – his wife?'

'Yes.'

'Good.' He stuffed their IDs in his pocket and jerked a thumb at the meadow. 'Tell him to drive over there. We will search your car.'

'But th – '

'Do it. NOW!' The squat man climbed on to the bumpers, his boots scratching the paintwork. 'What's that?' he asked, pointing to the blue cross on a white background that was painted on the roof.

'It's the Finnish flag,' Azadeh said. 'My husband's Finnish.'

'Why is it there?'

'It pleases him to have it there.'

The squat man spat, then pointed again towards the meadow. 'Hurry up! Over there.' When they were in an empty spot, the crowd following them, he slid off. 'Out. I want to search your car for arms and contraband.'

Azadeh said, 'We have no guns or contr – '

'Out! And you, woman, you hold your tongue!' The crones in the crowd hissed approvingly. Angrily he jerked a thumb at the two bodies left crumpled in the trampled slush. 'The people's justice is quick and final and don't forget it.' He stabbed a finger at Erikki. 'Tell your monster husband what I said – if he is your husband.'

'Erikki, he says, the people's . . . the people's justice is quick and final and don't forget it. Be careful, my darling. We, we have to get out of the car – they want to search the car.'

'All right. But slide over and come out my side.' Towering above the crowd, Erikki got out. Protectively, he put his arm around her, men, women and some children crowding them, giving them little space. The stench of unwashed bodies was overpowering. He could feel her trembling, as much as she tried to hide it. Together they watched the squat man and others clambering into their spotless car, muddy boots on the seats. Others unlocked the rear door, carelessly removing and scattering their possessions, grubby hands reaching into pockets, opening everything – his bags and her bags. Then one of the men held up her filmy underclothes and night things to catcalls and jeers. The crones muttered their disapproval. One of them reached out and touched her hair. Azadeh backed away but those behind her would not give her room. At once Erikki moved his bulk to help but the mass of the crowd did not move though those nearby cried out, almost crushed by him, their cries infuriating the others who moved closer, threateningly, shouting at him.

Suddenly Erikki knew truly, for the first time, he could not protect Azadeh. He knew he could kill a dozen of them before they overpowered and killed him, but that would not protect her.

The realisation shattered him.

His legs felt weak and he had an overpowering wish to urinate and the smell of his own fear choked him and he fought the panic that pervaded him. Dully he watched their possessions being defiled. Men were staggering away with their vital cans of petrol without which he could never make Tehran as all petrol stations were on strike and closed. He tried to force his legs into motion but they would not work, nor would his mouth. Then one of the crones shouted at Azadeh who numbly shook her head and men took up the cry, jostling him and jostling her, men closing on him, their fetid smell filling his nostrils, his ears clogged with the Farsi.

His arm was still around her, and in the noise she looked up and he saw her terror but could not hear what she said. Again he tried to ease more room for the two of them but again he failed. Desperately he tried to contain the soaring, claustrophobic, panic-savagery and need to fight beginning to overwhelm him, knowing that once he began it would start the riot that would destroy her. But he could not stop himself and lashed out blindly with his free elbow as a thickset peasant woman with strange, enraged eyes pushed though the cordon and thrust the chador into Azadeh's chest, spitting out a paroxysm of Farsi at her, diverting attention from the man who had collapsed behind him, and now lay under their feet, his chest caved in from Erikki's blow.

The crowd were shouting at her and at him, clearly telling her to put on the chador, Azadeh crying out, 'No, no, leave me alone . . .' completely disoriented. In her whole life she had never been threatened like this, never been in a crowd like this, never experienced such closeness of peasants, or such hostility.

'Put it on, harlot . . .

'In the Name of God, put on the chador . . .

'Not in the Name of God, woman, in the name of the People . . .

'God is Great, obey the word . . .

'Piss on God, in the name of the revolution . . .

'Cover your hair, whore and daughter of a whore . . .

'Obey the Prophet Whose Name be praised . . .'

The shouting increased and the jostling, their feet trampling the dying man on the ground, then someone tore at Erikki's arm that was around Azadeh and she felt his other hand go for the big knife and she screamed out, 'Don't, don't, Erikki, they'll kill you . . .'

In panic she pushed the peasant woman away and fought the chador into place, calling out repeatedly, 'Allah-u Akbarrr,' and this mollified those nearby somewhat, their jeers subsiding, though people at the back shoved forward to see better, crushing others against the Range Rover. In the mêlée Erikki and Azadeh gained a little more space around them though they were still trapped on all sides. She did not look up at him, just clutched him, shivering like a frozen puppy, enveloped in the coarse shroud. A roar of laughter as one of the men held her bra against his chest and minced around.

The vandalism went on until, suddenly, Erikki sensed a newness surrounding them. The squat man and his followers had stopped and they were looking fixedly towards Qazvin. As he watched he saw them begin to melt into the crowd. In seconds they had vanished. Other men near the roadblock were getting into cars and heading off down the Tehran road, picking up speed. Now villagers also stared towards the city, then others, until the whole crowd was transfixed. Approaching up the road, through the snarled lines of traffic, was another mob of men, mullahs at their head. Some of the mullahs and many of the men were armed. 'Allah-u Akbar,' they shouted, 'God and Khomeiniiiiii!' then broke into a run, charging the roadblock.

A few shots rang out, the fire was returned from the roadblock, the opposing forces clashed with staves, stones, iron bars, and some guns. Everyone else scattered. Villagers rushed for the protection of their homes, drivers and passengers fled from their cars for the ditches or lay on the ground.

The cries and counter-cries and shots and noise and screams of this minor skirmish snapped Erikki's paralysis. He shoved Azadeh towards their car, hastily picking up the nearest of their scattered possessions, throwing them into the back, and slammed the rear door. Half a dozen of the villagers began scavenging too but he shoved them out of the way, jumped into the driver's seat and gunned the engine, jerked the car into reverse, then ahead, then roared off across the meadow, paralleling the road. Just ahead and to the right he saw the squat man with three of his followers getting into a car and remembered that the man still had their papers. For a split second he considered stopping but instantly rejected the thought and held course for the trees that skirted the road. But then he saw the squat man pull the machine gun off his shoulder, aim, and fire. The burst was a little high and Erikki's maddened reflexes swung the wheel over and shoved his foot on the accelerator as he charged the gun. Their massive bumper rammed the man against the car broadside, crushing him and it, the machine gun firing until the magazine was spent, bullets howling off metal, splaying through the windshield, the Range Rover now a battering ram. Berserk, Erikki backed off then charged again, overturning the wreckage, killing them, and he would have got out and continued the carnage with his bare hands but then, in the rearview mirror, he saw men running for him and so he reversed and fled.

The Range Rover was built for this sort of terrain, its snow tyres gripping the surface of the rough ground. In a moment they were in the trees and safe from capture, and he turned for the road, shifted into low, locked both differentials and clambered over the deep joub, ripping the barbed-wire fence apart. Once on the road he unlocked the differentials, changed gear and whirled away.

Only when he was well away did the blood clear from his eyes. Aghast, he remembered the howl of the bullets spraying the car, and that Azadeh was with him. In panic he looked across at her. But she was all right though paralysed with fear and hunched down in the seat, hanging on with both hands to the side, bullet holes in the glass and roof nearby, but all right though he did not recognise her for a moment, saw just an Iranian face made ugly by the chador – like any one of the tens of thousands they had all seen in the mobs.

'Oh, Azadeh,' he gasped, then reached over and pulled her to him, driving with one hand. In a moment he slowed and pulled over to the side and held her to him as the sobs tore her. He did not notice that the fuel gauge read near empty, or that the traffic was building up, or the hostile looks of the passers, or that many cars contained revolutionaries fleeing their roadblock for Tehran.

Chapter 4

In the skies near Qazvin: 3:17 P.M. From the moment Charlie Pettikin had left Tabriz with Rakoczy – the man he knew as Smith – he had flown the 206 as straight and level as possible, hoping to lull the KGB man to sleep, or at least off guard. For the same reason he had avoided conversation by slipping his headset on to his neck. At length Rakoczy had given up, just watched the terrain below. But he stayed alert with his gun across his lap, his thumb on the safety catch. And Pettikin wondered about him, who he was, what he was, what band of revolutionaries he belonged to – army or SAVAK, and if so why it was so important to get to Tehran. It had never occurred to Pettikin that the man was Russian not Iranian.

At Bandar-e Pahlavi where refuelling had been laboriously slow and had taken hours, he had done nothing to break the monotony, just paid over his last remaining American dollars and watched while the tanks were filled, then signed the official IranOil chit. Rakoczy had tried to chat with the refueller but the man was hostile, clearly frightened of being seen refuelling this foreign helicopter, and even more frightened of the machine gun that was on the front seat.

All the time they were on the ground Pettikin had gauged the odds of trying to grab the gun. There was never a chance. In Korea they had been plentiful. And Vietnam. My God, he thought, those days seem a million years ago.

He had taken off from Bandar-e Pahlavi and was now heading south at 1,000 feet, following the Qazvin road. East he could see the beach where he had set down Captain Ross and his two paratroopers. Again he wondered how they had known he was making a flight to Tabriz and what their mission had been. Hope to God they make it – whatever they had to make. Had to be urgent and important. Hope I see Ross again, I'd like that . . .

'Why do you smile, Captain?'

The voice came through his earphones. Automatically on takeoff this time he had put them on. He looked across at Rakoczy and shrugged, then went back to monitoring his instruments and the ground below. Over Qazvin he banked southeast following the Tehran road, once more retreating into himself. Be patient, he told himself, then saw Rakoczy tense and put his face closer to the window, looking downward.

'Bank left . . . a little left,' Rakoczy ordered urgently, his concentration totally on the ground. Pettikin put the chopper into a gentle bank – Rakoczy on the low side. 'No more! Make a one eighty.'

'What is it?' Pettikin asked. He steepened the bank, suddenly aware the man had forgotten the machine gun in his lap. His heart picked up a beat.

'There below on the road. That truck.'

Pettikin paid no attention to the ground below. He kept his eyes on the gun, gauging the distance carefully, his heart racing. 'Where? I can't see anything.' He steepened the bank even more to come around quickly on to the new heading. 'What truck? You mean . . .'

His left hand darted out and grabbed the gun by the barrel and awkwardly jerked it through the sliding window into the cabin behind them. At the same time his right hand on the stick went harder left, then quickly right and left-right again, rocking the chopper viciously. Rakoczy was taken completely unaware and his head slammed against the side, momentarily stunning him. At once Pettikin clenched his left fist and inexpertly slashed at the man's jaw to put him unconscious. But Rakoczy, karate-trained, his reflexes good, managed to stop the blow with his forearm. Groggily he held on to Pettikin's wrist, gaining strength every second as the two men fought for supremacy, the chopper dangerously heeled over, Rakoczy still on the downside. They grappled with each other, cursing, seat belts inhibiting them. Both became more frenzied, Rakoczy with two hands free beginning to dominate.

Abruptly Pettikin gripped the stick with his knees, took his right hand off it, and smashed again at Rakoczy's face. The blow was not quite true but the strength of it shifted him off balance, destroyed the grip of his knees shoving the stick left and overrode the delicate balance of his feet on the rudder pedals. At once the chopper reeled on to its side, lost all lift – no chopper can fly itself even for a second – the centrifugal force further throwing his weight askew and in the mêlée the collective lever was shoved down. The chopper fell out of the sky, out of control.

In panic, Pettikin abandoned the fight. Blindly he struggled to regain control, engines screaming and instruments gone mad. Hands and feet and training against panic, overcorrecting, then overcorrecting again. They dropped nine hundred feet before he got her straight and level, his heart unbearable, the snow-covered ground fifty feet below.

His hands were trembling. It was difficult to breathe. Then he felt something hard shoved in his side and heard Rakoczy cursing. Dully he realised the language was not Iranian but did not recognise it. He looked across at him and saw the face twisted with anger and the grey metal of the automatic and cursed himself for not thinking of that. Angrily he tried to shove the gun away but Rakoczy stuck it hard into the side of his neck.

'Stop or I'll blow your head off, you *matyeryebyets!*'

At once Pettikin put the plane into a violent bank, but the gun pressed harder, hurting him. He felt the safety catch go off and the gun cock.

'Your last chance!'

The ground was very near, rushing past sickeningly. Pettikin knew he could not shake him off. 'All right – all right,' he said, conceding, and straightened her and began to climb. The pressure from the gun increased and with it, the pain. 'You're hurting me for God's sake and shoving me off balance! How can I fly if y – '

Rakoczy just jabbed the gun harder, shouting at him, cursing him, jamming his head against the door frame.

'For Christ's sake!' Pettikin shouted back in desperation, trying to adjust his headset that had been torn off in the struggle. 'How the hell can I fly with your gun in my neck?' The pressure eased off a fraction and he righted the plane. 'Who the hell are you, anyway?'

'Smith!' Rakoczy was equally unnerved. A split second later, he thought, and we would have been splattered like a pat of fresh cow dung. 'You think you deal with a *matyeryebyets* amateur?' Before he could stop himself his reflexes took his hand and backhanded Pettikin across the mouth.

Pettikin was rocked by the blow, and the chopper twisted but came back into control. He felt the burn spreading over his face. 'You do that again and I'll put her on her back,' he said with a great finality.

'I agree,' Rakoczy said at once. 'I apologise for . . . for that . . . for that stupidity, Captain.' Carefully he eased back against his door but kept the gun cocked and pointed. 'Yes, there was no need. I'm sorry.'

Pettikin stared at him blankly. 'You're sorry?'

'Yes. Please excuse me. It was unnecessary. I am not a barbarian.' Rakoczy gathered himself. 'If you give me your word you'll stop trying to attack me, I'll put my gun away. I swear you're in no danger.'

Pettikin thought a moment. 'All right,' he said. 'If you tell me who you are and what you are.'

'Your word?'

'Yes.'

'Very well, I accept your word, Captain.' Rakoczy put the safety on and the gun in his far pocket. 'My name is Ali bin Hassan Karakose and I'm a Kurd. My home – my village – is on the slopes of Mount Ararat on the Iranian-Soviet border. Through the Blessings of God I'm a Freedom Fighter against the Shah, and anyone else who wishes to enslave us. Does that satisfy you?'

'Yes – yes it does. Then if y – '

'Please, later. First go there – quickly.' Rakoczy pointed below. 'Level off and go closer.'

They were at 800 feet to the right of the Qazvin-Tehran road. A village straddled the road a mile back and he could see the smoke whirled away by a stiff breeze. 'Where?'

'There, beside the road.'

At first Pettikin could not see what the man pointed at – his mind jumbled with questions about the Kurds and their historic centuries of wars against the Persian shahs. Then he saw the collection of cars and trucks pulled up to one side, and men surrounding a modern truck with a blue cross on a rectangular white background on the roof, other traffic grinding past slowly. 'You mean there? You want to go over those trucks and cars?' he asked, his face still smarting and his neck aching. 'The bunch of trucks near the one with the blue cross on its roof?'

'Yes.'

Obediently Pettikin went into a descending bank. 'What's so important about them, eh?' he asked, then glanced up. He saw the man staring at him suspiciously. 'What? What the hell's the matter now?'

'You really don't know what a blue cross on a white background signifies?'

'No. What about it? What is it?' Pettikin had his eyes on the truck that was much closer now, close enough to see it was a red Range Rover, an angry crowd surrounding it, one of the men smashing at the back windows with the butt of a rifle. 'It's the flag of Finland' came through his earphones and Erikki leaped into Pettikin's mind. 'Erikki had a Range Rover,' he burst out and saw the rifle butt shatter the window. 'You think that's Erikki?'

'Yes . . . yes it's possible.'

At once he went faster and lower, his pain forgotten, his excitement overriding all the sudden questions of how and why this Freedom Fighter knew Erikki. Now they could see the crowd turning towards them and people scattering. His pass was very fast and very low but he did not see Erikki. 'You see him?'

'No. I couldn't see inside the cab.'

'Nor could I,' Pettikin said anxiously, 'but a few of those buggers are armed and they were smashing the windows. You see them?'

'Yes. They must be fedayeen. One of them fired at us. If you . . .' Rakoczy stopped, hanging on tightly as the chopper skidded into a 180-degree turn, twenty feet off the ground, and hurtled back again. This time the crowd of men and the few women fled, falling over one another. Traffic in both directions tried to speed away or shuddered to a halt, one overloaded truck skidding into another. Several cars and trucks turned off the road and one almost overturned in the joub.

Just abreast of the Range Rover, Pettikin swung into a sliding 90-degree turn to face it – snow boiling into a cloud – for just enough time to recognise Erikki, then into another 90 degrees to barrel away into the sky. 'It's him all right. Did you see the bullet holes in the windscreen?' he asked, shocked. 'Reach in the back for the machine gun. I'll steady her and then we'll go and get him. Hurry, I want to keep them off balance.'

At once Rakoczy unbuckled his seat belt, reached back through the small intercommunicating window but could not get the gun that lay on the floor. With great difficulty he twisted out of his seat and clambered head first, half through the window, groping for it, and Pettikin knew the man was at his mercy. So easy to open the door now and shove him out. So easy. But impossible.

'Come on!' he shouted and helped pull him back into the seat. 'Put your belt on!'

Rakoczy obeyed, trying to catch his breath, blessing his luck that Pettikin was a friend of the Finn, knowing that if their positions had been reversed

he would not have hesitated to open the door. 'I'm ready,' he said, cocking
the gun, appalled at Pettikin's stupidity. The British are so stupid the
mother-eating bastards deserve to lose. 'Wh – '

'Here we go!' Pettikin spun the chopper into a diving turn at maximum
speed. Some armed men were still near the truck, guns pointing at them. 'I'll
soften them up and when I say "fire" put a burst over their heads!'

The Range Rover rushed up at them, hesitated, then swirled away
drunkenly – no trees nearby – hesitated again and came at them as the
chopper danced around it. Pettikin flared to a sudden stop twenty yards
away, ten feet off the ground. 'Fire,' he ordered.

At once Rakoczy let off a burst through the open window, aiming not over
heads but at a group of men and women ducked down behind the back end
of Erikki's truck, out of Pettikin's line of sight, killing or wounding some
of them. Everyone nearby fled panic-stricken – screams of the wounded
mingling with the howl of the jets. Drivers and passengers jumped out of
cars and trucks, scrambling away in the snowdrifts as best they could. Another
burst and more panic, now everyone rushing in retreat, all traffic snarled. On
the road some youths came from behind a truck with rifles. Rakoczy sprayed
them and those nearby. 'Make a three-sixty!' he shouted.

Immediately the helicopter pirouetted but no one was near. Pettikin saw
four bodies in the snow. 'I said over their heads, for God's sake,' he began,
but at that moment the door of the Range Rover swung open and Erikki
jumped out, his knife in one hand. For a moment he was alone, then a
chador-clad woman was beside him. At once Pettikin set the chopper down
on the snow but kept her almost airborne. 'Come on,' he shouted, beckoning
them. They began to run, Erikki half carrying Azadeh whom Pettikin did
not yet recognise.

Beside him Rakoczy unlocked his side door and leaped out, opened the
back door and whirled on guard. Another short burst towards the traffic.
Erikki stopped, appalled to see Rakoczy. 'Hurry!' Pettikin shouted, not
understanding the reason for Erikki's hesitation. 'Erikki, come on!' Then
he recognised Azadeh. 'My God . . .' he muttered, then shouted, 'Come on,
Erikki!'

'Quick, I've not much ammunition left!' Rakoczy shouted in Russian.

Erikki whirled Azadeh up into his arms and ran forward. A few bullets
hummed past. At the side of the helicopter Rakoczy helped bundle Azadeh
into the back, suddenly shoved Erikki aside with the barrel of the gun. 'Drop
your knife and get in the front seat!' he ordered in Russian. 'At once.'

Half paralysed with shock, Pettikin watched Erikki hesitate, his face
mottled with rage.

Rakoczy said harshly, 'By God, there's more than enough ammunition for
her, you, and this mother-fucking pilot. Get in!'

Somewhere in the traffic a machine gun started to fire. Erikki dropped
his knife in the snow, eased his great height into the front seat, Rakoczy
slid beside Azadeh and Pettikin took off and sped away, weaving over the
ground like a panicked grouse, then climbed into the sky.

When he could talk he said, 'What the hell's going on?'

Erikki did not answer. He craned around to make sure Azadeh was all right. She had her eyes closed and was slumped against the side, panting, trying to get her breath. He saw that Rakoczy had locked her seat belt, but when Erikki reached back to touch her the Soviet motioned him to stop with the gun.

'She will be all right, I promise you.' He continued speaking in Russian, 'providing you behave as your friend has been taught to behave.' He kept his eyes on him as he reached into his small bag and brought out a fresh magazine. 'Just so you know. Now face forward, please.'

Trying to contain his fury, Erikki did as he was told. He put on the headset. There was no way they could be overheard by Rakoczy – there was no intercom in the back – and it felt strange for both of them to be so free and yet so imprisoned. 'How did you find us, Charlie, who sent you?' he said into the mouth mike, his voice heavy.

'No one did,' Pettikin said. 'What the hell's with that bastard? I went to Tabriz to pick up you and Azadeh, got kidnapped by the son of a bitch in the back, and then he hijacked me to Tehran. It was just luck for Christ's sake – what the hell happened to you?'

'We ran out of fuel.' Erikki told him briefly what had happened. 'When the engine stopped, I knew I was finished. Everyone seems to have gone mad. One moment it was all right, then we were surrounded again, just like at the roadblock. I locked all the doors but it was only a matter of time . . .' Again he craned around. Azadeh had her eyes open and had pulled the chador off her face. She smiled at him wearily, reached forward to touch him but Rakoczy stopped her. 'Please excuse me, Highness,' he said in Farsi, 'but wait till we land. You will be all right.' He repeated it in Russian, adding to Erikki, 'I have some water with me. Would you like me to give it to your wife?'

Erikki nodded. 'Yes. Please.' He watched while she sipped gratefully. 'Thank you.'

'Do you want some?'

'No thank you,' he said politely even though he was parched, not wishing any favours for himself. He smiled at her encouragingly. 'Azadeh, like manna from heaven, eh? Charlie like an angel!'

'Yes. . . yes. It was the Will of God. I'm fine, fine now, Erikki, praised be to God. Thank Charlie for me . . .'

He hid his concern. The second mob had petrified her. And him, and he had sworn that if he ever got out of this mess alive, never again would he travel without a gun and, preferably, hand grenades. He saw Rakoczy watching him. He nodded and turned back again. '*Matyeryebyets*,' he muttered, automatically checking the instruments.

'That bugger's a lunatic – no need to kill anyone, I told him to fire over their heads.' Pettikin dropped his voice slightly, uneasy at talking so openly even though there was no way Rakoczy could hear. 'The bastard damn near killed me a couple of times. How do you know him, Erikki? Were you or Azadeh mixed up with the Kurds?'

Erikki stared at him. 'Kurds? You mean the *matyeryebyets* back there?'

'Yes, him of course – Ali bin Hassan Karakose. He comes from Mount Ararat. He's a Kurd Freedom Fighter.'

'He's not a Kurd but a turd, Soviet and KGB!'

'Christ Almighty! You're sure?' Pettikin was openly shocked.

'Oh yes. He claims he's Muslim but I bet that's a lie too. "Rakoczy" he called himself to me, another lie. They're all liars – at least why should they tell us, the enemy, anything?'

'But he swore it was the truth and I gave him my word.' Angrily Pettikin told him about the fight and the bargain he had made.

'You're a fool, Charlie, not him – haven't you read Lenin? Stalin? Marx? He's only doing what all KGB and committed communists do: use anything and everything to forward the "sacred" Cause – absolute world power for the USSR Communist party – and get us to hang ourselves to save them the trouble. My God, I could use a vodka!'

'A double brandy'd be better.'

'Both together would be even better.' Erikki studied the ground below. They were cruising easily, the engines sounding good and plenty of fuel. His eyes searched the horizon for Tehran. 'Not long now. Has he said where to land yet?'

'No.'

'Perhaps we'll get a chance then.'

'Yes.' Pettikin's apprehension increased. 'You mentioned a roadblock. What happened there?'

Erikki's face hardened. 'We got stopped. Leftists. Had to make a run for it. We've no papers left, Azadeh and I. Nothing. A fat bastard at the roadblock kept everything and there wasn't time to get them back.' A tremor went through him. 'I've never been so scared, Charlie. Never. I was helpless in that mob and almost shitting with fear because I couldn't protect her. That stinking fat bastard took everything, passport, ID, flying licences, everything.'

'Mac'll get you more, your embassy'll give you passports.'

'I'm not worried about me. What about Azadeh?'

'She'll get a Finnish passport too. Like Sharazad'll get a Canadian one – no need to worry.'

'She's still in Tehran, isn't she?'

'Sure. Tom should be there too. He was due in from Zagros yesterday with mail from home . . .' Strange, Pettikin thought in passing. I still call England home even with Claire gone, everything gone. 'He's just back off leave.'

'That's what I'd like to do, go on leave. I'm overdue. Perhaps Mac can send a replacement.' Erikki punched Pettikin lightly. 'Tomorrow can take care of tomorrow, eh? Hey, Charlie, that was a great piece of flying. When I first saw you, I thought I was dreaming or already dead. You saw my Finnish flag?'

'No, that was Ali – what did you call him? Rekowsky?'

'Rakoczy.'

'Rakoczy recognised it. If he hadn't I wouldn't have been any the wiser. Sorry.' Pettikin glanced across. 'What's he want with you?'

'I don't know but whatever it is, it's for Soviet purposes.' Erikki cursed for a moment. 'So we owe our lives to him too?'

After a moment Pettikin said, 'Yes. Yes, I couldn't have done it alone.' He glanced around. Rakoczy was totally alert, Azadeh dozing, shadows over her lovely face. He nodded briefly, then turned back. 'Azadeh seems okay.'

'No, Charlie, no, she's not,' Erikki said, an ache inside him. 'Today was terrible for her. She said she'd never been that close to villagers ever . . . I mean surrounded, bottled in. Today they got under her guard. Now she's seen the real face of Iran, the reality of her people – that and the forcing of the chador.' Again a shiver went through him. 'That was a rape – they raped her soul. Now I think everything will be different for her, for us. I think she'll have to choose: family or me, Iran or exile. They don't want us here. It's time for us to leave, Charlie. All of us.'

'No, you're wrong. Perhaps for you and Azadeh it's different but they'll still need oil so they'll still need choppers. We're good for a few more years, good years. With – ' Pettikin stopped, feeling a tap on his shoulder, and he glanced around. Azadeh awake now. He could not hear what Rakoczy said so he slipped one earphone off. 'What?'

'Don't use the radio, Captain, and be prepared to land on the outskirts where I'll tell you.'

'I . . . I'll have to get clearance.'

'Don't be a fool! Clearance from whom? Everyone's too busy down there. Tehran Airport's under siege – so is Doshan Tappeh and so's Galeg Morghi. Take my advice and make your landfall the small airport of Rudrama after you've dropped me.'

'I have to report in. The military insist.'

Rakoczy laughed sardonically. 'Military? And what would you report? That you landed illegally near Qazvin, helped murder five or six civilians, and picked up two foreigners fleeing – fleeing from whom? From the People!'

Grimly Pettikin turned back to make the call but Rakoczy leaned forward and shook him roughly. 'Wake up! The military doesn't exist any more. The generals have conceded victory to Khomeini! The military doesn't exist any more – they've given in!'

They all stared at him blankly. The chopper lurched. Hastily Pettikin corrected. 'What're you talking about?'

'Late last night the generals ordered all troops back to their barracks. All services – all men. They've left the field to Khomeini and his revolution. Now there's no army, no police, no gendarmes between Khomeini and total power – the People have conquered!'

'That's not possible,' Pettikin said.

'No,' Azadeh said, frightened. 'My father would have known.'

'Ah, Abdollah the Great?' Rakoczy said with a sneer. 'He'll know by now – if he's still alive.'

'It's not true!'

'It's. . . it's possible, Azadeh,' Erikki said, shocked. 'That'd explain why we saw no police or troops – why the mob was so hostile!'

'The generals'd never do that,' she said shakily, then turned on Rakoczy. 'It would be suicide, for them and thousands. Tell the truth, by Allah!'

Rakoczy's face mirrored his glee, delighted to twist words and sow dissension to unsettle them. 'Now Iran's in the hands of Khomeini, his mullahs, and his revolutionary guards.'

'It's a lie.'

Pettikin said, 'If that's true Bakhtiar's finished. He'll nev – '

'That weak fool never even began!' Rakoczy started laughing. 'Ayatollah Khomeini has frightened the balls off the generals and now he'll cut their throats for good measure!'

'Then the war's over.'

'Ah, the war,' Rakoczy said darkly. 'It is. For some.'

'Yes,' Erikki said, baiting him. 'And if what you say is true, it's all over for you too – all the Tudeh and all Marxists. Khomeini will slaughter you all.'

'Oh, no, Captain. The Ayatollah was the sword to destroy the Shah, but the People wielded the sword.'

'He and his mullahs and the People will destroy you – he's as anti-communist as he is anti-American.'

'Better you wait and see and not further delude yourselves, eh? Khomeini's a practical man and exults in power, whatever he says now.'

Pettikin saw Azadeh whiten and he felt an equal chill. 'And the Kurds?' he asked roughly. 'What about them?'

Rakoczy leaned forward, his smile strange. 'I am a Kurd whatever the Finn told you about Soviet and KGB. Can he prove what he says? Of course not. As to the Kurds, Khomeini will try to stamp us out – if he's allowed to – with all tribal or religious minorities, and foreigners and the bourgeoisie, landowners, moneylenders, Shah supporters, and,' he added with a sneer, 'and any and all people who will not accept his interpretation of the Koran – and he'll spill rivers of blood in the name of *his* Allah, *his*, not the real One God – if allowed to.' He glanced out of the window below, checking his bearings, then added even more sardonically, 'This heretic Sword of God has served his purpose and now he's going to be turned into a ploughshare – and buried!'

'You mean murdered?' Erikki said.

'Buried' – again the laugh – 'at the whim of the People.'

Azadeh came to life and tried to claw his face, cursing him. He caught her easily and held her while she struggled. Erikki watched, grey-faced. There was nothing he could do. For the moment.

'Stop it!' Rakoczy said harshly. 'You of all people should want this heretic gone – he'll stamp out Abdollah Khan and all the Gorgons and you with them if he wins.' He shoved her away. 'Behave, or I shall have to hurt you. It's true, you of all people should want him dead.' He cocked the machine gun. 'Turn around, both of you.'

They obeyed, hating the man and the gun. Ahead, the outskirts of Tehran were about ten miles away. They were paralleling the road and railway, the

Elburz Mountains to their left, approaching the city from the west. Overhead the sky was overcast, the clouds heavy, and no sun showed through.

'Captain, you see the stream where the railway crosses it? The bridge?'

'Yes, I can see that,' Pettikin said, trying to make a plan to overcome him, as Erikki was also planning – wondering if he could whirl and grab him but he was on the wrong side.

'Land half a mile south, behind that outcrop. You see it?'

Not far from this outcrop was a secondary road that headed for Tehran. A little traffic. 'Yes. And then?'

'And then you're dismissed. For the moment.' Rakoczy laughed and nudged the back of Pettikin's neck with the barrel of the gun. 'With my thanks. But don't turn around any more. Stay facing ahead, both of you, and keep your seat belts locked and know that I'm watching you both very closely. When you land, land firmly and cleanly and when I'm clear, take off. But don't turn around or I may become frightened. Frightened men pull triggers. Understand?'

'Yes.' Pettikin studied the landing site. He adjusted his headset. 'It look all right to you, Erikki?'

'Yes. Watch the snow dunes.' Erikki tried to keep the nervousness out of his voice.

The landing was clean and simple. Snow, whipped up by the idling blades, billowed alongside the windows. 'Don't turn around!'

Both men's nerves were jagged. They heard the door open and felt the cold air. Then Azadeh screamed, 'Erikkiiii!'

In spite of the order both craned around. Rakoczy was already out, dragging Azadeh after him, kicking and struggling and trying to hang on to the door, but he overpowered her easily. The gun was slung over his shoulder. Instantly Erikki jerked his door open and darted out, slid under the fuselage, and charged. But he was too late. A short burst at his feet stopped him. Ten yards away, clear of the rotors, Rakoczy had the gun levelled at them with one hand, the other firm in the neck of her chador. For a moment she was equally still, then she redoubled her efforts, shouting and screaming, flailing at him, catching him unawares. Erikki charged.

Rakoczy grabbed her with both hands, shoved her violently at Erikki, breaking the charge and bringing Erikki down with her. At the same moment he leapt backward, turned, and raced away, whirled again, the gun ready, his finger tightening on the trigger. But there was no need to pull it, the Finn and the woman were still on their knees, half stunned. Beyond them the pilot was still in his seat. Then he saw Erikki come to his senses, and shove her behind him protectively, readying another charge.

'Stop!' he ordered, 'or this time I will kill you all. STOP!' He put a warning burst into the snow. 'Get back in the plane – both of you!' Now totally alert, Erikki watched him suspiciously. 'Go on – you're free. Go!'

Desperately afraid, Azadeh scrambled into the backseat. Erikki retreated slowly, his body shielding her. Rakoczy kept the gun unwavering. He saw the Finn sit on the backseat, the door still open, his feet propped against skid. At once the engines picked up speed. The chopper eased a foot off the ground, slowly swung around to face him, the back door closing. His heart pounded even more. Now, he thought, do you all die or do we live to fight another day?

The moment seemed to him to last for ever. The chopper backed away, foot by foot, still so tempting a target. His finger tightened slightly. But he did not squeeze the further fraction. A few more yards then she twisted, hurried away through the snowfields, and went into the sky.

Good, he thought, tiredness almost overcoming him. It would have been better to have been able to keep the woman as a hostage, but never mind. We can grab old Abdollah Khan's daughter tomorrow, or the day after. She can wait and so can Yokkonen. Meanwhile there's a country to possess, generals and mullahs and ayatollahs to kill . . . and other enemies.

Tuesday

Chapter 5

On the North Face of Mount Sabalan: 10:00 A.M. The night was bitterly cold under a cloudless sky, stars abundant, the moon strong and Captain Ross and his two Gurkhas were working their way cautiously under a crest following the guide and the CIA man, Rosemont, an American. The soldiers wore cowled, white snow coveralls over their battle dress, and gloves and thermal underwear but still the cold tormented them. They were about 8,000 feet, down wind of their target half a mile away the other side of the ridge. Above them the vast cone shape of the extinct volcano soared over 16,000.

'Meshghi, we'll stop and rest,' the CIA man said in Turkish to the guide. Both were dressed in rough tribesmen's clothes.

'If you wish it, agha, then let it be so.' The guide led the way off the path, through the snow, to a small cave that none of them had noticed. He was old and gnarled like an ancient olive tree, hairy and thin, his clothes ragged, and still the strongest of them after almost two days' climbing.

'Good,' the CIA man said. Then to Ross, 'Let's hole up here, till we're ready.'

Ross unslung his carbine, sat, and rested his pack gratefully, his calves and thighs and back aching. 'I'm all one big bloody ache,' he said disgustedly, 'and I'm supposed to be fit.'

'You're fit, sahib,' the Gurkha sergeant called Tenzing said in Gurkhali with a beam. 'On our next leave we go up Everest, eh?'

'Not on your Nelly,' Ross said in English and the three soldiers laughed together.

Then the CIA man said thoughtfully, 'Must be something to stand on top of that mother.'

Ross saw him look out at the night and the thousands of feet of mountain below. When they had first met at the rendezvous near Bandar-e Pahlavi two days ago, if he hadn't been told otherwise he would have thought him part Mongol or Nepalese or Tibetan, for the CIA man was dark-haired with a yellowish skin and Asian eyes and dressed like a nomad.

'Your CIA contact's Rosemont, Vien Rosemont, he's half Vietnamese – half American,' the CIA colonel had said at his briefing in Tehran. 'He's twenty-six, been here a year, speaks Farsi and Turkish, he's second-generation CIA, and you can trust him with your life.'

'It seems I'm going to have to, sir, one way or another, don't you think?'

'Huh? Oh, sure, yes. Yes, I guess so. You meet him just south of Bandar-e

Pahlavi at those coordinates and he'll have the boat. You'll hug the coast until you're just south of the Soviet border, then backpack in.'

'He's the guide?'

'No. He, er, he just knows about Mecca – that's our code name for the radar post. Getting the guide's his problem – but he'll deliver. If he's not at the rendezvous, wait throughout Saturday night. If he's not there by dawn, he's blown and you abort. Okay?'

'Yes. What about the rumours of insurrection in Azerbaijan?'

'Far as we know there's some fighting in Tabriz and the western part – nothing around Ardabil. Rosemont should know more. We, er, we know the Soviets are massed and ready to move in if the Azerbaijanis throw Bakhtiar supporters out. Depends on their leaders. One of them's Abdollah Khan. If you run into trouble go see him. He's one of ours – loyal.'

'All right. And this pilot, Charles Pettikin, say he won't take us?'

'Make him. One way or another. There's approval way up to the top for this op, both from your guys and ours, but we can't put anything into writing. Right, Bob?'

The other man at the briefing, a Robert Armstrong, an Englishman from Special Branch, whom he had also never met before, had nodded agreement. 'Yes.'

'And the Iranians? They've approved it?'

'It's a matter of, er, of national security – yours and ours. Theirs too but they're . . . they're busy. Bakhtiar's, well, he's – he may not last.'

'Then it's true – the U.S. are jerking the rug?'

'I wouldn't know about that, Captain.'

'One last question: why aren't you sending your fellows?'

Robert Armstrong had answered for the colonel. 'They're all busy – we can't get any more here quickly – not with your elite training.'

We're certainly well trained, Ross thought, easing his shoulders cut raw by his backpack straps – to climb, to jump, to ski, to snorkel, to kill silently or noisily, to move like the wind against terrorist or public enemy, and to blow everything sky-high if need be, above or under water. But I'm bloody lucky, I've everything I want: health, university, Sandhurst, paratroopers, special air services, and even my beloved Gurkhas. He beamed at both of them and said a Gurkhali obscenity in a vulgar dialect that sent them into silent fits of laughter. Then he saw Vien Rosemont and the guide looking at him. 'Your pardon, Excellencies,' he said in Farsi. 'I was just telling my brothers to behave themselves.'

Meshghi said nothing, just turned his attention back to the night.

Rosemont had pulled off his boots and was massaging the chill out of his feet. 'The guys I've seen, British officers, they're not friends with their soldiers, not like you.'

'Perhaps I'm luckier than others.' With the side of his eyes Ross was watching the guide who had got up and was now standing at the mouth of the cave, listening. The old man had become increasingly edgy in the last few hours. How far do I trust him? he thought, then glanced at

Gueng who was nearest. Instantly the little man got the message, nodded back imperceptibly.

'The captain is one of us, sir,' Tenzing was saying to Rosemont proudly. 'Like his father and grandfather before him – and they were both Sheng'khan.'

'What's that?'

'It's a Gurkhali title,' Ross said, hiding his pride. 'It means Lord of the Mountain. Doesn't mean much outside the regiment.'

'Three generations in the same outfit. That usual?'

Of course it's not usual, Ross wanted to say, disliking personal questions, though liking Vien Rosemont personally. The boat had been on time, the voyage up the coast safe and quick, them hidden under sacking. Easily ashore at dusk and on their way to the next rendezvous where the guide had been waiting, fast into the foothills, and into the mountains, Rosemont never complaining but pressing forward hard, with little conversation and none of the barrage of questions he had expected.

Rosemont waited patiently, noticing Ross was distracted. Then he saw the guide move out of the cave, hesitate, then come back and squat against the cave mouth, rifle cradled on his lap.

'What is it, Meshghi?' Rosemont asked.

'Nothing, agha. There are flocks in the valley, goats and sheep.'

'Good.' Rosemont leaned back comfortably. Lucky to find the cave, he thought, it's a good place to hole up in. He glanced back at Ross, saw him looking at him. After a pause he added, 'It's great to be part of a team.'

'What's the plan from now on?' Ross asked.

'When we get to the entrance of the cave, I'll lead. You and your guys stay back until I make sure, okay?'

'Just as you like, but take Sergeant Tenzing with you. He can protect your tail – I'll cover you both with Gueng.'

After a pause, Rosemont nodded. 'Sure, sounds good. Okay, Sergeant?'

'Yes, sahib. Please tell me what you want simply. My English is not good.'

'It's just fine,' Rosemont said, covering his nervousness. He knew Ross was weighing him like he was weighing them – too much at stake.

'You just blow Mecca to hell,' his director had told him. 'We've a specialist team to help you; we don't know how good they are but they're the goddam best we can get. Leader's a captain, John Ross, here's his photo and he'll have a couple of Gurkhas with him, don't know if they speak English but they come recommended. He's a career officer. Listen, as you've never worked close with Limeys before, a word of warning. Don't get personal or friendly or use first names too fast – they're as sensitive as a cat with a feather up its ass about personal questions, so take it easy, okay?'

'Sure.'

'Far as we know you'll find Mecca empty. Our other posts nearer Turkey are still operating. We figure to stay as long as we can – by that time the brass'll make a deal with the new jokers, Bakhtiar or

Khomeini. But Mecca – goddam those bastards who've put us at so much risk.'

'How much risk?'

'We think they just left in a hurry and destroyed nothing. You've been there, for crissake! Mecca's stuffed with enough top secret gizmos, listening gear, seeing gear, long-range radar, locked-in satellite ciphers and codes and computers to get our unfriendly KGB chief Andropov voted Man of the Year – if he gets them. Can you believe it – those bastards just hightailed it out!'

'Treason?'

'Doubt it. Just plain stupid, dumb – there wasn't even a contingency plan at Sabalan, for crissake – anywhere else either. Not all their fault, I guess. None of us figured the Shah'd fold so goddam quick, or that Khomeini'd get Bakhtiar by the balls so fast. We got no warning – not even from SAVAK . . .'

And now we have to pick up the pieces, Vien thought. Or, more correctly, blow them to hell. He glanced at his watch, feeling very tired. He gauged the night and the moon. Better give it another half an hour. His legs ached, and his head. He saw Ross watching him and he smiled inside: I won't fail, Limey. But will you?

'An hour, then we'll move out,' Vien said.

'Why wait?'

'The moon'll be better for us. It's safe here and we've time. You're clear what we do?'

'Mine everything in Mecca you mark, blow it and the cave entrance simultaneously, and run like the clappers all the way home.'

Rosemont smiled and felt better. 'Where's home for you?'

'I don't know really,' Ross said caught unawares. He had never asked himself the question. After a moment, more for himself than the American, he added, 'Perhaps Scotland – perhaps Nepal. My father and mother are in Katmandu, they're as Scots as I am but they've been living there off and on since '51 when he retired. I was even born there though I did almost all my schooling in Scotland.' Both are home, for me, he thought. 'What about you?'

'Washington, D.C. – really Falls Church, Virginia, which is almost part of Washington. I was born there.' Rosemont wanted a cigarette but knew it might be dangerous. 'Pa was CIA. He's dead now but he was at Langley for his last few years, which's close by – CIA HQ's at Langley.' He was happy to be talking. 'Ma's still in Falls Church, haven't been back in a couple of years. You ever been to the States?'

'No, not yet.' The wind had picked up a little and they both studied the night for a moment.

'It'll die down after midnight,' Rosemont said confidently.

Ross saw the guide shift position again. Is he going to make a run for it? 'You've worked with the guide before?'

'Sure. I tramped all over the mountains with him last year – I spent a month here. Routine. Lotta the opposition infiltrate through this area and we try to keep tabs on 'em – like they do us.' Rosemont watched the guide. 'Meshghi's a good joe. Kurds don't like Iranians, or Iraqis or our friends across the border. But you're right to ask.'

Ross switched to Gurkhali. 'Tenzing, watch everywhere and the pathfinder – you eat later.' At once Tenzing slipped out of his pack and was gone into the night. 'I sent him on guard.'

'Good,' Rosemont said. He had watched them all very carefully on the climb up and was very impressed with the way they worked as a team, leapfrogging, always one of them flanking, always seeming to know what to do, no orders, always safety catches off. 'Isn't that kinda dangerous?' he had said early on.

'Yes, Mr. Rosemont – if you don't know what you're doing,' the Britisher had said to him with no arrogance that he could detect. 'But when every tree or corner or rock could hide hostiles, the difference between safety on and off could mean killing or being killed.'

Vien Rosemont remembered how the other had added guilelessly, 'We'll do everything we can to support you and get you out,' and he wondered again if they would get in, let alone out. It was almost a week since Mecca had been abandoned. No one knew what to expect when they got there – it could be intact, already stripped, or even occupied. 'You know this whole op's crazy?'

'Ours not to reason why.'

'Ours but to do or die? I think that's the shits!'

'I think that's the shits too if it's any help.'

It was the first time they had laughed together. Rosemont felt much better. 'Listen, haven't said it before, but I'm happy you three're aboard.'

'We're, er, happy to be here.' Ross covered his embarrassment at the open compliment. 'Agha,' he called out in Farsi to the guide, 'please join us at food.'

'Thank you, agha, but I am not hungry,' the old man replied without moving from the cave mouth.

Rosemont put his boots back on. 'You got a lot of special units in Iran?'

'No. Half a dozen – we're here training Iranians. You think Bakhtiar will weather it?' He opened his pack and distributed the cans of bully beef.

'No. The word in the hills among the tribes is that he'll be out – probably shot – within the week.'

Ross whistled, 'Bad as that?'

'Worse: that Azerbaijan'll be a Soviet protectorate within the year.'

'Bloody hell!'

'Sure. But you never know' – Vien smiled – 'that's what makes life interesting.'

Casually Ross offered the flask. 'Best Iranian rotgut money can buy.'

Rosemont grimaced and took a careful sip, then beamed. 'Jesus H. Christ, it's real Scotch!' He prepared to take a real swallow but Ross was ready and he grabbed the flask back.

'Easy does it – it's all we've got, agha.'

Rosemont grinned. They ate quickly. The cave was snug and safe. 'You ever been to Vietnam?' Rosemont asked, wanting to talk, feeling the time right.

'No, never have. Almost went there once when my father and I were en route to Hong Kong but we were diverted to Bangkok from Saigon.'

'With the Gurkhas?'

'No, this was years ago, though we do have a battalion there now. I was,' Ross thought a moment, 'I was seven or eight, my father has some vague Hong Kong relations, Dunross, yes, that was their name, and there was some sort of clan gathering. I don't remember much of Hong Kong except a leper who lay in the dirt by the ferry terminal. I had to pass him every day – almost every day.'

'My dad was in Hong Kong in '63,' Vien said proudly. 'He was Deputy Director of Station – CIA.' He picked up a stone, toyed with it. 'You know I'm half-Vietnamese?'

'Yes, they told me.'

'What else did they tell you?'

'Just that I could trust you with my life.'

Rosemont smiled wryly. 'Let's hope they're right.' Thoughtfully he began checking the action of his M16. 'I've always wanted to visit Vietnam. My pa, my real pa, was Vietnamese, a planter, but he was killed just before I was born – that was when the French owned Indochina. He got clobbered by Viet Cong just outside Dien Bien Phu. Ma . . .' The sadness dropped off him and he smiled. 'Ma's as American as a Big Mac and when she remarried she picked one of the greatest. No real pa could've loved me more . . .'

Abruptly Gueng cocked his carbine. 'Sahib!' Ross and Rosemont grabbed their weapons, then there was a keening on the wind, Ross and Gueng relaxed. 'It's Tenzing.'

The sergeant appeared out of the night as silently as he had left. But now his face was grim. 'Sahib, many trucks on the road below – '

'In English, Tenzing.'

'Yes, sahib. Many trucks, I counted eleven, in convoy, on the road at the bottom of the valley . . .'

Rosemont cursed. 'That road leads to Mecca. How far away were they?'

The little man shrugged. 'At the bottom of the valley. I went the other side of the ridge and there's a . . .' He said the Gurkhali word and Ross gave him the English equivalent. 'A promontory. The road in the valley twists, then snakes as it climbs. If the tail of the snake is in the valley and the head wherever the road ends, then four trucks were already well past tail.'

Rosemont cursed again. 'An hour at best. We'd bett – ' At that moment there was a slight scuffle and their attention flashed to the cave mouth. They just had time to see the guide rushing away, Gueng in pursuit.

'What the hell . . .'

'For whatever reason, he's abandoning ship,' Ross said. 'Forget him. Does an hour give us a chance?'

'Sure. Plenty.' Quickly they got into their packs and Rosemont armed his light machine gun. 'What about Gueng?'

'He'll catch us up.'

'We'll go straight in. I'll go first – if I run into trouble you abort. Okay?'

The cold was almost a physical barrier they had to fight through but Rosemont led the way well, the snow not bad on the meandering path, the moon helping, their climbing boots giving them good traction. Quickly they topped the ridge and headed down the other side. Here it was more slippery, the mountainside barren, just a few clumps of weeds and plants fighting to get above the snow. Ahead now was the maw of the cave, the road running into it, many vehicle tracks in the snow.

'They could've been made by our trucks,' Rosemont said, covering his disquiet. 'There's been no snow for a couple of weeks.' He motioned the others to wait and went forward, then stepped out on the road and ran for the entrance. Tenzing followed, using the ground for cover, moving as rapidly.

Ross saw Rosemont disappear into the darkness. Then Tenzing. His anxiety increased. From where he was he could not see far down the road, for it curled away, falling steeply. The strong moonlight made the crags and the wide valley more ominous, and he felt naked and lonely and hated the waiting. But he was confident. 'If you've Gurkhas with you, you've always a chance, my son,' his father had said. 'Guard them – they'll always guard you. And never forget, with luck, one day you'll be Sheng'khan.' Ross had smiled to himself, so proud, the title given so rarely: only to one who had brought honour to the regiment, who had scaled a worthy Nepalese peak alone, who had used the kukri and had saved the life of a Ghurka in the service of the Great Raj. His grandfather, Captain Kirk Ross, MC, killed in 1915 at the Battle of the Somme, had been given it posthumously; his father Lieutenant-Colonel Gavin Ross, DSO, was given it in Burma, 1943. And me? Well, I've scaled a worthy peak – K4 – and that's all so far but I've lots of time . . .

His fine-tuned senses warned him and he had his kukri out, but it was only Gueng. The little man was standing over him, breathing hard. 'Not fast enough, sahib,' he whispered happily in Gurkhali. 'I could have taken you moments ago.' He held up the severed head and beamed. 'I bring you a gift.'

It was the first that Ross had seen. The eyes were open. Terror still contorted the face of the old man. Gueng killed him but I gave the order, he thought, sickened. Was he just an old man who was scared fartless and wanted to get out while the going was good? Or was he a spy or a traitor rushing to betray us to the enemy?

'What is it, sahib?' Gueng whispered, his brow furrowed.

'Nothing. Put the head down.'

Gueng tossed it aside. The head rolled a little down the slope then stopped. 'I searched him, sahib, and found this.' He handed him the amulet. 'It was around his throat and this' – he gave him the small leather bag – 'this hung down around his balls.'

The amulet was just a cheap blue stone worn against the evil eye. Inside the little bag was a small card, wrapped in plastic. Ross squinted at it and his heart skipped a beat. At that moment there was another keening on the wind, the note different. Immediately they picked up their guns and ran for the cave mouth, knowing that Tenzing had given them the all clear signal and to hurry. Inside the throat of the cavern the darkness seemed deeper and then, as their eyes adjusted, they saw a fleck of light. It was a flashlight, the lens partially covered.

'Over here, Captain.' Though it was softly said, Rosemont's voice echoed loudly. 'This way.' He led them farther into the cave and when he was sure it was safe he shone the light on the rock walls and all around to get his bearings. 'It's okay to use your flashes.' The cave was immense, many tunnels and passages leading off it, some natural, some man-made, the rock dome fifty feet overhead. 'This's the unloading area,' he said. When he found the tunnel he sought he shone the light down it. At the end was a thick steel door, half open. 'It should be locked,' he whispered, his voice raw. 'I don't know if it was left like that or what, but that's where we have to go.'

Ross motioned to Tenzing. At once the kukri came out and the soldier went forward to vanish inside. Automatically Ross and Gueng took up defensive positions. Against whom? Ross asked himself helplessly, feeling trapped. There could be fifty men hidden in any one of those other tunnels.

The seconds dragged. Again there was the keening. Ross led the rush through the doorway, then Gueng, then Rosemont. As Rosemont passed the door he saw that Tenzing had taken up a position nearby and was covering them. He pulled the door to and switched on the lights. The suddenness made the others gasp.

'Hallelujah!' Rosemont said, openly relieved. 'The brass figured if the generators were still working, we'd have a good shot. This door's lightproof.' He slid heavy bolts into place, hung his flashlight on his belt.

They were in another cave, much smaller, that had been adapted, the floor levelled and carpeted roughly, the walls made more flat. It was a form of anteroom with desks and phones and litter everywhere. 'The guys sure didn't waste any time getting to hell out, did they?' he said bitterly, hurrying across the room to another tunnel, down it and into another caveroom with more desks, a few radar screens, and more phones, grey and green.

'The grey're internal, greens go to the tower and masts on the crest, from there by satellite to Tehran, our HQ switchboard in the embassy, and various top-secret places – they've built-in scramblers.' Rosemont picked one up. It was dead. 'Maybe the communications guys did their job after all.' At the far end of the room was a tunnel. 'That goes down to the generator room for this section which has all the gear we've to blow. Living quarters, kitchens, mess halls, repair shops, are in other caves off the unloading area. About eighty guys worked here around the clock.'

'Is there any other way out of here?' Ross asked. His feeling of being closed in was greater than ever.

'Sure, topside, where we're going.'

Rough steps led upward through the domed roof. Rosemont started climbing them. On the landing was a door: TOP SECURITY AREA – NO ADMITTANCE WITHOUT SPECIAL AUTHORITY. It too was open. 'Shit,' he muttered. This cave was well appointed, floor flatter, walls whitewashed. Dozens of computers and radar screens, and banked electronic equipment. More desks and chairs and phones, grey and green. And two red on a central desk.

'What're those for?'

'Direct to Langley by military satellite.' Rosemont picked one up. It was dead. So was the other. He pulled out a piece of paper and checked it, then went over to a bank of switches and turned some on. Another obscenity as a soft hum began, computers started chattering, warming up, and three of the radar screens came to life, the central white trace-line turning, leaving a scatter pattern in its wake. 'Bastards! Bastards to leave everything like this.' His finger stabbed at four corner computers. 'Blow those mothers – they're the core.'

'Gueng!'

'Yes, sahib.' The Gurkha took off his pack and began to lay out the plastic explosives and detonators.

'Half-hour fuses?' Rosemont said.

'Half-hour fuses it is.' Ross was staring at one of the screens, fascinated. Northward he could see most of the Caucasus, all of the Caspian, eastward even part of the Black Sea, all with extraordinary clarity. 'That's a lot of space to peer into.'

Rosemont went over to its keyboard and turned a switch.

For a moment Ross was dumbfounded. He tore his eyes off the screen. 'Now I understand why we're here.'

'That's only part.'

'Christ! Then we'd better get cracking. What about the cave mouth?'

'We've no time to do a decent job – and the other side of our door's routine junk they've stolen anyway. We'll blow our tunnels after us and use the escapeway.'

'Where's that?'

The American went over to a door. This one was locked. He took out a bunch of tagged keys and found the one he wanted. The door swung open. Behind the door a narrow flight of stairs spiralled upward steeply. 'It leads out on to the mountain.'

'Tenzing, make sure the way's clear.' Tenzing went up the stairs two at a time. 'Next?'

'Code room and the safes, we'll mine those. Then communications. Generator room last, okay?'

'Yes.' Ross liked the incisive strength more and more. 'Before we do you'd better look at this.' He took out the small, plastic-covered card. 'Gueng caught up with our guide. This was on him.'

All colour left Rosemont's face. On the card was a thumbprint, some writing in Russian script and a signature. 'An ID!' he burst out. 'A commie ID!' Behind them Gueng paused momentarily.

'That's what I thought. What's it say exactly?'

'I don't know, I can't read Russian either but I'll bet my life it's a safe-conduct pass.' A wave of sickness came up from his stomach as he remembered all the days and nights he had spent in the old man's company, wandering the mountains, sleeping alongside him in the open, feeling very safe. And all the time he'd been pegged. Numbly he shook his head. 'Meshghi was with us for years – he was one of Ali bin Hassan Karakose's band – Ali's an underground leader and one of our best contacts in the mountains. Great guy who even operates as far north as Baku. Jesus, maybe he's been betrayed.' He looked at the card again. 'Just doesn't figure.'

'I think it figures we could have been deliberately set up, sitting ducks,' Ross said. 'Perhaps the convoy's part of it, full of troops to track us. We'd better hurry it up, eh?'

Rosemont nodded, fighting to dominate the fear that swept through him, helped by the calmness of the other man. 'Yes, yes, you're right.' Still shattered, he went through a small passage to another door. Locked. As he looked for the key on the tabbed ring of keys he said, 'I owe you and your men an apology. I don't know how we – I – got taken in or how that bastard escaped the security check but he did and you're probably right – we're set up. Sorry, but, shit, that doesn't help a goddam bit.'

'It helps.' Ross grinned and the fear dropped off both of them. 'It helps. Okay?'

'Okay. Thanks, yes, thanks. Gueng killed him?'

'Well,' Ross said dryly. 'He handed me his head. They usually just bring back ears.'

'Jesus. You been with them long?'

'The Gurkhas? Four years.'

The key slid into the lock and the door opened. The code room was pedantically neat. Telex and teleprinter and copy machines. A curious computer printer with a keyboard was on its own desk. 'That's the decoder – worth any money you'd like to ask the opposition.' On the desks pencils were lined up. Half a dozen manuals.

Rosemont picked them up. 'Good sweet Jesus . . .' All were codebooks marked MECCA – ONE COPY ONLY. 'Well, at least the master code's locked up.' He went to the modern safe with its electronic, 0–9 digital lock that was set into one wall, read the combination from his piece of paper and touched the digits. But the open light didn't come on. 'Maybe I missed a number. Read them to me, okay?'

'Sure.' Ross began reading out the long series of numbers. Behind them Tenzing came in noiselessly. Neither man heard him . . . then both men felt the presence at the same instant and whirled, momentarily panicked.

Tenzing kept the delight off his face and closed his ears to the profanity. Hadn't the Sheng'khan told him to train the son and make him wise in the ways of stealth and killing? Hadn't he sworn to guard him and be his silent teacher? 'But, Tenzing, for the love of God don't let my son know I told you to. Keep his secret between us. . . .' It's been very hard to catch the sahib unawares for weeks, he thought happily. But Gueng caught him tonight and so did I. Much better we do than an enemy – and now they surround us like bees and their queen.

'The staircase leads upward for seventy-five steps to an iron door,' Tenzing said in his best reporting voice. 'The door is rusty but I forced it. Outside is a cave, outside the cave is the night – a good escape route, sahib. Not good is that from there I saw the first of the convoy.' He paused, not wanting to be wrong. 'Perhaps half an hour of time is left.'

'Go back to the first door, Tenzing, the one we barred. Mine the tunnel this side of the door to leave the door unharmed – twenty-minute fuse from now. Tell Gueng to set his fuses the same from now exactly. Tell Gueng what I've ordered.'

'Yes, sahib.'

Ross turned back. He noticed the sweat on Rosemont's forehead. 'Okay?'

'Sure. We got to 103.'

'The last two numbers are 660 and 31.' He saw the American touch the numbers. The Open light began winking. Rosemont's right hand went for the lever. 'Hold it!' Ross wiped the sweat from his own chin, the golden stubble rasping. 'I suppose there's no chance it could be booby-trapped?'

Rosemont stared at him, then at the safe. 'It's possible. Sure, it's possible.'

'Then let's just blow the bugger and not risk it.'

'I – I've gotta check. I've got to check if Mecca's master code's inside or not. That and the decoder are priority.' Again he looked at the light winking at him. 'You go back in the other room, take cover with Gueng, shout when you're ready I – it's my shot.'

Ross hesitated. Then he nodded, picked up both packs that contained explosives and detonators. 'Where's the communication room?'

'Next door.'

'Is – is the generator room important?'

'No. Just this one, the decoder and those four mothers back there, though it'd be best if this whole goddam floor went to hell.' Rosemont watched Ross walk away then turned and looked back at the lever. There was a bad tightness in his chest. That sonofabitch Meshghi! I'd've bet my life – you ready?' he called out impatiently.

'Wait!' Again his stomach surged. Ross was back beside him before he had heard him, in his hands a long, thin, nylon climbing rope that, quickly, he lashed to the lever. 'Turn the lever when I say but don't open the door. We'll jerk it open from back there.' Ross hurried out. 'Now!'

Rosemont took a deep breath to slow his heart and turned the lever to Open then ran through the passage into the other cave. Ross beckoned him down beside the wall. 'I sent Gueng to warn Tenzing. Ready?'

'Sure.'

Ross tightened the rope, then tugged hard. The rope remained taut. He tugged even harder, then it slackened a foot but came no farther. Silence. Nothing. Both men were sweating. 'Well,' Ross said, greatly relieved, and

got up. 'Better safe than sorr – ' The explosion obliterated his words, a great
cloud of dust and bits of metal blew out of the passage into their cave, jerking
the air from their lungs, scattering tables and chairs. All radar screens burst,
lights vanished, one of the red phones tore loose and hurtled across the room
to smash through the steel casing of a computer. Gradually the dust settled,
both men coughing their hearts out in the darkness.

Rosemont was the first to recover. His flashlight was still on his belt. He
groped for it.

'Sahib?' Tenzing called out anxiously, rushing into the room, his flash on,
Gueng beside him.

'I'm all – right,' Ross said, still coughing badly. Tenzing found him lying
in the rubble. A little blood was running down his face but it was only a
superficial wound from the flying glass. 'Bless all gods,' Tenzing muttered
and helped him up.

Ross fought to stay upright. 'Christalmighty!' Blankly he looked around
at the wreckage, then stumbled after Rosemont through the passage into the
code room. The safe had vanished, with it the decoder, manuals, phones,
leaving a huge hole in the living rock. All electronic equipment was just a
mess of twisted metal and wires. Small fires had already started.

'Jesus,' was all Rosemont could say, his voice little more than a croak, his
psyche revolted by the nearness to extinction, mind screaming: run, escape
this place of your death . . .

'Christ all bloody mighty!'

Helplessly, Rosemont tried to say something more, couldn't, his legs took
him into a corner and he was violently sick.

'We'd better – ' Ross found it hard to talk, his ears still ringing, a
monstrous ache in his head, adrenalin pumping, trying to dominate his own
wish to run. 'Tenzing, are – are you finished?'

'Two minutes, sahib.' The man rushed off.

'Gueng?'

'Yes sahib. Two minutes also.' He hurried away.

Ross went to the other corner and retched. Then he felt better. He found
the flask and took a long swig, wiped his mouth on the sleeve of his battle
dress, went over and shook Rosemont who was leaning against the wall.
'Here.' He gave it to him. 'You all right?'

'Yes. Sure.' Rosemont still felt queasy, but now his mind was working.
His mouth tasted foul and he spat the foulness into the rubble. Small fires
burned, throwing crazy shadows on the walls and roof. He took a careful sip.
After a moment he said, 'Nothing on God's earth like Scotch.' Another sip
and he handed the flask back. 'We'd better get the hell out of here.'

With the flashlight he made a quick search of the wreckage, found the
twisted remains of the all-important decoder, and picked his way carefully
into the next cave and laid the remains near the charge at the base of the
corner computers. 'What I don't understand,' he said helplessly, 'is why the
whole goddam place didn't go up and blow us all to hell anyway – with all
our explosives scattered around.'

'I – before I came back with the rope and sent Gueng off to Tenzing, I told Gueng to remove the explosives and the detonators for safety.'

'You always think of everything?'

Ross smiled weakly. 'All part of the service,' he said. 'Communications room?'

It was mined quickly. Rosemont glanced at his watch. 'Eight minutes to blast-off. We'll forget the generator room.'

'Good. Tenzing, you lead.'

They went up the escape staircase. The iron hatch creaked as it opened. Once in the cave Ross took the lead. Cautiously he peered out at the night and all around. The moon was still high. Three or four hundred yards away the lead truck was grinding up the last incline. 'Which way, Vien?' he asked and Rosemont felt a glow.

'Up,' he said, hiding the warmth. 'We climb. If there're troops after us, we forget the coast and head for Tabriz. If no troops we circle and go back the way we came.'

Tenzing led. He was like a mountain goat but he picked the easiest path, knowing the two men were still very shaky. Here the slope was steep but not too difficult with little snow to impede them. They had barely started when the ground shook beneath them, the sound of the first explosion almost totally muffled. In quick succession there were other small quakes.

One to go, Rosemont thought, glad of the cold which was clearing his head. The last explosion – the communications room – where they had used all their remaining explosive was much bigger and really shuddered the earth. Below and to their right, part of the mountain gave way, smoke billowing out of the resulting crater.

'Christ,' Ross muttered.

'Probably an air vent.'

'Sahib. Look down there!'

The lead truck had stopped at the entrance to the cave. Men were jumping out of it, others staring up at the mountainside, illuminated by the lights of the following trucks. The men all had rifles.

Ross and the others slid deeper into the shadows. 'We'll climb up to that ridge,' Rosemont said softly, pointing above and to their left. 'We'll be out of their sight and covered. Then we head for Tabriz, almost due east. Okay?'

'Tenzing, on you go!'

'Yes, sahib.'

They made the ridge and hurried over it to climb again, working their way eastward, not talking, conserving their energy for there were many, many miles to go. The terrain was rough and the snow harried them. Soon their gloves were torn, hands and legs bruised, calves aching but, no longer encumbered by heavy packs, they made good progress and their spirits were high.

They came to one of the paths that crisscrossed the mountains. Whenever the path forked, their choice was always to keep to the heights. There were villages in the valley, very few up this high. 'Better we stay up here,' Rosemont said, 'and . . . and hope we don't run into anyone.'

'You think they'll all be hostile?'

'Sure. It's not only anti-Shah country here but anti-Khomeini, anti-everyone.' Rosemont was breathing heavily. 'It's village against village most of the time and good bandit country.' He waved Tenzing onward, thankful for the moonlight and that he was with the three of them.

Tenzing kept up the pace but it was a mountaineer's pace, measured and unhurried and constant and punishing. After an hour Gueng took over the lead then Ross, Rosemont, and then Tenzing again. Three minutes' rest an hour, then on again.

The moon sank lower in the sky. They were well away now, the going easier, lower down the mountainside. The path meandered but it led generally eastward towards a curiously shaped cleft in the range. Rosemont had recognised it. 'Down in that valley's a side road that goes to Tabriz. It's little more than a track in winter but you can get through okay. Let's go on till dawn, then rest up and make a plan. Okay?'

Now they were down the tree line and into the beginnings of the pine forest, going much slower and feeling the tiredness.

Tenzing still led. Snow muffled their footsteps and the good clean air pleased him greatly. Abruptly he sensed danger and stopped. Ross was just behind him and he stopped also. Everyone waited motionless. Then Ross went forward carefully. Tenzing was peering into the dark ahead, the moon casting strange shadows. Slowly both men used their peripheral vision. Nothing. No sign or smell. They waited. Some snow fell from one of the trees. No one moved. Then a night bird left a branch ahead and to the right and flew noisily away. Tenzing pointed in that direction, motioned Ross to wait, slid his kukri out and went forward alone, melting into the night.

After a few yards Tenzing saw a man crouched behind a tree fifty yards ahead and his excitement picked up. Closer he could see that the man was oblivious of him. Closer. Then his peripheral vision saw a shadow move to his left, another to his right and he knew. 'Ambush!' he shouted at the top of his lungs and dived for cover.

The first wave of bullets passed near him but missed. Part of the second punctured his left lung, ripped a hole out of his back, slamming him against a fallen tree. More guns opened up on the opposite side of the pathway, the crossfire racking Ross and the others, who had scrambled behind tree trunks and into gullies.

For a moment Tenzing lay there helplessly. He could hear the firing but it seemed far away though he knew that it must be near. With a last mighty effort he dragged himself to his feet and charged the guns that had killed him. He saw some of their attackers turn back on him and heard bullets pass him, some tugging at his cowl. One went through his shoulder but he did not feel it, pleased that he was dying as men in the regiment were supposed to die. Going forward. Fearlessly. I am truly without fear. I am Hindu and I go to meet Shiva contentedly, and when

I am reborn I pray Brahma, Vishnu, Shiva that I will be born again Gurkha.

As he reached the ambush, his kukri hacked off someone's arm, his legs gave out, a monstrous, peerless light went off in his head and he strode into death without pain.

'Hold all fire,' Ross called out, getting his bearings, pulling the strings of battle back into his hands. He pegged two groups of guns against them, but there was no way that he could get at either. The ambush had been well chosen and the crossfire deadly. He had seen Tenzing hit. It had taken all of his willpower not to go to his aid but first there was this battle to win and the others to protect. The shots were echoing and re-echoing off the mountainside. He had wriggled out of his pack, found the grenades, made sure his carbine was fully automatic, not knowing how to lead the way out of the trap. Then he had seen Tenzing reel to his feet with a battle cry and charge up the slope, creating the diversion Ross needed. At once he ordered Rosemont, 'Cover me,' and to Gueng, 'Go!' pointing towards the same group Tenzing was attacking.

Immediately Gueng jumped out of his gully and rushed them, their attention diverted by Tenzing. When he saw his comrade go down, his rage burst, he let the lever on his grenade fly off, hurled it into their midst and hit the snow. The instant the grenade exploded he was up, his carbine spraying the screams, stopping most of them. He saw one man rushing away, another desperately crawling off into the underbrush. One slash of the kukri took off part of the crawler's head. A short burst cut the other to pieces and again Gueng whirled into cover, not knowing where the next danger would come from. Another grenade exploding took his attention to the other side of the path.

Ross had crawled forward out of safety. Bullets straddled him but Rosemont opened up with short bursts, drawing fire, giving Ross the help he needed, and he made the next tree safely, found a deep trough in the snow and fell into it. For a second he waited, collecting his breath, then scrambled along the hard, frozen snow towards the firing. Now he was out of sight of the attackers and he made good time. Then he heard the other grenade go off and the screaming, and he prayed that Gueng and Tenzing were all right.

The enemy firing was getting closer, and when he judged that he was in position, he pulled the pin out of the first grenade and with his carbine in his left hand went over the top. The instant he was in the open he saw the men, but not where he had expected them. There were five, barely twenty yards away. Their rifles turned on him but his reactions were just a little faster and he was on the ground behind a tree, the lever off and counting before the first barrage ripped into it. On the fourth second he reached around the tree and lobbed the grenade at them, buried his head under his arms. The explosion lifted him off the ground, blew the trunk of a nearer tree to pieces, burying him under branches and snow from its limbs.

Down by the path Rosemont had emptied his magazine into where he thought the attackers would be. Cursing in his anxiety, he slapped in a new magazine and fired another burst.

Across the path on the other slope, Gueng was huddled behind a rock waiting for someone to move. Then, near the exploded tree, he saw one man running away, bent double. He aimed and the man died, the shot echoing. Now silence.

Rosemont felt his heart racing. He could wait no longer. 'Cover me, Gueng,' he shouted and leaped to his feet and rushed for the tree. A flicker of firing to his right, bullets hissed past, then Gueng opened up from the other slope. A bubbling scream and the firing ceased. Rosemont ran onward until he was straddling the ambush point, his carbine levelled. Three men were in pieces, the last barely alive, their rifles bent and twisted. All wore rough tribal clothes. As he watched, the last man choked and died. He turned away and rushed for the other tree, pulling branches away, fighting his way through the snow to Ross.

On the other slope Gueng waited and watched to kill anything that moved. There was a slight stir amid the carnage behind the rocks where his grenade had ripped the three men apart. He waited, hardly breathing, but it was only a rodent feeding. Soon they will clean the ground and make it whole again, he thought, awed by the cycle of the gods. His eyes ranged slowly. He saw Tenzing crumpled to one side of the rock, his kukri still locked in his grasp. Before I leave I will take it, Gueng thought; his family will cherish it and his son will wear it with equal honour. Tenzing Sheng'khan lived and died like a man and will be reborn as the gods decide. Karma.

Another movement. Ahead in the forest. He concentrated.

The other side of the path Rosemont was pulling at the branches, fighting them away, his arms aching. At last he reached Ross and his heart almost stopped. Ross was crumpled on the ground, his arms over his head, his carbine nearby. Blood stained the snow and the back of the white coveralls. Rosemont knelt and turned him over and almost cried out with relief that Ross was still breathing. For a moment his eyes were blank, then they focused. He sat up and winced. 'Tenzing? And Gueng?'

'Tenzing got clobbered, Gueng's the other side covering us. He's okay.'

'Thank God. Poor Tenzing.'

'Test your arms and legs.'

Gingerly Ross moved his limbs. Everything worked. 'My head hurts like hell, but I'm okay.' He looked around and saw the crumpled attackers. 'Who are they?'

'Tribesmen. Bandits maybe.' Rosemont studied the way ahead. Nothing moved. The night was fine. 'We'd better get the hell out of here before more of the bastards jump us. You think you can go on?'

'Yes. Give me a couple of seconds.' Ross wiped some snow over his face. The cold helped. 'Thanks, eh? You know. Thanks.'

Rosemont smiled back. 'All part of the service,' he said wryly. His eyes went to the tribesmen. Keeping well down he went over to them and searched where he could. He found nothing. 'Probably locals – or just bandits. These bastards can be real cruel if they catch you alive.'

Ross nodded and another spasm of pain soared. 'I'm okay now, I think. We'd better move – the firing must have been heard for miles and this's no place to hang around.'

Rosemont had seen the pain. 'Wait some more.'

'No. I'll feel better moving.' Ross gathered his strength, then called out in Gurkhali, 'Gueng, we'll go on.' He started to get up, stopped as an abrupt keening for danger answered him. 'Get down!' he gasped and pulled Rosemont with him.

A single rifle bullet came out of the night and chose Rosemont and buried itself in his chest, mortally wounding him. Then there was firing from the other slope and a scream and silence once more.

In time, Gueng joined Ross. 'Sahib, I think that was the last. For the moment.'

'Yes.' They waited with Vien Rosemont until he died, then did what they had to do for him and for Tenzing. And then they went on.

Chapter 6

Tehran: At Sharazad's Apartment: 7:30 P.M. Sharazad was lying in a foam bath, her head propped on a waterproof pillow, eyes closed, her hair tied up in a towel. 'Oh, Azadeh, darling,' she said drowsily, perspiration beading her forehead, 'I'm so happy.'

Azadeh was also in the bath and she lay with her head at the other end, enjoying the heat and the intimacy and the sweet perfumed water and the luxury – her long hair also up in a pure white towel – the bath large and deep and comfortable for two. But there were still dark rings under her eyes, and she could not shake off the terrors of yesterday at the roadblock or in the helicopter. Outside the curtains, night had come. Gunfire echoed in the distance. Neither paid it any attention.

'I wish Erikki would come back,' Azadeh said.

'He won't be long, there's lots of time, darling. Mac has much to talk over with him. Dinner's not till nine, so we've almost two hours to get ready.' Sharazad opened her eyes and put her hand on Azadeh's slender thighs, enjoying the touch of her. 'Don't worry, darling Azadeh, he'll be back soon, your redheaded giant! And don't forget I'm spending the night with my parents so you two can run naked together all night long! Enjoy our bath, be happy, and swoon when he returns.' They laughed together. 'Everything's wonderful now, you're safe, we're all safe, Iran's safe – with the Help of God the Imam has conquered and Iran's safe and free.'

'I wish I could believe it, I wish I could believe it as you do,' Azadeh said. 'I can't explain how terrible those people near the roadblock were – it was as though I was being choked by their hate. Why should they hate us – hate me and Erikki? What had we done to them? Nothing at all and yet they hated us.'

'Don't think about them, my dear one.' Sharazad stifled a yawn. 'Leftists are all mad, claiming to be Muslim and at the same time Marxist. They're anti-God and therefore cursed. The villagers? Villagers are uneducated as you know too well, and most of them simple. Don't worry – that's past, now everything is going to be better, you'll see.'

'I hope, oh how I hope you're right. I don't want it better but just as it was, normal, like it's always been, normal again.'

'Oh, it will be.' Sharazad felt so contented, the water so silky and so warm and womblike. Ah, she thought, only three more days and then my Tommy comes back, and then, the next day, the great day, I should know for certain though I'm certain now. Haven't I always been so regular? Then I can give Tommy my gift of God and he'll be so proud. 'The Imam does the work of God. How can it be otherwise than good?'

'I don't know, Sharazad, but never in our history have mullahs been worthy of trust – just parasites on the backs of the villagers.'

'Ah, but now it's different,' Sharazad told her, not really wanting to discuss such serious matters. 'Now we have a real leader. Now he's in control of Iran for the first time ever. Isn't he the most pious of men, the most learned of Islam and the law? Doesn't he do God's work? Hasn't he achieved the impossible, throwing out the Shah and his nasty corruption, stopping the generals from making a coup with the Americans? Father says we're safer now than we've ever been.'

'Are we?' Azadeh remembered Rakoczy in the chopper and what he had said about Khomeini and stepping backwards in history, and she knew he had spoken the truth, a lot of truth, and she had clawed at him, hating him, wanting him dead, for of course he was one of those who would use the simple-minded mullahs to enslave everyone else. 'You want to be ruled by Islamic laws of the Prophet's time, almost fifteen hundred years ago – enforced chador, the loss of our hard-won rights of voting, working and being equal, Sharazad?'

'I don't want to vote, or work, or be equal – how can a woman equal a man? I just want to be a good wife to my Tommy, and in Iran I prefer the chador on the streets.' Delicately Sharazad covered another yawn, drowsed by the warmth. 'Insha'Allah, Azadeh, darling. Of course everything will be as before but Father says more wonderful because now we possess ourselves, our land, our oil, and everything in our land. There'll be no nasty foreign generals or politicians to disgrace us and with the evil Shah gone, we'll all live happily ever after, you with your Erikki, me with my Tommy, and lots and lots of children. How else could it be? God is with the Imam and the Imam is with us! We're so lucky.' She smiled at her and put her arm around her friend's legs affectionately. 'I'm so glad you're staying with me, Azadeh. It seems such a long time since you were in Tehran.'

'Yes.' They had been friends for many years. First in Switzerland where they had met at school, up in the High Country, though Sharazad had only stayed one term, unhappy to be away from her family and Iran, then later at the university in Tehran. And now, for a little over a year, because both had married foreigners in the same company, they had become even closer, closer than sisters, helping each other adapt to foreign idiosyncrasies.

'Sometimes I just don't understand my Tommy at all, Azadeh,' Sharazad had said tearfully in the beginning. 'He enjoys being alone, I mean quite alone, just him and me, the house empty, not even one servant – he even told me he likes to be alone by himself, just reading, no family around or children, no conversation or friends. Oh, sometimes it's just awful.'

'Erikki's just the same,' Azadeh had said. 'Foreigners aren't like us – they're very strange. I want to spend days with friends and children and

family, but Erikki doesn't. It's good that Erikki and Tommy work during
the days – you're luckier, Tommy's off for two weeks at a time when you
can be normal. Another thing, you know, it took me months to get used to
sleeping in a bed.'

'I never could! Oh, so high off the floor, so easy to fall off, always a huge
dip on his side, so you're always uncomfortable and you wake up with an ache
in your back. A bed's so awful compared with soft quilts on beautiful carpets
on the floor, so comfortable and civilised.'

'Yes. But Erikki won't use quilts and carpets, he insists on a bed. He just
won't try it any more – sometimes it's such a relief when he's away.'

'Oh, we sleep correctly now, Azadeh. I stopped the nonsense of a Western
bed after the first month.'

'How did you do it?'

'Oh, I'd sigh all night long and keep my poor darling awake – then I'd
sleep during the day to be fresh again to sigh all night long.' Sharazad had
laughed delightedly. 'Seven nights and my darling collapsed, slept like a baby
for the next three nights correctly, and now he always sleeps like a civilised
person should – he even does so when he's at Zagros! Why don't you try it? I
guarantee you'll be successful, darling, particularly if you also complain just
a tiny bit that the bed has caused a backache and of course you would still
adore to make love but please be a little careful.'

Azadeh had laughed. 'My Erikki's cleverer than your Tommy – when
Erikki tried the quilts on our carpet *he* sighed all night and turned and turned
and kept me awake – I was so exhausted after three nights I quite liked the bed.
When I visit my family I sleep civilised, though when Erikki's at the palace
we use a bed. You know, darling, another problem: I love my Erikki but
sometimes he's so rude I almost die. He keeps saying "yes" and "no" when I
ask him something – how can you have a conversation after yes or no?'

She smiled to herself now. Yes, it's very difficult living with him, but living
without him now is unthinkable – all his love and good humour and size and
strength and always doing what I want but only just a little too easily so I
have little chance to sharpen my wiles. 'We're both very lucky, Sharazad,
aren't we?'

'Oh, yes, darling. Can you stay for a week or two – even if Erikki has to go
back, you stay, please?'

'I'd like to. When Erikki gets back . . . perhaps I'll ask him.'

Sharazad shifted in the bath, moving the bubbles over her breasts, blowing
them off her hands. 'Mac said they'd come here from the airport if they were
delayed. Genny's coming straight from the apartment but not before nine – I
also asked Paula to join us, the Italian girl, but not for Nogger, for Charlie.'
She chuckled. 'Charlie almost swoons when she just looks at him!'

'Charlie Pettikin? Oh, but that's wonderful. Oh, that's very good. Then
we should help him – we owe him so much! Let's help him snare the sexy
Italian!'

'Wonderful! Let's plan how to give Paula to him.'

'As a mistress or wife?'

'Mistress. Well, let me think! How old is she? She must be at least twenty-seven. Do you think she'd make him a good wife? He should have a wife. All the girls Tommy and I have shown him discreetly, he just smiles and shrugs – I even brought my third cousin who was fifteen thinking that would tempt him, but nothing. Oh good, now we have something to plan. We've plenty of time to plan and dress and get ready – and I've some lovely dresses for you to choose from.'

'It feels so strange, Sharazad, not to have anything – anything. Money, papers . . .' For an instant Azadeh was back in the Range Rover near the roadblock, and there before her was the fat-faced mujhadin who had stolen their papers, his machine gun blazing as Erikki rammed him against the other car, crushing him like a cockroach, blood and filth squeezed from his mouth. 'Having nothing,' she said, forcing the bad away, 'not even a lipstick.'

'Never mind, I've lots of everything. And Tommy'll be so pleased to have you and Erikki here. He doesn't like me to be alone either. Poor darling, don't worry. You're safe now.'

I don't feel safe at all, Azadeh told herself, hating the fear that was so alien to her whole upbringing – that even now seemed to take away the warmth of the water. I haven't felt safe since we left Rakoczy on the ground and even that had only lasted a moment, the ecstasy of escaping that devil – me, Erikki, and Charlie unhurt. Even the joy of finding a car with petrol in it at the little airstrip didn't take my fear away. I hate being afraid.

She ducked down a little in the tub, then reached up and turned on the hot-water tap, swirling the hot currents.

'That feels so good,' Sharazad murmured, the foam heavy, and the water sensuous. 'I'm so pleased you wanted to stay.'

Last evening, by the time Azadeh, Erikki and Charlie had reached McIver's apartment it was after dark. There was no room for them – Azadeh had been too frightened to want to stay in her father's apartment, even with Erikki – so she had asked Sharazad if they could move in with her until Lochart returned. Sharazad had delightedly agreed at once, glad for the company. Everything had begun to be fine and then, during dinner, there was gunfire nearby, making her jump.

'No need to worry, Azadeh,' McIver had said. 'Just a few hotheads letting off steam, celebrating probably. Didn't you hear Khomeini's order to lay down all arms?' Everyone agreeing and Sharazad saying, 'The Imam will be obeyed,' always referring to Khomeini as 'the Imam', almost associating him with the Twelve Imams of Shi'ism – the direct descendants of Mohammed the Prophet, near divinity – surely a sacrilege: 'But what the Imam's accomplished is almost a miracle, isn't it?' Sharazad had said with her beguiling innocence. 'Surely our freedom's a gift of God?'

Then so warm and toasty in bed with Erikki, but him strange and brooding and not the Erikki she had known. 'What's wrong, what's wrong?'

'Nothing, Azadeh, nothing. Tomorrow I'll make a plan. There was no time tonight to talk to Mac. Tomorrow we'll make a plan, now sleep, my darling.'

Twice in the night she had awakened from violent dreams, trembling and terrified, crying out for Erikki.

'It's all right, Azadeh, I'm here. It was only a dream, you're quite safe now.'

'No, no, we're not. I don't feel safe, Erikki – what's happening to me? Let's go back to Tabriz, or let's go away, go away from these awful people.'

This morning Erikki had left her to join McIver, and she had slept some more but gathered little strength from the sleep. Passing the rest of the morning daydreaming or hearing Sharazad's news about going to Galeg Morghi, or listening to the hourly crop of rumours from her servants: many more generals shot, many new arrests, the prisons burst open by mobs. Western hotels set on fire or shot up. Rumours of Bazargan taking the reins of government, mujhadin in open rebellion in the south, Kurds rebelling in the north, Azerbaijan declaring independence, the nomad tribes of the Kash'kai and Bakhtiari throwing off the yoke of Tehran; everyone laying down their arms or no one laying down their arms. Rumours that Prime Minister Bakhtiar had been captured and shot or escaped to the hills or to Turkey, to America; President Carter preparing an invasion or Carter recognising Khomeini's government; Soviet troops massing on the border ready to invade or Brezhnev coming to Tehran to congratulate Khomeini; the Shah landing in Kurdistan supported by American troops or the Shah dead in exile.

Then going to lunch with Sharazad's parents at the Bakravan house near the bazaar, but only after Sharazad had insisted she wear the chador, hating the chador and everything it stood for. More rumours at the huge, family house, but benign there, no fear and absolute confidence. Abundance as always, just as in her own home in Tabriz, servants smiling and safe and thanks be to God for victory, Jared Bakravan had told them jovially, and now with the bazaar going to open and all foreign banks closed, business will be marvellous as it was before the ungodly laws the Shah instituted.

After lunch they had returned to Sharazad's apartment. By foot. Wrapped in the chador. Never a problem for them and every man deferential. The bazaar was crowded, with pitifully little for sale though every merchant foretold abundance ready to be trucked, trained, or flown in – ports clogged with hundreds of ships, laden with merchandise. On the street, thousands walked this way and that, Khomeini's name on every lip, chanting 'Allah-u Akbarrr,' almost all men and boys armed – none of the old people. In some areas Revolutionary Guards, in place of police, haphazardly and amateurishly directed traffic, or stood around truculently. In other areas police as always. Two tanks rumbled past driven by soldiers, masses of guards and civilians on them, waving to the cheering pedestrians.

Even so, everyone was tense under the patina of joy, particularly the women enveloped in their shrouds. Once, they had turned a corner and seen ahead a group of youths surrounding a dark-haired woman dressed in Western clothes, jeering at her, abusing her, shouting insults and making obscene signs, several of them exposing themselves, waggling their penises at her. The woman was in her thirties, dressed neatly, a short coat over her skirt, long legs and long hair under a little hat. Then she was joined by a man who shoved through the crowd to her. At once he began shouting that they were English and to leave them alone, but the men paid no attention to him, jostling him, concentrating on the woman. She was petrified.

There was no way for Sharazad and Azadeh to walk around the crowd that grew quickly, hemming them in, so they were forced to watch. Then a mullah arrived and told the crowd to leave, harangued the two foreigners to obey Islamic customs. By the time they got home they were tired and both felt soiled. They had taken off their clothes and collapsed on the quilt bed.

'I'm glad I went out today,' Azadeh had said wearily, deeply concerned. 'But we women better organise a protest before it's too late. We better march through the streets, without chador or veils, to make our point with the mullahs: that we're not chattel, we have rights, and wearing the chador's up to us – not to them.'

'Yes, let's! After all, we helped win the victory too!' Sharazad had yawned, half asleep. 'Oh, I'm so tired.'

The nap had helped.

Idly Azadeh was watching the bubbles of foam crackling, the water hotter now, the sweet-smelling vapour very pleasing. Then she sat up for a moment, smoothing the foam on her breasts and shoulders. 'It's curious, Sharazad, but I was glad to wear chador today – those men were so awful.'

'Men on the street are always awful, darling Azadeh.' Sharazad opened her eyes and watched her, golden skin glistening, nipples proud. 'You're so beautiful, Azadeh darling.'

'Ah, thank you – but you're the beautiful one.' Azadeh rested her hand on her friend's stomach and patted her. 'Little mother, eh?'

'Oh, I do so hope so.' Sharazad sighed, closed her eyes and gave herself back to the heat. 'I can hardly imagine myself a mother. Three more days and then I'll know. When are you and Erikki going to have children?'

'In a year or two.' Azadeh kept her voice calm as she told the same lie she had told so many times already. But she was deeply afraid that she was barren, for she had used no contraceptives since she was married and had wished, with all her heart, to have Erikki's child from the beginning. Always the same nightmare welling up: that the abortion had taken away any chance of children as much as the German doctor had tried to reassure her. How could I have been so stupid?

So easy. I was in love. I was just seventeen and I was in love, oh, how deeply in love. Not like with Erikki, for whom I will give my life gladly. With Erikki it is true and for ever and kind and passionate and safe. With my Johnny Brighteyes it was dreamlike.

Ah, I wonder where you are now, what you're doing, you so tall and fair with your blue-grey eyes and oh, so British. Who did you marry? How many hearts did you break like you broke mine, my darling?

That summer he was at school in Rougemont – the next village to where she was at finishing school – ostensibly to learn French. It was after Sharazad had left. She had met him at the Sonnenhof, basking in the sun, overlooking all the beauty of Gstaad in its bowl of mountains. He was nineteen then, she three days seventeen, and all that summer long they had wandered the High Country – so beautiful, so beautiful – up in the mountains and the forests, swimming in streams, playing, loving, ever more adventurous, up above the clouds.

More clouds than I care to think of, she told herself dreamily, my head in the clouds that summer, knowing about men and life, but not knowing. Then in the fall him saying, 'Sorry, but I must go now, go back to university but I'll be back for Christmas.' Never coming back. And long before Christmas finding out. All the anguish and terror where there should have been only happiness. Petrified that the school would find out, for then her parents would have to be informed. Against the law to have an abortion in Switzerland without parents' consent – so going over the border to Germany where the act was possible, somehow finding the kindly doctor who had assured her and reassured her. Having no pain, no trouble, none – just a little difficulty borrowing the money. Still loving Johnny. Then the next year, school finished, everything secret, coming home to Tabriz. Stepmother finding out somehow – I'm sure Najoud, my step-sister, betrayed me, wasn't it she who lent me the money? Then Father knowing.

Kept like a spiked butterfly for a year. Then a peace – a form of peace. Begging for university in Tehran. 'I agree, providing you swear by God, no affairs, absolute obedience and you marry only whom I choose,' the Khan had said.

Top of her class. Then begging for the Teaching Corps, any excuse to get out of the palace. 'I agree, but only on our lands. We've more than enough villages for you to look after,' he had said.

Many men of Tabriz wanting to marry her but her father refusing them, ashamed of her. Then Erikki.

'And when this foreigner, this . . . this impoverished, vulgar, ill-mannered, spirit-worshipping monster who can't speak a word of Farsi or Turkish, who knows nothing of our customs or history or how to act in civilised society, whose only talent is that he can drink enormous quantities of vodka and fly a helicopter – when he finds out you're not virgin, that you're soiled, spoiled, and perhaps ruined inside for ever?'

'I've already told him, Father,' she had said through her tears. 'Also that without your permission I cannot marry.'

Then the miracle of the attack on the palace and Father almost killed – Erikki like an avenging warrior from the ancient storybooks. Permission to marry, another miracle. Erikki understanding, another miracle. But as yet no child. Old Dr. Nutt says I'm perfect and normal and to be patient. With the Help of God soon I will have a son, and this time there will be only happiness, like with Sharazad, so beautiful with her lovely face and breasts and flanks, hair like silk and skin like silk.

She felt the smoothness of her friend beneath her fingers and it pleased her greatly. Absently she began to caress her, letting herself drift in the warmth and tenderness. We're blessed to be women, she thought, able to bathe together and sleep together, to kiss and touch and love without guilt. 'Ah Sharazad,' she murmured, surrendering too, 'how I love your touch.'

In the Old City: 7:52 P.M. Jared Bakravan, Sharazad's father, was in his upper-storey, private inner room over the open-fronted shop in the Street of the Moneylenders deep in the huge bazaar that had been in his family for five generations and was in one of the best positions. His speciality was banking and financing. He was seated on thick pile carpets, drinking tea with his old friend, Ali Kia, who had managed to be appointed an official in the Bazargan government. Ali Kia was clean-shaven with glasses, Bakravan white-bearded and heavy. Both were in their sixties and had known each other most of their lives.

'And how will the loan be repaid, over what time period?' Bakravan asked.

'Out of oil revenues, as always,' Kia said patiently, 'just as the Shah would have done, the time period over five years, at the usual one percent per month. My friend Mehdi, Mehdi Bazargan, says Parliament will guarantee the loan the moment it meets.' He smiled and added, exaggerating slightly, 'As I'm not only in Mehdi's cabinet but also in his inner cabinet as well, I can personally watch over the legislation. Of course you know how important the loan is, and equally important to the bazaar.'

'Of course.' Bakravan tugged at his beard to prevent himself guffawing. Poor Ali, he thought, just as pompous as ever! 'It's certainly not my place to mention it, old friend, but some of the bazaaris have asked me what about the millions in bullion already advanced to support the revolution? Advanced for Ayatollah Khomeini – may God protect him,' he added politely, in his heart thinking may God remove him from us quickly now that we've won, before he and his rapacious, blinkered, parasitical mullahs do too much damage. As for you, Ali, old friend, bender of the truth, exaggerater of your own importance, you may be my oldest friend, but I don't trust you further than a camel can cast dung.

'Of course these loans will be repaid immediately we have the money – the very second! The Tehran bazaari loans are the first in line to be repaid of all internal debts – we, in government, realise how important your help has been. But Jared, Excellency, old friend, before we can do anything we must get oil production going and to do this we must have some cash. The Pr – '

The door burst open and Emir Paknouri rushed into the room. He was in his sixties, distraught and dishevelled. 'Jared, they're going to arrest me!' he cried out, tears now running down his face.

'Who? Who's going to arrest you and for what?' Bakravan spluttered, the customary calm of his house obliterated, the faces of frightened assistants, clerks, teaboys, and managers now crowding the doorway.

'For . . . for crimes against Islam!' Paknouri wept openly.

'There must be some mistake! It's impossible!'

'Yes, it's impossible but they . . . they came to my house with my name. . . . half an hour ago we – '

'Who? Give me their names and I'll destroy their fathers! Who came?'

'I told you! Revolutionary Guards, Green Bands, yes, them of course,' Paknouri said and rushed on, oblivious of the sudden hush. Ali Kia blanched and someone muttered, God protect us! 'Half an hour or so ago, with my name on a piece of paper . . . my name, Emir Paknouri, chief of the league of goldsmiths who gave millions of rials . . . they came to my house accusing me . . . by God and the Prophet, Jared,' he cried out as he fell to his knees, 'I've committed no crimes – I'm an Elder of the Bazaar, I've given millions and – ' Suddenly he stopped, seeing Ali Kia. 'Kia, Ali Kia, Excellency, you know only too well what I did to help the revolution!'

'Of course.' Kia was white-faced, his heart thumping. 'There has to be a mistake.'

'Of course there's a mistake!' Bakravan put his arm around the poor man and tried to calm him. 'Fresh tea at once!' he ordered.

'A whisky. Please, do you have a whisky?' Paknouri mumbled. 'I'll have tea afterwards, do you have whisky?'

'Not here, my poor friend, but of course there's vodka.' It came at once. Paknouri downed it and choked a little. He refused another. In a minute or two he became a little calmer and began again to tell what had happened. 'The leader of the Guards – there were five of them – the leader was waving this piece of paper and demanding to see me. He told us the paper was signed by someone called Uwari, on behalf of the Revolutionary Komiteh – in the Name of God, who're they? Who's this man Uwari? Who are they – this Revolutionary Komiteh? Ali Kia, surely you'd know?'

'Many names have been mentioned,' Kia said importantly, hiding his instant unease every time 'Revolutionary Komiteh' was uttered. Like everyone else in government or outside it, he did not have any real information about its actual makeup or when or where it meets, only that it seemed to come into being the moment Khomeini returned to Iran, barely two weeks ago and, since yesterday when Bakhtiar fled into hiding, it had been acting like it was a law unto itself, ruling in Khomeini's name and with his authority, precipitously appointing new judges, most with no legal training whatsoever, authorising arrests, revolutionary courts, and immediate executions, totally outside normal law and jurisprudence – and against the Constitution!

'Only this morning my friend Mehdi . . .' he began confidentially, passing on the rumour as though it was private knowledge, 'only this morning, with, er, with our blessing, he went to the Ayatollah and threatened to resign unless the Revolutionary Komiteh stopped bypassing him and his authority and so put them in their place for all time.'

'Praise be to God!' Paknouri said, very relieved. 'We didn't win the revolution to let more lawlessness take the place of SAVAK, foreign domination and the Shah!'

'My poor friend,' Bakravan said. 'My poor friend, how you must have suffered! Never mind, you're safe now. Stay here tonight. Ali, directly after first prayer tomorrow, go to the prime minister's office and make sure this matter is dealt with and those fools are punished. We all know Emir Paknouri's a patriot, that he and all the goldsmiths supported the revolution and are essential to this loan.' Wearily he closed his ears to all the platitudes that Ali Kia was uttering now, stifled a yawn, tired now and hungry. *A nap before dinner would do me good.* 'So sorry, Excellencies, so sorry but I have urgent business to attend to. Paknouri, old friend, I'm glad everything is resolved. Stay here tonight, servants will arrange quilts and cushions, and don't worry! Ali, my friend, walk with me to the bazaar gate – do you have transport?' he asked thinly, knowing that the first perk of a deputy minister would be a car and chauffeur and unlimited petrol.

'Yes, thank you, the PM insisted I arrange it, insisted – the importance of our department, I suppose.'

'As God wants!' Bakravan said.

Well satisfied, they all went out of the room, down the narrow stairs and into the small passageway that led to the open-fronted shop. Their smiles vanished and bile filled their mouths.

Waiting there were the five Green Bands, Revolutionary Guards, lolling on the desks and chairs, all armed with U.S. Army carbines, all in their early twenties, unshaven or bearded, their clothes poor and soiled, some with holed shoes, some sockless. The leader picked his teeth silently, the rest were smoking, carelessly dropping their ash on Bakravan's priceless Kash'kai carpets. One of these youths coughed badly as he smoked, his breath wheezing.

Bakravan felt his knees weakening. All of his staff stood frozen against one of the walls. Everyone. Even his favourite teaboy. Out in the street it was very quiet, no one about – even the owners of the moneylending shops across the alley seemed to have vanished.

'Salaam, agha, the Blessing of God on you,' he said politely, his voice sounding strange. 'What can I do for you?'

The leader paid no attention to him, just kept his eyes boring into Paknouri, his face handsome but scarred by the parasite disease, carried by sandflies and almost endemic in Iran. He was in his early twenties, dark eyes and hair and work-scarred hands that toyed with the carbine. His name was Yusuf Senvar – Yusuf the bricklayer.

The silence grew and Paknouri could stand the strain no longer. 'It's all a mistake,' he screamed. 'You're making a mistake!'

'You thought you'd escape the Vengeance of God by running away?' Yusuf's voice was soft, almost kind – though with a coarse village accent that Bakravan could not place.

'What Vengeance of God?' Paknouri screamed. 'I've done nothing wrong, nothing.'

'Haven't you worked for and with foreigners for years, helping them to carry off the wealth of our nation?'

'Of course not to do that but to create jobs and help the econ – '

'Nothing? Haven't you served the Satan Shah for years?'

Again Paknouri shouted, 'No, I was in opposition, everyone knows I . . .
I was in oppo – '

'But you still served him and did his bidding?'

Paknouri's face was twisted and almost out of control. His mouth worked
but he could not get the words out. Then he croaked, 'Everyone served him
– of course everyone served him, he was the Shah, but we worked for the
revolution – the Shah was the Shah, of course everyone served him while he
was in power . . .'

'The Imam didn't,' Yusuf said, his voice suddenly raw. 'Imam Khomeini
never served the Shah. In the Name of God, did he?' Slowly he looked from
face to face. No one answered him.

In the silence, Bakravan watched the man reach into his torn pocket and
find a piece of paper and peer at it and he knew that he was the only one here
who could stop this nightmare.

'By Order of the Revolutionary Komiteh,' Yusuf began, 'and Ali'allah
Uwari: Miser Paknouri, you are called to judgment. Submit yo – '

'No, Excellency,' Bakravan said firmly but politely, his heart pounding in
his ears. 'This is the bazaar. Since the beginning of time you know the bazaar
has its own laws, its own leaders. Emir Paknouri is one of them, he cannot be
arrested or taken away against his will. He cannot be touched – that is bazaari
law from the beginning of time.' He stared back at the young man, fearlessly,
knowing that the Shah, even SAVAK had never dared to challenge their laws
or right of sanctuary.

'Is bazaari law greater than God's law, Moneylender Bakravan?'

He felt a wave of ice go through him. 'No – no, of course not.'

'Good. I obey God's law and do God's work.'

'But you may not arres – '

'I obey God's law and do only God's work.' The man's eyes were brown
and guileless under his black brows. He gestured at his carbine. 'I do not
need this gun – none of us need guns to do God's work. I pray with all
my heart to be a martyr for God, for then I'll go straight to Paradise
without the need to be judged, my sins forgiven me. If it's tonight, then
I will die blessing him who kills me because I know I will die doing
God's work.'

'God is Great,' one of the men said, the others echoed him.

'Yes, God is Great. But you, Moneylender Bakravan, did you pray five times
today as the Prophet ordered?'

'Of course, of course,' Bakravan heard himself say, knowing his lie to be
sinless because of *taqiyah* – concealment – the Prophet's permission to any
Muslim to lie about Islam if he feels his life threatened.

'Good. Be silent and be patient, I come back to you later.' Another chill
racked him as he saw the man turn his attention back to Paknouri. 'By order
of the Revolutionary Komiteh and Ali'allah Uwari: Miser Paknouri, submit
yourself to God for crimes against God.'

Paknouri's mouth struggled. 'I . . . I . . . you cannot . . . there . . .'

Ali Kia cleared his throat. 'Now listen, perhaps it would be better to leave this until tomorrow,' he began, trying to keep his voice important. 'Emir Paknouri's clearly upset by the mista – '

'Who're you?' The leader's eyes bored into him as they had into Paknouri and Bakravan. 'Eh?'

'I'm Deputy Minister Ali Kia,' Ali replied, keeping his courage under the strength of the eyes, 'of the Department of Finance, member of Prime Minister Bazargan's cabinet and I suggest you wait u – '

'In the Name of God: you, your Department of Finance, your cabinet, your Bazargan has nothing to do with me or us. We obey the mullah Uwari, who obeys the Komiteh, who obeys the Imam, who obeys God.' The man scratched absently and turned his attention back to Paknouri. 'In the street!' he ordered, his voice still gentle. 'Or we'll drag you.'

Paknouri collapsed with a groan and lay inert. The others watched helplessly, someone muttered, 'The Will of God,' and the little teaboy began sobbing.

'Be quiet, boy,' Yusuf said without anger. 'Is he dead?'

One of the men went over and squatted over Paknouri. 'No. As God wants.'

'As God wants. Hassan, pick him up, put his head in the water trough and if he doesn't wake up, we'll carry him.'

'No,' Bakravan interrupted bravely, 'no, he'll stay here, he's sick an – '

'Are you deaf, old man?' An edge had crept into Yusuf's voice. Fear stalked the room. The little boy crammed his fist into his mouth to prevent himself from crying out. Yusuf kept his eyes on Bakravan as the man called Hassan, broad-shouldered and strong, lifted Paknouri easily and went out of the shop and up the alley. 'As God wants,' he said, eyes on Bakravan. 'Eh?'

'Where . . . please, where will you be taking him?'

'To jail, of course. Where else should he go?'

'Which . . . which jail, please?'

One of the other men laughed. 'What does it matter what jail?'

For Jared Bakravan and the others, the room was now stifling and cell-like even though the air had not changed and the open front on to the alley was as it had ever been.

'I would like to know, Excellency,' Bakravan said, his voice thick, trying to mask his hatred. 'Please.'

'Evin.' This had been the most infamous of Tehran's prisons. Yusuf sensed another wave of fear. They must all be guilty to be so afraid, he thought. He glanced behind him at his younger brother. 'Give me the paper.'

His brother was barely fifteen, grubby and coughing badly. He took out half a dozen pieces of paper and shuffled through them. He found the one he sought. 'Here it is, Yusuf.'

The leader peered at it. 'Are you sure it's the right one?'

'Yes.' The youth pointed a stubby finger at the name. Slowly he spelled out the characters. 'J-a-r-e-d B-a-k-r-a-v-a-n.'

Someone muttered, 'God protect us!' and in the vast silence Yusuf took the paper and held it out to Bakravan. The others watched, frozen.

Hardly breathing, the old man took it, his fingers trembling. For a moment he could not focus his eyes. Then he saw the words: 'Jared Bakravan of the Tehran bazaar, by order of the Revolutionary Komiteh and Ali'allah Uwari, you are summoned to the Revolutionary Tribunal at Evin Prison tomorrow immediately after first prayer to answer questions.' The paper was signed, Ali'allah, the writing illiterate.

'What questions?' he asked dully.

'As God wills.' The leader shouldered his carbine and got up. 'Until dawn. Bring the paper with you and don't be late.'

He stalked out.

Near the U.S. Embassy: 8:15 P.M. Erikki had been waiting for almost four hours. From where he sat in the first-floor window of his friend Christian Tollonen's apartment, he could see the high walls surrounding the floodlit U.S. compound down the road, uniformed marines near the huge iron gates stamping their feet against the cold, and the big embassy building beyond. Traffic was still heavy, snarled here and there, everyone honking and trying to get ahead, pedestrians as impatient and self-centred as usual. No traffic lights working. No police. Not that they'd make any difference, he thought, Tehranis don't give a damn for traffic regulations, never have, never will. Like those madmen on the road down through the mountains who killed themselves. Like Tabrizis. Or Qazvinis.

His great fist bunched at the thought of Qazvin. At the Finnish embassy this morning there had been reports of Qazvin in a state of revolt, that Azerbaijan nationalists in Tabriz had rebelled again and fighting was going on against forces loyal to the Khomeini government and that the whole oil-rich and vastly strategic border province had again declared its independence of Tehran, independence it had fought for over the centuries, always aided and abetted by Russia, Iran's permanent enemy and gobbler of her territory. Rakoczy and others like him must be swarming all over Azerbaijan.

'Of course the Soviets are after us,' Abdollah Gorgon Khan had said angrily, during the quarrel, just before he and Azadeh had left for Tehran. 'Of course your Rakoczy and his men are here in strength. We walk the thinnest tightrope in the whole world because we're their key to the Gulf and the key to Hormuz, the jugular of the West. If it hadn't been for us Gorgons, our tribal connections and some of our Kurdish allies, we'd be a Soviet province now – joined to the other half of Azerbaijan that the Soviets stole from us years ago, helped as always by the insidious British – oh, how I hate the British, even more than Americans who are just stupid and ill-mannered barbarians. It's the truth, isn't it?'

'They're not like that, not the ones I've met. And S-G's treated me fairly.'

'So far. But they'll betray you – the British betray everyone who's not British and even then they'll betray them if it suits them.'

'Insha'Allah.'

Abdollah Gorgon Khan had laughed without humour. 'Insha'Allah! And Insha'Allah the Soviet army retreated over the border and then we smashed their quislings, and stamped out their "Democratic Azerbaijan Republic" and the "Kurdish People's Republic". But I admire the Soviets, they play only to win and change the rules to suit themselves. The real winner of your world war was Stalin. He was the colossus. Didn't he dominate everything at Potsdam, Yalta and Tehran – didn't he outmanoeuvre Churchill and Roosevelt? Didn't Roosevelt even stay with him in Tehran in the Soviet embassy? How we Iranians laughed! The Great President gave Stalin the future when he had the power to stuff him behind his own borders. What a genius! Beside him your ally Hitler was a craven bungler! As God wills, eh?'

'Finland sided with Hitler only to fight Stalin and get back our lands.'

'But you lost, you chose the wrong side and lost. Even a fool could see Hitler would lose – how could Reza Shah have been so foolish? Ah, Captain, I never understood why Stalin let you Finns live. If I'd been him I would have laid waste Finland as a lesson – as he decimated a dozen other lands. Why did he let you all live? Because you stood up to him in your Winter War?'

'I don't know. Perhaps. I agree the Soviets will never give up.'

'Never, Captain. But neither will we. We Azerbaijanis will always out-manoeuvre them and keep them at bay. As in '46.'

But then the West was strong, there was the Truman Doctrine towards the Soviets of hands off or else, Erikki thought grimly. And now? Now Carter's at the helm? What helm?

Heavily, he leaned forward and refilled his glass, impatient to get back to Azadeh. It was cold in the apartment and he still wore his overcoat – the central heating was off and the windows draughty. But the room was large and pleasant and masculine with old easy chairs, the walls decorated with small but good Persian carpets and bronze. Books, magazines and journals were scattered everywhere, on tables and chairs and bookshelves – Finnish, Russian, Iranian – a pair of girl's shoes carelessly on one of the shelves. He sipped the vodka, loving the warmth it gave him, then looked out of the window once more at the embassy. For a moment he wondered if it would be worth emigrating to the U.S. with Azadeh. 'The bastions are falling,' he muttered out loud. 'Iran no longer safe, Europe so vulnerable, Finland on the sword's edge . . .'

His attention focused below. Now the traffic was totally blocked by swarms of youths collecting on both roads – the U.S. embassy complex was on the corner of Tahkt-e-Jamshid and the main road called Roosevelt. Used to be called Roosevelt, he reminded himself idly. What's the road called now? Khomeini Street? Street of the Revolution?

The front door of the apartment opened. 'Hey, Erikki,' the young Finn said with a grin. Christian Tollonen wore a Russian-style fur hat and fur-lined trench coat that he had bought in Leningrad on a drunken weekend with other university friends. 'What's new?'

'Four hours I've been waiting.'

'Three hours and twenty-two minutes and half a bottle of my best contraband Russian Moskava money can buy anywhere, and we agreed three or four hours.' Christian Tollonen was in his early thirties, a bachelor, fair and grey-eyed, deputy cultural attaché at the Finnish embassy. They had been friends since he came to Iran, some years ago. 'Pour me one, by God, I need it – there's another demonstration simmering, and I had a hell of a time getting through.' He kept his trench coat on and went to the window.

The two sections of crowds had joined now, the people milling about in front of the embassy complex. All gates had been closed. Uneasily Erikki noticed that there were no mullahs among the youths. They could hear shouting.

'Death to America, death to Carter,' Christian interpreted – he could speak fluent Farsi because his father too had been a diplomat here and he had spent five years of his youth at school in Tehran. 'Just the usual shit, down with Carter and American imperialism.'

'No Allah-u Akbar,' Erikki said. For a moment his mind took him back to the roadblock, and ice swept into his stomach. 'No mullahs.'

'No. I didn't see one anywhere around.' In the street the tempo picked up with different factions swirling around the iron gates. 'Most of them are university students. They thought I was Russian and they told me there'd been a pitched battle at the university, leftists versus the Green Bands – with perhaps twenty or thirty killed or wounded and it was still going on.' While they watched, fifty or sixty youths began rattling the gates. 'They're spoiling for a fight.'

'And no police to stop them.' Erikki handed him the glass.

'What would we do without vodka?'

Erikki laughed. 'Drink brandy. Do you have everything?'

'No – but a start.' Christian sat in one of the armchairs near the low table opposite Erikki and opened his briefcase. 'Here's a copy of your marriage and birth certificates – thank God we had copies. New passports for both of you – I managed to get someone in Bazargan's office to stamp yours with a temporary residence permit good for three months.'

'You're a magician!'

'They promised they'd issue you a new Iranian pilot's licence but when, they wouldn't say. With your S-G ID and the photocopy of your British licence they said you were legal enough. Now, Azadeh's passport's temporary.' He opened it and showed him the photograph. 'It's not standard – I took a Polaroid of the photo you gave me – but it'll pass until we can get a proper one. Get her to sign it as soon as you see her. Has she been out of the country since you were married?'

'No, why?'

'If she travels out on a Finnish passport – well, I don't know how it will affect her Iranian status. The authorities have always been touchy, particularly about their own nationals. Khomeini seems even more xenophobic so his regime's bound to be tougher. It might look to them as though she'd renounced her nationality. I don't think they'll let her back.'

A muted burst of shouting from the massed youths in the street diverted them for a moment. Hundreds were waving clenched fists and somewhere someone had a loudspeaker and was haranguing them. 'The way I feel right now, as long as I can get her out, I don't care,' Erikki said.

The younger man glanced at him. After a moment he said, 'Perhaps she should be aware of the danger, Erikki. There's no way I can get her replacement papers or any Iranian passport, but it'd be very risky for her to leave without them. Why don't you ask her father to arrange them for her? He could get them for her easily. He owns most of Tabriz, eh?'

Bleakly Erikki nodded. 'Yes, but we had another row just before we left. He still disapproves of our marriage.'

After a pause Christian said, 'Perhaps it's because you don't have a child yet, you know how Iranians are.'

'Plenty of time for children,' Erikki said, sick at heart. We'll have children in good time, he thought. Dr. Nutt says she's fine. Shit! If I tell her what Christian said about her Iranian papers she'll never leave; if I don't tell her and she's refused re-entry she'll never forgive me, and anyway she'd never leave without her father's permission. 'To get her new papers means we'll have to go back and, well, I don't want to go back.'

'Why, Erikki? Usually you can't wait to get to Tabriz.'

'Rakoczy.' Erikki had told him everything that had happened – except the killing of the mujhadin at the roadblock and Rakoczy killing others during the rescue. Some details are best untold, he thought grimly.

Christian Tollonen sipped his vodka. 'What's the real problem?'

'Rakoczy.' Erikki held his gaze steady.

Christian shrugged. Two refills emptied the bottle. 'Prosit!'

'Prosit! Thanks for the papers and passports.'

Shouting outside distracted them again. The crowd was well disciplined though it was becoming noisier. In the American courtyard more floodlights were on now, and they could see faces clearly in the embassy windows. 'Just as well they've their own generators.'

'Yes – and their own heating units, gasoline pumps, PX, everything.' Christian went over to the sideboard and brought out a fresh bottle. 'That and their special status in Iran – no visas necessary, not being subject to Iranian laws – has caused a lot of the hatred.'

'By God, it's cold in here, Christian. Don't you have any wood?'

'Not a damned bit. The damned heat's been off ever since I moved in here – three months, that's almost all winter.'

'Perhaps that's just as well.' Erikki motioned at the pair of shoes. 'You have heat enough. Eh?'

Christian grinned. 'Sometimes. I will admit Tehran is one of the – used to be one of the great places on earth for all sorts of pleasures. But now, now, old friend . . .' a shadow went over his face. 'Now I think Iran won't be the paradise those poor bastards out there believe they've won, but a hell on earth for most of them. Particularly the women.' He sipped his vodka. There was an eddy of excitement beside the compound wall as a youth, with his U.S. Army rifle slung, climbed on the shoulders of others and tried unsuccessfully to reach the top. 'I wonder what I'd do if that was my wall and those bastards started coming over at me in strength.'

'You'd blow their heads off – which'd be quite legal. Wouldn't it?'

Christian laughed suddenly. 'Only if you got away with it.' He looked back
at Erikki. 'What about you? What's your plan?'

'I don't have one. Not until I talk to McIver – there was no chance this
morning. He and the others were busy trying to track down the Iranian
partners, then they had meetings at the British embassy with someone called
– I think they said Talbot . . .'

Christian masked his sudden interest. 'George Talbot?'

'Yes, that's right. D'you know him?'

'Yes, he's second secretary.' Christian did not add: Talbot's also covert chief
of British Intelligence in Iran, has been for years, and is one very important
operator. 'I didn't know he was still in Tehran – I thought he'd left a couple
of days ago. What did McIver want with him?'

Erikki shrugged, absently watching more youths trying to scale the wall,
his mind concerned with what to do about Azadeh's papers.

'Did they find out what they wanted to know?'

Again Erikki shrugged. 'I don't know. I never caught up with them. I
was . . .' He stopped and studied the other man. 'Is it important?'

'No – no, not at all. You hungry? Are you and Azadeh free for dinner?'

'Sorry, not tonight.' Erikki glanced at his watch. 'I'd better be getting back.
Thanks again for the help.'

'Nothing. You were saying about McIver? They have a plan to change
operations here?'

'I don't think so. I was supposed to meet them at 3 p.m. to go to the airport
but seeing you and getting the passports was more important to me.' Erikki
stood up and put out his hand, towering over him. 'Thanks again.'

'Nothing.' Christian shook hands warmly. 'See you tomorrow.'

Now in the street the shouting had ceased and there was an ominous silence.
Both men ran for the window. All attention turned towards the main road once
called Roosevelt. Then they heard the growing, 'Allahhhh-uuuu Akbarrrr!'

Erikki muttered, 'Is there a back way out of the building?'

'No. No, there isn't.'

The new oncoming horde had mullahs and Green Bands in their front
ranks, most of them armed like the following mass of the young men. All
were shouting in unison, God is Great, God is Great, totally outnumbering
the student demonstration in front of the embassy, though the men there were
equally armed.

At once the leftists poured into well-chosen defensive positions in doorways
and among the traffic. Men, women and children trapped in cars and trucks
began to scatter. The Islamics approached fast. As the front ranks flowed
along the sidewalks and through the stalled vehicles and approached the
floodlit walls, the tempo of their shouting increased, their pace quickened,
and everyone readied. Then, astonishingly, the students began to retreat.
Silently. The Green Bands hesitated, nonplussed.

The retreat was peaceful and so the horde became peaceful. Soon the
protesters had moved away and now none of them threatened the embassy.
Mullahs and Green Bands began directing traffic. Those bystanders who

had fled or abandoned their vehicles breathed again, thanked God for His intercession and swarmed back. At once the hooting and cursing opened up in a growing frenzy as cars and trucks and pedestrians fought for space. The great iron gates of the embassy did not open, though a side door did.

Christian's throat felt dry. 'I'd've bet my life there was going to be a pitched battle.'

Erikki was equally astonished. 'It's almost as though . . . as though it was a rehearsal for som – ' He stopped and went closer to the window, his face suddenly flushed. 'Look! Down there in that doorway, that's Rakoczy.'

'Where? Wh – oh, you mean the man in the flight jacket talking to the short guy?' Christian squinted into the darkness below. The two men were half in shadow, then they shook hands and came into the light. It was Rakoczy all right. 'Are you sure that . . .'

But Erikki had already pulled the front door open and was halfway down the stairs. Christian had a fleeting glimpse of him as he pulled the great pukoh knife from his belt holster and slipped it into his sleeve, haft in his palm. 'Erikki, don't be a fool,' he shouted but Erikki had already vanished. Christian rushed back to the window and was just in time to see Erikki run out of the doorway below, shove through the crowds in pursuit, Rakoczy nowhere to be seen.

But Erikki had him in view. Rakoczy was half a hundred yards away and he just caught sight of him turning south into Roosevelt to disappear. When Erikki got to the corner, he saw the Soviet ahead, walking quickly but not too quickly, many pedestrians between them, the traffic slow and very noisy. Making a detour around a tangle of trucks, Rakoczy stepped out into the road, waited for a hooting, battered old Volkswagen to squeeze past and glanced around. He saw Erikki. It would have been almost impossible to miss him – almost a foot taller than almost everyone else. Without hesitation Rakoczy took to his heels, weaving through the crowds, and cut down a side street, running fast. Erikki saw him go and raced after him. Pedestrians cursed both of them, one old man sent flying into the filthy dirt as Rakoczy shoved past into another turning.

The side street was narrow, refuse strewn everywhere, no stalls or shops open now and no streetlights, a few weary pedestrians trudging homewards with multitudes of doorways and archways leading to hovels and staircases of more hovels – the whole area smelling of urine and waste and offal and rotting vegetables.

Rakoczy was a little more than forty yards ahead. He turned into a smaller alley, crashing through the street stalls where families were sleeping – howls of rage in his wake – changed direction and fled into a passageway and into another, cut across it into an alley, quite lost now, into another, down this and into another. Aghast, he stopped, seeing that this was a cul-de-sac. His hand went for his automatic, then he noticed a passageway just ahead and rushed for it.

The walls were so close he could touch both of them as he charged down it, his chest heaving, going ever deeper into the curling, twisting warren. Ahead an old woman was emptying night soil into the festering joub and he sent her sprawling as others cowered against the walls to get out of his way. Now Erikki was only twenty yards behind, his rage feeding his strength, and he jumped over the old woman who was still sprawled, half in and half out of the joub, and redoubled his efforts, closing the gap. Just around the corner his adversary stopped, pulled an ancient street stall into the way, and, before Erikki could avoid it, he crashed into it and went down half stunned. With a bellow of rage he groped to his feet, swayed dizzily for a moment, climbed over the wreckage, then rushed onward again, the knife now openly in his hand, and turned the corner.

But the passageway ahead was empty. Erikki skidded to a stop. His breath was coming in great, aching gasps and he was bathed in sweat. It was hard to see though his night vision was very good. Then he noticed the small archway. Carefully he went through it, knife ready. The passage led to an open courtyard strewn with rubble and the rusty skeleton of a ravaged car. Many doorways and openings led off this dingy space, some with doors, some leading to rickety stairways and upper storeys. It was silent – the silence ominous. He could feel eyes watching him. Rats scuttled out of some refuse and vanished under a pile of rubble.

To one side was another archway. Above it was an ancient inscription in Farsi that he could not read. Through the archway the darkness seemed deeper. The pitted vaulted entrance stopped at an open doorway. The door was wooden and girt with bands of ancient iron and half off its hinges. Beyond, there seemed to be a room. As he went closer he saw a candle guttering.

'What do you want?'

The man's voice came out of the darkness at him, the hair on Erikki's neck twisted. The voice was in English – not Rakoczy's – the accent foreign, a gruff eeriness to it.

'Who – who're you?' he asked uneasily, his senses searching the darkness, wondering if it was Rakoczy pretending to be someone else.

'What do you want?'

'I – I want – I'm following a man,' he said, not knowing where to talk to, his voice echoing eerily from the unseen, high-vaulted roof above.

'The man you seek is not here. Go away.'

'Who're you?'

'It doesn't matter. Go away.'

The candle flame was just a tiny speck of light in the darkness, making the darkness seem more strong. 'Did you see anyone come this way – come running this way?'

The man laughed softly and said something in Farsi. At once rustling and some muted laughter surrounded Erikki and he whirled, his knife protectively weaving in front of him. 'Who are you?'

The rustling continued. All around him. Somewhere water dripped into a cistern. The air smelled dank and rancid. Sound of distant firing. Another rustle. Again he whirled, feeling someone close by but seeing no one, only the archway and the dim night beyond. The sweat was running down his face.

Cautiously he went to the doorway and put his back against a wall, sure now that Rakoczy was here. The silence grew heavier.

'Why don't you answer?' he said. 'Did you see anyone?'

Again a soft chuckle. 'Go away.' Then silence.

'Why're you afraid? Who are you?'

'Who I am is nothing to you, and there's no fear here, except yours.' The voice was as gentle as before. Then the man added something in Farsi and another ripple of amusement surrounded him.

'Why do you speak English to me?'

'I speak English to you because no Iranian or reader of the language of the Book would come here by day or by night. Only a fool would come here.'

Erikki's peripheral vision saw something or someone go between him and the candle. At once his knife came on guard. 'Rakoczy?'

'Is that the name of the man you seek?'

'Yes – yes that's him. He's here, isn't he?'

'No.'

'I don't believe you, whoever you are!'

Silence, then a deep sigh. 'As God wants,' and a soft order in Farsi that Erikki did not understand.

Matches flickered all around him. Candles caught, and small oil lamps. Erikki gasped. There were ragged bundles against the walls and columns of the high-domed cavern. Hundreds of them. Men and women. The diseased, festering remains of men and women lying on straw or beds of rags. Eyes in ravaged faces staring at him. Stumps of limbs. One old crone was almost beside his feet and he leapt away in panic to the centre of the doorway.

'We are all lepers here,' the man said. He was propped against a nearby column, a helpless mound of rags. Another rag half covered the sockets of his eyes. Almost nothing was left of his face except his lips. Feebly he waved the stump of an arm. 'We're all lepers here – unclean. This is a house of lepers. Do you see this man among us?'

'No – no. I'm – I'm sorry,' Erikki said shakily.

'Sorry?' The man's voice was heavy with irony. 'Yes. We are all sorry. Insha'Allah! Insha'Allah.'

Erikki wanted desperately to turn and flee but his legs would not move. Someone coughed, a hacking, frightful cough. Then his mouth said, 'Who – who are you?'

'Once I was a teacher of English – now I am unclean, one of the living dead. As God wants. Go away. Bless God for His mercy.'

Numbed, Erikki saw the man motion with the remains of his arms. Obediently, around the cavern the lights began to go out, eyes still watching him.

Outside in the night air, he had to make a grim effort to stop himself from running away in terror, feeling filthy, wanting to cast off his clothes at once and bathe and soap and bathe and soap and bathe again.

'Stop it,' he muttered, his skin crawling, 'there's nothing to be afraid of.'

Wednesday

Chapter 7

Tehran: 4:17 P.M. Both men were staring anxiously at the telex machine in the S-G penthouse office. 'Come on for God's sake!' McIver muttered and glanced again at his watch.

Pettikin was rocking absently in a creaky old chair. 'Soon as Gen arrives we'll leave.'

This was the first day the komiteh had allowed any foreigners back into the building. Most of the morning had been spent cleaning up and restarting their generator that had, of course, run out of fuel. Almost at once the telex machine had chattered into life: 'Urgent! Please confirm your telex is working and inform Mr. McIver I have an Avisyard telex for him.' The telex was from S-G HQ in Aberdeen. 'Avisyard' was a company code, used rarely, meaning a top classified message for McIver's eyes only and to operate the machine himself. It took him four tries to get the Aberdeen callback.

'So long as we haven't lost a bird,' Pettikin said with an inward prayer.

'I was thinking that too.' McIver eased his shoulders.

'Anything I can do?'

'Don't think so. Squeezing our two remaining partners helped a lot.' McIver had tracked them down, and had extracted five million rials in cash – a little over sixty thousand, a pittance against what the partners owed – with promises for more every week, in return for a promise, and a handwritten note, to reimburse them personally 'outside the country, should it be necessary, and passage on the company 125 should it be necessary'.

'All right, but there's the matter of almost four million dollars owing on work already completed, apart from our aircraft lease payments overdue, long overdue.'

'If the banks were open you'd have the money. It's not our fault the Shah's pestilential allies ruined him and ruined Iran. We are not to blame for any of the catastrophes, none. As to the monies owed, haven't we paid in the past?'

'Yes. Usually six months late, but I agree, dear friend, eventually we have extracted our share. But if all joint ventures are suspended as the mullah Tehrani told me, how do we operate from now on?'

'*Some* joint ventures, not all – your information is exaggerated and incorrect. We are on notice to get back to normal as soon as possible – crews can leave once their replacements are safely here. Oil fields must be returned to full production. There will be no problems. But to forestall any trouble, once more we have bailed out the partnership. Tomorrow my illustrious cousin, Finance Minister Ali Kia joins the board a – '

'Hold on a minute! I have prior approval of any change in the board!'

'You used to have that power, but the board voted to change that byelaw. If you wish to go against the board you can bring it up at the next meeting in London – but under the circumstances the change is necessary and reasonable. Minister Kia has assured us we'll be exempt. Of course Minister Kia's fees and percentage will come out of your share . . .'

McIver tried not to watch the telex machine but he found it difficult, trying to think a way out of the trap. 'One moment everything seems okay, the next it's rotten again.'

'Yes. Talbot was today's clincher.'

This morning, early, they had met Talbot briefly. 'Oh, yes, old boy, joint ventures are definitely persona non grata now, so sorry,' he had told them dryly. 'The "On High" have decreed that *all* joint ventures are suspended, pending instructions, though what instructions and from whom, they didn't impart. Or who the "On High" are. We presume the Olympian decree is from the dear old Rev Komiteh, whoever they are! On the other side of the coin, old chap, the Ayatollah and Prime Minister Bazargan have both said all foreign debts will be honoured. Of course Khomeini overrides Bazargan and issues counter-instructions, Bazargan issues instructions which the Revolutionary Komiteh overrules, the local komitehs are vigilantes who're taking their own version of law as gospel, and not one rotten little urchin has yet handed in a weapon. The jails are filling up nicely, heads rolling – and apart from the tumbrils it all has a jolly old tediously familiar ring, old boy, and rather suggests we should all retire to Margate for the duration.'

'You're serious?'

'Our advice to evacuate all unessential personnel still stands the moment the airport opens which is God knows when but promised for Saturday – we've got BA to cooperate with chartered 747s. Be prepared to get out fast.'

'But what about our aircraft and spares and hangars for God's sake! Our whole corporate capital is tied up here.'

'Ours not to wonder, old boy. As to the illustrious Ali Kia, he's very minor indeed, with no power and a good weather friend to all sides. By the way we've just heard that the U.S. ambassador in Kabul was abducted by anti-communist, Shi'ite fundamentalist mujhadin who tried to exchange him for other mujhadin held by the pro-Soviet government. In the following shoot-out he was killed. Things are heating up rather nicely . . .'

The telex clicked on, their attention zeroed, but the machine did not function. Both of them cursed.

McIver glanced at the door as it opened. To their surprise it was Erikki – he and Azadeh had been due to meet them for dinner. Erikki was smiling his usual smile but there was no light behind it.

'Hi, Erikki. What's up?' McIver looked at him keenly.

'Slight change of plan. We're, er, well, Azadeh and I are going back to Tabriz first.'

Yesterday evening McIver had suggested that Erikki and Azadeh take immediate leave. 'We'll find a replacement. Go tomorrow – we've got clearance for the company 125 to land and, hopefully, to maintain a shuttle to Al Shargaz across the Gulf – we're sending out everyone not essential. No sweat. Perhaps we could get Azadeh replacement papers in London . . .'

'Why the change, Erikki?' he asked. 'Azadeh's had second thoughts about leaving Iran without Iranian papers?'

'No. An hour ago we got a message – I got a message from her father. Here, read it for yourself.' Erikki gave it to McIver. The handwritten note said: 'From Abdollah Khan to Captain Yokkonen: I require my daughter to come back here at once and ask you to grant her permission.' It was signed, Abdollah Khan. The message was repeated in Farsi on the other side.

'You're sure it's his handwriting?'

'Azadeh's sure, and she also knew the messenger.' Erikki added, 'The messenger told us nothing else, only that there's lots of fighting going on there.'

'By road's out of the question.' McIver turned to Pettikin. 'Maybe our mullah Tehrani'd give Erikki a clearance? According to Nogger, he was like a dog-eating wallah after his joyride this morning. We could fit your 206 with long-range tanks. Erikki could take her, maybe with Nogger or one of the others to bring her right back?'

'Erikki, you know the risk you're taking?'

'Yes.' Erikki had not yet told them about the killings.

'You've thought it through – everything? Rakoczy, the roadblock, Azadeh herself? We could send Azadeh back alone and you could get on the 125 and we'd put her on Saturday's flight.'

'Come on, boss, you'd never do that and neither will I – I couldn't leave her.'

'Of course, but it had to be said. All right. Erikki, you take care of the long-range tanks, we'll try for the clearance. I'd suggest you both come back to Tehran as quickly as possible and take the 125 on Saturday. Both of you. It might be wise for you to transfer and do a tour somewhere else – Australia, Singapore perhaps – or Aberdeen, but that might be too cold for Azadeh, you let me know.' McIver cheerfully stuck out his hand. 'Happy Tabriz, eh?'

'Thanks.' Erikki hesitated. 'Any news of Tom Lochart?'

'No, not yet – still can't raise Kowiss or Bandar-e Delam. Why? Sharazad's getting anxious?'

'More than that. Her father's in Evin Jail an – '

'JesusChrist,' McIver exploded, Pettikin equally shocked, knowing the rumours of arrests and firing squads. 'What for?'

'For questioning – by a komiteh – no one knows what for or how long he'll be held.'

'Well, if it's only for questioning. . . what happened?'

'Sharazad came home half an hour or so ago in tears. When she went back last night after dinner to her parents' house all hell had broken loose. Apparently some Green Bands went into the bazaar, grabbed Emir Paknouri, a friend of his, for "crimes against Islam" and ordered Bakravan to appear at dawn for questioning – for what reason no one knows.' Erikki took a breath. 'They went with him to the prison this morning, she, her mother, sisters and brother. They got there just after dawn and waited and waited and would be still waiting if they hadn't been told to clear off around 2 p.m. by Green Bands on guard there.'

There was a stunned silence.

Erikki broke it. 'Mac, try Kowiss. Get them to contact Bandar-e Delam – Tom should know about Sharazad's father. Well, I'll be off. Sorry for bringing bad news but I thought you'd better know.' Erikki forced a smile. 'Sharazad wasn't in good shape. See you in Al Shargaz!'

'Sooner the better, Erikki. Listen, if the stuff hits the fan – for *ANY* reason – go over the border to Turkey by any way you can.'

'I will, don't worry about me.'

'These are lousy times – choppers and pilots are gold dust in a revolution. Just in case, if I send you a message, *Take a powder*, that means drop everything at once, grab Azadeh and go over the border because it's really going to hit the fan. At once, okay?'

'All right. Don't worry about me.'

McIver said, 'If you bump into Gen – don't mention about Sharazad's father, eh?'

'Of course,' Erikki said and left.

McIver broke the silence. 'Bakravan's a pretty important bazaari to summarily arrest.'

'I agree.' After a pause Pettikin said, 'Hope to God Erikki's not going into a trap. That message bit's very smelly, very sm – '

The telex chattering made them both jump. They read the telex, line by line, as it came through.

It read: *Duncan, sorry to advise a top secret Foreign Office directive says all our aircraft in Iran will be impounded and all pilots refused permission to leave without* NEW SPECIAL VISAS, *within five or six days.*

I will go to Al Shargaz. Sorry, but prepare to evacuate all personnel as soon as possible.

The signature was Andy Gavallan, chairman of S.G. Helicopters.

McIver felt his heart pumping. That's it, he thought. Twenty years up the spout. Everything we've worked for, Andy and Gen and me. We're dead. . . .

'Duncan?'

He looked up and he saw it was Genny, Pettikin by the door, both of them watching him. 'Oh, hello, Genny, sorry, I was a million miles away.' He got up. 'It – I think it was the Avisyard that set me thinking.'

Genny's eyes widened. 'Oh, an Avisyard telex? Not a bird down?'

'No, no, thank God.'

'Oh, thank God too,' Genny said, openly relieved. She was dressed in a heavy coat and nice hat. 'Can I read it?' she asked, concerned with her husband's pallor, at once understanding why. She put the telex back on the table. 'I'll make a cuppa.'

The two men went through their options. Each time they came back to the same gloomy conclusion: they had to hope the situation came back to normal, the banks reopened, they got the money owing to them, that their joint venture was exempt and they weren't nailed, and the Foreign Office were wrong.

Genny listened attentively, also more than a little worried. It's obvious there's no future for us here, and I'd be very glad to leave – provided Duncan comes too. Even so, we can't just meekly run away with our tails between our legs and let all of Duncan's work and life's nest egg be stolen, that'd kill him as certainly as any bullet. Ugh! I do wish he'd do what he's told – he should have retired last year when the Shah was still in power. Men! Bloody stupid, the whole lot of them! Christ Almighty! What fools men are!

She started pouring the tea into the three cups. The silence tightened. Seeing her husband's misery a tear trickled down her cheek. She added condensed milk to the tea and gave one cup to Pettikin. Then she took the other cup to McIver.

'Thanks, Gen.' Tenderly he brushed away her tears. 'Come Saturday, Gen, when the 125 goes you're on it,' he told her gently. 'I promise only until we sort this all out – but this time you must go.'

She nodded. He drank his tea. It tasted very good. He smiled down at her. 'You make a damn good cuppa, Gen,' he said, but that did not take away her fear or her misery – or her fury at all the killing and uselessness and tragedy and the blatant usurping of their livelihood, or the age that it was putting on her husband. The worry's killing him. It's killing him, she thought with growing rage. Then all at once the answer came to her.

'Duncan,' she whispered, 'if you don't want those bastards to steal our future, why don't we leave and take everything with us?'

'Eh?'

'Planes, spares and personnel.'

'We can't do that, Gen, I've already told you fifty times.'

'Oh, yes, we can if we want to and if we have a plan.' She said it with such utter confidence it swept him. 'There's Andy to help. He's going to Al Shargaz. Andy can make the plan, we can't. You can carry it out, he can't. They don't want us here, so be it, we'll leave – but with our planes and our spares and our self-respect. We'll have to be very secretive but we can do it. We can do it, I know we can.'

BOOK TWO

Saturday

Chapter 8

Near Tabriz 11:49 A.M. Erikki was climbing the 206 through the high pass that led at length to the city, Nogger Lane beside him with Azadeh in the back. She wore a bulky flight jacket over her ski clothes, but in the carryall beside her was a chador: 'Just for safety,' she had said. On her head was a third headset that Erikki had rigged for her.

'Tabriz One, do you read?' he said again. They waited. Still no answer and well within range. 'Could be abandoned, could be a trap, like with Charlie.'

'Best take a jolly good look before we land,' Nogger said uneasily, his eyes scanning the sky and the land.

The sky was clear. It was well below freezing, the mountains heavy with snow. They had refuelled without incident at an IranOil depot just outside Bandar-e Pahlavi – already renamed – by arrangement with Tehran ATC. 'Khomeini's got everything by the short and curlies, with ATC helpful and the airport opened up again,' Erikki had said, trying to shove away the depression that sat heavily on all of them.

Azadeh was still badly shaken by the news of Emir Paknouri's execution for crimes against Islam and by the even more terrible news about Sharazad's father, also executed. 'That's murder,' she had burst out, horrified, when she had heard. 'What crimes could he commit, he who has supported Khomeini and mullahs for generations?'

None of them had had any answers. The family had been told to collect the body and now were in deep and abject mourning, Sharazad demented with grief – the house closed even to Azadeh and Erikki. Azadeh had not wanted to leave Tehran but a second message had arrived from her father to Erikki, repeating the first: 'Captain, I require my daughter in Tabriz urgently.'

And now they were almost home.

Once it was home, Erikki thought. Now I'm not so sure.

Near Qazvin he had flown over the place where his Range Rover had run out of petrol and Pettikin and Rakoczy had rescued Azadeh and him from the mob. The Range Rover was no longer there. Then over the miserable village where the roadblock had been, and he had escaped to crush the fat-faced mujhadin who had stolen their papers. Madness to come back, he thought.

'Mac's right,' Azadeh had pleaded with him. 'Go to Al Shargaz. Let Nogger fly me to Tabriz and fly me back to get on the next shuttle. I'll join you in Al Shargaz whatever my father says.'

'I'll take you home and bring you back,' he had said. 'Finish.'

They had taken off from Doshan Tappeh just after dawn. The base was almost empty, with many buildings and hangars now burned-out shells, wrecked Iranian Air Force airplanes, trucks, and one fire-gutted tank with the Immortals emblem on its side. No one cleaning up the mess. No guards. Scavengers taking away anything burnable – still hardly any fuel oil for sale, or food, but many daily and nightly clashes between Green Bands and leftists.

The S-G hangar and repair shop were hardly damaged. Many bullet holes in the walls but nothing had been looted yet and it was operating, more or less, with a few mechanics and office staff about their normal work. Some back salary from the money McIver had squeezed from the partners had been the magnet. He had given some cash to Erikki to pay the staff at Tabriz One: 'Start praying, Erikki! Today I've an appointment at the Ministry to iron out our finances and the money we're owed,' he had told them just before they took off, 'and to renew all our out-of-date licences. Talbot at the embassy fixed it for me – he thinks there's a better than good chance Bazargan and Khomeini can get control now and disarm the leftists. We've just got to keep our bottle, keep our cool.'

Easy for him, Erikki thought.

Now they crested the pass. He banked and came down fast. 'There's the base!' Both pilots concentrated. The wind sock was the only thing that moved. No transport parked anywhere. No smoke from any of the cabins. 'There should be smoke.' He circled tightly at 700 feet. No one came out to greet them. 'I'll take a closer look.'

They whirled in quickly and out again. Still nothing moved so they went back up to a thousand feet. Erikki thought a moment. 'Azadeh, I could set her down in the forecourt of the palace just outside the walls.'

At once Azadeh shook her head: 'No, Erikki, you know how nervous his guards are and how, how sensitive he is about anyone arriving unasked.'

'But we're asked, at least you are. Ordered is the real word. We could go over there, circle and take a look, and if it seems all right, we could land.'

'We could land well away and walk in t – '

'No walking. Not without guns.' He had been unable to obtain one in Tehran. Every damned hooligan has as many as he wants, he thought irritably. Have to get one. Don't feel safe any more. 'We'll go and look and then I'll decide.' He switched to the Tabriz Tower frequency and called. No answer. He called again, then banked and went for the city. As they passed over their village of Abu Mard, Erikki pointed downward and Azadeh saw the little schoolhouse where she had spent so many happy hours, the glades nearby and there, just by the stream, was where she had first seen Erikki and thought him a giant of the forest and had fallen in love, miracle of miracles, to be rescued by him from a life of torment. She reached forward and touched him through the small window.

'You all right? Warm enough?' He smiled at her.

'Oh, yes, Erikki. The village was so lucky for us, wasn't it?' She kept her hand on his shoulder. The contact pleased both of them.

Soon they could see the airport and the railway that went north to Soviet Azerbaijan a few miles away, then on to Moscow, southeast it curled back to Tehran, three hundred and fifty miles away. The city was large. Now they could pick out the citadel and the Blue Mosque and polluting steel factories, the huts and hovels and houses of the 600,000 inhabitants.

'Look over there!' Part of the railway station was smouldering, smoke billowing. More fires near the citadel and no answer from Tabriz Tower and no activity on the airfield apron, though some small, feeder airplanes were parked there. A lot of activity at the military base, trucks and cars coming and going, but as far as they could see, no firing or battles or crowds in the streets, the whole area near the mosque curiously empty. 'Don't want to go too low,' he said, 'don't want to tempt some trigger-happy crackpot.'

'You like Tabriz, Erikki?' Nogger asked, to cover his disquiet. He had never been here before.

'It's a grand city, old and wise and open and free – the most cosmopolitan in Iran. I've had some grand times here, the food and drink of all the world cheap and available – caviar and Russian vodka and Scottish smoked salmon and once a week, in the good times, Air France brought fresh French breads and cheeses. Turkish goods and Caucasian, British, American, Japanese – anything and everything. It's famous for its carpets, Nogger, and the beauty of its girls . . .' He felt Azadeh pinch his earlobe and he laughed. 'It's true, Azadeh, aren't you Tabrizi? It's a fine city, Nogger. They speak a dialect of Farsi which is more Turkish than anything else. For centuries it's been a big trading centre, part Iranian, part Russian, part Turkish, part Kurd, part Armenian, and always rebellious and independent and always wanted by the tsars and now the Soviets . . .'

Here and there knots of people stared up at them. 'Nogger, see any guns?'

'Plenty, but no one's firing at us. Yet.'

Cautiously Erikki skirted the city and headed eastward. There the land climbed into close foothills and there was the walled palace of the Gorgons on a crest with the road leading up to it. No traffic on the road. Many acres of land within the high walls: orchards, a carpet factory, garages for twenty cars, sheds for wintering herds of sheep, huts and outhouses for a hundred-odd servants and guards, and the sprawling main cupolaed building of fifty rooms and small mosque and tiny minaret. A number of cars were parked near the main entrance. He circled at 700 feet.

'That's some pad,' Nogger Lane said, awed.

'It was built for my great-grandfather by Prince Zergeyev on orders of the Romanov tsars, Nogger, as a pishkesh,' Azadeh said absently, watching the grounds below. 'That was in 1890 when the tsars had already stolen our Caucasian provinces and once more were trying to split Azerbaijan from Iran and wanted the help of the Gorgon Khans. But our line has always been loyal to Iran though they have sought to maintain a balance.' She was watching the palace below. People were coming out of the main house and some of the outhouses – servants and armed guards. 'The mosque was built in 1907 to celebrate the signing of the new Russian-British accord on their partitioning of us, and spheres of infl – oh, look, Erikki, isn't that Najoud and Fazulia and Zadi . . . and, oh, look, Erikki, isn't that my brother Hakim – what's Hakim doing there?'

'Where? Oh, I see him. No, I don't th – '

'Perhaps . . . perhaps Abdollah Khan's forgiven him,' she said excitedly. 'Oh wouldn't that be wonderful!'

Erikki peered at the people below. He had only met her brother once, at their wedding, but he had liked him very much. Abdollah Khan had released Hakim from banishment for this day only, then sent him back to Khvoy in the northern part of Azerbaijan near the Turkish border where he had extensive mining interests. 'All Hakim has ever wanted was to go to Paris to study the piano,' Azadeh had told him. 'But my father wouldn't listen to him, just cursed him and banished him for plotting . . .'

'It's not Hakim,' Erikki said, his eyes much better than hers.

'Oh!' Azadeh squinted against the wind. 'Oh.' She was so disappointed. 'Yes, yes, you're right, Erikki.'

'There's Abdollah Khan!' There was no mistaking the imposing, corpulent man with the long beard, coming out of the main door to stand on the steps, two armed guards behind him. With him were two other men. All were dressed in heavy overcoats against the cold. 'Who're they?'

'Strangers,' she said, trying to get over her disappointment. 'They haven't guns and there's no mullah, so they're not Green Bands.'

'They're Europeans,' Nogger said. 'You have any binoculars, Erikki?'

'No.' Erikki stopped circling and came down to five hundred feet and hovered, watching Abdollah Khan intently. He saw him point at the chopper and then talk with the other men, then go back to watching the chopper again. More of her sisters and family, some wearing chador, and servants had collected, bundled against the cold. Down another hundred feet. Erikki slipped off his dark glasses and headset and slid the side window back, gasped as the freezing air hit him, stuck his head out so they could see him clearly and waved. All eyes on the ground went to Abdollah Khan. After a pause the Khan waved back. Without pleasure.

'Azadeh! Take your headset off and do what I did.'

She obeyed at once. Some of her sisters waved back excitedly, chattering among themselves. Abdollah Khan did not acknowledge her, just waited. *Matyeryebyets*, Erikki thought, then leaned out of the cockpit and pointed at the wide space beyond the mosaic, frozen pool in the courtyard, obviously asking permission to land. Abdollah Khan nodded and pointed there, spoke briefly to his guards, then turned on his heel and went back into the house. The other men followed. One guard stayed. He walked down the steps towards the touchdown point, checking the action of his assault rifle.

'Nothing like a friendly reception committee,' Nogger muttered.

'No need to worry, Nogger,' Azadeh said with a nervous laugh. 'I'll get out first, Erikki, safer for me to be first.'

They landed at once, Azadeh opened her door and went to greet her sisters and her stepmother, her father's third wife and younger than her. His first wife, the Khananam, was of an age with him but now she was bedridden and never left her room. His second wife, Azadeh's mother, had died many years ago.

The guard intercepted Azadeh. Politely. Erikki breathed easier. It was too far away to hear what was said – in any event, neither he nor Nogger spoke Farsi or Turkish. The guard motioned at the chopper. She nodded then turned and beckoned them. Erikki and Nogger completed the shutdown, watching the guard who watched them seriously.

'You hate guns as much as I do, Erikki?' Nogger said.

'More. But at least that man knows how to use one – it's the amateurs that scare me.' Erikki slipped out the circuit breakers and pocketed the ignition key.

They went to join Azadeh and her sisters but the guard stood in the way. Azadeh called out, 'He says we are to go to the Reception Room at once and wait there. Please follow me.'

Nogger was last. One of the pretty sisters caught his eye and he smiled to himself and went up the stairs two at a time.

The Reception Room was vast and cold and draughty and smelled of damp, with heavy Victorian furniture and many carpets and lounging cushions and old-fashioned water heaters. Azadeh tidied her hair at one of the mirrors. Her ski clothes were elegant and fashionable. Abdollah Khan had never required any of his wives or daughters or household to wear chador, did not approve of chador. Then why was Najoud wearing one today? she asked herself, her nervousness increasing. A servant brought tea. They waited half an hour, then another guard arrived and spoke to her. She took a deep breath. 'Nogger, you're to wait here,' she said. 'Erikki, you and I are to go with this guard.'

Erikki followed her, tense but confident that the armed peace he had worked out with Abdollah Khan would hold. The touch of his pukoh knife reassured him. The guard opened a door at the end of the corridor and motioned them forward.

Abdollah Khan was leaning against some cushions, reclining on a carpet facing the door, guards behind him, the room rich, Victorian and formal – and somehow decadent and soiled. The two men they had seen on the steps were seated cross-legged beside him. One was European, a big, well-preserved man in his late sixties with heavy shoulders and Slavic eyes set in a friendly face. The other was younger, in his thirties, his features Asiatic and the colour of his skin yellowish. Both wore heavy winter suits. Erikki's caution soared and he waited beside the doorway as Azadeh went to her father, knelt in front of him, kissed his pudgy, jewelled hands, and blessed him. Impassively her father waved her to one side and kept his dark, dark eyes on Erikki who greeted him politely from the door but stayed near it. Hiding her shame and fear, Azadeh knelt again on the carpet, and faced him. Erikki saw both the strangers flick their eyes over her appreciatively, and his temperature went up a notch. The silence intensified.

Beside the Khan was a plate of halvah, small squares of the honey-rich Turkish delicacies that he adored, and he ate some of them, light dancing off his rings. 'So,' he said harshly, 'it seems you kill indiscriminately like a mad dog.'

Erikki's eyes narrowed and he said nothing.

'Well?'

'If I kill it's not like a mad dog. Whom am I supposed to have killed?'

'One old man in a crowd outside Qazvin with a blow from your elbow, his chest crushed in. There are witnesses. Next, three men in a car and one outside it – he an important fighter for freedom. There are more witnesses. Farther down the road five dead and more wounded in the wake of the helicopter rescue. More witnesses.' Another silence. Azadeh had not moved though the blood had left her face. 'Well?'

'If there are any witnesses you will know also that we were peacefully trying to get to Tehran, we were unarmed, we were set upon by a mob and if it hadn't been for Charlie Pettikin and Rakoczy, we'd probably be – ' Erikki stopped momentarily, noticing the sudden glance between the two strangers. Then, even more warily, he continued, 'We'd probably be dead. We were unarmed – Rakoczy wasn't – we were fired on first.'

Abdollah Khan had also noticed the change in the men beside him. Thoughtfully, he glanced back at Erikki. 'Rakoczy? The same with the Islamic-Marxist mullah and men who attacked your base? The Soviet Muslim?'

'Yes.' Erikki looked at the two strangers, hard-eyed. 'The KGB agent, who claimed he came from Georgia, from Tbilisi.'

Abdollah Khan smiled thinly. 'KGB? How do you know that?'

'I've seen enough of them to know.' The two strangers stared back blandly; the older wore a friendly smile and Erikki was chilled by it.

'This Rakoczy, how did he get into the helicopter?' the Khan said.

'He captured Charlie Pettikin at my base last Sunday – Pettikin's one of our pilots and he'd come to Tabriz to pick us up, Azadeh and me. I'd been asked by my embassy to check with them about my passport – that was the day most governments, mine too, had ordered non-essential expats out of Iran,' he said, the exaggeration easy. 'On Monday, the day we left here, Rakoczy forced Pettikin to fly him to Tehran.' He told briefly what had happened. 'But for him noticing the Finnish flag on the roof we'd be dead.'

The man with Asiatic features laughed softly. 'That would have been a great loss, Captain Yokkonen,' he said in Russian.

The older man with the Slavic eyes said, in faultless English, 'This Rakoczy, where is he now?'

'I don't know. Somewhere in Tehran. May I ask who you are?' Erikki was playing for time and expected no answer. He was trying to decide if Rakoczy was friend or enemy to these two, obviously Soviet, obviously KGB or GRU – the secret police of the armed forces.

'Please, what was his first name?' the older man asked pleasantly.

'Fedor, like the Hungarian revolutionary.' Erikki saw no further reaction and could have gone on but was far too wise to volunteer anything to KGB or GRU. Azadeh was kneeling on the carpet, stiff-backed, motionless, her hands at rest in her lap, her lips red against the whiteness of her face. Suddenly he was very afraid for her.

'You admit killing those men?' the Khan said and ate another sweetmeat.

'I admit I killed men a year or so ago saving your life, Highness, an – '

'And yours!' Abdollah Khan said angrily. 'The assassins would have killed you too – it was the Will of God we both lived.'

'I didn't start that fight or seek it either.' Erikki tried to choose his words wisely, feeling unwise and unsafe and inadequate. 'If I killed those others it was not of my choosing but only to protect your daughter and my wife. Our lives were in danger.'

'Ah, you consider it your right to kill at any time you consider your life to be in danger?'

Erikki saw the flush in the Khan's face, and the two Soviets watching him, and he thought of his own heritage and his grandfather's stories of the olden days in the North Lands, when giants walked the earth and trolls and ghouls were not myth, long long ago when the earth was clean and evil was known as evil, and good as good, and evil could not wear the mask.

'If Azadeh's life is threatened – or mine – I will kill anyone,' he said evenly. The three men felt ice go through them. Azadeh was appalled at the threat, and the guards, who spoke neither Russian nor English, shifted uneasily, feeling the violence.

The vein in the centre of Abdollah's Khan's forehead knotted. 'You will go with this man,' he said darkly. 'You will go with this man and do his bidding.'

Erikki looked at the man with the Asiatic features. 'What do you want with me?'

'Just your skills as a pilot, and the 212,' the man said, not unfriendly, speaking Russian.

'Sorry, the 212's on a fifteen-hundred-hours check and I work for S-G and Iran-Timber'

'The 212 is complete, already ground-tested by your mechanics, and Iran-Timber has released you to . . . to me.'

'To do what?'

'To fly,' the man said irritably. 'Are you hard of hearing?'

'No, but it seems you are.'

Air hissed out of the man's mouth. The older man smiled strangely. Abdollah Khan turned on Azadeh, and she almost jumped with fright. 'You will go to the Khananam and pay your respects!'

'Yes. . . yes. . . Father,' she stuttered and jumped up. Erikki moved half a step but the guards were ready, one had him covered and she said, near tears, 'No, Erikki, it's . . . I . . . must go . . .' She fled before he could stop her.

The man with the Asiatic face broke the silence. 'You've nothing to fear. We just need your skills.'

Erikki Yokkonen did not answer him, sure that he was at bay, that both he and Azadeh were at bay and lost, and knowing that if there were no guards here he would have attacked now, without hesitation, killed Abdollah Khan now and probably the other two. The three men knew it.

'Why did you send for my wife, Highness?' he said in the same quiet voice, knowing the answer now. 'You sent two messages.'

Abdollah Khan said with a sneer, 'She's of no value to me, but she is to my friends: to bring you back and to make you behave. And by God and the Prophet, you will behave. You will do what this man wants.'

One of the guards moved his snub-nosed machine gun a fraction and the noise he made echoed in the room. The Soviet with the Asiatic features got up. 'First your knife. Please.'

'You can come and take it. If you wish it seriously.'

The man hesitated. Abruptly Abdollah Khan laughed. The laugh was cruel, and it edged all of them. 'You will leave him his knife. That will make your life more interesting.' Then to Erikki, 'It would be wise to be obedient and to behave.'

'It would be wise to let us go in peace.'

'Would you like to watch your co-pilot hung up by his thumbs now?' Erikki's eyes flattened even more. The older Soviet leaned over to whisper to the Khan whose gaze never left Erikki. His hands played with his jewelled dagger. When the man had finished, he nodded. 'Erikki, you will tell your co-pilot that he is to be obedient too, while he is in Tabriz. We will send him to the base, but your small helicopter will remain here. For the moment.' He motioned the man with the Asiatic features to leave.

'My name is Cimtarga, Captain.' The man was not nearly as tall as Erikki but strongly built with wide shoulders. 'First we g – '

'Cimtarga's the name of a mountain, east of Samarkand. What's your real name? And rank?'

The man shrugged. 'My ancestors rode with Timour Tamburlaine, the Mongol, he who enjoyed erecting mountains of skulls. First we go to your base. We will go by car.' He walked past him and opened the door, but Erikki did not move, still looked at the Khan.

'I will see my wife tonight.'

'You will see her when – ' Abdollah Khan stopped as again the older man leaned forward and whispered. Again the Khan nodded. 'Good. Yes, Captain, you will see her tonight, and every second night. Providing.' He let the word hang. Erikki turned on his heel and walked out.

As the door closed after them, tension left the room. The older man chuckled. 'Highness, you were perfect, perfect as usual.'

Abdollah Khan eased his left shoulder, the ache in the arthritic joint annoying him. 'He'll be obedient, Petr,' he said, 'but only as long as my disobedient and ungrateful daughter is within my reach.'

'Daughters are always difficult,' Petr Oleg Mzytryk answered. He came from north of the border, from Tbilisi – Tiflis.

'Not so, Petr. The others obey and give me no trouble but this one – she infuriates me beyond words.'

'Then send her away once the Finn has done what's required. Send them both away.' The Slavic eyes crinkled and he added lightly, 'If I were thirty years younger and she was free I would petition to take her off your hands.'

'If you'd asked before that madman appeared, you could have had her with my blessing,' Abdollah Khan said sourly, though he had noted the underlying hope, hid his surprise, and put it aside for later consideration. 'I regret giving her to him – I thought she'd drive him mad too – regret my oath before God to leave him alive – it was a moment of weakness.'

'Perhaps not. It's good to be magnanimous, occasionally. He did save your life.'

'Insha'Allah! That was God's doing – he was just an instrument.'

'Of course,' Mzytryk said soothingly. 'Of course.'

'That man's a devil, an atheist devil who stinks of bloodlust. If it hadn't been for my guards – you saw for yourself – we would be fighting for our lives.'

'No, not so long as she's in your power to be dealt with. . . improperly.' Petr smiled strangely.

'God willing, they'll both be soon in hell,' the Khan said, still infuriated that he had had to keep Erikki alive to assist Petr Oleg Mzytryk, when he could have given him to the leftist mujhadin and thus be rid of him for ever. The mullah Mahmud, one of the Tabriz leaders of the Islamic-Marxist mujhadin faction that had attacked the base, had come to him two days ago and told him what happened at the roadblock. 'Here are their papers as proof,' the mullah had said truculently, 'both of the foreigner who must be CIA and of the lady, your daughter. The moment he returns to Tabriz we will stand him before our komiteh, sentence him, take him to Qazvin and put him to death.'

'By the Prophet you won't, not until I give you approval,' he had said imperiously, taking their papers. 'That mad dog foreigner is married to my daughter, is not CIA, is under my protection until I cancel it, and if you touch so much as one foul red hair or interfere with him or the base until I approve it, I'll withdraw all my secret support and nothing will stop the Green Bands from stamping out the leftists of Tabriz! He'll be given to you in my time, not yours.' Sullenly the mullah had gone away and Abdollah had at once added Mahmud to his list of imperatives. When he had examined the papers carefully and found Azadeh's passport and ID and other permits he had been delighted, for these gave him an added hold over her, and her husband.

Yes, he thought, looking up at the Soviet, she will do whatever I require of her now. Anything. 'As God wants, but she may be a widow very soon.'

'Let's hope not too soon!' Mzytryk's laugh was good and infectious. 'Not until her husband's finished his assignment.'

Abdollah Khan was warmed by the man's presence and wise counsel and

pleased that Mzytryk would do what was required of him. But I'll still have
to be a better puppeteer than ever before, he thought, if I'm to survive, and
Azerbaijan to survive.

All over the province and in Tabriz the situation now was very delicate,
with insurrections of various kinds and factions fighting factions, with tens
of thousands of Soviet soldiers poised just over the border. And tanks. And
nothing between them and the Gulf to hinder them. Except me, he thought.
And once they possessed Azerbaijan – with Tehran indefensible as history's
proved time and time again – then Iran will fall into their hands like the
rotten apple Khrushchev forecast. With Iran the Gulf, the world's oil, and
Hormuz.

He wanted to howl with rage. God curse the Shah who wouldn't listen,
wouldn't wait, hadn't the sense to crush a minor mullah-inspired rebellion
not twenty years ago and send Ayatollah Khomeini into hell as I advised and
so put into jeopardy our absolute, unstoppable, inevitable stranglehold over
the entire world outside of Russia, Tsarist or Soviet – our real enemy.

We were so close: the U.S. was eating out of our hands, fawning and
pressing on us their most advanced weapons, begging us to police the Gulf
and so dominate the vile Arabs, absorb their oil, make vassals of them and
their flyblown, foul Sunni sheikdoms from Saudi to Oman. We could have
overrun Kuwait in a day, Iraq in a week, the Saudi and Emirate sheiks
would have fled to their Riviera flesh pots screaming for mercy! We could
get whatever technology we wanted, whatever ships, airplanes, tanks, arms
for the asking, even the Bomb, by God! – our German-built reactors would
have made them for us!

So close to doing God's will, we Shi'as of Iran, with our superior
intelligence, our ancient history, our oil, and our command of the strait
that must eventually bring all the People of the Left Hand to their knees. So
close to gaining Jerusalem and Mecca, control of Mecca – Holy of Holies.

So close to being First on Earth, as is our right, but now, now all in
jeopardy and we have to start again, and again outmanoeuvre the Satanic
barbarians from the North and all because of one man.

Insha'Allah, he thought, and that took some of his anger away. Even so,
if Mzytryk had not been in the room he would have ranted and raved and
beaten someone, anyone. But the man was here and had to be dealt with, the
problems of Azerbaijan arranged, so he controlled his anger and pondered
his next move. His fingers picked up the last of the halvah and popped it
into his mouth.

'You'd like to marry Azadeh, Petr?'

'You'd like me, older than you, as a son-in-law?' the man said with a
deprecating laugh.

'If it was the Will of God,' he replied with the right amount of sincerity
and smiled to himself for he had seen the sudden light in his friend's eyes,
quickly covered. So, he thought, the first time you see her you want her.
Now if I really gave her to you when the monster's disposed of, what would
that do for me? Many things! You're eligible, you're powerful, politically it

would be wise, and you'd beat sense into her and deal with her as she should be dealt with, not like the Finn who fawns on her. You'd be an instrument of revenge on her. There are many advantages . . .

Three years ago Petr Oleg Mzytryk had taken over the immense dacha and lands that had belonged to his father – also an old friend of the Gorgons – near Tbilisi where, for generations, the Gorgons also had had very important business connections. Since then Abdollah Khan had got to know him intimately, staying at the dacha on frequent business trips. He had found Petr Oleg like all Russians, secretive, volunteering little. But, unlike most, helpful and friendly – and more powerful than any Soviet he knew, a widower with a married daughter, a son in the navy, grandchildren – and rare habits. He lived alone in the huge dacha except for servants and a strangely beautiful, strangely venomous Russian-Eurasian woman called Vertinskya, in her late 30s, whom he had brought out twice in three years, almost like a unique private treasure. She seemed to be part slave, part prisoner, part drinking companion, part whore, part tormentor and part wildcat. 'Why don't you kill her and have done with her, Petr?' he had said when a raging violent quarrel had erupted and Mzytryk had physically whipped her out of the room, the woman spitting and cursing and fighting till servants hauled her away.

'Not . . . not yet,' Mzytryk had said, his hands trembling, 'she's far . . . far too valuable.'

'Ah, yes . . . yes, now I understand,' Abdollah Khan had said, equally aroused, having almost the same feeling about Azadeh – the reluctance to cast away such an object until she was truly cowed, truly humble and crawling – and he remembered how he had envied Mzytryk that Vertinskya was mistress and not daughter so the final act of revenge could be consummated.

God curse Azadeh, he thought. Curse her who could be the twin of the mother who gave me so much pleasure, who reminds me constantly of my loss, she and her evil brother, both patterns of the mother in face and manner but not in quality, she who was like a houri from the Garden of God. I thought both of our children loved and honoured me, but no, once Napthala had gone to Paradise their true natures came to pass. I know Azadeh was plotting with her brother to murder me – haven't I the proof? Oh, God, I wish I could beat her like Petr does his nemesis, but I can't, I can't. Every time I raise my hand against her I see my Beloved, God curse Azadeh to hell . . .

'Be calm,' Mzytryk said gently.

'What?'

'You were looking so upset, my friend. Don't worry, everything will be all right. You will find a way to exorcise her.'

Abdollah Khan nodded heavily. 'You know me too well.' That's true, he thought, ordering tea for himself and vodka for Mzytryk, the only man he had ever felt at ease with.

I wonder who you really are, he thought, watching him. In years gone by, in your father's time at the dacha when we met, you used to say you were on leave, but you'd never say on leave from what, nor could I ever find out, however much I tried. At first I presumed it was the Soviet army for once when you were drunk you told me you'd been a tank commander during World War II at Sebastopol, and all the way to Berlin. But then I changed my mind and thought it more likely you and your father were KGB or GRU, for no one in the whole USSR retires to such a dacha with such lands in Georgia, the best part of the empire, without very particular knowledge and influence. You say you're retired now – retired from what?

Experimenting to find out the extent of Mzytryk's power in the early days, Abdollah Khan had mentioned that a clandestine communist Tudeh cell in Tabriz was plotting to assassinate him and he would like the cell stamped out. It was only partially true, the real reason being that a son of a man he hated secretly and could not attack openly was part of the group. Within the week all their heads were stuck on spikes near the mosque with a sign, THUS WILL ALL ENEMIES OF GOD PERISH, and he had wept cold tears at the funeral and laughed in privacy. That Petr Mzytryk had the power to eliminate one of their own cells was power indeed – and also, Abdollah knew, a measure of his own importance to them.

He looked at him. 'How long will you need the Finn?'

'A few weeks.'

'What if the Green Bands prevent him flying or intercept him?'

The Soviet shrugged. 'Let's hope he will have finished the assignment. I doubt if there would be any survivors – either him or Cimtarga – if they're found this side of the border.'

'Good. Now, back to where we were before we were interrupted: you agreed there'll be no massive support for the Tudeh here, so long as the Americans stay out and Khomeini doesn't start a pogrom against them?'

'Azerbaijan has always been within our frame of interest. We've always said it should be an independent state – there's more than enough wealth, power, minerals and oil to sustain it and . . .' Mzytryk smiled, 'and enlightened leadership. You could lift the flag, Abdollah. I'm sure you'd get all the support you need to be president – with our immediate recognition.'

And then I'd be assassinated the next day while the tanks roll over the borders, the Khan told himself without venom. Oh, no, my fine friend, the Gulf is too much temptation even for you. 'It's a wonderful idea,' he said earnestly, 'but I would need time – meanwhile I can count also on the communist Tudeh being turned on the insurrectionists?'

Petr Mzytryk's smile remained the same but his eyes changed. 'It would be curious for the Tudeh to attack their stepbrothers. Islamic-Marxism is advocated by many Muslim intellectuals – I hear even you support them.'

'I agree there should be a balance in Azerbaijan. But who ordered leftists to attack the airfield? Who ordered them to attack and burn our railway station? Who ordered the blowing up of the oil pipeline? Obviously no one sensible. I hear it was the mullah Mahmud of the Hajsra mosque.' He watched Petr carefully. 'One of yours.'

'I've never heard of him.'

'Ah,' Abdollah Khan said with pretended joviality, disbelieving him. 'I'm glad, Petr, because he's a false mullah, not even a real Islamic-Marxist, a rabble-rouser – he's the one who invaded Yokkonen's base. Unfortunately he has as many as five hundred fighters supporting him, equally ill-disciplined. And money from somewhere. And helpers like Fedor Rakoczy. What does Rakoczy mean to you?'

'Not much,' Petr said at once, his smile the same and voice the same, far too clever to avoid the question. 'He's a pipeline engineer from Ashara, on the border, one of our Muslim nationals who is believed to have joined the mujhadin as a Freedom Fighter, strictly without permission or approval.'

Petr kept his face bland but inside he was swearing obscenely, wanting to shout, My son, my son, have you betrayed us? You were sent to spy, to infiltrate the mujhadin and report back, that's all! And this time you were sent to try to recruit the Finn, then to go to Tehran and organise university students, not to ally yourself to a mad dog mullah nor to attack airfields or kill scum beside a road. Have you gone mad? You stupid fool, what if you'd been wounded and caught? How many times have I told you they – and we – can break anyone in time and empty him or her of their secrets? Stupid to take such risks! The Finn's temporarily important but not important enough to disobey orders, to risk your future, your brother's future – and mine!

If the son's suspect, so is the father. If the father's suspect so is the family. How many times have I told you that the KGB works by the Book, destroys those who won't obey the Book, who think for themselves, take risks, and exceed instructions.

'This Rakoczy's unimportant,' he said smoothly. Be calm, he ordered himself, beginning the litany: There's nothing to worry about. You know too many secrets to be touched. So does my son. He's good, they must be wrong about him. He's been tested many times, by you and by other experts. You're safe. You're strong, you've your health, and you could beat and bed that little beauty Azadeh and still rape Vertinskya the same day. 'What's important is that you are the focus of Azerbaijan, my friend,' he said in the same soothing voice. 'You will get all the support you need and your views on the Islamic-Marxists will reach the right source. The balance you require, you will have.'

'Good. I will count on it,' the Khan said.

'Meanwhile,' Mzytryk said, coming back to the main reason for his sudden trip here. 'What about the British captain? Can you help us?'

The day before yesterday a top secret, priority-coded telex from Centre had arrived at his home near Tbilisi telling him that the CIA's covert radar listening post on Sabalan's north face had been blown up by saboteurs just before friendly local teams sent to remove all cipher books, cipher machine, and computers had arrived. 'See Ivanovitch personally at once,' the telex had continued, using Abdollah Khan's undercover name. 'Tell him that the saboteurs were British – a captain and two Gurkhas – and an American CIA agent Rosemont (code name Abu Kurd), guided by one of our mercenaries who was murdered by them before he could lead them into an ambush. One soldier and the CIA agent were killed during their escape and the two survivors are believed to be heading towards Ivanovitch's sector – arrange his cooperation. Section 16/a. Acknowledge.' The Section 16 command meant: this person or persons are priority enemies who are to be intercepted, detained and brought back for interrogation by whatever means necessary. The added 'a' meant: if this cannot be done, eliminate them without fail.

Mzytryk sipped the vodka, waiting. 'We would appreciate your help.'

'You've always got my help,' Abdollah said. 'But to find two expert saboteurs in Azerbaijan who are certain to be disguised by now is almost an impossibility. They're bound to have safe houses to go to – there's a British consulate in Tabriz, and dozens of routes out of the mountains that would bypass us.' He got up and went to the window and stared out of it. From here he could see the 206 parked in the forecourt under guard. The day was still cloudless. 'If I'd been leading that operation I'd pretend to head for Tabriz, but then I'd double back and go out by the Caspian. How did they go in?'

'Caspian. But they were tracked this way. Two bodies were found in the snow, and tracks of the two others headed this way.'

The failure of the Sabalan venture had sent a tremor of rage up the line. That there was so much CIA top secret equipment so near at hand had been a magnet for covert acquisition and infiltration for many years. In the last two weeks information that some of the radar posts had been evacuated but not destroyed in the retreat and panic they had helped foster, had had the hawks ready to move in immediately, in strength. Mzytryk, senior counsellor in this area, had advised caution, to use locals rather than Soviet teams so as not to antagonise Abdollah Khan – his exclusive contact and prize agent – nor risk an international incident.

'It's totally unwise to risk a confrontation,' he had said, keeping to the Book – and his private plan. 'What do we gain by immediate action – if we've not been fed disinformation and Sabalan's not one great booby trap which is probable? A few cipher books that we may or may not already have. As to the advanced computers – our whole Operation Zatopek has that well in hand.'

This was a highly controversial and innovative KGB covert operation – named after the Czech long-distance runner – set up in '65. With an initial budget of ten million dollars of terribly scarce foreign currency, Operation Zatopek was to acquire a continuing supply of the most advanced and best Western technology *by simple purchase through a network of bogus companies* and not by the conventional and very expensive method of theft and espionage.

'The money is nothing compared to the gains,' his top-secret initial report to Centre had said when he had first returned from the Far East in '64. 'There are tens of thousands of corrupt businessmen and fellow travellers who will sell us the best and the most up to date for a profit. A huge profit to any individual would be a pittance to us – because we will save billions in research and development which we can spend on our navy, air force, and army. And, just as important, we save years of sweat, toil, and failure. At almost no cost we maintain parity with anything their minds can conceive. A few dollars under their rotten little tables will get us all their treasures.'

Petr Mzytryk felt a glow when he remembered how his plan had been accepted – though naturally and rightly taken over by his superiors as their idea, as he had taken it from one of his own deep-cover agents in Hong Kong, a French national called Jacques de Ville in the big conglomerate of Struan's who had opened his eyes: 'It's not against U.S. law to ship technology to France or West Germany or a dozen other countries, and not against these countries' laws for a company to ship it on to other countries, where there are no laws against shipping goods to the Soviet Union. Business is business, Gregor, and money makes the world go around. Through Struan's alone we could supply you tons of equipment the U.S. has forbidden you. We service China – why not you? Gregor, you seafarers don't understand business . . .'

Mzytryk smiled to himself. In those days he had been known as Gregor Suslev, captain of a small Soviet freighter that plied from Vladivostok to Hong Kong, his cover for his top-secret job of deputy controller for Asia for the KGB's First Directorate.

Over the years since '64, when I first proposed the scheme, he thought so proudly, with a total outlay so far of eighty-five million dollars, Operation Zatopek has saved Mother Russia billions and provided a constant, ever-growing flow of NASA, Japanese, and European-developed gadgetry, electronic marvels, hardware, software, plans, robots, chips, micros, medicines, and all manner of magic to duplicate and manufacture at our leisure – with equipment developed by the same enemy, and bought and paid for with loans they provide that we'll never repay. What fools they are!

He almost laughed out loud. Even more important, Zatopek gives me a free hand to continue to operate and manoeuvre as I choose in this area, to play the Great Game the stupid British let slip from their grasp.

He watched Abdollah Khan standing at the window, waiting patiently for him to decide on the favour he wanted in return for catching the saboteurs. Come on, Bad Fats, he thought grimly, using his secret nickname for him, we both know you can catch those *matyeryebyets* if you want to – if they're still in Azerbaijan.

'I'll do what I can,' Abdollah Khan said, still with his back to him, and Mzytryk did not hide his smile. 'If I intercept them, what then, Petr?'

'Tell Cimtarga. He will make all arrangements.'

'Very well.' Abdollah Khan nodded to himself and came and sat down again. 'That's settled, then.'

'Thank you,' Petr said, very satisfied. Such finality from Abdollah Khan promised quick success.

'This mullah we were discussing, Mahmud,' the Khan said, 'he's very dangerous. Also his band of cut-throats. I think they're a threat to everyone. The Tudeh should be directed to deal with him. Covertly, of course.'

Mzytryk wondered how much Abdollah knew about their secret support for Mahmud, one of their best and most fanatic converts. 'The Tudeh must be guarded, and their friends too.' He saw the immediate flash of irritation, so he compromised and added at once, 'Perhaps this man could be moved and replaced – a general split and fratricide would only help the enemy.'

'The mullah's a false mullah and not a true believer in anything.'

'Then he should go. Quickly.' Petr Mzytryk smiled, Abdollah Khan didn't.

'Very quickly, Petr. Permanently. And his group broken.'

The price was steep, but the Section 16/a gave him authority enough. 'Why not quickly and permanently, since you say it's necessary? I agree to, er, pass on your recommendation.' Mzytryk smiled and now Abdollah Khan smiled, also satisfied.

'I'm glad we agree, Petr. Become a Muslim for your eternal soul.'

Petr Mzytryk laughed. 'In time. Meanwhile, become a communist for your earthly pleasure.'

The Khan laughed, leaned forward, and refilled Petr's glass. 'I can't persuade you to stay for a few days?'

'No, but thanks. After we've eaten, I think I'll start back for home.' The smile broadened. 'There's a lot for me to do.'

The Khan was very content. So now I can forget the troublesome mullah and his band and another tooth's been drawn. But I wonder what you would do, Petr, if you knew your saboteur captain and his saboteur soldier were at the other side of my estate, waiting for safe passage out? But out to where? To Tehran or to you? I haven't yet decided.

Oh, I knew you'd come to beg my help, why else did I keep them safe, why else did I meet them secretly in Tabriz two days ago and bring them here secretly if not for you? Perhaps. Pity Vien Rosemont got killed, he was useful. Even so, the information and warning contained in the code he gave the captain for me is more than useful. He'll be difficult to replace.

Yes, and also true that if you receive a favour you must return a favour. The Infidel Erikki is only one. He rang a bell and when the servant appeared, he said, 'Tell my daughter Azadeh she will join us for food.'

Chapter 9

At Tehran: 4:17 P.M. Jean-Luc Sessonne banged the brass knocker on the door of McIver's apartment. Beside him was Sayada Bertolin. Now that they were off the street and alone, he cupped her breasts through her coat and kissed her. 'I promise we won't be long, then back to bed!'

She laughed. 'Good.'

'You booked dinner at the French Club?'

'Of course. We'll have plenty of time!'

'Yes, *chérie*.' He wore an elegant, heavy raincoat over his flying uniform and his flight from Zagros had been uneasy, no one answering his frequent radio calls though the airwaves were filled with excitable Farsi which he did not speak or understand.

He had kept at regulation height and made a standard approach to Tehran's International Airport. Still no answer to his calls. The wind sock was full and showed a strong crosswind. Four jumbos were on the apron near the terminal along with a number of other jets, one a burned-out wreck. He saw some were loading, surrounded by too many men, women and children with no order to them, the fore and aft steps to the cabins dangerously overcrowded, discarded suitcases and luggage scattered everywhere. No police or traffic wardens that he could see, nor at the other side of the terminal building where all approach roads were clogged with standstill traffic that was jammed nose to tail. The car park was solid but more cars were trying to squeeze in, the sidewalks packed with laden people.

Jean-Luc thanked God that he was flying and not walking and he landed at the nearby airfield of Galeg Morghi without trouble, bedded the 206 in the S-G hangar, and organised an immediate ride into town with the help of a ten-dollar bill. First stop at the Schlumberger office and a dawn date fixed to fly back to Zagros. Then to her apartment. Sayada had been at home. As always the first time after being so long apart was immediate, impatient, rough, selfish and mutually explosive.

He had met her at a Christmas party in Tehran a year and two months and three days ago. He remembered the evening exactly. The room was crowded and the moment he arrived, he saw her as though the room was empty. She was alone, sipping a drink, her dress sheer and white.

'*Vous parlez français, madame?*' he had asked, stunned by her beauty.

'Sorry, *m'sieur*, only a few words. I would prefer English.'

'Then in English: I am overjoyed to meet you but I have a dilemma.'

'Oh? What?'

'I wish to make love to you immediately.'

'Eh?'

'You are the manifestation of a dream. . . .' It would sound so much better in French but never mind, he had thought. 'I've been looking for you for ever and I need to make love to you, you are so desirable.'

'But . . . but my . . . husband is over there. I'm married.'

'That is a condition, *madame*, not an impediment.'

She had laughed and he had known she was his. Only one thing more would make everything perfect. 'Do you cook?'

'Yes,' she had said with such confidence that he knew she would be superb, that in bed she would be divine, and that what she lacked he would teach her. How lucky she is to have met me, he thought happily, and banged on the door again. The door swung open. It was Charlie Pettikin. 'Good God, Jean-Luc, what the hell're you doing here? Hi, Sayada, you look more beautiful than ever, come on in!' He shook hands with Jean-Luc and gave her a friendly kiss on both cheeks and felt the warmth of her.

Her long, heavy coat and hood hid most of her. She knew the dangers of Tehran and dressed accordingly: 'It saves so much bother, Jean-Luc; I agree it's stupid and archaic but I don't want to be spat on, or have some rotten thug wave his penis at me or masturbate as I pass by – it's not and never will be France. I agree it's unbelievable that now in Tehran I have to wear some form of chador to be safe, yet a month ago I didn't. Whatever you say, *chérie*, the old Tehran's gone for ever. . . .'

Pity in some ways, she thought, going into the apartment. It had had the best of the West and best of the East – and the worst. But now, now I pity Iranians, particularly the women. Why is it Muslims, particularly Shi'as, are so narrow-minded and won't let their women dress in a modern way? Is it because they're so repressed and sex besotted? Or is it because they're frightened they'd be shown up? Why can't they be open-minded like us Palestinians, or Egyptians, Shargazi, Dubaians, or Indonesians, Pakistanis, or so many others? It must be impotence. Well nothing's going to keep me from joining the Women's Protest March. How dare Khomeini try to betray us women who went to the barricades for him!

It was cold inside the apartment, the electric fire still down to half power, so she kept her coat on, just opened it to be more comfortable, and sat on one of the sofas. Her dress was warm and Parisian and slit to the thigh. Both men noticed. She had been here many times and thought the apartment drab and uncomfortable though she liked Genny very much. 'Where's Genny?'

'She went to Al Shargaz this morning on the 125.'

'Then Mac's gone?' Jean-Luc said.

'No, just her, Mac's out at the – '

'I don't believe it!' Jean-Luc said. 'She swore she'd never leave without old Dirty Duncan!'

'I didn't believe it either but she went like a lamb.' Time enough to tell Jean-Luc the real reason why she went, he thought.

'Things've been bad here?'

'Yes, and getting worse. Lots more executions.' Pettikin thought it better not to mention Sharazad's father in front of Sayada. No point in worrying her. 'How about tea? I've just made some. You hear about Qasr Jail today?'

'What about it?'

'A mob stormed it,' Pettikin said, going into the kitchen for extra cups. 'They broke down the door and released everyone, strung up a few SAVAKs and police, and now the rumour is Green Bands have set up shop with kangaroo courts and they're filling the cells with whom the hell ever and emptying them as quickly in front of firing squads. Mac went to the airport with Genny early, then to the Ministry, then here. He'll be back soon. How was the traffic at the airport, Jean-Luc?'

'Jammed for miles.'

'The Old Man's stationed the 125 at Al Shargaz for a couple of weeks to get all our people out – if necessary – or bring in fresh crews.'

'Good. Scot Gavallan's overdue for leave and also a couple of our mechanics – can the 125 get clearance to stop at Shiraz?'

'We're trying next week. Khomeini and Bazargan want full oil production back, so we think they'll cooperate. The rumours about having to close down . . . well, let's hope. What're you doing here and how're things at Zagros? You'll stay for dinner – I'm cooking tonight.'

Jean-Luc hid his horror. 'Sorry, *mon vieux*, tonight is impossible. As to Zagros, at Zagros things are perfect, as always; after all it is the French sector. I'm here to fetch Schlumberger – I return at dawn tomorrow and will have to bring them back in two days – how can I resist the extra flying?' He smiled at Sayada and she smiled back.

The warning buzzer went on the High Frequency transmitter-receiver on the sideboard. He got up and turned up the volume. 'HQ Tehran, go ahead!'

'This is Captain Ayre in Kowiss for Captain McIver. Urgent.' The voice was mixed with static and low.

'This is Captain Pettikin, Captain McIver's not here at the moment. You're two by five.' This was a measure, one to five, of the signal strength. 'Can I help?'

'Standby One.'

Jean-Luc grunted. 'What's with Freddy and you? Captain Ayre and Captain Pettikin?'

'It's just a code,' Pettikin said absently, staring at the set, and Sayada's attention increased. 'It just sort of developed and means someone's there or listening in who shouldn't. A hostile. Replying with the same formality means you got the message.'

'That's very clever,' Sayada said. 'Do you have lots of codes, Charlie?'

'No, but I'm beginning to wish we had. It's a bugger not knowing what's going on really – no face-to-face contact, no mail, phones and the telex ropey with so many trigger-happy nutters muscling us all. Why don't they turn in their guns and let's all live happily ever after?'

The HF was humming nicely. Outside the windows, the day was overcast and dull, the clouds promising more snow, the late afternoon light making all the city roofs drab and even the mountains beyond. They waited impatiently.

'This is Captain Ayre at Kowiss . . .' Again the voice was eroded by static and they had to concentrate to hear clearly. '. . . first I relay a message received from Zagros Three a few minutes ago from Captain Scot Gavallan.' Jean-Luc stiffened. 'The message said exactly: "Pan pan pan"' – the international aviation distress signal just below Mayday – ' "I've just been told by the local komiteh we are no longer persona grata in Zagros and to evacuate the area with all expatriates from all our rigs within 48 hours, or else. Request immediate advice on procedure." End of message. Did you copy?'

'Yes,' Pettikin said hastily, jotting some notes.

'That's all he said except, he sounded chocker.'

'I'll inform Captain McIver and call you back as soon as possible.' Jean-Luc leaned forward and Pettikin let him take the mike.

'This's Jean-Luc, Freddy, please call Scot and tell him I'll be back as planned tomorrow before noon. Good to talk to you, thanks, here's Charlie again.' He handed the mike back, all of his *bonhomie* vanished.

'Will do, Captain Sessonne. Nice to talk to you. Next: the 125 picked up our outgoings along with Mrs. Starke, including Captain Jon Tyrer who'd been wounded in an aborted leftist counter-attack at Bandar-e Delam . . .'

'What attack?' Jean-Luc muttered.

'First I've heard of it.' Pettikin was just as concerned.

'. . . and, according to plan, will bring back replacement crews in a few days. Next: Captain Starke.' They all heard the hesitation and underlying anxiety and the curious stilted delivery as though this information was being read: 'Captain Starke has been taken into Kowiss for questioning by a komiteh . . .' Both men gasped. '. . . to ascertain facts about a mass helicopter escape of pro-Shah air force officers from Isfahan on the 13th, last Tuesday, believed to have been piloted by a European. Next: air operations continue to improve under close supervision of the new management. Mr. Esvandiary is now our IranOil area manager and wants us to take over all Guerney contracts. To do this would require three more 212s and one 206. Please advise. We need spares for HBN, HKJ and HGX and money for overdue wages. That's all for now.'

Pettikin kept scribbling, his brain hardly working. 'I've, er, I've noted everything and will inform Captain McIver as soon as he returns. You said, er, you said "an attack on Bandar-e Delam". Please give the details.'

The airwaves were silent but for static. They waited. Then again Ayre's voice, not stilted now: 'I've no information other than there was an anti-Ayatollah Khomeini attack that Captains Starke and Lutz helped put down. Afterwards Captain Starke brought the wounded here for treatment. Of our personnel only Tyrer was creased. That is all.'

Pettikin felt a bead of sweat on his face and he wiped it off. 'What . . . what happened to Tyrer?'

Silence. Then: 'A slight head wound. Dr. Nutt said he'd be okay.'

Jean-Luc said, 'Charlie, ask him what was that about Isfahan.'

As though in dreamtime, Pettikin saw his fingers click on the sender switch. 'What was that about Isfahan?'

They waited in the silence. Then: 'I have no information other than what I gave you.'

'Someone's telling him what to say,' Jean-Luc muttered.

Pettikin pressed the sending button, changed his mind. So many questions to ask that Ayre clearly could not answer. 'Thank you, Captain,' he said, glad that his voice sounded firmer. 'Please ask Hotshot to put his request for the extra choppers in writing, with suggested contract time and payment schedule. Put it on our 125 when they bring your replacements. Keep . . . keep us informed about Captain Starke. McIver'll get back to you as soon as possible.'

'Wilco. Out.'

Now only static. Pettikin fiddled with the switches. The two men looked at each other, oblivious of Sayada who sat quietly on the sofa, missing nothing. ' "Close supervision"? That sounds bad, Jean-Luc.'

'Yes. Probably means they have to fly with armed Green Bands.' Jean-Luc swore, all his thinking on Zagros and how young Scot Gavallan would cope without his leadership. '*Merde!* When I left this morning everything was five by five with Shiraz ATC as helpful as a Swiss hotelier off-season. *Merde! Mon Dieu*, doesn't sound too good either for Captain Starke – these komitehs're breeding like lice. Bazargan and Khomeini better deal with them quickly before the two of them're bitten to death.' Jean-Luc got up, very concerned, then saw Sayada curled up on the sofa, smiling at him.

At once his *bonhomie* returned. There's nothing more I can do for young Scot at the moment, but there is for Sayada. 'Sorry, *chérie*,' he said with a beam. 'You see, without me there are always problems at Zagros. Charlie, we'll leave now – I've got to check the apartment but we'll return before dinner. Say 8 p.m.; by then Mac should be back, eh?'

'Yes. Won't you have a drink? Sorry, we've no wine. Whisky?' He offered it halfheartedly as this was their last three-quarters of a bottle.

'No thanks, *mon vieux*.' Jean-Luc got into his coat, noticed in the mirror that he was looking as dashing as ever, and thought of the cases of wine and the tins of cheese he had had the wisdom to tell his wife to stock in their apartment. '*A bientôt*, I'll bring you some wine.'

'There's a rumour Bakhtiar's slipped out of the country and fled to Paris.'

'I don't believe that, Charlie,' Sayada said.

Jean-Luc said, 'I do. If I was an Iranian of wealth, I would have gone months ago with all I could collect. It's been clear for months that the Shah was out of control. Now it's the French Revolution and the Terror all over again but without our style, sense, civilised heritage, or manners.' He shook his head disgustedly. 'What a waste! When you think of all the centuries of teaching and wealth we French've put in trying to help these people crawl out of the Dark Ages and what have they learned? Not even how to make a decent loaf of bread!'

Sayada laughed and, on tiptoe, kissed him. 'Ah, Jean-Luc, I love you and your confidence. Now, *mon vieux*, we should go, you've lots to accomplish!'

After they had left, Pettikin went to the window and stared out at the rooftops. There was the inevitable sporadic gunfire and some smoke near Jaleh. Not a big fire but enough. A stiff breeze scattered the smoke. Clouds reached down the mountains. The cold from the windows was strong, ice and snow on the sills. In the street below were many Green Bands. Walking or in trucks. Then from minarets everywhere muezzins began calling to afternoon prayer. Their calls seemed to surround him.

Suddenly he was filled with dread.

At the Ministry of Aviation: 5:04 P.M. Duncan McIver was sitting wearily on a wooden chair in a corner of the crowded antechamber of the deputy minister. He was cold and hungry and very irritable. His watch told him he had been waiting almost three hours.

Scattered around the room were a dozen other men, Iranians, some French, American, British, and one Kuwaiti wearing a galabia – a long-flowing Arabian robe – and headband. A few moments ago the Europeans had politely stopped chatting as, in response to the muezzins' calls that still came through the tall windows, the Muslims had knelt, faced Mecca, and prayed the afternoon prayer. It was short and quickly over and once more the desultory conversation picked up – never wise to discuss anything important in a government office, particularly now. The room was draughty, the air chilly. They all still wore their overcoats, were equally weary, a few stoic, most seething, for all, like McIver, had long overdue appointments.

'Insha'Allah,' he muttered but that didn't help him.

With any luck Gen's already at Al Shargaz, he thought. I'm damned glad she's safely out, and damned glad she came up with the reason herself: 'I'm the one who can talk to Andy. You can't put anything into writing.'

'That's true,' he had said, in spite of his misgivings, reluctantly adding, 'Maybe Andy can make a plan that we could carry out – might carry out. Hope to God we don't have to. Too bloody dangerous. Too many lads and too many planes spread out. Too bloody dangerous. Gen, you forget we're not at war though we're in the middle of one.'

'Yes, Duncan, but we've nothing to lose.'

'We've people to lose, as well as birds.'

'We're only going to see if it's feasible, aren't we, Duncan?'

Old Gen's certainly the best go-between we could have – if we really needed one. She's right, much too dangerous to put in a letter: '*Andy, the only way we can safely extract ourselves from this mess is to see if we can come up with a plan to pull out all our planes – and spares – that're presently under Iranian registry and technically owned by an Iranian company called IHC . . .'*

Christ! Isn't that a conspiracy to defraud!

Leaving is not the answer. We've got to stay and work and get our money when the banks open. Somehow I've got to get the partners to help – or maybe this minister can give us a hand. If he'll help, whatever it costs, we could wait out the storm here. Any government's got to have help to get their oil up, they've got to have choppers and we'll get our money . . .

He looked up as the inner door opened and a bureaucrat beckoned one of the others into the inner room. By name. There never seemed to be a logic to the manner of being called. Even in the Shah's time it was never first come, first served. Then it was only influence. Or money.

Talbot of the British embassy had arranged the appointment for him with the deputy prime minister and had given him a letter of introduction. 'Sorry, old boy, even I can't get into the PM, but his deputy Antazam's a good sort, speaks good English – not one of these rev twits.'

McIver had got back from the airport just before lunch and had parked as near as he could to the government offices. When he had presented the letter in English and Farsi to the guard on the main door in plenty of time, the man had sent him with another guard down the street to another building and more inquiries and then, from there, down another street to this building and from office to office until he arrived here, an hour late and fuming.

'Ah, don't worry, agha, you're in plenty of time,' the friendly reception clerk said to his relief in good English, and handed back the envelope containing the introduction. 'This is the right office. Please go through that door and take a seat in the anteroom. Minister Kia will see you as soon as possible.'

'I don't want to see him,' he had almost exploded. 'My appointment's with Deputy Prime Minister Antazam!'

'Ah, Deputy Minister Antazam, yes, agha, but he's no longer in Prime Minister Bazargan's government. Insha'Allah,' the young man said pleasantly. 'Minister Kia deals with everything to do with, er, foreigners, finances and airplanes.'

'But I must insist th – ' McIver stopped as the name registered and he remembered what Talbot had said and how remaining IHC partners had implanted this man on the board with an enormous retainer and no guarantees of assistance. 'Agha Minister Ali Kia?'

'Yes, agha. Minister Ali Kia will see you as soon as possible.' The receptionist was a pleasant, well-dressed young man in a suit and white shirt and blue tie, just like in the old days. McIver had had the foresight to enclose a pishkesh of 5,000 rials in the envelope with the introduction, just like in the old days. The money had vanished.

Perhaps things are really getting back to normal, McIver thought, went into the other room and took a chair in the corner and began to wait. In his pocket was another wad of rials and he wondered if he should refill the envelope with the appropriate amount. Why not, he thought, we're in Iran, minor officials need minor money, high officials, high money – sorry, pishkesh. Making sure no one observed him, he put some high denomination notes into the envelope, then added a few more for safety. Maybe this bugger can really help us – the partners used to have the court buttoned up, perhaps they've done the same to Bazargan.

From time to time harassed bureaucrats hurried importantly through the anteroom into the inner room, papers in their hands, and came out again. Occasionally, one of the men waiting would be politely ushered in. Without exception they were inside for just a few minutes and emerged taut-faced or red-faced, furious, and obviously empty-handed. Those who still waited felt more and more frustrated. Time passed very slowly.

'Agha McIver!' The inner door was open now, a bureaucrat beckoning him.

Ali Kia was seated behind a very large desk with no papers on it. He wore a smile but his eyes were hard and small and McIver instinctively disliked him.

'Ah, Minister, how kind of you to see me,' McIver said, forcing *bonhomie*, offering his hand. Ali Kia smiled politely and shook hands limply.

'Please sit down, Mr. McIver. Thank you for coming to see me. You have an introduction I believe?' His English was good, Oxford-accented, where he had gone to university just before World War Two on a Shah grant, staying for the duration. He waved a tired hand at the bureaucrat beside the door.

'Yes, it, er, it was to Deputy Minister Antazam, but I understand it should have been directed to you.' McIver handed him the envelope. Kia took out the introduction, noticed the amount of the notes exactly, tossed the envelope carelessly on to the desk to indicate more should be forthcoming, read the handwritten note with care, then put it down in front of him.

'Mr. Talbot is an honoured friend of Iran though a representative of a hostile government,' Kia said, his voice smooth. 'What particular help can I give the friend of such an honoured person?'

'There're three things, Minister. But perhaps I may be allowed to say how happy we are at S-G that you've considered giving us the benefit of your valuable experience by joining our board.'

'My cousin was most insistent. I doubt I can help, but, as God wants.'

'As God wants.' McIver had been watching him carefully, trying to read him, and could not explain the immediate dislike he took great pains to hide. 'First, there's a rumour that all joint ventures are suspended, pending a decision of the Revolutionary Komiteh.'

'Pending a decision of the government,' Kia corrected him curtly. 'So?'

'How will that affect our joint company, IHC?'

'I doubt if it will affect it at all, Mr. McIver. Iran needs helicopter service for oil production. Other helicopter companies have fled. It would seem the future looks better than ever for our company.'

McIver said carefully, 'But we haven't been paid for work done for many months. We've been carrying all lease payments for the aircraft from

Aberdeen and we're heavily overcommitted here in aircraft for the amount of work we have on the books.'

'Tomorrow the Central Bank is due to open. By order of the PM – and the Ayatollah, of course. A proportion of the money owed will, I'm sure, be forthcoming.'

'Would you conjecture how much we can expect, Minister?' McIver's hope quickened.

'More than enough to . . . to keep our operation going. I've already arranged for you to take out crews once their replacements are here.' Ali Kia took a thin file from a drawer and gave him a paper. It was an order directed to Immigration at Tehran, Abadan, and Shiraz airports to allow out accredited IHC pilots and engineering crews, one for one, against incoming crew. The order was badly typed but legible, in Farsi and English, and signed on behalf of the komiteh responsible for IranOil and dated yesterday.

'Thank you. May I also have your approval for the 125 to make at least three trips a week for the next few weeks – of course only until your international airports are back to normal – to bring in crews, spares, and equipment, replacement parts, and so on, and,' he added matter-of-factly, 'to take out redundancies.'

'It might be possible to approve that,' Kia said.

McIver handed him the set of papers. 'I took the liberty of putting it into writing – to save you the bother, Minister – with copies addressed to Air Traffic Control at Kish, Kowiss, Shiraz, Abadan, and Tehran.'

Kia read the top copy carefully. It was in Farsi and English, simple, direct, and with the correct formality. His fingers trembled. To sign them would far exceed his authority but now that the deputy prime minister was in disgrace, as well as his own superior – both supposedly dismissed by this still mysterious Revolutionary Komiteh – and with mounting chaos in the government, he knew he had to take the risk. The absolute need for him, his family, and his friends to have ready access to a private jet, made the risk worthwhile.

I can always say my superior told me to sign it, he thought, keeping his nervousness away from his face and eyes. The 125 is a gift from God – just in case lies are spread about me. Damn Jared Bakravan! My friendship with that bazaari dog almost embroiled me in his treason against the state; I've never lent money in my life, or engaged in plots with foreigners, or supported the Shah.

To keep McIver off balance he tossed the papers beside the introduction almost angrily. 'It might be possible for this to be approved. There would be a landing fee of $500 per landing. Was that everything, Mr. McIver?' he asked, knowing it was not. Devious British dog! Do you think you can fool me?

'Just one thing, Excellency.' McIver handed him the last paper. 'We've three aircraft that're in desperate need of servicing and repair. I need the exit permit signed so I can send them to Al Shargaz.' He held his breath.

'No need to send valuable airplanes out, Mr. McIver; repair them here.'

'Oh, I would if I could, Excellency, but there's no way I can do that.

We don't have the spares or the engineers – and every day that one of our choppers're not working costs the partners a fortune. A fortune,' he repeated.

'Of course you can repair them here, Mr. McIver, just bring the spares and the engineers from Al Shargaz.'

'Apart from the cost of the aircraft there're the crews to support and pay for. It's all very expensive; perhaps I should mention that's the Iranian partners' cost – that's part of their agreement . . . to supply all the necessary exit permits.' McIver continued to wheedle. 'We need to get every available piece of equipment ready to service all the new Guerney contracts if the Ay – if, er, the government's decree to get oil production to normal is to be obeyed. Without equipment . . .' he left the word hanging and again held his breath, praying he'd chosen the right bait.

Kia frowned. Anything that cost the Iranian partnership money came partially out of his own pocket now. 'How soon could they be repaired and brought back?'

'If I can get them out in a couple of days, less than two weeks.'

Again Kia hesitated. The new contracts, added to existing IHC contracts, helicopters, equipment, fixtures and fittings were worth millions of which he now had a sixth share – for no investment, he chortled deep inside. Particularly if everything was provided, without cost, by these foreigners! Exit permits for three helicopters? He glanced at his watch. It was Cartier and bejewelled – a pishkesh from a banker who, two weeks ago, had needed a private half an hour access to a working telex. In a few minutes he had an appointment with the chairman of Air Traffic Control and could easily embroil him in this decision.

'Very well,' he said, delighted to be so powerful, an official on the rise, to be able to assist the implementation of government oil policy, and save the partnership money at the same time. 'Very well, but the exit permits will only be valid for two weeks, the licence will be' – he thought a moment – 'will be $5,000 U.S. per aircraft in cash prior to exit, and they must be back in two weeks.'

'I, I can't get that money in cash in time. I could give you a note, or cheques payable on a Swiss bank – for $2,000 per aircraft.'

They haggled for a moment and settled on $3,100. 'Thank you, Agha McIver,' Ali Kai said politely. 'Please leave downcast lest you encourage those rascals waiting outside.'

When McIver was once more in his car he took out the papers and stared at the signatures and official stamps. 'It's almost too good to be true,' he muttered out loud. Maybe pushing the panic button wasn't necessary. The 125's legal now, Kia says the suspension won't apply to us, we've exit permits for three 212s that're needed in Nigeria – $9,000-odd against their value of 3 million's more than fair! I never thought I'd get away with it! 'McIver,' he said happily, 'you deserve a Scotch! A very large Scotch!'

Sunday

Chapter 10

At the Khan's Palace, Tabriz: 3.13 A.M. In the darkness of the small room Captain Ross opened the leather cover of his watch and peered at the luminous figures. 'All set, Gueng?' he whispered in Gurkhali.

'Yes, sahib,' Gueng whispered, glad that the waiting was over.

Carefully and quietly both men got off their pallets that lay on old, smelly carpets on the hard-packed, earthen floor. They were fully dressed and Ross picked his way across to the window and peered out. Their guard was slumped down beside the door, fast asleep, his rifle in his lap. Two hundred yards away beyond the snow-covered orchards and outbuildings was the four-storey palace of the Gorgon Khan. The night was dark and cold with some clouds, a nimbus around the moon that came through brightly from time to time.

More snow, he thought, then eased the door open. Both men stood there, searching the darkness with all their senses. No lights anywhere. Noiselessly Ross moved over to the guard and shook him but the man did not wake from the drugged sleep that was good for at least two hours. It had been easy to give him the drug in a piece of chocolate, kept for just that purpose in their survival kit – some of the chocolate drugged, some poisoned. Once more he concentrated on the night, waiting patiently for the moon to go behind a cloud. Absently he scratched at the bite of a bedbug. He was armed with his kukri, and one grenade: 'If we're stopped, Gueng, we're only going for a stroll,' he had told him earlier. 'Better to leave our weapons here. Why have kukris and one grenade? It's an old Gurkha custom – an offence against our regiment to be unarmed.'

'I think I would like to take all our weapons now and slip back into the mountains and make our way south, sahib.'

'If this doesn't work, we'll have to but it's a rotten gamble,' Ross had said. 'It's a rotten gamble. We'll be trapped in the open – those hunters're still searching and they won't give up till we're caught. Don't forget we only just made it to the safe house. It was only the clothes that saved us.' After the ambush where Vien Rosemont and Tenzing had been killed, he and Gueng had stripped some of their attackers and put tribesmen's robes over their uniforms. He had considered dumping their uniforms entirely but thought that unwise. 'If we're caught we're caught and that's the end of it.'

Gueng had grinned. 'Therefore better you become a good Hindu now. Then if we get killed, it's not an end but a beginning.'

'How do I do that, Gueng? Become a Hindu?' He smiled wryly, remembering the perplexed look on Gueng's face and the vast shrug. Then they had tidied the bodies of Vien Rosemont and Tenzing and left them together in the snow according to the custom of the High Lands: 'This body has no more value to the spirit and, because of the immutability of rebirth, it is bequeathed to the animals and to the birds that are other spirits struggling in their own Karma towards Nirvana – the place of Heavenly Peace.'

The next morning they had spotted those who followed relentlessly. When they came down out of the hills into the outskirts of Tabriz, their pursuers were barely half a mile behind. Only their camouflage had saved them, allowing them to be lost in the crowds, many tribesmen as tall as he and with blue eyes, many as well armed. More luck was with them and he had found the back door of the filthy little garage the first time, used Vien Rosemont's name, and the man there had hidden them. That night Abdollah Khan had come with his guards, very hostile and suspicious. 'Who told you to ask for me?'

'Vien Rosemont. He also told us about this place.'

'Who is this Rosemont? Where is he now?'

Ross had told him what had happened at the ambush and noticed something new behind the man's eyes now, even though he remained hostile.

'How do I know you're telling me the truth? Who are you?'

'Before Vien died he asked me to give you a message – he was delirious and his dying bad, but he made me repeat it three times to make sure. He said: "Tell Abdollah Khan that Peter's after the Gorgon's head and Peter's son is worse than Peter. The son plays with curds and whey and so does the father who'll try to use a Medusa to catch the Gorgon."' He saw the older man's eyes light up at once but not happily. 'So it means something to you?'

'Yes. It means you know Vien. So Vien's dead. As God wants, but that's a pity. Vien was good, very good, and a great patriot. Who are you? What was your mission? What were you doing in our mountains?'

Again he hesitated, remembering that Armstrong had told him at his briefing not to trust this man too far. Yet Rosemont whom he had trusted had said in his dying, 'You can trust that old bastard with your life. I have, half a dozen times, and he's never failed me. Go to him, he'll get you out . . .'

Abdollah Khan was smiling, his mouth cruel like his eyes. 'You can trust me – I think you have to.'

'Yes.' But not very far at all, he added silently, loathing the word, the word that costs millions their lives, more millions their freedom and every adult on earth peace of mind at some time or another. 'It was to neutralise Sabalan,' he said and told him what had happened there.

'God be praised! I will pass word to Wesson and Talbot.'

'Who?'

'Ah, doesn't matter. I'll get you south. Come with me, it's not safe here – the hue and cry's out, with a reward, for "two British saboteurs, two enemies of Islam". Who are you?'

'Ross. Captain Ross and this is Sergeant Gueng. Who were the men chasing us? Iranians – or Soviets? Or Soviet led?'

'Soviets don't operate openly in my Azerbaijan – not yet.' The Khan's lips twisted into a strange smile. 'I have a station wagon outside. Get into it quickly and lie down in the back. I'll hide you and when it's safe, get you both back to Tehran – but you have to obey my orders. Explicitly.'

That was two days ago, but then the coming of the Soviet strangers and the arrival of the helicopter had made everything different. He saw the moon go behind a cloud and he tapped Gueng on the shoulder. The small man vanished into the orchard. When the all-clear signal came out of the night, he followed. They leapfrogged each other, moving very well until they were beside the corner of the north wing of the great house. No guards or guard dogs yet though Gueng had seen some Doberman pinschers chained up.

It was an easy climb up a balustrade to the first-floor balcony. Gueng led. He hurried down half its length, passed the corridor of shuttered windows to the staircase that climbed to the next balcony. At the top he waited, getting his bearings. Ross came alongside. Gueng pointed at the second set of windows and took out his kukri but Ross shook his head and motioned to a side door that he had noticed, deep in shadow. He tried the handle. The door squeaked loudly. Some night birds skeetered out of the orchard, calling to one another. Both men concentrated on where the birds had come from, expecting to see a patrol. None appeared. Another moment to make sure, then Ross led the way inside, adrenalin heightening his tension.

The corridor was long, many doors on either side, some windows to the south. Outside the second door he stopped, warily tried the handle. This door opened silently and he went in quickly, Gueng following, his kukri out and grenade ready. The room seemed to be an anteroom – carpets, lounging pillows, old-fashioned Victorian furniture and sofas. Two doors led off it. Praying it was the correct choice, Ross opened the door nearest the corner of the building and went in. The curtains were drawn but a crack of moonlight to one side showed them the bed clearly and the man he sought and a woman asleep there under the thick quilt. It was the right man but he had not expected a woman. Gueng eased the door closed. Without hesitation they went to either side of the bed, Ross taking the man and Gueng the woman. Simultaneously they clapped the bunched handkerchiefs over the mouths of the sleepers, holding them down with just enough pressure under their noses to keep them from crying out.

'We're friends, pilot, don't cry out,' Ross whispered, close to Erikki's ear, not knowing his name or who the woman was, only recognising him as the pilot. He saw the blank fright of the sudden awakening transformed into blinding rage as sleep vanished and the great hands came up to rip him apart. He avoided their grasp, increasing the pressure just under Erikki's nose, holding him down easily. 'I'm going to release you, don't cry out, pilot. We're friends, we're British. British soldiers. Just nod if you're awake and you understand.' He waited, then felt more than saw the huge man nod, watching his eyes. The eyes shouted danger. 'Keep her gagged, Gueng, until we're all set this side,' he said softly in Gurkhali, then to Erikki, 'Pilot, don't be afraid, we're friends.'

He released the pressure and leaped out of the way as Erikki lunged at him, then squirmed in the bed to get at Gueng but stopped rigid. Moonlight glinted off the curved kukri held near her throat. Azadeh's eyes were wide open and she was petrified.

'Don't! Leave her alone . . .' Erikki said hoarsely in Russian, seeing only Gueng's Oriental eyes, thinking it must be one of Cimtarga's men, still confused and in panic. He was heavy with sleep, his head aching from hours of flying, mostly on instruments in bad conditions. 'What do you want?'

'Speak English. You're English, aren't you?'

'No, no, I'm Finnish.' Erikki peered at Ross, little more than a silhouette in the shaft of moonlight. 'What the hell do you want?'

'Sorry to wake you like this, pilot,' Ross said hastily, coming a little closer, keeping his voice down, 'sorry, but I had to talk to you secretly. It's very important – '

'Tell this bastard to let my wife go! Now!'

'Wife? Oh, yes . . . yes, of course, sorry. She . . . she won't scream? Please tell her not to scream.' He watched the huge man turn towards the woman who lay motionless under the heavy quilt, her mouth still covered, the kukri unwavering. He saw him reach out warily and touch her, eyes on the kukri. His voice was gentle and encouraging but he did not speak English or Farsi but another language. In panic Ross thought it was Russian and he was further disoriented, expecting a British S-G pilot, without a bed partner, not a Finn with a Russian wife, and he was petrified he had led Gueng into a trap. The big man's eyes came back on him and more danger was there.

'Tell him to let my wife go,' Erikki said in English, finding it hard to concentrate. 'She won't scream.'

'What did you say to her? Was it Russian?'

'Yes, it was Russian and I said, "This bastard's going to release you in a second. Don't shout out. Don't shout out, just move behind me. Don't move quickly, just behind me. Don't do anything unless I go for the other bastard, then fight for your life." '

'You're Russian?'

'I told you, Finnish, and I tire quickly of men with knives in the night, British, Russian, or even Finnish.'

'You're a pilot with S-G helicopters?'

'Yes, hurry up and let her go whoever you are or I'll start something.'

Ross was not yet over his own panic. 'Is she Russian?'

'My wife's Iranian, she speaks Russian and so do I,' Erikki said icily, moving slightly to get out of the narrow beam of moonlight into shadows. 'Move into the light, I can't see you, and for the last time tell this little bastard to release my wife, tell me what you want, and then get out.'

'Sorry about all this. Gueng, let her go now.'

Gueng did not move. Nor did the curved blade. In Gurkhali he said, 'Yes, sahib, but first take the knife from under the man's pillow.'

In Gurkhali Ross replied, 'If he goes for it, brother, even touches it, kill her, I'll get him.' Then in English he said pleasantly, 'Pilot, you have a knife under your pillow. Please don't touch it, sorry, but if you do until this is all okay . . . please be patient. Let her go, Gueng,' he said, his attention never leaving the man. With the side of his eyes he saw the vague shape of a face, long hair tousled and half covering her, then she moved behind the great shoulders, bunching her long-sleeved, winter nightclothes closer. Ross had his back to the light and he saw little of her, only the hatred in her half-seen eyes, even from the shadows. 'Sorry to arrive like a thief in the night. Apologies,' he said to her. She did not answer. He repeated the apology in Farsi. She still did not answer. 'Please apologise to your wife for me.'

'She speaks English. What the hell do you want?' Erikki felt a little better now that she was safe, still very aware how close the other man with the curved knife was.

'We're sort of prisoners of the Khan, pilot, and I came to warn you and to ask your help.'

'Warn me about what?'

'I helped one of your captains a few days ago – Charles Pettikin.' He saw the name register at once so he relaxed a little. Quickly he told Erikki about Doshan Tappeh and the SAVAK attack and how they had escaped, describing Pettikin accurately so there could be no mistake.

'Charlie told us about you,' Erikki said, astonished, no longer afraid, 'but not that he'd dropped you off near Bandar-e Pahlavi – only that some British paratroopers had saved him from a SAVAK who'd have blown his head off.'

'I asked him to forget my name. I, er, we were on a job.'

'Lucky for Charlie you, we – ' Ross saw the woman whisper in her husband's ear, distracting him. The man nodded and turned his eyes back again. 'You can see me, I can't see you, move into the light – as to Abdollah, if you were his prisoners, you'd be chained up, or in a dungeon, not loose in the palace.'

'I was told the Khan would help us if we had trouble and he said he'd hide us until he could get us back to Tehran. Meanwhile he put us in a hut, out of sight, across the estate. There's a permanent guard on us.'

'Hide you from what?'

'We were on a, er, classified job, and being hunted an – '

'What classified job? I still can't see you, move into the light.'

Ross moved but not enough. 'We had to blow some secret American radar stuff to prevent it being pinched by Soviets or their supporters. I rec – '

'Sabalan?'

'How the hell did you know that?'

'I'm being forced to fly a Soviet and some leftists to ransack radar sites near the border, then take the stuff down to Astara on the coast. One of them was wrecked on the north face – they got nothing out of that one and so far the rest haven't produced anything worthwhile – as far as I know. Go on – warn me about what?'

'You're being forced?'

'My wife's hostage to the Khan and the Soviets – for my cooperation and good behaviour,' Erikki said simply.

'Christ!' Ross's mind was working overtime. 'I, er, I recognised the S-G decal when you were circling and came to warn you Soviets were here, they came here early this morning, and they're planning to kidnap you with the friendly help of the Khan – it seems he's playing both ends against the middle, double agent.' He saw Erikki's astonishment. 'Our people should know that quickly.'

'Kidnap me to do what?'

'I don't know exactly. I sent Gueng on a recce after your chopper arrived – he slipped out of a back window. Tell them, Gueng.'

'It was after they had eaten lunch, sahib, the Khan and the Soviet, and they were beside the Soviet's car when he was leaving – I was in the undergrowth near and could hear well. They were talking English. The Soviet said, Thanks for the information and the offer. The Khan said, Then we have an agreement? Everything, Patar? The Soviet said, Yes I'll recommend everything you want. I'll see the pilot never bothers you again. When he's finished here he'll be brought north . . .' Gueng stopped as the air hissed out of Azadeh's mouth. 'Yes, memsahib?'

'Nothing.'

Gueng concentrated, wanting to get it perfect for them: 'The Soviet said: I'll see that the pilot never bothers you again. When he's finished here he'll be brought north, permanently. Then. . .' He thought a moment. 'Ah, yes! Then he said, the mullah won't trouble you again and in return you'll catch the British saboteurs for me? Alive, I'd like them alive if possible. The Khan said, Yes, I'll catch them, Patar, Do y – '

'Petr,' Azadeh said, her hand on Erikki's shoulder. 'His name was Petr Mzytryk.'

'Christ!' Ross muttered as it fell into place.

'What?' Erikki said.

'I'll tell you later. Finish, Gueng.'

'Yes, sahib. The Khan said, I'll catch them, Patar, alive if I can. What's my favour if they're alive? The Soviet laughed. Anything, within reason, and mine? The Khan said, I'll bring *her* with me on my next visit. Sahib, that was all. Then the Soviet got into his car and left.'

Azadeh shuddered.

'What?' Erikki said.

'He means me,' she said, her voice small.

Ross said, 'I don't follow.'

Erikki hesitated, the tightness in his head greater than before. She had told him about being summoned for lunch by her father, and about Petr Mzytryk inviting her to Tbilisi – 'and your husband, of course, if he's free, I would love to show you our countryside . . .' and how attentive the Soviet had been. 'It's . . . it's personal. Not important,' he said. 'It seems you've done me a big favour. How can I help?' He smiled tiredly and stuck out his hand. 'My name's Yokkonen, Erikki Yokkonen and this is my wife, Az – '

'Sahib!' Gueng hissed warningly.

Ross jerked to a stop. Now he saw Erikki's other hand was under the pillow. 'Don't move a muscle,' he said, kukri suddenly out of its scabbard. Erikki recognised the tone and obeyed. Cautiously Ross moved the pillow aside but the hand was not near the knife. He picked the knife up. The blade glinted in the shaft of moonlight. He thought a moment, then handed it back to Erikki, haft first. 'Sorry, but it's better to be safe.' He shook the outstretched hand that had never wavered and felt the enormous strength. He smiled at him and turned slightly, the light now on his face for the first time. 'My name's Ross, Captain John Ross, and this's Gueng . . .'

Azadeh gasped and jerked upright. They all looked at her and now Ross saw her clearly for the first time. It was Azadeh, his Azadeh of ten years ago, Azadeh Gorden as he had known her then, Azadeh Gorden of the High Country staring up at him, more beautiful than ever, eyes bigger than ever, still heaven sent. 'My God, Azadeh, I didn't see your face . . .'

'Nor I yours, Johnny.'

'Azadeh . . . good God,' Ross stammered. He was beaming and so was she, and then he heard Erikki and looked down and saw him staring up at him, the great knife in his fist, and a shaft of fear rushed through him and through her.

'You're "Johnny Brighteyes"?' Erikki said it flat.

'Yes, yes, I'm . . . I had the privilege of knowing your wife years ago, many years ago . . . Good Lord, Azadeh, how wonderful to see you!'

'And you . . .' Her hand had not left Erikki's shoulder.

Erikki could feel her hand and it was burning him but he did not move, mesmerised by the man in front of him. She had told him about John Ross and about their summer and the result of the summer, that the man had not known about the almost child, nor had she ever tried to find him to tell him, nor did she want him ever to know. 'The fault was mine, Erikki, not his,' she had told him simply. 'I was in love, I was just a few days seventeen and he nineteen – Johnny Brighteyes I called him; I had never seen a man with such blue eyes before. We were deeply in love but it was only a summer love, not like ours which is for ever, mine is, and yes, I will marry you if Father will allow it, oh yes, please God, but only if you can live happily with knowing that once upon a time, long long ago, I was growing up. You must promise me, swear to me you can be happy as a man and a husband for perhaps one day we will meet him – I will be happy to meet him and will smile at him but my soul will be yours, my body yours, my life yours, and all that I have . . .'

He had sworn as she had wished, truly and with all his soul, happily brushing aside her concern. He was modern and understanding and Finnish – wasn't Finland always progressive, hadn't Finland been the second country on earth after New Zealand to give women the vote? There was no worry in him. None. He was only sad for her that she had not been careful, for she had told him of her father's anger – an anger he could understand.

And now here was the man, fine and strong and young, far nearer her size than he, nearer her age than he. Jealousy ripped him apart.

Ross was trying to collect his wits, her presence possessing him. He pulled his eyes off her and the memory of her and looked back at Erikki. He read his eyes clearly. 'A long time ago I knew your wife, in Switzerland at . . . I was at school there for a short time.'

'Yes, I know,' Erikki said. 'Azadeh told me about you. I'm . . . I'm . . . it's a . . . it's a sudden meeting for all of us.' He got out of bed, towering over Ross, the knife still in his hand, all of them aware of the knife. Gueng on the other side of the bed still had his kukri out. 'So. Again, Captain, again thanks for the warning.'

'You said you're being forced to fly the Soviets?'

'Azadeh's hostage, for my good behaviour,' Erikki said simply.

Thoughtfully Ross nodded. 'Not much you can do about that if the Khan's hostile. Christ, that's a mess! My thought was that as you were threatened too, you'd want to escape too and that you'd give us a ride in the chopper.'

'If I could I would, yes . . . yes, of course. But I've twenty guards on me all the time I'm flying and Azadeh . . . my wife and I are watched very closely when we're here. There's another Soviet called Cimtarga who's like my shadow, and Abdollah Khan's . . . very careful.' He had not yet decided what to do about this man Ross. He glanced at Azadeh and saw that her smile was true, her touch on his shoulder true, and that clearly this man meant nothing more than an old friend to her now. But this did not take away his almost blinding urge to run amok. He made himself smile at her. 'We must be careful, Azadeh.'

'Very.' She had felt the surge under her hand when he had said 'Johnny Brighteyes' and knew that, of the three of them, only she could control this added danger. At the same time, Erikki's jealousy that he sought so hard to hide excited her, as did the open admiration of her long-lost love. Oh, yes, she thought, Johnny Brighteyes, you are more wonderful than ever, slimmer than ever, stronger than ever – more exciting, with your curved knife and unshaven face and filthy clothes and man smell – how could I not have recognised you? 'A moment ago when I corrected this man's "Patar" to "Petr" it meant something to you, Johnny. What?'

'It was a code message I had to give the Khan,' Ross said, achingly aware she still bewitched him. '"Tell Abdollah Khan that Peter" – that could be Gueng's Patar or Petr, the Soviet – "that Peter's after the Gorgon's head and Peter's son is worse than Peter. The son plays with curds and whey and so does the father, who'll try to use a Medusa to catch the Gorgon."'

Azadeh said, 'That's easy. Erikki?'

'Yes,' Erikki said, distracted. 'But why "curds and whey"?'

'Perhaps this,' she said, her excitement rising. 'Tell Abdollah Khan that Petr Mzytryk, KGB, is after his head, that Mzytryk's son – let's presume also KGB – is worse than his father. The son plays at curds and whey –

perhaps that means the son is involved with the Kurds and their rebellion that threatens Abdollah Khan's power base in Azerbaijan, that the KGB, the father, and the son are also involved – and that Petr Mzytryk will use a Medusa to catch the Gorgon.' She thought a moment. 'Could that be another pun and mean "use a woman", perhaps even an evil woman to catch my father?'

Ross was shocked. 'The Khan's . . . My God, the Khan's your father?'

'Yes, I'm afraid so. Gorgon's my family name,' Azadeh said. 'Not Gorden. But the principal of the school at Château d'Or told me the first day I could hardly have a name like Gorgon – I would get teased to death – so I was to be just Azadeh Gorden. It was fun for me, and the principal thought it better for me that I was just plain Azadeh Gorden and not the daughter of a Khan.'

Erikki broke the silence. 'If the message's correct, the Khan won't trust that *matyeryebyets* at all.'

'Yes, Erikki. But my father trusts no one. No one at all. If Father's playing both sides as Johnny thinks – there's no telling what he'll do. Johnny, who gave you the message to give to him?'

'A CIA agent who said I could trust your father with my life.'

Erikki said witheringly, 'I always knew the CIA were . . . were crazy.'

'This one was all right,' Ross said more sharply than he meant. He saw Erikki flush and her smile vanish.

Another silence. More jagged. The moonlight in the room faded as the moon went behind a bank of cloud. It was uneasy in the gloom. Gueng who had watched and listened felt the increased disquiet and he silently called on all gods to extricate them from Medusa, the pagan devil with snakes for hair that the missionaries had taught about in his first school in Nepal. Then his special sense felt the approaching danger, he hissed a warning and went to the window and peered out. Two armed guards with a Doberman pinscher on a leash were coming up the staircase opposite.

The others were equally rigid now. They heard the guards pad along the terrace, the dog sniffing and straining on the leash. Then go towards the outside door. Again it creaked open. The men came into the building.

Muffled voices outside the door of the bedroom and the sound of the dog snuffling. Then near the door of the anteroom. Gueng and Ross moved into ambush, kukris ready. In time the guards moved down the corridor, out of the building and down the staircase again. Azadeh shifted nervously. 'They don't come here normally. Ever.'

Ross whispered back hastily, 'Maybe they saw us coming up here. We'd better leave. If you hear firing, you don't know us. If we're still free tomorrow night, could we come here, say just after midnight? We could perhaps make a plan?'

'Yes,' Erikki said. 'But make it earlier. Cimtarga warned me we might have to leave before dawn. Make it around 11 p.m. We'd better have several plans ready – to get out is going to be very difficult, very.'

'How long will you be working for them – before you're finished?'

'I don't know. Perhaps three or four days.'

'Good. If we don't make contact with you – forget us. Okay?'

'God protect you, Johnny,' Azadeh told him anxiously; 'don't trust my father, you mustn't let him . . . mustn't let him or them take you.'

Ross smiled and it lit up the room, even for Erikki. 'No problem – good luck to all of us.' He waved a devil-may-care salute and opened the door. In a few seconds he and Gueng were gone as quietly as they had arrived. Erikki watched out of the window and saw them only as shadows going down the steps, noting how cleverly and silently the two men used the night, envying Ross his careless elegance of manner and movement.

Azadeh was standing alongside him, a head smaller, her arm around his waist, also watching. After a moment, his arm went around her shoulders. They waited, expecting shouting and firing, but the night remained undisturbed. The moon came out from the clouds again. No movement anywhere. He glanced at his watch. It was 4.23.

He looked at the sky, no sign of any dawn yet. At dawn he had to leave, not to the north face of Sabalan but to other radar sites further west. Cimtarga had told him that the CIA still operated certain sites nearer the Turkish border but that today the Khomeini government had ordered them closed, evacuated, and left intact. 'They'll never do that,' Erikki had said. 'Never.'

'Perhaps, perhaps not.' Cimtarga had laughed. 'The moment we get orders, you and I will just fly there with my "tribesmen" and hurry them up . . .'

Matyer! And *matyer* Johnny Brighteyes arriving to complicate our lives. Even so, thank all gods for the warning he brought. What's Abdollah planning for Azadeh? I should kill that old swine and have done with it. Yes, but I can't, I swore by the Ancient Gods an oath that may not be broken, not to touch her father – as he himself swore by the One God not to hinder us though he'll find a way to break that oath. Can I do the same? No. An oath is an oath. Like the one you swore to her that you could live happily with her, knowing about him – *him* – didn't you? His mind blackened and he was glad of the darkness.

So the KGB plan to kidnap me. If it's a real plan I'm done for. Azadeh? What's that devil Abdollah planning for her now? And now this Johnny arrives to harass us all – I never thought he'd be so good-looking and tough and no man to mix with, him with that sodding great knife, killing knife . . .

'Come back to bed, Erikki,' she said. 'It's very cold, isn't it?'

He nodded and followed and got in his side, greatly troubled. When they were back under the great quilt, she snuggled against him. Not enough to provoke a reaction but just enough to appear normal and untouched. 'How extraordinary to find it was him, Erikki! John Ross – in the street I certainly wouldn't have recognised him. Oh, that was such a long time ago, I'd forgotten all about him. I'm so pleased you married me, Erikki,' she said, her voice calm and loving, sure that his mind was grinding her long-lost love to dust. 'I feel so safe with you – if it hadn't been for you I would have died of fright.' She said it as though expecting an answer. But I don't expect one, my darling, she thought contentedly and sighed.

He heard her sigh and wondered what it meant, feeling her warmth against him, loathing the rage that possessed him. Was it because she's sorry she had smiled at her lover as she did? Or is she furious with me – she must have seen my jealousy. Or is she saddened that I have forgotten my oath, or is she hating me because I hate that man? I swear I'll exorcise him from her . . .

Ah, Johnny Brighteyes, she was thinking, what ecstasy I enjoyed in your arms, even the first time when it was supposed to hurt, but it never did. Just a pain that became a burning that became a melting that tore away life and gave life back to me again, better than before, oh how so much better than before! And then Erikki . . .

It was much warmer now under the quilt. Her hand went across his loins. She felt him move slightly and she hid her smile, sure that her warmth was reaching him now, so easy to warm him further. But unwise. Very unwise, for then she knew he would only take her with Johnny in the forefront of his mind, taking her to spite Johnny and not to love her – perhaps even thinking that in her acquiescence she was feeling guilty and was trying to make up for her guilt. Oh, no, my love, I'm not a foolish child, you're the guilty one, not me. And though you'd be stronger than usual and more rough, which would normally increase my pleasure, this time it would not, for, like it or not, I would resist even more than you, aware of my other love. So, my darling, it is ten thousand times better to wait. Until the dawn. By then, my darling, if I'm lucky you will have persuaded yourself that you are wrong to hate him and be jealous and you will be my Erikki again. And if you haven't? Then I will begin again – there are ten thousand ways to heal my man. 'I love you, Erikki,' she said and kissed the cloth that covered his chest, turned over, and settled her back against him and went into sleep, smiling.

Tuesday

Chapter 11

Tabriz: 5:12 A.M. In the small hut on the edge of the Khan's estate, Ross was suddenly awake. He lay motionless, keeping his breathing regular but all of his senses concentrated. Seemingly nothing untoward, just the usual insects and closeness of the room. Through the window he could see that the night was dark, the sky mostly overcast. Across the room on the other pallet, Gueng slept curled up, breathing normally. Because of the cold, both men had gone to bed with their clothes on. Noiselessly, Ross went to the window and searched the darkness. Still nothing. Then, close to his ear, Gueng whispered, 'What is it, sahib?'

'I don't know. Probably nothing.'

Gueng nudged him and pointed. There was no guard in the seat outside on the veranda.

'Perhaps he's just gone to take a leak.' There had always been at least one guard. By day or night. Last night there had been two so Ross had made a mock dummy in his bed and left Gueng to divert them and had slipped out of the back window and gone to see Erikki and Azadeh alone. Coming back he had almost stumbled into a patrol but they had been sleepy and unattentive so he had passed them by.

'Take a look out the back window,' Ross whispered.

Again they watched and waited. Dawn in about an hour, Ross thought.

'Sahib, perhaps it was just a spirit of the mountain,' Gueng said softly. In the Land Atop the World it was a superstition that by night, spirits visited the beds of sleeping men and women and children, for good purposes or ill, and that dreams were the stories they whispered.

The little man kept his eyes and ears feeling out the darkness. 'I think perhaps we'd better pay attention to the spirits.' He went back to his bed and pulled on his boots, put the talisman he had kept under his pillow back into his uniform pocket, then put on the tribesman robes and turban. Nimbly he checked his grenades and carbine and settled the rough backpack that contained ammunition, grenades, water and a little food. No need to check his kukri, that was never out of reach, always oiled and cleaned nightly – just before sleep.

Now Ross was equally ready. But ready for what? he asked himself. It's hardly five minutes since you awoke and here you are, kukri loose in the scabbard, safety catch off and for what? If Abdollah meant you harm, he would've already taken away your weapons – or tried to take them.

Yesterday afternoon they had heard the 206 take off and shortly afterwards Abdollah Khan had visited them. 'Ah, Captain, sorry for the delay but the hue and cry is worse than ever. Our Soviet friends have put a very large price on your heads,' he had said jovially. 'Enough even to tempt me, perhaps.'

'Let's hope not, sir. How long will we have to wait?'

'A few days, no more. It seems the Soviets want you very much. I've had another deputation from them asking me to help capture you, the first was before you arrived. But don't worry, I know where the future of Iran lies.'

Last night Erikki had confirmed about the reward: 'Today I was near Sabalan, cleaning out another radar site. Some of the workers thought I was Russian – lots of Russian speakers among the border people – and said they hoped they'd be the ones to catch the tall British saboteur and his helper. The reward's five horses and five camels and fifty sheep. That's a fortune, and if they know about you that far north you can bet they're looking here.'

'Were Soviets supervising you?'

'Only Cimtarga, but even then he didn't seem to be in charge. Just of me and the aircraft. The Russian speakers kept asking me when we were coming over the border in strength.'

'My God – did they have anything to base that on?'

'I doubt it, just more rumours. People here feed on them. I said, "Never", but this man scoffed and said he knew we had "leagues" of tanks and armies waiting, that he'd seen them. I can't speak Farsi so I don't know if he was another KGB plant disguised as a tribesman.'

'The "stuff" you're carrying? Is it anything important?'

'I don't know. Some computers and lots of black boxes and papers – they keep me away from it but none of it's dismantled by experts, just pulled out of walls, wires cut, and hanging loose and stacked carelessly. The only thing the workers're interested in is stores, cigarettes particularly.'

They had talked about escaping. Impossible to make plans. Too many imponderables. 'I don't know how long they want me to keep flying,' Erikki had said. 'This bastard Cimtarga told me Prime Minister Bazargan has ordered the Yanks out of two sites, far to the east, near Turkey, the last they've got here, ordered them to evacuate at once and to leave the equipment intact. We're supposed to fly up there tomorrow.'

'Did you use the 206 today?'

'No. That was Nogger Lane, one of our captains. He came here with us – to take the 206 back to Tehran. Our base manager told me they've co-opted Nogger to recce some places where fighting's going on. When McIver doesn't hear from us he'll go into shock and send out a search party. That might give us another chance. What about you?'

'We might sneak off. I'm getting very nervous in that rotten little hut. If we evacuate, we might head for your base and hide out in the forest. If we can, we'll contact you – but don't expect us. All right?'

'Yes – but don't trust anyone at the base – except our two mechanics, Dibble and Arberry.'

'Anything I can do for you?'

'Could you leave me a grenade?'

'Of course, have you ever used one?'

'No, but I know how they work.'

'Good. Here. Pull the pin and count to three – not four – and heave it. Do you need a gun?'

'No, no thanks. I've my knife – but the grenade might come in handy.'

'Remember they can be rather messy. I'd better be going. Good luck.'

Ross had been looking at Azadeh when he had said it, seeing how beautiful she was, so very aware that their time was already written among the stars or on the wind or in the chimes of the bells that were as much a part of the summer High Country as the peaks themselves. Wondering why she never replied to his letters, then the school telling him she had gone. Gone home. Gone. On their last day she had said, 'All this that has come to pass may not come to pass again, my Johnny Brighteyes.'

'I know. If it doesn't, I can die happy because I know what love is. Truly. I love you, Azadeh.'

Last kiss. Then down to his train and waving goodbye, waving until she was lost. Lost for ever. Perhaps we both knew that it was forever, he thought, waiting here in the darkness of the little hut, trying to decide what to do, to wait more, to sleep or to flee. Maybe it's as the Khan said and we're safe here – for the moment. No reason to mistrust him completely. Vien Rosemont was no fool and he said to trust h –

'Sahib!'

He had heard the stealthy footsteps at the same instant. Both men moved into ambush, one covering the other, both of them glad that the time for action had arrived. The door opened quietly. It was a ghoulish spirit of the mountain standing there peering into the greater darkness of the hut – a shape and vague face. To his astonishment he recognised Azadeh, the chador blending her with the night, her face puffy from crying.

'Johnny?' she whispered anxiously.

For a moment Ross did not move, gun still levelled and expecting enemies. 'Azadeh, here, beside the door,' he whispered back, trying to adjust.

'Quick, follow me, you're both in danger! Hurry!' At once she ran off into the night.

He saw Gueng shake his head uneasily and he hesitated. Then he decided, 'We go.' He slid out of the doorway and ran after her, the moonlight small, Gueng following, flanking, automatically covering him. She was waiting beside some trees. Before he reached her, she beckoned him to follow, unerringly led the way through the orchard and around some farm buildings. The snow muffled their way but left tracks and he was very aware of them. He was ten paces behind her, watching the terrain carefully, wondering what danger and why had she been crying and where's Erikki?

Clouds were toying with the moon, hiding it mostly. Whenever it came clear, she would stop and motion him to stop and to wait, then she would move on again, using cover well, and he wondered where she had learned woodsmanship then remembered Erikki and his great knife and Finns and Finland – land of lakes and forests and mountains and trolls and hunting. Concentrate, fool, time enough to let your mind wander later, not now when you're endangering everyone! Concentrate!

His eyes searched, expecting trouble, wanting it to begin. Soon they were near the perimeter wall. The wall was ten feet high and made of hewn stone, with a wide, empty swathe between it and the trees. Again she motioned him to stop in cover and walked forward into the open, seeking a special place. Finding it without trouble, she beckoned him. Before he was beside her she was already climbing, her feet fitting easily into the notches and cracks with sufficient hand holds, some natural, some cleverly embedded to make the climb easy. The moon came into a bare patch of sky and he felt naked and climbed more quickly. When he reached the top she was already halfway down the other side. He slithered over and found some footholds, ducked down to wait for Gueng. His anxiety mounted until he saw the shadow darting over the ground, reaching the wall safely.

The climb down was more difficult and he slipped and fell the last six feet, cursed and looked around to get his bearings. She was already across the boundary road and heading for a rocky outcrop on the steep mountainside two hundred yards away. Below and to the left he could see part of Tabriz, fires on the far side of the city near the airport. Now he could hear distant guns.

Gueng landed neatly beside him, grinned and motioned him onward. When he reached the outcrop she had vanished.

'Johnny! Here!'

He saw the small crack in the rock and went forward. Just enough room to squeeze through. He waited until Gueng came up, and then went through the rock into darkness. Her hand came out and guided him to one side. She beckoned Gueng and did the same for him, then moved a heavy leather curtain across the crack. Ross reached into his pack for his flash but before he could pull it out the match flamed. Her hand was cupped around it. She was kneeling and lit the candle that was in a niche. Quickly he looked around. The curtain over the entrance seemed lightproof, the cave spacious, warm and dry, some blankets, old carpets on the ground, a few drinking and eating utensils – some books and toys on a natural shelf. Ah, a child's hideout, he thought and looked back at her. She had stayed kneeling by the candle, her back to him, and now, as she pulled the chador away from her head, she became Azadeh again.

'Here.' He offered her some water from his water bottle. She accepted it gratefully but avoided his eyes. He glanced at Gueng and read his mind. 'Azadeh, do you mind if we put the light out – now that we see where we are – then we can pull the curtain back and keep watch and hear better. I've a flash if we need it.'

'Oh, oh, yes . . . yes, of course.' She turned back to the candle. 'I . . . oh, just a minute, sorry . . .' There was a mirror on the shelf he had not noticed. She picked it up and peered at herself, hated what she saw, the streaks of sweat

and puffy eyes. Hastily she brushed away some smudges, picked up the comb
and tidied herself as best she could. A final check in the mirror and she blew
out the candle. 'Sorry,' she said.

Gueng moved the curtain away and went through the rock and stood there
listening. More gunfire from the city. A few buildings burning beyond the
single runway of the airfield below and to the right. No lights there and very
few on in the city itself. A few car headlights in the streets. The palace still
dark and silent and he could sense no danger. He came back and told Ross
what he had seen, speaking Gurkhali, and added, 'Better I stay outside, safer,
there's not much time, sahib.'

'Yes.' Ross had heard disquiet in his voice but did not comment. He knew
the reason. 'You all right, Azadeh?' he asked softly.

'Yes. Yes I am now. It's better in the dark – sorry I looked such a mess.
Yes, I'm better now.'

'What's this all about – and where's your husband?' He used the word
deliberately and heard her move in the darkness.

'Just after you left last night, Cimtarga and a guard came and told Erikki he
had to dress at once and leave – this man Cimtarga said he was sorry but there'd
been a change of plan and he wanted to leave at once. And I, I was summoned
to see my father. At once. Before I went into his room I overheard him giving
orders for you both to be captured and disarmed, just after dawn.' There was
a catch to her voice. 'He was planning to send for you both to discuss your
departure tomorrow, but you would be led into ambush near the farmhouses
and bound up and put into a truck and sent north at once.'

'Where north?'

'Tbilisi.' Nervously she hurried onward: 'I didn't know what to do, there
was no way to warn you – I'm watched as closely as you and kept away from
the others. When I saw my father, he said Erikki wouldn't be back for a few
days, that today he, my father, he was going on a business trip to Tbilisi and
that . . . that I would be going with him. He . . . he said we would be away
two or three days and by that time Erikki would be finished and then we
would go back to Tehran.' She was almost in tears. 'I'm so frightened. I'm
so frightened something's happened to Erikki.'

'Erikki will be all right,' he said, not understanding about Tbilisi, trying
to decide about the Khan. Always back to Vien: "Trust Abdollah with
your life and don't believe the lies about him." And yet here was Azadeh
saying the opposite. He looked across at her, unable to see her, hating the
darkness, wanting to see her face, her eyes, thinking that perhaps he could
read something from them. Wish to Christ she'd told me all this the other side
of the bloody wall or at the hut, he thought, his nervousness increasing. Christ,
the guard! 'Azadeh, the guard, do you know what happened to him?'

'Oh, yes I . . . I bribed him, Johnny, I bribed him to be away for half an
hour. It was the only way I could get . . . it was the only way.'

'God Almighty,' he muttered. 'Can you trust him?'

'Oh, yes. Ali is . . . he's been with Father for years. I've known him
since I was seven and I gave him a pishkesh of some jewellery, enough

for him and his family for years. But, Johnny, about Erikki . . . I'm so worried.'

'No need to worry, Azadeh. Didn't Erikki say they might send him near to Turkey?' he said encouraging her, anxious to get her back safely. 'I can't thank you enough for warning us. Come on, first we'd better get you an – '

'Oh, no, I can't,' she burst out. 'Don't you understand? Father'll take me north and I'll never get away, never – my father hates me and he'll leave me with Mzytryk, I know he will, I know he will.'

'But what about Erikki?' he said shocked. 'You can't just run away!'

'Oh, yes, I have to, Johnny, I have to. I daren't wait, I daren't go to Tbilisi, it's much safer for Erikki that I run away now. Much safer.'

'What're you talking about? You can't run away just like that! That's madness! Say Erikki comes back tonight and finds you gone? Wh – '

'I left him a note – we made an arrangement that in an emergency I'd leave a note in a secret place in our room. We had no way of telling what Father would do while he was away. Erikki'll know. There's something else. Father's going to the airport today, around noon. He has to meet a plane, someone from Tehran, I don't know who or what about but I thought perhaps you could . . . perhaps there are other planes . . . you could persuade them to take us back to Tehran or we could sneak aboard or you . . . you could force them to take us.'

'You're crazy,' he said angrily. 'This's all crazy, Azadeh. It's madness to run off and leave Erikki – how do you know it's not just as your father says, for God's sake? You say the Khan hates you – my God, if you run off like this, whether he does or doesn't he'll blow a gasket. Either way you put Erikki into more danger.'

'How can you be so blind? Don't you see? So long as I'm here Erikki has no chance, none. If I'm not here he has to think only of himself. If he knows I'm in Tbilisi he'll go there and be lost for ever. Don't you see? I'm the bait. In the Name of God, Johnny, open your eyes! Please help me!'

He heard her crying now, softly but still crying, and this only increased his fury. Christ Almighty, we can't take her along. There's no way I could do that. That'd be murder – if what she says about the Khan's true the dragnet'll be out for us in a couple of hours and we'll be lucky if we see sunset – the dragnet's already out for God's sake, think clearly! Bloody nonsense about running away! 'You have to go back. It's better,' he said.

The crying stopped. 'Insha'Allah,' she said in a different voice. 'Whatever you say, Johnny. It's better you leave quickly. You've not much time. Which way will you go?'

'I – I don't know.' He was glad for the darkness that hid his face from her. My God, why must it be Azadeh? 'Come on, I'll see you safely back.'

'There's no need. I'll . . . I'll stay here for a while.'

He heard the falsehood and his nerves jangled even more. 'You're going to go back. You've got to.'

'No,' she said defiantly. 'I can never go back. I'm staying here. He won't find me, I've hidden here before. Once I was here two days. I'm safe here.

Don't worry about me. I'll be all right. You go on. That's what you've got to do.'

Exasperated, he managed to control his urge to drag her to her feet, and instead sat back against the wall of the cave. I can't leave her, can't carry her back against her will, can't take her. Can't leave her, can't take her. Oh you can take her with you but for how long and then, when she's captured, she's mixed up with saboteurs and Christ only knows what else they'd accuse her of and they stone women for that. 'When we're found missing – if you are not – the Khan'll know you tipped us off. If you stay here, eventually you'll be found and anyway the Khan'll know you gave us the tip and that'll make it worse than ever for you, and worse for your husband. You must go back.'

'No, Johnny. I'm in the Hands of God and not afraid.'

'For God's sake, Azadeh, use your head!'

'I am. I'm in God's hands, you know that. Didn't we talk about that in our High Country a dozen times? I'm not afraid. Just leave me a grenade like the one you gave to Erikki. I'm safe in God's hands. Please go now.'

In the other time they had talked about God often. On a Swiss mountaintop it was easy and ordinary and nothing to be shy about – not with your beloved who knew the Koran and could read Arabic and felt very close to the Infinite and believed in Islam absolutely. Here in the darkness of the small cave it was not the same. Nothing was the same.

'Insha'Allah it is,' he said and decided. 'We'll go back, you and I, and I'll send Gueng on.' He got up.

'Wait.' He heard her get up too and felt her breath and nearness. Her hand touched his arm. 'No, my darling,' she said, her voice as it used to be. 'No, my darling, that would destroy my Erikki – and you and your soldier. Don't you see, I'm the lodestone to destroy Erikki. Remove the lodestone and he has a chance. Outside my father's walls, you too have a chance. When you see Erikki, tell him . . . tell him.'

What should I tell him? he was asking himself. In the darkness he took her hand in his and, feeling its warmth, was back in time again in the darkness together in the great bed, a vast summer storm lashing the windows, the two of them counting the seconds between the lightning flashes and the thunder that bounced off the sides of the high valley – sometimes only one or two seconds, oh, Johnny it must be almost overhead, Insha'Allah if it hits us, never mind we're together – holding hands together just like this. But not like this, he thought sadly. He put her hand to his lips and kissed it. 'You can tell him yourself,' he said. 'We'll give it a go – together. Ready?'

'You mean go on – together?'

'Yes.'

After a pause she said, 'First ask Gueng.'

'He does what I say.'

'Yes, of course. But please ask him. Another favour. Please?'

He went to the neck of the cleft. Gueng was leaning against the rocks outside. Before he could say anything Gueng said softly in Gurkhali, 'No danger yet, sahib. Outside.'

'Ah, you heard?'

'Yes, sahib.'

'What do you think?'

Gueng smiled. 'What I think, sahib, has no weight, affects nothing. Karma is karma. I do what you say.'

At Tabriz Airport: 12:40 P.M. They were in the trees at the edge of the airport. Ross had his binoculars trained. The terminal was empty but for soldiers, a few burnt-out wrecks of passenger aircraft.

'Not a hope in hell,' he said. 'We'll try Erikki's airport. Perhaps we can hide there until a chopper arrives.' He led the way deeper into the forest, of necessity keeping to the crude path.

On the edge of this clump of forest were frozen fields that in the summer would be abundant with crops, most of it belonging to a few landowners, in spite of the Shah's land reforms. Beyond the fields were the outlying slums of Tabriz. They could see the minarets of the Blue Mosque and smoke from many fires pulled away by the wind. 'Can we skirt the city, Azadeh?'

'Yes,' she said, 'but it's . . . it's quite a long way.'

They heard her underlying concern. So far she had moved quickly and without complaint. But she was still a hazard. They wore their tribesmen's clothes over their uniforms. Their scrubby boots would pass. So would their weapons. And her chador. He looked at her, still not used to the ugliness that it made of her. She felt his glance and tried to smile. She understood. Both about the chador and about being a burden.

'Let's go through the town,' she said. 'We can stay in the side streets. I have some . . . some money and we can buy food. Johnny, you could pretend to be Caucasian from, say, from Astara, I could pretend to be your wife. Gueng, you speak Gurkhali or a foreign tongue and be rough and arrogant like the Turkomen from the north – you'd pass for one of them – they were descended from the Mongols, many Iranians are. Or perhaps I could buy some green scarves and make you Green Bands . . . That's the best I can do.'

'That's good, Azadeh. Perhaps we'd better not stay bunched up. Gueng, you tail us.'

Azadeh said, 'In the streets Iranian wives follow their husbands. I . . . I will stay a pace behind you, Johnny.'

'It's a good plan, memsahib,' Gueng said. 'Very good. You guide us.'

Her smile thanked him. Soon they were in the markets and the streets and alleys of the slums. Once a man shoved into Gueng carelessly. Without hesitation Gueng slammed his fist into the man's throat, sending him sprawling into the joub senseless, cursing him loudly in a dialect of Ghurkali. There was a moment's silence in the crowd, then noise picked up again and those nearby kept their eyes down and passed onward, a few surreptitiously making a sign against the evil eye that all those who came from the north, the descendants of the hordes who knew not the One God, were known to possess.

Azadeh bought food from street vendors, fresh bread from the kilns, charcoaled lamb kebab and bean and vegetable horisht, heavy with rice.

They sat on rough benches and gorged, then went on again. No one paid any attention to them. Occasionally someone would ask him to buy something but Azadeh would intervene and protect him well, coarsening her voice and talking the local Turkish dialect. When the muezzins called for afternoon prayer, she stopped, afraid. Around them, men and women searched for a piece of carpet or material or newspaper or cardboard or box to kneel on and began to pray. Ross hesitated, then following her pleading look, pretended to pray also and the moment passed. In the whole street only four or five remained standing, Gueng among them, leaning against a wall. No one bothered those who stood. Tabrizi came from many races, many religions.

They continued onward, making their way southeast and now were in the outlying suburbs, shantytowns filled with refuse and mangy, half-starved dogs, the joub the only sewer. Soon the hovels would end, the fields and orchards would begin, then the forest and the main Tehran road that curled upward to the pass that would lead them to Tabriz One. What he would do when they got there, Ross did not know, but Azadeh had said that she knew of several caves nearby where they could hide until a helicopter landed.

They went through the last of the slums, out on to the crude, snow-banked track. The snow of the surface was stained from mule and donkey droppings, pitted and treacherous, and they joined others who trudged along, some leading burdened donkeys, others bent over under the weight of their loads, others relieving themselves, men and women and children – a handful of snow with the left hand, then on again – a polyglot of people, tribesmen, nomads, townspeople – only their poverty in common, and their pride.

Azadeh was feeling very tired, the strain of crossing the city heavy on her. She had been afraid she would make a mistake, afraid they would be spotted, frantic with worry over Erikki and worried how they would get to the base and what then? Insha'Allah, she told herself, over and over. God will look after you and after him and after Johnny.

When they came near the junction of the track and the Tehran road they saw Green Bands and armed men standing beside a makeshift roadblock, peering into vehicles and watching the people filing past. There was no way to avoid them.

'Azadeh, you go first,' Ross whispered. 'Wait for us up the road – if we get stopped, don't interfere, just go on – head for the base. We'll split up, safer.' He smiled at her. 'Don't worry.' She nodded, her fear making her face more pale, and walked off. She was carrying his rucksack. Coming out of the town she had insisted: 'Look at all the other women, Johnny. If I don't carry something, I'll stand out terribly.'

The two men waited, then went to the side of the track and urinated into the snowbank. People plodded by. Some noticed them. A few cursed them as Infidels. One or two wondered about them – unknowingly, they were relieving themselves towards Mecca, an act no Muslim would ever do.

'Once she's through, you next, Gueng. I'll follow in ten minutes.'

'Better you next,' Gueng whispered back. 'I'm a Turkoman.'

'All right, but if I'm stopped – do not interfere. Sneak by in the fracas and get her to safety. Don't fail me!'

The little man grinned, his teeth very white. 'Don't you fail, sahib. You have much yet to do before you're a Lord of the Mountain.' Gueng looked past him towards the roadblock, a hundred yards away. He saw that Azadeh was in line now. One of the Green Bands said something to her, but she kept her eyes averted, replied, and the man waved her through. 'Don't wait for me on the road, sahib. I may cross the fields. Don't worry about me – I'll track you.' He pushed through the pedestrians and joined the stream going back towards the town. After a hundred yards or so, he sat on an upturned crate and unlaced his boot as though it were hurting him. His socks were in shreds but that did not matter. The soles of his feet were like iron. Taking his time, he relaced his boots, enjoying being a Turkoman.

At the roadblock Ross joined the line of those leaving Tabriz. He noticed police standing around with the Green Bands, watching the people. The people were irritable, hating any authority as always and any infringement of their right to go where and how and when they pleased. Many were openly angry and a few almost came to blows. 'You,' a Green Band said to him, 'where are your papers?'

Angrily Ross spat on the ground. 'Papers? My house is burned, my wife burned, and my child burned by leftist dogs. I have nothing left but this gun and some ammunition. God's will – but why don't you go and burn Satanists and do the work of God instead of stopping honest men?'

'We're honest!' the man said angrily. 'We're doing the Work of God. Where do you come from?'

'Astara. Astara on the coast.' He let the anger come out. 'Astara. And you?'

The next man in line and the one behind him began cursing and telling the Green Band to hurry up and not cause them to wait around in the cold. A policeman was edging over towards them, so Ross decided to chance it and he shoved past with another curse, the man behind followed, and the next and now they were out in the open. The Green Band sullenly shouted an obscenity after them, then went back to watching others file through.

It took Ross a little while to breathe easier. He tried not to hurry and his eyes searched ahead. No sign of Azadeh. Cars and trucks were passing now, grinding up the incline or coming down too fast, people scattering from time to time with the inevitable stream of curses. The man who had been behind him at the roadblock came up alongside, pedestrians thinning out now, turning off into the side paths that led to hovels beside the road or to villages within the forest. He was a middle-aged man with a lined, very strong face, poorly dressed, his rifle well serviced. 'That Green Band son of a dog,' he said with a thick accent. 'You're right, agha, they should be doing God's work, the Imam's work, not Abdollah Khan's.'

Ross was instantly on guard. 'Who?'

'I come from Astara and from your accent I know you don't come from Astara, agha. Astaris never piss towards Mecca or with their backs to Mecca

– we're all good Muslims in Astara. From your description you must be the saboteur the Khan's put a price on.' The man's voice was easy, curiously friendly, the old Enfield rifle over his shoulder.

Ross said nothing, just grunted, not changing his pace.

'Yes, the Khan's put a good price on your head. Many horses, a herd of sheep, ten or more camels. A Shah's ransom to ordinary folk. The ransom's better for alive than dead – more horses and sheep and camels then, enough to live for ever. But where's the woman Azadeh, his daughter, the daughter that you kidnapped, you and another man?'

Ross gaped at him and the man chuckled. 'You must be very tired to give yourself away so easily.' Abruptly the face hardened, his hand went into the pocket of his old jacket, pulled out a revolver and shoved it into Ross's side. 'Walk ahead of me a pace, don't run or do anything or I shall just shoot you in the spine. Now where's the woman – there's a reward for her too.'

At that moment a truck coming down from the pass careened around the bend ahead, lurched to the wrong side of the road, and charged them, hooting loudly. People scattered. Ross's reflexes were faster and he sidestepped, shoved his shoulder into the man's side and sent him reeling into the truck's path. The truck's front wheels went over the man and the back wheels. The truck skidded to a stop a hundred feet below.

'God protect us, did you see that?' someone said. 'He lurched into the truck.'

Ross dragged the body out of the road. The revolver had vanished into the snow.

'Ah, is the sacrifice of God your father, agha?' an old woman said.

'No . . . no,' Ross said with difficulty, everything so fast, in panic. 'I . . . he's a stranger. I've never seen him before.'

'By the Prophet, how careless walkers are! Have they no eyes? Is he dead?' the truck driver called out, coming back up the hill. He was a rough, bearded, swarthy man. 'God witness that he moved into my path as all could see! You,' he said to Ross, 'you were beside him, you must have seen it.'

'Yes . . . yes, it is as you say. I was behind him.'

'As God wants.' The trucker went off happily, everything correct and finished. 'His Excellency saw it. Insha'Allah!'

Ross pushed away through the few who had bothered to stop and walked up the hill, not fast, not slow, trying to get himself together, not daring to look back. Around the bend in the road, he quickened his pace, wondering if it was right to react so quickly – almost without thought. But the man would have sold her and sold them. Put him away, karma is karma. Another bend and still no Azadeh. His anxiety increased.

Here the road was twisting, the grade steep. He passed a few hovels half hidden in the forest verge. Mangy dogs were scavenging. The few that came near him he cursed away, rabies usually rampant among them. Another bend, sweat pouring off him, and there she was squatting beside the road, resting like any of a dozen other old crones. She saw him at the same moment, shook her head cautioning him, got up, and started off up the road again. He fell into place twenty yards behind her. Then there was firing below them. With everyone else, they stopped and looked back. They could see nothing. The roadblock was far behind, around many corners, half a mile or more away. In a moment the firing ceased. No one said anything, just began climbing more hurriedly.

The road was not good. They walked on for a mile or so, stepping aside for traffic. Occasionally a bus groaned past but always overloaded and none would stop. These days you could wait a day or two even at a correct stop before there was space. Trucks sometimes would stop. For payment.

Later one chugged past him and as it came alongside Azadeh, it slowed to her pace. 'Why walk when those who are tired can ride with the help of Cyrus the trucker – and God,' the driver called out, leering at her, nudging his companion, a dark-bearded man of his own age. They had been watching her for some time, watching the sway of her hips that not even a chador could hide. 'Why should a flower of God walk when she could be warm in a truck or on a man's carpet?'

She looked up at him and gave him a gutter curse and called back to Ross, 'Husband, this leprous son of a dog dared to insult me and made lewd remarks against the laws of God . . .' Ross was already alongside her, and the driver found himself looking into the barrel of a gun. 'Excellency . . . I was asking if . . . if you and she would . . . would like to ride,' the driver said in panic. 'There's room in the back . . . if his Excellency would honour my vehicle . . .'

The truck was half-filled with scrap iron, but it would be better than walking. 'On your head, driver, where do you go?'

'To Qazvin, Excellency, Qazvin. Would you honour us?'

The truck did not stop but it was easy for Ross to help her climb up over the tailgate. Together they ducked down out of the wind. Her legs were shaking and she was chilled and very nervous. He reached out and put his arms around her and held her.

'Oh, Johnny, if you hadn't been there . . .'

'Don't worry, don't worry.' He gave her of his warmth. Qazvin, Qazvin? Isn't that halfway to Tehran? Of course it is! We'll stick with the truck until Qazvin, he told himself, gathering strength. Then we can get another ride, or find a bus, or steal a car, that's what we'll do.

'The turnoff to the base is two or three miles ahead,' she said, shivering in his arms. 'To the right.'

Base? Ah, yes, the base. And Erikki. But more important, what about Gueng? What about Gueng? Get your mind working. What are you going to do?

'What's the . . . what's the land like there, open and flat or a ravine or what?' he asked.

'It's fairly flat. Our village is soon, Abu Mard. We pass our village, then shortly afterwards, the land flattens into a kind of a wooded plateau where our own road is. Then the main road climbs again up to the pass.'

Ahead he could see the road curling away, occasionally coming into view

as it wound precariously along the mountainside. 'We'll get off the other side
of the village, before the flat, circle through the forest, and get to the base.
That possible?'

'Yes. I know the country very well. I . . . I taught in the village school and
used to take the children for . . . for walks. I know the paths.' Again she
trembled.

'Keep down out of the wind. You'll soon be warm.'

The old truck was labouring on the incline not much faster than walking
but better than walking. He kept his arm around her and in time she stopped
trembling. Over their tailgate, he noticed a car overtaking them fast, gears
shrieking, followed by a mottled green half truck. The driver of the car kept
his hand on the horn. There was nowhere for their truck to pull over, so
the car swung over to the wrong side of the road and charged ahead. Hope
you bloody kill yourself, he thought, angered by the noise and the incredible
stupidity. Idly he had noticed that it had been filled with armed men. So was
the following half truck though all these men stood in the back, hanging on
to metal stanchions, the tailgate down and banging wildly. As it roared past,
he caught a glimpse of a body slumped under their feet. At first he thought
it was the old man. But it wasn't. It was Gueng. No mistaking the remains of
the uniform. Or the kukri one of the men had stuck in his belt.

'What is it, Johnny?'

He found himself beside her, not feeling her or anything, only that he had
failed the second of his men. His eyes were filled with tears.

'What is it, what's the matter?'

'Nothing. It's just the wind.' He brushed the tears away, then knelt and
looked ahead. Curling away, the road disappeared and appeared again. So
did the car and half truck. He could see the village now. Beyond it the road
climbed again, then flattened, just as she had said. The car and half truck went
through the village full tilt. In his pocket were his small but very powerful
binoculars. Steadying himself against the rocking of the truck, he focused on
the car. Once the car came up on to the flat it speeded up, then turned right
on to the side road to the base and disappeared. When the half truck reached
the intersection it stopped, blocking most of the road outward bound. Half a
dozen of the men jumped down, spread out across the road and stood facing
Tabriz. Then, the half truck turned right and vanished after the car.

Their truck slowed as the driver shifted noisily into bottom gear. Just ahead
was a short, steeper grade, a path nearby, no pedestrians on this section of
road. 'Where does that go, Azadeh?'

She got on to her knees and looked where he pointed. 'Towards Abu Mard,
our village,' she said. 'It wanders this way and that but that's where it ends.'

'Get ready to jump out – there's another roadblock ahead.'

At the right moment he slipped over the side, helped her down, and they
scrambled into hiding. The truck did not stop nor the driver look around.
Soon it was well away. Hand in hand, they fled into the trees.

Chapter 12

At Tehran Airport: 6:40 P.M. McIver watched Talbot and Andrew Gavallan through his office window. Gavallan was a big, imposing man and had just arrived from Al Shargaz in the 125 for an urgent conference.

He saw Talbot drive off. Gavallan stalked back into the office that was well staffed today. Not back to normal yet but getting there – radio op, telex op, office manager, stores men and no women. 'Mac, let's take a walk.'

'Sure,' he said, seeing the gravity.

They had had no time to talk privately yet.

The two men went out on to the freight apron. A JAL jumbo roared into the sky. 'They say there're still a thousand Japanese techs kicking their heels at Iran-Toda,' McIver said absently.

'Their consortium's taking a hell of a beating. Today's *Financial Times* said their override's already half a billion dollars, no way they can get finished this year and no way to pull out – that and the world shipping glut must be hurting Toda badly.' Gavallan saw there was no one near. 'At least our capital investment's mobile, Mac, most of it.'

McIver looked up at him, seeing the craggy face, grey bushy eyebrows, brown eyes. 'That's the reason for "imperative conference"?'

'One of them,' Gavallan said. 'Talbot told me, following the advice of our fellow board member, Ali Kia, *they* intend nationalising all foreign aircraft companies, particularly ours. That means we lose the lot – unless we do something about it. Genny's right, you know. We've got to do it ourselves.'

'I don't think it's possible. Did she tell you that?'

'Of course, but I think we can. Try this on for size: say today's Day One. All non-essential personnel begin to quit Iran for reassignment or on leave; we get out all the spares we can – either by our 125 or on regular airlines when they start up again – as obsolete, redundant, for repair or as personal baggage. Zagros Three retreats to Kowiss, Tabriz closes "temporarily" and Erikki's 212 goes to Al Shargaz, then to Nigeria along with Tom Lochart from Zagros, and one 212 from Kowiss. You close HQ in Tehran and relocate at Al Shargaz to run operations and control our three remaining bases of Lengeh, Kowiss and Bandar-e Delam "pending return to normality" from there – we're all still under our government orders to evacuate all nonessential personnel.'

'Right, but th – '

'Let me finish, laddie. Say we can do the prep and planning and all that in thirty days. Day Thirty-one's D-day. At an exact time on D-day – or D plus One or Two depending on weather or Christ knows what – we radio a code word from Al Shargaz. Simultaneously all remaining pilots and choppers take off, head across the Gulf for Al Shargaz. There we remove the rotors, stow the choppers into 747 freighters I've chartered from somewhere, they'll fly to Aberdeen and Bob's your bloody uncle,' Gavallan ended with a beam.

McIver stared at him blankly. 'You're crazy! You're stark raving bonkers, Chinaboy. It's got so many holes in it . . . you're bonkers.'

'Name one hole.'

'I can give you fifty, firs – '

'One at a time, laddie, and remember your bloody pressure. How is it by the way – Genny asked me to ask?'

'Fine, and don't you bloody start. First, the same takeoff time: choppers from the different bases'll take vastly different times because of the distances they have to go. Kowiss'll have to refuel – can't make it in one hop, even across the Gulf.'

'I know that. We make separate subplans for each of the three bases. Each base commander makes his own plan how to get out – we'll take over on arrival. Scrag can zip across the Gulf easy, so can Rudi from Bandar-e De – '

'He can't. Neither Rudi from Bandar-e Delam nor Starke from Kowiss can make it in one hop all along the Gulf to Al Shargaz – even if they can get across the Gulf in the first place. They'll have to go through Kuwait, Saudi and Emirate airspace and God only knows if they'd impound us, jail, or fine us – Al Shargaz too, no reason why they should be any different.' McIver shook his head. 'The Sheikdoms can't do anything without proper Iranian clearances – rightly they're all scared fartless Khomeini's revolution'll spread to them, they've all got big Shi'a minorities, they're no match for Iranian Navy, Army and Air Force if he decides to get mean.'

'One point at a time,' Gavallan said calmly. 'You're right about Rudi and Starke's planes, Mac. But say they have permission to fly through all those territories?'

'Eh?'

'I telexed all Gulf ATC's individually for permission and I've got telex confirms that S-G choppers in transit can go through.'

'Yes, but – '

'But one point at a time, laddie. Next, say all our planes were back on British registry – they are British, they *are* our planes, we're paying for them, we own them whatever the partners try to pull. On British registry they're not subject to Iran or anything to do with them. Right?'

'Once they're out, yes, but you won't get Iran Civil Aviation Authority to agree to the transfer, therefore you can't get them back to British.'

'Say I could get them on to British registry regardless.'

'How in the hell would you do that?'

'Ask. You ask, laddie, you ask the registry lads in London to do it. In fact I did before I left London. "Things are kind of ropey in Iran," says I. "Totally snafu, old boy, yes," says they. "I'd like you to put my birds back on British registry, temporarily," says I, "I may bring them out until the situation normalises – of course, the powers that be in Iran'd approve but I can't get a bloody piece of paper signed there at the moment, you know how it is." "Certainly, old boy," says they, "same with our bloody government – any bloody government. Well, they are your kites, no doubt about that, it's a tiny bit irregular but I imagine it might be all right. Are you going to the Old Boys' beer-up?" '

McIver had stopped walking and stared at him in wonder. 'They agreed?'

'Not yet, laddie. Next?'

'I've got a hundred "nexts" but!' Irritably McIver started walking again, too cold to stand still.

'But?'

'But if I give them one at a time, you'll give me an answer – and a *possible* solution but they still won't all add up.'

'I agree with Genny, we have to do it ourselves.'

'Maybe, but it has to be feasible. Another thing: we've permission to take three 212s out, maybe we could get out the rest.'

'The three aren't out yet, Mac. The partners, let alone ICAA, won't let us out of their grasp. Look at Guerney – all their choppers are impounded. Forty-eight, including all their 212s – maybe 30 million dollars rotting, they can't even service them.' They glanced at the runway. An RAF Hercules was landing. Gavallan watched it. 'Talbot told me by the end of the week all British Army, Navy and Air Force technicians and training personnel'll be out and at the embassy they'll be down to three, including him. It seems that in the fracas at the U.S. embassy – someone sneaked in under cover of it, blew open safes, grabbed ciphers . . .'

'They still had secret stuff there?' McIver was appalled.

'Seems so. Anyway, Talbot said the infiltration caused every diplomatic sphincter in Christendom – and Sovietdom – and Arabdom – to palpitate. All embassies are closing. The Arabs are the most fractured of all – not one of the oil sheiks wants Khomeinism across the Gulf and they're anxious, willing and able to spend petro dollars to prevent it. Talbot said: "Fifty pounds against a bent hat pin that Iraq privately now has an open chequebook, the Kurds likewise, and anyone else who's Arab, pro-Sunni and anti-Khomeini. The whole Gulf's poised to explode." '

'But meanwhile th – '

'Meanwhile, he's not so bullish as he was a few days ago and not so sure that Khomeini's going to quietly retire to Qom. "It's jolly old Iran for the Iranians, old boy, so long as they're Khomeini and mullahs," he said. "It's in with Khomeinism if the leftists don't assassinate him first and out with the old. That means us." ' Gavallan banged his gloved hands together to keep the circulation going. 'I'm bloody frozen. Mac, it's clear from the books we're in dead trouble here. We've got to look after ourselves.'

'It's a hell of a risk. I think we'd lose some birds.'

'Only if luck's against us.'

'You're asking a lot from luck, Andy. Remember those two mechanics in

Nigeria who've been jailed for fourteen years just for servicing a 125 that was flown out illegally?'

'That was Nigeria, the mechanics stayed behind. We'd leave no one.'

'If just one expat gets left behind, he'll be grabbed, tossed into jail and become a hostage for all of us and all the birds – unless you're prepared to let him take the flak. If you're not, they'll use him to force us back and when we come back they'll be plenty bloody irritated. What about all our Iranian employees?'

Doggedly Gavallan said, 'If luck's against us it'll be a disaster whatever we do. I think we should come up with a proper plan with all the final details, *in case*. That'll take weeks – and we'd better keep the planning super secret, just between us.'

McIver shook his head. 'We'll have to consult Rudi, Scragger, Lochart, Erikki and Starke, if you want to be serious.'

'Just as you say.' Gavallan's back was aching and he stretched. 'Once it's properly planned . . . We don't have to press the final tit until then.'

They walked for a while in silence, snow crunching loudly. Now they were almost at the end of the apron. 'We'd be asking a hell of a lot from the lads,' McIver said.

Gavallan did not appear to have heard him. 'We can't just leave fifteen years of work, can't toss away all our savings, yours, Scrag's, and everything,' he said. 'Our Iran's gone. Most of the fellows we've worked with over the years have fled, are in hiding, dead – or against us if they like it or not. Work's at a minimum. We've got nine choppers working out of twenty-six here. We're not being paid for the little we do, or any back money. I think that's all a write-off.'

Doggedly McIver said, 'It's not as bad as you think. The partn – '

'Mac, you've got to understand I can't write off the money we're owed *plus our birds and spares* and stay in business. I can't. Our thirteen 212s are worth 13 million U.S., nine 206s another one point three odd million, three Alouettes another million and a half, and 3 million of spares – 20 million give or take a few dollars. I can't write that off. Can't be done.'

'You'd be asking a hell of a lot from the lads, Chinaboy.'

'And from you, Mac, don't forget you. It'd be a team effort, not just for me, for them too – because it's that or go under.'

'Most of our lads can get jobs with no problem. The market's desperate for trained chopper pilots who're oilers.'

'So what? Bet you all of them'd rather be with us, we look after them, pay top dollar, we've the best safety record – S-G's the best chopper company on earth, and they know it! You and I know we're part of the Noble House, by God, and that means something too.' Gavallan's eyes suddenly lit up with his irrepressible twinkle. 'It'd be a great caper if we pulled it off. When the time comes we'll ask the lads. Meanwhile all systems go, eh, laddie?'

'All right,' McIver said without enthusiasm. 'For the planning.'

Gavallan looked at him. 'I know you too well, Mac. Soon you'll be raring to go and I'll be the one saying, Hold it, what about so-and-so . . .'

But McIver wasn't listening. His mind was trying to formulate a plan, despite the impossibility of it – except for the British registry. Could that make the difference?

'Andy, about the plan. We'd better have a code name.'

'Genny says to call it "Whirlwind" – that's what we're mixed up in.'

Thursday

Chapter 13

Northwest of Tabriz: 11:20 A.M. From where he sat on the cabin steps of his parked 212 high up on the mountainside, Erikki could see deep into Soviet Russia. Far below the river Aras flowed eastward towards the Caspian, twisting through gorges and marking much of the Iran–USSR border. To his left he could see into Turkey, to soaring Mount Ararat, 15,500 feet, and the 212 was parked not far from the cave mouth where the secret American listening post was.

Was, he thought with grim amusement. When he had landed here yesterday afternoon – the altimeter reading 8,562 feet – the motley bunch of leftist fedayeen fighters he had brought with him had stormed the cave, but the cave was empty of Americans and when Cimtarga inspected it he found all the important equipment destroyed and no cipher books. Much evidence of a hasty departure, but nothing of real value to be scavenged. 'We'll clean it out anyway,' Cimtarga had said to his men, 'clean it out like the others.' To Erikki he had added, 'Can you land there?' He pointed far above where the complex of radar masts stood. 'I want to dismantle them.'

'I don't know,' Erikki had said. The grenade Ross had given him was still taped in his left armpit – Cimtarga and his captors had not searched him – and his pukoh knife was still in its back scabbard. 'I'll go and look.'

'*We'll* look, Captain. We'll look together,' Cimtarga had said with a laugh. 'Then you won't be tempted to leave us.'

He had flown him up there. The masts were secured to deep beds of concrete on the northern face of the mountain, a small flat area in front of them. 'If the weather's like today it'd be okay, but not if the wind picks up. I could hover and winch you down.' He had smiled wolfishly.

Cimtarga had laughed. 'Thanks, but no. I don't want an early death.'

'For a Soviet, particularly a KGB Soviet, you're not a bad man.'

'Neither are you – for a Finn.'

Since Sunday, when Erikki had begun flying for Cimtarga, he had come to like him – not that you can like or trust any KGB, he thought. But the man had been polite and fair, had given him a correct share of all food. Last night he had split a bottle of vodka with him and had given him the best place to sleep. They had slept in a village twenty kilometres south on carpets on a dirt floor. Cimtarga had said that though this was all mostly Kurdish territory the village was secretly fedayeen and safe. 'Then why keep the guard on me?'

'It's safe for us, Captain – not safe for you.'

The night before last at the Khan's palace when Cimtarga and guards had come for him just after Ross had left, he had been driven to the air base and, in darkness and against IATC regulations, had flown to the village in the mountains north of Khvoy. There, in the dawn, they had collected a full load of armed men and had flown to the first of the two American radar posts. It was destroyed and empty of personnel like this one. 'Someone must have tipped them we would be coming,' Cimtarga said disgustedly. '*Matyeryebyets* spies!'

Later Cimtarga told him locals whispered that the Americans had evacuated the night before last, whisked away by helicopters, unmarked and very big. 'It would have been good to catch them spying. Very good. Rumour says the bastards can see a thousand miles into us.'

'You're lucky they weren't here, you might have had a battle and that would have created an international incident.'

Cimtarga had laughed. 'Nothing to do with us – nothing. It was the Kurds again, more of their rotten work – bunch of thugs, eh? They'd've been blamed. Rotten *yezdvas*, eh? Eventually the bodies would have been found – on Kurdish land. That'd be proof enough for Carter and his CIA.'

Erikki shifted on the plane's steps, his seat chilled by the metal, depressed and weary. Last night he had slept badly again – nightmares about Azadeh. He hadn't slept well since Ross had appeared.

You're a fool, he thought for the thousandth time. I know, but that doesn't help. Nothing seems to help. Maybe the flying's getting to you. You've been putting in too many hours in bad conditions, too much night flying. Then there's Nogger to worry about – and Rakoczy to brood about and the killings. And Ross. And most of all Azadeh. Is she safe?

He had tried to make his peace with her about her Johnny Brighteyes the next morning. 'I admit I was jealous. Stupid to be jealous. I swore by the ancient gods of my forefathers that I could live with your memory of him – I can and I will,' he had said, but saying the words had not cleansed him. 'I just didn't think he'd be so . . . so much a man and so . . . so dangerous. That kukri would be a match for my knife.'

'Never, my darling. Never. I'm so glad you're you and I'm me and we're together. How can we get out of here?'

'Not all of us, not together at the same time,' he had told her honestly. 'The soldiers'd be better to get out while they can. With Nogger, and them, and while you're here – I don't know, Azadeh. I don't know how we can escape yet. We'll have to wait. Maybe we could get into Turkey . . .'

He looked eastwards into Turkey now, so close and so far with Azadeh still in Tabriz – thirty minutes by air to her. But when? If we got into Turkey and if my chopper wasn't impounded, and if I could refuel we could fly to Al Shargaz, skirting the border. If if if! Gods of my ancestors, help me!

Over vodka last night Cimtarga had been as taciturn as ever, but he had drunk well and they had shared the bottle glass to glass to the last drop. 'I've another for tomorrow night, Captain.'

'Good. When will you be through with me?'

'It'll take two to three days to finish here, then back to Tabriz.'

'Then?'

'Then I'll know better.'

But for the vodka Erikki would have cursed him. He got up and watched the Iranians piling the equipment for loading. Most of it seemed to be very ordinary. As he strolled over the broken terrain, his boots crunching the snow, his guard went with him. Never a chance to escape. In all five days he had never had a single chance. 'We enjoy your company,' Cimtarga had said once, reading his mind, his Oriental eyes crinkling.

Above, he could see some men working on the radar masts, dismantling them. Waste of time, he thought. Even I know there's nothing special about them. 'That's unimportant, Captain,' Cimtarga had said. 'My Master enjoys bulk. He said get everything. More is better than less. Why should you worry – you're paid by the hour.' Again the laugh, not taunting.

Feeling his neck muscles taut, Erikki stretched and touched his toes and, in that position, let his arms and head hang freely, then waggled his head in as big a semicircle as he could, letting the weight of his head stretch the tendons and ligaments and muscles and smooth out the kinks, forcing nothing, just using the weight. 'What're you doing?' Cimtarga asked, coming up to him.

'It's great for neck ache.' He put his dark glasses back on – without them the reflected light from the snow was uncomfortable. 'If you do it twice a day you'll never get neck ache.'

'Ah, you get neck aches too? Me, I'm always getting them – have to go to a chiropractor at least three times a year. That helps?'

'Guaranteed. A waitress told me about it – carrying trays all day gives them plenty of neck and backache, like pilots; it's a way of life. Try it and you'll see.' Cimtarga bent over as Erikki had done and moved his head. 'No, you're doing it wrong. Let your head and arms and shoulders hang freely, you're too stiff.'

Cimtarga did as he was told and felt his neck crack and the joints ease and when he raised himself again, he said, 'That's wonderful, Captain. I owe you a favour.'

'It's a return for the vodka.'

'It's worth more than a bottle of vod – '

Erikki stared at him blankly as blood spurted out of Cimtarga's chest in the wake of the bullet that pierced him from behind, then came a thraaakkk followed by others as tribesmen poured out of ambush from the rocks and trees, shrieking battle cries and 'Allah-u Akbarrr', firing as they came. The attack was brief and violent and Erikki saw Cimtarga's men going down all over the plateau, quickly overwhelmed. His own guard, one of the few who was carrying a weapon, had opened up at the first bullet but was hit at once, and now a bearded tribesman stood over him and gleefully finished him with the rifle butt. Others charged into the cave. More firing, then silence again.

Two men rushed him and he put his hands up, feeling naked and foolish, his heart thundering. One of these turned Cimtarga over and shot him again. The other bypassed Erikki and went to the cabin of the 212 to make sure no one was hiding there. Now the man who had shot Cimtarga stood in front of Erikki, breathing hard. He was small and olive-skinned and bearded, dark eyes and hair and wore rough garments and stank.

'Put your hands down,' he said in heavily accented English. 'I am Sheik Bayazid, chief here. We need you and helicopter.'

'What do you want with me?'

Around them the tribesmen were finishing off the wounded and stripping the dead of anything of value. 'CASEVAC.' Bayazid smiled thinly at the look on Erikki's face. 'Many of us work the oil and rigs. Who is this dog?' He motioned at Cimtarga with his foot.

'He called himself Cimtarga. He was a Soviet. I think also KGB.'

'Of course Soviet,' the man said roughly. 'Of course KGB – all Soviets in Iran KGB. Papers, please.' Erikki gave him his ID. The tribesman read it and nodded half to himself. And, to Erikki's further surprise, handed it back. 'Why you flying Soviet dog?' He listened silently, his face darkening as Erikki told him how Abdollah Khan had entrapped him. 'Abdollah Khan no man to offend. The reach of Abdollah the Cruel very wide, even in the lands of the Kurds.'

'You're Kurds?'

'Kurds,' Bayazid said, the lie convenient. He knelt and searched Cimtarga. No papers, a little money that he pocketed, nothing else. Except the holstered automatic and ammunition which he also took. 'Have you full fuel?'

'Three-quarter full.'

'I want go twenty miles south. I direct you. Then pick up CASEVAC, then go Rezaiyeh, to hospital there.'

'Why not Tabriz – it's much closer.'

'Rezaiyeh in Kurdistan. Kurds are safe there, sometimes. Tabriz belong to our enemies: Iranians, Shah or Khomeini no difference. Go Rezaiyeh.'

'All right. The Overseas Hospital would be best. I've been before and they've a helipad. They're used to CASEVACs. We can refuel there – they've chopper fuel, at least they had in . . . the old days.'

Bayazid hesitated. 'Good. Yes. We go at once.'

'And after Rezaiyeh – what then?'

'And then, if serve us safely, perhaps you released to take your wife from the Gorgon Khan.' Sheik Bayazid turned away and shouted for his men to hurry up and board the airplane. 'Start up, please.'

'What about him?' Erikki pointed at Cimtarga. 'And the others?'

'The beasts and birds soon make here clean.'

It took them little time to board and leave, Erikki filled with hope now. No problem to find the site of the small village. The CASEVAC was an old woman. 'She is our chieftain,' Bayazid said.

'I didn't know women could be chieftains.'

'Why not, if wise enough, strong enough, clever enough, and from correct family? We Sunni Muslims – not leftists or heretic Shi'a cattle who put mullahs between man and God. God is God. We leave at once.'

'Does she speak English?'

'No.'

'She looks very ill. She may not last the journey.'

'As God wants.'

But she did last the hour's journey and Erikki landed on the helipad. The Overseas Hospital had been built, staffed and sponsored by foreign oil companies. He had flown low all the way, avoiding Tabriz and military airfields. Bayazid had sat up front with him, six armed guards in the back with their high chieftain. She lay on the stretcher, awake but motionless. In great pain but without complaining.

A doctor and orderlies were at the helipad seconds after touchdown. The doctor wore a white coat with a large red cross on the sleeve over heavy sweaters, and he was in his thirties, American, dark rings around bloodshot eyes. He knelt beside the stretcher as the others waited in silence. She groaned a little when he touched her abdomen even though his hands were healing hands. In a moment he spoke to her gently in halting Turkish. A small smile went over her and she nodded and thanked him. He motioned to the orderlies and they lifted the stretcher out of the cabin and carried her away. At Bayazid's order, two of his men went with her.

The doctor said to Bayazid in halting dialect, 'Excellency, I need name and age and . . .' he searched for the word, 'history, medical history.'

'Speak English.'

'Good, thank you, agha. I'm Doctor Newbegg. I'm afraid she's near the end, agha, her pulse is almost zero. She's old and I'd say she was haemorrhaging – bleeding – internally. Did she have a fall recently?'

'Speak slower, please. Fall? Yes, yes, two days ago. She slip in snows and fell against a rock, on her side against a rock.'

'I think she's bleeding inside. I'll do what we can but . . . sorry, I can't promise good news.'

'Insha'Allah.'

'You're Kurds?'

'Kurds.' More firing, closer now. They all looked off to where the sound came from. 'Who?'

'I don't know, just more of the same, I'm afraid,' the doctor said uneasily. 'Green Bands against leftists, leftists against Green Bands, against Kurds – many factions – and all're armed.' He rubbed his eyes. 'I'll do what I can for the old lady – perhaps you'd better come with me, agha, you can give me the details as we go.' He hurried off.

'Doc, do you still have fuel here?' Erikki called after him.

The doctor stopped and looked at him blankly. 'Fuel? Oh, chopper fuel? I don't know. Gas tank's in back.' He went up the stairs to the main entrance, his white coat-tail flapping.

'Captain,' Bayazid said, 'you will wait till I return. Here.'

'But the fuel? I ca – '

'Wait here. Here.' Bayazid rushed after the doctor. Two of his men went with him. Two stayed with Erikki.

While Erikki waited, he checked everything. Tanks almost empty. From time to time cars and lorries arrived with wounded to be met by doctors and medics. Many eyed the chopper curiously but none approached. The guards made sure of that.

During the flight here Bayazid had said: 'For centuries we Kurds try for independent. We a separate people, separate language, separate customs. Now perhaps 6 million Kurds in Azerbaijan, Kurdistan, over Soviet border, this side of Iraq, and Turkey.' He had almost spat the word. 'For centuries we fight them all, together or singly. We hold the mountains. We are good fighters. Salah-al-din – he was Kurd. You know of him?' Salah-al-din – Saladin – was the chivalrous Muslim opponent of Richard the Lionheart during the crusades of the twelfth century, who made himself Sultan of Egypt and Syria and captured the Kingdom of Jerusalem in AD 1187 after smashing the allied might of the Crusaders.

'Yes, I know of him.'

'Today other Salah-al-dins among us. One day we recapture again all the Holy places – after Khomeini, betrayer of Islam, is stamped into joub.'

Erikki had asked, 'You ambushed Cimtarga and the others and wiped them out just for the CASEVAC?'

'Of course. They enemy. Yours and ours.' Bayazid had smiled his twisted smile. 'Nothing happens in our mountains without us knowing. Our chieftain sick – you nearby. We see the Americans leave, see scavengers arrive, and you were recognised.'

'Oh? How?'

'Redhead of the Knife? The Infidel who kills assassins like lice, then given a Gorgon whelp as reward! CASEVAC pilot?' The dark, almost sloe eyes were amused. 'Oh, yes, Captain, know you well. Many of us work timber as well as oil – a man must work. Even so, it's good you not Soviet or Iranian.'

'After the CASEVAC will you and your men help me against Gorgon Khan?'

Bayazid had laughed. 'Your blood feud is your blood feud, not ours. Abdollah Khan is for us, at the moment. We not go against him. What you do is up to God.'

It was cold in the hospital forecourt, a slight wind increasing the chill factor. Erikki was walking up and down to keep his circulation going. I've got to get back to Tabriz. I've got to get back and then somehow I'll take Azadeh and we'll leave for ever.

Firing nearby startled him and the guards. Outside the hospital gates, the traffic slowed, horns sounding irritably, then quickly snarled. People began running past. More firing and those trapped in their vehicles got out and took cover or fled. Inside the gates the expanse was wide, the 212 parked on the helipad to one side. Wild firing now, much closer. Some glass windows on the top floor of the hospital blew out. The two guards were hugging the snow behind the plane's undercarriage, Erikki fuming that his airplane was so exposed and not knowing where to run or what to do, no time to take off, and not enough fuel to go anywhere. A few ricochets, and he ducked down as the small battle built outside the walls. Then it died as quickly as it had begun. People picked themselves up out of cover, horns began sounding, and soon the traffic was as normal and as spiteful as ever.

'Insha'Allah,' one of the tribesmen said, then cocked his rifle and came on guard. A small petrol truck was approaching from behind the hospital, driven by a young Iranian with a broad smile. Erikki went to meet it.

'Hi, Cap,' the driver said happily, his accent heavily New York. 'I'm to gas you up. Your fearless leader, Sheik Bayazid fixed it.' He greeted the tribesmen in Turkish dialect. At once they relaxed and greeted him back. 'Cap, we'll fill her brimming. You got any temp tanks, or special tanks?'

'No. Just the regular. I'm Erikki Yokkonen.'

'Sure. Red the Knife.' The youth grinned. 'You're kinda a legend in these parts. I gassed you once, maybe a year ago.' He stuck out his hand. 'I'm "Gasoline" Ali – Ali Reza that is.'

They shook hands and, while they talked, the youth began the refuel. 'You went to American school ?' Erikki asked.

'Hell, no. I was sort of adopted by the hospital, years ago, long before this one was built, when I was a kid. In the old days the hospital worked out of one of the Golden Ghettos on the east side of town – you know, Cap, U.S. Personnel Only, an ExTex depot.' The youth smiled, screwed the tank cap back carefully, and started to fill the next. 'The first doc who took me in was Abe Weiss. Great guy, just great. He put me on the payroll, taught me about soap and socks and spoons and toilets – hell, all sorts of gizmos un-Iranian for street rats like me, with no folks, no home, no name and no nothing. He used to call me his hobby. He even gave me my name. Then, one day, he left.'

Erikki saw the pain in the youth's eyes, quickly hidden. 'He passed me on to Doc Templeton, and he did the same. At times it's kinda hard to figure where I'm at. Kurd but not, Yank but not – Iranian but not, Jew but not, Muslim but not Muslim.' He shrugged. 'Kinda mixed up, Cap. The world, everything. Huh?'

'Yes.' Erikki glanced towards the hospital. Bayazid was coming down the steps with his two fighters beside orderlies carrying a stretcher. The old woman was covered now, head to foot.

'We leave soon as fuel,' Bayazid said shortly.

'Sorry,' Erikki said.

'Insha'Allah.' They watched the orderlies put the stretcher into the cabin. Bayazid thanked them and they left. Soon the refuel was complete.

'Thanks, Mr. Reza.' Erikki stuck out his hand. 'Thanks.'

The youth stared at him. 'No one's ever called me mister before, Cap, never.' He pummelled Erikki's hand. 'Thanks – any time you want gas, you got it.'

Bayazid climbed in beside Erikki, fastened his belt, and put on the headset, the engines building. 'Now we go to village from whence we came.'

'What then?' Erikki asked.

'I consult new chieftain,' Bayazid said, but he was thinking, this man and the helicopter will bring a big ransom, perhaps from the Khan, perhaps from the Soviets, or even from his own people. My people need every rial we can get.

Near Tabriz One – in the Village of Abu Mard: 6:16 P.M. Azadeh picked up the bowl of rice and the bowl of horisht, thanked the headman's wife, and walked across the dirty, refuse-fouled snow to the hut that was set a little apart. Her face was pinched, her cough not good. She knocked, then went through the low doorway. 'Hello, Johnny. How do you feel? Any better?'

'I'm fine,' he said. But he wasn't.

The first night they had spent in a cave not far away, huddled together, shivering from the cold. 'We can't stay here, Azadeh,' he had said in the dawn. 'We'll freeze to death. We'll have to try the base.' They had gone through the snows and watched from hiding. They saw the two mechanics and even Nogger Lane from time to time – and the 206 – but all over the base were armed men. Dayati, the base manager, had moved into Azadeh and Erikki's cabin – he, his wife and children. 'Sons and daughters of dogs,' Azadeh hissed, seeing the wife wearing a pair of her boots. 'Perhaps we could sneak into the mechanics' huts. They'll hide us.'

'They're escorted everywhere; I'll bet they've even guards at night. But who are the guards, Green Bands, the Khan's men, or who?'

'I don't recognise any of them, Johnny.'

'They're after us,' he said, feeling very low, the death of Gueng preying on him. Both Gueng and Tenzing had been with him since the beginning. And there was Rosemont. And now Azadeh. 'Another night in the open and you'll have had it, we'll have had it.'

'Our village, Johnny. Abu Mard. It's been in our family for more than a century. They're loyal, I know they are. We'd be safe there for a day or two.'

'With a price on my head? And you? They'd send word to your father.'

'I'd ask them not to. I'd say Soviets were trying to kidnap me and you were helping me. That's true. I'd say that we needed to hide until my husband comes back – he's always been very popular, Johnny, his CASEVACs saved many lives over the years.'

He looked at her, a dozen reasons against. 'The village's on the road, almost right on the road an – '

'Yes, of course, you're quite right and we'll do whatever you say, but it sprawls away into the forest. We could hide there – no one'd expect that.'

He saw her tiredness. 'How do you feel? How strong do you feel?'

'Not strong, but fine.'

'We could hike out, go down the road a few miles – we'd have to skirt the roadblock, it's a lot less dangerous than the village. Eh?'

'I'd . . . I'd rather not. I could try.' She hesitated, then said, 'I'd rather not, not today. You go on. I'll wait. Erikki may come back today.'

'And if he doesn't?'

'I don't know. You go on.'

He looked back at the base. A nest of vipers. Suicide to go there. From where they were on a rise, he could see as far as the main road. Men still manned the roadblock – he presumed Green Bands and police – a line of traffic backed up and waiting to leave the area. No one'll give us a ride now, he thought, not unless it's for the reward. 'You go to the village. I'll wait in the forest.'

'Without you they'll return me to my father – I know them, Johnny.'

'Perhaps they'll betray you anyway.'

'As God wants. But we could get some food and warmth, perhaps even a night's rest. In the dawn we could sneak away. Perhaps we could get a car or truck from them – the kalandar has an old Ford.' She stifled a sneeze. Armed men were not far away. More than likely there were patrols out in the forest – coming here they had had to detour to avoid one. The village's madness, he thought. To get around the roadblock'll take hours in daylight, and by night – we can't stay outside another night.

'Let's go to the village,' he said.

So they had gone yesterday and Mostafa, the kalandar, had listened to her story and kept his eyes away from Ross. News of their arrival had gone from mouth to mouth and in moments all the village knew and this news was added to the other, about the reward for the saboteur and kidnapper of the Khan's daughter. The kalandar had given Ross a disused, one-room hut with dirt floor and old mildewed carpets. The hut was well away from the road, on the far edge of the village, and he noticed the steel hard eyes and matted hair and stubbled beard – his carbine and kukri and ammunition-heavy knapsack. Azadeh he invited into his home. It was a two-room hovel. No electricity or running water. The joub was the toilet.

At dusk last night, hot food and a bottle of water had been brought to Ross by an old woman.

'Thank you,' he said, his head aching and the fever already with him. 'Where is Her Highness?' The woman shrugged. She was heavily lined, pockmarked, with brown stubs of teeth. 'Please ask her to receive me.'

Later he was sent for. In the headman's room, watched by the headman, his wife, some of his brood, and a few elders, he greeted Azadeh carefully – as a stranger might a highborn. She wore chador of course and knelt on carpets facing the door. Her face had a yellowish, unhealthy pallor, but he thought it might be from the light of the spluttering oil lamp. 'Salaam, Highness, your health is good?'

'Salaam, agha, yes, thank you, and yours?'

'There is a little fever I think.' He saw her eyes flick up from the carpet momentarily. 'I have medicine. Do you need any?'

'No. No, thank you.'

With so many eyes and ears what he wanted to say was impossible. 'Perhaps I may greet you tomorrow,' he said. 'Peace be upon you, Highness.'

'And upon you.'

It had taken him a long time to sleep. And her. With the dawn the village awoke, fires were stoked, goats milked, vegetable horisht set to stew – little to nourish it but a morsel of chicken, in some huts a piece of goat or sheep, the meat old, tough and rancid. Bowls of rice but never enough. Food twice a day in good times, morning and before last light. Azadeh had money and she paid for their food. This did not go unnoticed. She asked that a whole chicken be put in to tonight's horisht to be shared by the whole household, and she paid for it. This, too, did not go unnoticed.

Before last light she had said, 'Now I will take food to him.'

'But, Highness, it's not right for you to serve him,' the kalandar's wife said. 'I'll carry the bowls. We can go together if you wish.'

'No, it's better if I go alone beca – '

'God protect us, Highness. Alone? To a man not your husband? Oh no, that would be unseemly, that would be very unseemly. Come, I will take it.'

'Good, thank you. As God wants. Thank you. Last night he mentioned fever. It might be plague. I know how Infidels carry vile diseases that we are not used to. I only wished to save you probable agony. Thank you for sparing me.'

Last night everyone in the room had seen the sheen of sweat on the Infidel's face. Everyone knew how vile Infidels were, most of them Satan worshippers and sorcerers. Almost everyone secretly believed that Azadeh had been bewitched, first by the Giant of the Knife, and now again by the saboteur. Silently the headman's wife had handed Azadeh the bowls and she had walked across the snow.

Now she watched him in the semidarkness of the room that had as window a hole in the adobe wall, no glass, just sacking covering most of it. The air was heavy with the smell of urine and waste from the joub outside.

'Eat, eat while it's hot. I can't stay long.'

'You okay?' He had been lying under the single blanket, fully dressed, dozing, but now he sat crosslegged and alert. The fever had abated somewhat with the help of drugs from his survival kit but his stomach was upset. 'You don't look so good.'

She smiled. 'Neither do you. I'm fine. Eat.'

He was very hungry. The soup was thin but he knew that was better for his stomach. Another spasm started building but he held on and it went away. 'You think we could sneak off?' he said between mouthfuls, trying to eat slowly.

'You could, I can't.'

While he had been dozing all day gathering his strength, he had tried to make a plan. Once he had started to walk out of the village. A hundred eyes were on him, everyone watching. He went to the edge of the village then came back. But he had seen the old truck. 'What about the truck?'

'I asked the headman. He said it was out of order. Whether he was lying or not I don't know.'

'We can't stay here much longer. A patrol's bound to come here. Or your father will hear about us or be told. Our only hope is to run.'

'Or to hijack the 106 with Nogger.'

He looked at her. 'With all those men there?'

'One of the children told me that they went back to Tabriz today.'

'You're sure?'

'Not sure, Johnny.' A wave of anxiety went over her. 'But there's no reason for the child to lie. I, I used to teach here before I was married – I was the only teacher they had ever had and I know they liked me. The child said there's only one or two left there.' Another chill swirled up and made her weak. So many lies, so many problems the last few weeks, she thought. Is it only weeks? So much terror since Rakoczy and the mullah burst in on Erikki and me after our sauna. Everything so hopeless now. Erikki, where are you? she wanted to scream, where are you?

He finished the soup and the rice and picked at the last grain, weighing the odds, trying to plan. She was kneeling opposite him and she saw his matted hair and filth, his exhaustion and gravity. 'Poor Johnny,' she murmured and touched him. 'I haven't brought you much luck, have I?'

'Don't be silly. Not your fault – none of this is.' He shook his head. 'None of it. Listen, this's what we'll do: we'll stay here tonight, tomorrow after first light we'll walk out. We'll try the base – if that doesn't work then we'll hike out. You try to get the headman to help us by keeping his mouth shut, his wife too. The rest of the villagers should behave if he orders it, at least to give us a start. Promise them a big reward when things are normal again, and here . . .' He reached into his pack into the secret place, found the gold rupees, ten of them. 'Give him five, keep the other five for emergency.'

'But. . . but what about you?' she said, wide-eyed and filled with hope at so much potential pishkesh.

'I've ten more,' he said, the lie coming easily. 'Emergency funds, courtesy of Her Majesty's Government.'

'Oh, Johnny, I think we've a chance now – this is so much money to them.'

They both glanced at the window as a wind picked up and rustled the sacking that covered it. She got up and adjusted it as best she could. Not all the opening could be covered. 'Never mind,' he said. 'Come and sit down.' She obeyed, closer than before. 'Here. Just in case.' He handed her the grenade. 'Just hold the lever down, pull the pin out, count three, and throw. Three, not four.'

She nodded and pulled up her chador and carefully put the grenade into one of her ski jacket pockets. Her tight ski pants were tucked into her boots. 'Thanks. Now I feel better. Safer.' Involuntarily, she touched him and wished she hadn't for she felt the fire. 'I'd . . . I'd better go. I'll bring you food at first light. Then we'll leave.'

He got up and opened the door for her. Outside it was dark. Neither saw the figure scuttle away from the window, but both felt eyes feeding on them from every side.

'What about Gueng, Johnny? Do you think he'll find us?'

'He'll be watching, wherever he is.' He felt a spasm coming. ''Night, sweet dreams.'

'Sweet dreams.'

They had always said it to each other in the olden times. Their eyes touched and their hearts and both of them were warmed and at the same time filled with foreboding. Then she turned, the darkness of her chador making her at once almost invisible. He saw the door of the headman's hut open and she went in and then the door closed. He heard a truck grinding up the road not far off, then a honking car that went past and soon faded away. A spasm came and it was too much so he squatted. The pain was big but little came out and he was thankful that Azadeh had gone. His left hand groped for some snow and he cleansed himself. Eyes were still watching him, all around. Bastards, he thought, then went back into the hut and sat on the crude straw mattress.

In the darkness he oiled the kukri. No need to sharpen it. He had done that earlier. Lights glinted off the blade. He slept with it out of its scabbard.

At the Palace of the Khan: 11:19 P.M. The doctor held the Khan's wrist and checked his pulse again. 'You must have plenty of rest, Highness,' he said worriedly, 'and one of these pills every three hours.'

'Every three hours . . . yes,' Abdollah Khan said, his voice small and breathing bad. He was propped on cushions in the bed that was made up on deep carpets. Beside the bed was Najoud, his eldest daughter, thirty-five, and Aysha, his third wife, seventeen. Both women were white-faced. Two guards stood at the door and Ahmed knelt beside the doctor. 'Now . . . leave me.'

'I'll come back at dawn with the ambulance an – '

'No ambulance! I stay here!' The Khan's face reddened, another pain went through his chest. They watched him, hardly breathing. When he could speak he said throatily, 'I stay . . . here.'

'But Highness, you've already had one heart attack, God be thanked just a mild one,' the doctor said, his voice quavering. 'There's no telling when you could have . . . I've no equipment here; you should have immediate treatment and observation.'

'What . . . whatever you need, bring it here. Ahmed, see to it!'

'Yes Highness.' Ahmed looked at the doctor.

The doctor put his stethoscope and blood pressure equipment into his old-fashioned bag. At the door he slipped his shoes on and went out. Najoud and Ahmed followed him. Aysha hesitated. She was tiny and had been married two years and had a son and a daughter. The Khan's face had an untoward pallor and his breath rasped heavily. She knelt closer and took his hand but he pulled it away angrily, rubbing his chest, cursing her. Her fear increased.

Outside in the hall, the doctor stopped. His face was old and lined, older than his age, his hair white. 'Highness,' he said to Najoud, 'better he should be in hospital. Tabriz is not good enough. Tehran would be much better. He should be in Tehran though the trip there might . . . Tehran is better than here. His blood pressure's too high, it's been too high for years but, well, as God wants.'

'Whatever you need we'll bring here,' Ahmed said.

Angrily the doctor said, 'Fool, I can't bring an operating theatre and dispensary and aseptic surroundings!'

'He's going to die?' Najoud said, her eyes wide.

'In God's time, only in God's time. His pressure's much too high . . . I'm not a magician and we're so short of supplies. Have you any idea what caused the attack – was there a quarrel or anything?'

'No, no quarrel, but it was surely Azadeh. It was her again, that half-sister of mine.' Najoud began wringing her hands. 'It was her, running off with a saboteur yesterday morning, it wa – '

'What saboteur?' the doctor asked astonished.

'The saboteur everyone is looking for, the enemy of Iran. But I'm sure he didn't kidnap her, I'm sure she ran off with him – how could he kidnap her from inside the palace? She's the one who caused His Highness such rage – we've all been in terror since yesterday morning. . . .'

Stupid hag! Ahmed thought. The insane, roaring outburst was because of Hashemi Fazir, the chief of Intelligence, who had arrived by plane from Tehran, and what he had demanded of my Master and what my Master had to agree to. Such a little thing, giving over to them a Soviet, a pretended friend who was an enemy, surely no cause to explode? Clever of my Master to set everything into motion: the day after tomorrow the burnt offering comes back over the border into the web and the enemies from Tehran come back into the web. Soon my Master will decide and then I will act. Meanwhile, Azadeh and the saboteur are safely bottled in the village, at my Master's will – word sent to him by the headman the first moment. Few men on earth are as clever as Abdollah Khan and only God will decide when he should die, not this dog of a doctor. 'Let us go on,' he said. 'Please excuse me, Highness, but we should fetch a nurse and drugs and some equipment. Doctor, we should hurry.'

The door at the far end of the corridor opened. Aysha was even paler. 'Ahmed, His Highness wants you for a moment.'

When they were alone, Najoud caught the doctor by the sleeve and whispered, 'How bad is His Highness? You must tell me the truth. I've got to know.'

The doctor lifted his hands helplessly. 'I don't know, I don't know. I've been expecting worse than this for . . . for a year or more. The attack was mild. The next could be massive or mild, in an hour or a year, I don't know.'

Najoud had been in a panic ever since the Khan had collapsed a couple of hours before. If the Khan died, then Hakim, Azadeh's brother, was his legitimate heir – Najoud's own two brothers had died in infancy. Aysha's son was barely a year old. The Khan had no living brothers, so his heir should be Hakim. But Hakim was in disgrace and disinherited so there would have to be a regency. Her husband, Mahmud, was senior of the sons-in-law. He would be regent, unless the Khan ordered otherwise.

Why should he order otherwise? she thought, her stomach once more a bottomless pit. The Khan knows I can guide my husband and make us all strong. Aysha's son – pshaw, a sickly child, as sickly as the mother. As God wants, but infants die. He's not a threat, but Hakim – Hakim is.

She remembered going to the Khan when Azadeh had returned from school in Switzerland: 'Father, I bring you bad tidings but you must know the truth. I overheard Hakim and Azadeh. Highness, she told him she'd been with child but with the help of a doctor had cast it out.'

'*What?*'

'Yes . . . yes, I heard her say it.'

'*Azadeh could not . . . Azadeh would not, could not do that!*'

'Question her – I beg you do not say from where you heard it – ask her before God, question her, have a doctor examine her, but wait, that's not all. Against your wishes, Hakim's still determined to become a pianist and he told her he was going to run away, asking Azadeh to come with him to Paris "then you can marry your lover", he said, but she said, Azadeh said, "Father will bring you back, he'll force us back. He'll never permit us to go without his prior permission, never." Then Hakim said, "I *will* go. I'm not going to stay here and waste my life. I'm going!" Again she said, "Father will never permit it, never." "Then better he's dead," Hakim said and she said, "I agree."'

'*I – I don't – believe it!*'

Najoud remembered the face gone purple, and how terrified she had been. 'Before God,' she had said, 'I heard them say it, Highness, before God. Then they said we must plan, we m – ' She had quailed as he shouted at her, telling her to tell it exactly.

'Exactly he said, Hakim said, "a little poison in his halvah, or in a drink, we can bribe a servant, perhaps we could bribe one of his guards to kill him or we could leave the gates open at night for assassins – there are a hundred ways for any one of a thousand enemies to do it for us, everyone hates him. We must think and be patient. . . ."'

It had been easy for her to weave her spell, deeper and deeper into the fabrication so that soon she was believing it as she believed it now. Except for the protestation 'Before God' it would be the truth.

God will forgive me, she told herself confidently as she always told herself. God will forgive me. Azadeh and Hakim have always hated us, the rest of the family, wanted us dead, outcast, to take all our heritage unto themselves, they and their witch of a mother who cast an evil spell over Father to turn his face from us for so many years. Eight years he was under the spell – Azadeh this and Azadeh that, Hakim this and Hakim that. Eight years he dismissed us and our mother, his first wife, took no notice of me, carelessly married me to this clod, Mahmud, this foul-smelling, now impotent, vile snoring clod, and so ruined my life. I hope my husband dies, eaten by worms, but not before he becomes Khan so my son will become Khan after him.

Father must get rid of Hakim before he dies. God keep him alive to do that – he must do it before he dies – and Azadeh must be humbled, cast out, destroyed too – even better, caught in her adultery with the saboteur, oh yes, then my revenge would be complete.

Friday

Chapter 14

Near Tabriz One, at the Village of Abu Mard. 6:17 A.M. In the dawn, the face of another Mahmud, the phoney Islamic-Marxist mullah, was contorted with rage. 'Have you lain with this man?' he shouted. 'Before God have you lain with him?'

Azadeh was on her knees in front of him, panic-stricken. 'You've no right to burst into th – '

'Have you lain with this man?'

'I . . . I am faithful to my . . . my husband,' she gasped. It was only seconds ago that she and Ross had been sitting on the carpets in the hut, hastily eating the meal she had brought him, happy together, ready for immediate departure. The headman had gratefully and humbly accepted his pishkesh – four gold rupees to him and one she had secretly given to his wife – telling them to sneak out of the village by the forest side the moment they had finished eating, blessing her – then the door had burst open, aliens had rushed them, overpowering him and dragging them both into the open, shoving her at Mahmud's feet and battering Ross into submission. 'I'm faithful, I swear it. I'm faithf – '

'Faithful? Why aren't you wearing chador?' he had shouted down at her, most of the village collected around them now, silent and afraid. Half a dozen armed men leaned on their weapons, two stood over Ross who was face downward in the snow, unconscious, blood trickling from his forehead.

'I was . . . I was wearing chador but I . . . I took it off while I was eat – '

'You took off your chador in a hut with the door closed eating with a stranger? What else had you taken off?'

'Nothing, nothing,' she said in more panic, pulling her unzipped parka closer about her, 'I was just eating and he's not a stranger but an old friend of mi . . . old friend of my husband,' she corrected herself hastily but the slip had not gone unnoticed. 'Abdollah Khan is my father and you have no r – '

'Old friend? If you're not guilty you've nothing to fear! Before God, have you lain with him? Swear it!'

'Kalandar, send for my father, send for him!' The kalandar did not move. All eyes were grinding into her. Helplessly she saw the blood on the snow, her Johnny groaned, coming around. 'I swear by God I'm faithful to my husband!' she screamed. The cry went over them all and into Ross's mind and seared him awake.

'Answer the question, woman! Is it yes or no! In the Name of God, have you lain with him?' The mullah was standing over her like a diseased crow, the villagers waiting, everyone waiting, the trees and the wind waiting – even God.

Insha'Allah.

Her fear left her. In its place was hate. She stared back at this man Mahmud as she got up. 'In the Name of God, I am and have always been faithful to my husband,' she pronounced. 'In the Name of God, yes, I loved this man, years upon years ago.'

Her words made many that were there shudder and Ross was appalled that she had admitted it.

'Harlot! Loose woman! You openly admit yourself guilty. You will be punished accord – '

'No,' Ross shouted over him. He dragged himself on to his knees and though the two mujhadin had guns at his head, he ignored them. 'It was not the fault of Her Highness. I – I'm to blame, only me, only me!'

'You'll be punished, Infidel, never fear,' Mahmud said, then turned to the villagers. 'You all heard the harlot admit fornication, you all heard the Infidel admit fornication. For her there is but one punishment – for the Infidel – what should happen to the Infidel?'

The villagers waited. The mullah was not their mullah, nor of their village, nor a real mullah but an Islamic-Marxist. He had come uninvited. No one knew why he had come here, only that he had appeared suddenly like the wrath of God with leftists – also not of their village. Not true Shi'as, only madmen. Hadn't the Imam said fifty times all such men were madmen who only paid lip service to God, secretly worshipping the Satan Marx-Lenin.

'Well? Should he share her punishment?'

No one answered him. The mullah and his men were armed.

Azadeh felt all eyes boring into her but she could no longer move or say anything. She stood there, knees trembling, the voices distant, even Ross's shouting, 'You've no jurisdiction over me – or her. You defile God's name . . .' as one of the men standing over him gave him a brutal shove to send him sprawling then put a booted foot on his neck pinioning him. 'Castrate him and be done with it,' the man said and another said, 'No, it was the woman who tempted him – didn't I see her lift her chador to him last night in the hut. Look at her now, tempting us all. Isn't the punishment for him a hundred lashes?'

Another said, 'He put his hands on her, take off his hands.'

'Good,' Mahmud said. 'First his hands, then the lash. Tie him up!'

Azadeh tried to cry out against this evil but no sound came out, the blood roaring in her ears now, her stomach heaving, her mind unhinged as they dragged her Johnny to his feet, fighting, kicking, to tie him spread-eagled between the rafters that jutted from the hut – remembering the time she and Hakim were children and he, filled with bravado, had picked up a stone and thrown it at a cat, and the cat squealed as it rolled over and got up, now injured, and tried to crawl away, squealing all the time until a guard shot it, but now . . . now she knew no one would shoot her. She lurched at Mahmud with a scream, her nails out, but her strength failed her and she fainted.

Mahmud looked down at her, 'Put her against that wall,' he said to some of his men, 'then bring her her chador.' He turned and looked at the villagers. 'Who is the butcher here? Who is the butcher of the village?' No one replied. His voice roughened. 'Kalandar, who is your butcher?'

Quickly the headman pointed to a man in the crowd, a small man with rough clothes. 'Abrim, Abrim is our butcher.'

'Go and get your sharpest knife,' Mahmud told him. 'The rest of you collect stones.'

Abrim went to do his bidding. As God wants, the others muttered to each other. 'Have you ever seen a stoning?' someone asked. A very old woman said, 'I saw one once. It was in Tabriz when I was a little girl.' Her voice quavered. 'The adulteress was the wife of a bazaari, yes, I remember she was the wife of a bazaari. Her lover was a bazaari too and they hacked off his head in front of the mosque, then the men stoned her. Women could throw stones too if they wanted but they didn't, I didn't see any woman do it. It took a long time, the stoning, and for years I heard the screams.'

'Adultery is a great evil and must be punished, whoever the sinner, even *her*. The Koran says a hundred lashes for the man . . . the mullah is the lawgiver, not us,' the kalandar said.

'But he's not a true mullah and the Imam has warned against their evil!'

'The mullah is the mullah, the law, the law,' the kalandar said darkly, secretly wanting the Khan humbled and this woman who had taught new, disturbing thoughts to their children destroyed. 'Collect the stones.'

Mahmud stood in the snow, ignoring the cold and the villagers and the saboteur who cursed and moaned and, frenzied, tried to fight out of his bonds, and the woman inert at the wall.

This morning, before dawn, coming to take over the base, he had heard about the saboteur and *her* being in the village. She of the sauna, he had thought, his anger gathering, she who had flaunted herself, the highborn whelp of the cursed Khan who pretends to be our patron but who has betrayed us and betrayed me, already engineering an assassination attempt on me last night, a burst of machine-gun fire outside the mosque after last prayer that killed many but not me. The Khan tried to have me murdered, me who is protected by the Sacred Word that Islam together with Marx-Lenin is the only way to help the world rise up.

He looked at her, seeing the long legs encased in blue ski pants, hair uncovered and flowing, breasts bulging against the blue and white ski jacket. Harlot, he thought, loathing her for tempting him. One of his men threw the chador over her. She moaned a little but did not come out of her stupor.

'I'm ready,' the butcher said, fingering his knife.

'First the right hand,' Mahmud said to his men. 'Bind him above the wrists.'

They bound strips of sacking ripped from the window tightly, villagers pressing forward to see better, and Ross used all his energy to stop his terror from bursting the dam, saw only the pockmarked face above the carving knife, the bedraggled moustache and beard, the eyes blank, the man's thumb testing the blade absently. Then his eyes focused. He saw Azadeh come out of her spell and he remembered.

'The grenade!' he shrieked. 'Azadeh, the grenade!'

She heard him clearly and fumbled for it in her side pocket as he shrieked again and again, further startling the butcher, dragging everyone's attention to himself. The butcher came forward cursing him, took hold of his right hand firmly, fascinated by it, moved it a little this way and that, the knife poised, deciding where to slice through the sinews of the joint, giving Azadeh just enough time to pick herself up and hurtle across the small space to shove him in the back, sending him flying and the knife into the snow, then to turn on Mahmud, pull the pin out, and stand there trembling, the lever held in her small hand.

'Get away from him,' she screamed. 'Get away!'

Mahmud did not move. Everyone else scattered, trampling some, rushing for safety across the square, cursing and shouting.

'Quick, over here, Azadeh,' Ross called out. 'Azadeh!' She heard him through her mist and obeyed, backing towards him, watching Mahmud, flecks of foam at the corner of her mouth. Then Ross saw Mahmud turn and stalk off towards one of his men out of range and he groaned, knowing what would happen now. 'Quick, pick up the knife and cut me loose,' he said to distract her. 'Don't let go of the lever – I'll watch them for you.' Behind her he saw the mullah take the rifle from one of his men, cock it and turn towards them. Now she had the butcher's knife and she reached for the bonds on his right hand and he knew the bullet would kill or wound her, the lever would fly off, four seconds of waiting, and then oblivion for both of them – but quick and clean and no obscenity. 'I've always loved you, Azadeh,' he whispered and smiled and she looked up startled, and smiled back.

The rifle shot rang out, his heart stopped, then another and another, but they did not come from Mahmud but from the forest and now Mahmud was screaming and twisting in the snow. Then a voice followed the shots: 'Allah-u-Akbar! Death to all enemies of God! Death to all leftists, death to all enemies of the Imam!'

With a bellow of rage one of the mujhadin charged the forest and died. At once the rest fled, falling over themselves in their panic-stricken rush to hide. Within seconds the village square was empty but for the babbling howls of Mahmud, his turban no longer on his head. In the forest the leader of the four-man Tudeh assassination team who had tracked him since dawn silenced him with a burst of machine-gun fire, then the four of them retreated as silently as they had arrived.

Blankly Ross and Azadeh looked at the emptiness of the village. 'It can't be . . . can't be . . .' she muttered, still deranged.

'Don't let go of the lever,' he said hoarsely. 'Don't let go of the lever. Quick, finish cutting me loose . . . quick!'

The knife was very sharp. Her hands were trembling and slow and she cut him once but not badly. The moment he was free he grabbed the grenade, his hands tingling and hurting, but held the lever, began to breathe again. He staggered into the hut, found his kukri that had been mixed up in the blanket in the initial struggle, stuck it in its scabbard and picked up his carbine. At the doorway he stopped. 'Azadeh, quick, get your chador and the pack and follow me.' She stared at him. 'Quick!'

She obeyed like an automaton, and he led her out of the village into the forest, grenade in his right hand, gun in the left. After a faltering run of a quarter of an hour, he stopped and listened. No one was following them. Azadeh was panting behind him. He saw she had the pack but had forgotten the chador. Her pale blue ski clothes showed clearly against the snow and trees. He hurried on again. She stumbled after him, beyond talking. Another hundred yards and still no trouble.

No place to stop yet. He went on, slower now, a violent ache in his side, near vomiting, grenade still ready, Azadeh flagging even more. He found the path that led to the back of the base. Still no pursuit. Near the rise, at the back of Erikki's cabin, he stopped, waiting for Azadeh, then his stomach heaved, he staggered and went down on his knees and vomited. Weakly, he got up and went up the rise to better cover. When Azadeh joined him she was labouring badly, her breath coming in great gulping pants. She slumped into the snow beside him, retching.

Down by the hangar he could see the 206, one of the mechanics washing it down. Good, he thought, perhaps it's being readied for a flight. Three armed revolutionaries were huddled on a nearby veranda under the overhang of a trailer in the lee of the small wind, smoking. No sign of life over the rest of the base, though chimney smoke came from Erikki's cabin and the one shared by the mechanics, and the cook house. He could see as far as the road. The roadblock was still there, men guarding it, some trucks and cars held up.

His eyes went back to the men on the veranda and he thought of Gueng and how his body had been tossed like a sack of old bones into the filth of the half truck under their feet, perhaps these men, perhaps not. For a moment his head ached with the strength of his rage. He glanced back at Azadeh. She was over her spasm, still more or less in shock, not really seeing him, a dribble of saliva on her chin and a streak of vomit. With his sleeve he wiped her face. 'We're fine now, rest a while then we'll go on.' She nodded and sank back on her arms, once more in her own private world. He returned his concentration to the base.

Ten minutes passed. Little change. Above, the cloud cover was a dirty blanket, snow heavy. Two of the armed men went into the office and he could see them from time to time through the windows. The third man paid little attention to the 206. No other movement. Then a cook came out of the cookhouse, urinated on the snow, and went back inside again. More time. Now one of the guards walked out of the office and trudged across the snow to the mechanics' trailer, an M16 slung over his shoulder. He opened the door and went inside. In a moment he came out again. With him was a tall European in flight gear and another man. Ross recognised the pilot Nogger Lane and the other mechanic. The mechanic said something to Lane, then waved and went back inside his trailer again. The guard and the pilot walked off towards the 206.

Everyone pegged, Ross thought, his heart fluttering. Awkwardly he checked his carbine, the grenade in his right hand inhibiting him, then put the last two spare magazines and the last grenade from his haversack into his side pocket. Suddenly fear swept into him and he wanted to run, oh, God help me, to run away, to hide, to weep, to be safe at home, away anywhere . . .

'Azadeh, I'm going down there now,' he forced himself to say. 'Get ready to rush for the chopper when I wave or shout. Ready?' He saw her look at him and nod and mouth yes, but he wasn't sure if he had reached her. He said it again and smiled encouragingly. 'Don't worry.' She nodded mutely.

Then he loosened his kukri and went over the rise like a wild beast after food.

He slid behind Erikki's cabin, covered by the sauna. Sounds of children and a woman's voice inside. Dry mouth, grenade warm in his hand. Slinking from cover to cover, huge drums or piles of pipe and saws and logging spares, always closer to the office trailer. Peering around to see the guard and the pilot nearing the hangar, the man on the veranda idly watching them. The office door opened, another guard came out, and beside him a new man, older, bigger, clean-shaven, possibly European, wearing better quality clothes and armed with a Sten gun. On the thick leather belt around his waist was a scabbard kukri.

Ross released the lever. It flew off. 'One, two, three,' and he stepped out of cover, hurled the grenade at the men on the veranda forty yards away and ducked behind the tank again, already readying another.

They had seen him. For a moment they were shock-still, then as they dropped for cover the grenade exploded, blowing most of the veranda and overhang away, killing one of them, stunning another, and maiming the third. Instantly Ross rushed into the open, carbine levelled, the new grenade held tightly in his right hand, index finger on the trigger. There was no movement on the veranda, but down by the hangar door the mechanic and pilot dropped to the snow and put their arms over their heads in panic, the guard rushed for the hangar and for an instant was in the clear. Ross fired and missed, charged the hangar, noticed a back door, and diverted for it. He eased it open and leaped inside. The enemy was across the empty space, behind an engine, his gun trained on the other door. Ross blew his head off, the firing echoing off the corrugated iron walls, then ran for the other door. Through it he could see the mechanic and Nogger Lane hugging the snow near the 206. Still in cover, he called to them. 'Quick! How many more hostiles're here?' No answer. 'For Christ sake, answer me!'

Nogger Lane looked up, his face white. 'Don't shoot, we're civilians, English – don't shoot!'

'How many more hostiles are here?'

'There . . . there were five . . . five . . . this one here and the rest in . . . in the office . . . I think in the office . . .'

Ross ran to the back door, dropped to the floor, and peered out at ground level. No movement. The office was fifty yards away – the only cover a detour around the truck. He sprang to his feet and charged for it. Bullets howled off the metal and then stopped. He had seen the automatic fire coming from a broken office window.

Beyond the truck was a little dead ground, and in the dead ground was a ditch that led within range. If they stay in cover they're mine. If they come out and they should, knowing I'm alone, the odds are theirs.

He slithered forward on his belly for the kill. Everything quiet, wind, birds, enemy. Everything waiting. In the ditch now. Progress slow. Getting near. Voices and a door creaking. Silence again. Another yard. Another. Now! He got his knees ready, dug his toes into the snow, eased the lever off the grenade, counted three, lurched to his feet, slipped but just managed to keep his balance, and hurled the grenade through the broken window, past the man standing there, gun pointing at him, and hit the snow again. The explosion stopped the burst of gunfire, almost blew out his own eardrums and once again he was on his feet charging the trailer, firing as he went. He jumped over a corpse and went on in still firing. Suddenly his gun stopped and his stomach turned over, until he could jerk out the empty mag and slam in the new. He killed the machine gunner and stopped.

Silence. Then a scream nearby. Cautiously he kicked the broken door away and went on to the veranda. The screamer was legless, demented, but still alive. Around his waist was the leather belt and kukri that had been Gueng's. Fury blinded Ross and he tore it out of the scabbard. 'You got that at the roadblock?' he shouted in Farsi.

'Help me help me help me . . .' A paroxysm of some foreign language then ' . . . whoareyou who . . . help meeee . . .' The man continued screaming and mixed with it was, '. . . helpmehelpmeee yes I killed the saboteur . . . helpme . . .'

With a bloodcurdling scream Ross hacked downward and when his eyes cleared he was staring into the face of the head that he held up in his left hand. Revolted, he dropped it and turned away. For a moment he did not know where he was, then his mind cleared, his nostrils were filled with the stench of blood and cordite, he found himself in the remains of the trailer and looked around.

The base was frozen, but men were running towards it from the roadblock. Near the chopper Lane and the mechanic were still motionless in the snow. He rushed for them, hugging cover.

Nogger Lane and the mechanic Arberry saw him coming and were panic-stricken – the stubble-bearded, matted-haired, wild-eyed maniac tribesman mujhadin or fedayeen who spoke perfect English, whose hands and sleeves were bloodstained from the head that only moments ago they had seen him hack off with a single stroke and a crazed scream, the bloody short sword-knife still in his hand, another in a scabbard, carbine in the other. They scrambled to their knees, hands up. 'Don't kill us – we're friends, civilians, don't kill u – '

'Shut up! Get ready to take off. Quick!'

Nogger Lane was dumbfounded. 'What?'

'For Christ sake, hurry,' Ross said angrily, infuriated by the look on their faces, completely oblivious of what he looked like. 'You,' he pointed at the mechanic with Gueng's kukri. 'You, see that rise there?'

'Yes . . . yes, sir,' Arberry croaked.

'Go up there as fast as you can, there's a lady there, bring her down . . .' He stopped, seeing Azadeh come out of the forest edge and start running down the little hill towards them. 'Forget that, go and get the other mechanic, hurry for Christ's sake, the bastards from the roadblock'll be here any minute. Go on, hurry!' Arberry ran off, petrified but more petrified of the men he could see coming down the road. Ross whirled on Nogger Lane. 'I told you to get started.'

'Yes . . . Yessir . . . that . . . that woman . . . that's not Azadeh, Erikki's Azadeh is it?'

'Yes – I told you to start up!'

Nogger Lane never got a 206 into takeoff mode quicker, nor did the mechanics ever move faster. Azadeh still had a hundred yards to go and already the hostiles were too close. So Ross ducked under the whirling blades and got between her and them and emptied the magazine at them. Their heads went down and they scattered, and he threw the empty in their direction with a screaming curse. A few heads came up. Another burst and another, conserving ammunition, kept them down, Azadeh close now but slowing. Somehow she made a last effort and passed him, reeling drunkenly for the back seat to be half pulled in by the mechanics. Ross fired another short burst retreating, groped into the front seat and they were airborne and away.

Chapter 15

At Tehran International Airport: 11:58 A.M. The cabin door of the 125 closed. From the cockpit John Hogg gave Gavallan and McIver who stood on the tarmac beside his car a thumbs-up and taxied away. Gavallan had just arrived from Al Shargaz and this was the first moment he and McIver had been alone.

'What's up, Mac?' he said, the chill wind tugging at their winter clothes and billowing the snow around them.

'Trouble, Andy.'

'I know that. Tell it to me quickly.'

McIver leaned closer. 'I've just heard we've barely a week before we're grounded pending nationalisation.'

'What?' Gavallan was suddenly numb. 'Talbot told you?'

'Yes.' McIver's face twisted, so worried that he was stumbling over the words. 'The bastard told me with his smooth, put-on politeness, "I wouldn't bet on more than ten days if I were you – a week'd be safe – and don't forget, Mr. McIver, a closed mouth catches no flies."'

'My God, does he know we are planning something?' A gust speckled them with powdered snow. They got into the car.

'I don't know. I just don't know, Andy.'

The windows were fogged up. McIver switched the defrost and fan to maximum, heat already at maximum, then pushed the music cassette home, jacked the sound up, turned it down again, cursing.

'What else's up, Mac?'

'Just about everything,' McIver blurted out. 'Erikki's been kidnapped by Soviets or the KGB and he's somewhere up near the Turkish border with his 212, doing Christ knows what – Nogger thinks he's being forced to help them clean out secret U.S. radar sites. Nogger, Azadeh, two of our mechanics and a British captain barely escaped from Tabriz with their lives, they got back yesterday and they're at my place at the moment – at least they were when I left this morning. My God, Andy, you should have seen the state they were in when they arrived. The captain was the same one who saved Charlie at Doshan Tapeh, who Charlie dropped off at Bandar-e Pahlavi . . .'

'He what?'

'It was a secret op. He's a captain in the Gurkhas . . . name's Ross, John Ross, he and Azadeh were both pretty incoherent, Nogger too was pretty excited and at least they're safe now back home.' McIver's voice became brittle. 'Sorry to tell you we've lost a mechanic at Zagros, Effer Jordon, he was shot an – '

'Jesus Christ! Old Effer dead?'

'Yes . . . yes I'm afraid so and your son was nicked . . . not badly,' McIver added hastily as Gavallan blanched. 'Scot's all right, he's okay an – '

'How badly?'

'Bullet through the fleshy part of the right shoulder. No bones touched, just a flesh wound – Jean-Luc said they've penicillin, a medic, the wound's clean. Scot won't be able to ferry the 212 out tomorrow to Al Shargaz so I asked Jean-Luc to do it and take Scot with him, then come back to Tehran on the next 125 flight and we'll get him back to Kowiss.'

'You're sure? That Scot was just nicked?'

'Yes, Andy. Sure.'

'What the hell happened?'

'I don't know exactly. I got a relayed message from Starke this morning who'd just picked it up from Jean-Luc. It seems that terrorists are operating in the Zagros, I suppose the same bunch that attacked the oil rigs Bellissima and Rosa, they must've been hiding in ambush in the forests around our base. Effer Jordon and Scot were loading spares into the 212 just after dawn this morning and got sprayed. Poor old Effer got most of the bullets and Scot just one . . .' Again McIver added hurriedly, seeing Gavallan's face, 'Jean-Luc assured me Scot's all right, Andy, honest to God!'

'I wasn't thinking just about Scot,' Gavallan said heavily. 'Effer's been with us damn nearly since we started – hasn't he got three kids?'

'Yes, yes he has. Terrible.' McIver let in the clutch and eased the car through the snow back towards the office. 'They're all still at school, I think.'

'I'll do something about them soon as I get back.' Gavallan was in dismay, so many questions to ask and to be answered, everything in jeopardy, here and at home. A week to doomsday? Thank God that Scot . . . poor old Effer . . . Christ Almighty, Scot shot! Gloomily he looked out of the windshield and saw they were nearing the freight area. 'Stop the car for a minute, Mac, better to talk in private, eh?'

'Sorry, yes, I'm not thinking too clearly.'

'You're all right? I mean your health?'

'Oh, that's fine, if I get rid of this cough . . . It's just that . . . it's just that I'm afraid.' McIver said it flat but the admission spiked through Gavallan. 'I'm out of control, I've already lost one man, old Erikki's in danger, we're all in danger, S-G and everything we've worked for.' He fiddled with the wheel. 'Gen's fine?'

'Yes, yes, she is,' Gavallan said patiently. This was the second time he had answered that question. McIver had asked him the moment he had come down the steps of the 125. 'Genny's fine, Mac,' he said, repeating what he had said earlier, 'I've mail from her, she's talked to both Hamish and Sarah, both families're fine and young Angus has his first tooth. Everyone's well at home, all in good shape and I've a bottle of Loch Vay in my briefcase from her. She tried to talk her way past Johnny Hogg on to the 125 – to stowaway in the loo – even after I'd said no, so sorry.' For the first time he saw a glimmer of a smile on McIver.

'Gen's bloody-minded, no doubt about it. Glad she's there and not here, very glad, curious though how you miss 'em.' McIver stared ahead. 'Thanks, Andy.'

'Nothing.' Gavallan thought a moment. 'Let's go into Tehran – do we have time?' Gavallan glanced at his watch. It read 12:25.

'Oh, yes. We've got a load of "redundant" stores to put aboard. We'll have time if we leave now.'

'Good. I'd like to see Azadeh and Nogger – and this man Ross – and particularly Talbot. We could go past the Bakravan house on the off chance. Eh?'

'Good idea. I'm glad you're here, Andy, very glad.' He eased in the clutch, the wheels skidding.

'So 'm I, Mac. Actually I've never been so down either,' Gavallan said. Inside he was churning. 'What about Whirlwind?' he asked, not able to bottle it up any longer.

'Well, whether it's seven days or seventy . . .' McIver swerved to avoid another accident neatly, returned the obscene gesture, and drove on again. 'Let's pretend we're all agreed, and we could push the button if we wanted on D-day, in seven days – no, Talbot said best not to count on more than a week so let's make it six, six days from today, Friday next – a Friday'd be best anyway, right?'

'Because it's their Holy Day, yes, my thought too.'

'Then adapting what we've come up with – Charlie and me: Phase One: From today on we send out every expat and spare we can, every way we can, by the 125, by truck out to Iraq or Turkey, or as baggage and excess baggage by BA. Somehow I'll get Bill Shoesmith to increase our seat reservations and get priority of freight space. We've already got two of our 212s out "for repair" and the Zagros one's due off tomorrow. We've five birds left here in Tehran, one 212, two 206s and two Alouettes. We send the 212 and the Alouettes to Kowiss ostensibly to service Hotshot's request for choppers though why he wants them, God only knows – Duke says his birds are not all employed as it is. Anyway, we leave our 206s here as camouflage.'

'Leave them?'

'There's no way we get all our choppers out, Andy, whatever our lead time. Now, D minus Two, next Wednesday, the last of our headquarter staff – Charlie, Nogger, our remaining pilots and mechanics and me – we get on the 125 Wednesday and flit the coop to Al Shargaz, unless of course we can get some of them out beforehand by BA. Don't forget we're supposed to be up to strength, one in for one out. Next we th – '

'What about papers, exit permits?'

'I'll try to get blanks from Ali Kia – I'll need some blank Swiss cheques, he understands pishkesh but he's also a member of the board, very clever, hot and hungry but not anxious to risk his skin. If we can't, then we'll just pishkesh our way on to the 125. Our excuse to the partners, Kia or whomever, when they discover we've gone is that you've called an urgent conference at Al Shargaz – it's a lame excuse but that's beside the point. That ends Phase One. If we're prevented from going then that ends Whirlwind because we'd be used as hostages for the return of all birds and I know you won't agree to expend us. Phase Two: we set up sh – '

'What about all your household things? And all those of the chaps who have apartments or houses in Tehran?'

'The company'll have to pay fair compensation – that should be part of Whirlwind's profit and loss. Agreed?'

'What'll that add up to, Mac?'

'Not a lot. We've no option but to pay compensation.'

'Yes, yes, I agree.'

'Phase Two: We set up shop at Al Shargaz by which time several things have happened. You've arranged for the 747 jumbo freighters to arrive at Al Shargaz the afternoon of D minus One. By then, Starke somehow has secretly cached enough 40 gallon drums on the shore to carry them across the Gulf. Someone else's cached more fuel on some godforsaken island off Saudi or the Emirates for Starke if he needs them, and for Rudi and his lads from Bandar-e Delam who definitely will. Scrag has no fuel problems. Meanwhile, you've arranged British registry for all birds we plan to "export", and you've got permission to fly through Kuwait, Saudi and Emirate airspace. I'm in charge of Whirlwind's actual operation. At dawn on D-day you say to me, go or no-go. If it's no-go, that's final. If it's go, I can abort the go order if I think it's prudent, then that becomes final too. Agreed?'

'With two provisos, Mac: you consult with me before you abort, as I'll consult with you before go or no-go, and second, if we can't make D-day we try again D plus one and D plus two.'

'All right.' McIver took a deep breath. 'Phase Three: at dawn on D-day, or D plus One or D plus Two – three days is the maximum I think we could sweat out – we radio a code message which says "Go!" The three bases acknowledge and at once all escaping birds get airborne and head for Al Shargaz. There's likely to be a four-hour difference between Scrag's arrivals and the last ones, probably Starke's – if everything goes well. The moment the birds land anywhere outside Iran we replace the Iranian registry numbers with British ones and that makes us partially legal. The moment they land at Al Shargaz the 747s are loaded, and then take off into the wild blue with everyone aboard.' McIver exhaled. 'Simple.'

Gavallan did not reply at once, sifting the plan, seeing the holes – the vast expanse of dangers. 'It's good, Mac.'

'It isn't, Andy, it isn't good at all.'

At McIver's Apartment: 4:20 P.M. Ross said, 'I don't know, Mr. Gavallan, I don't remember much after I left Azadeh on the hill and went into the base, more or less up to the time we got here.' He was wearing one of Pettikin's uniform shirts and a black sweater and black trousers and black shoes and was shaved and neat, but his faced showed his utter exhaustion. 'But before that, everything happened as . . . as I told you.'

'Terrible,' Gavallan said. 'But thank God for you, Captain. But for you the others'd be dead. Without you they'd all be lost. Let's have a drink, it's so damned cold. We've some whisky.' He motioned to Pettikin. 'Charlie?'

Pettikin went to the sideboard. 'Sure, Andy.'

'I won't, thanks, Mr. McIver,' Ross said.

'I'm afraid I will and the sun's not over the yardarm,' McIver said.

'So will I,' Gavallan said. The two of them had arrived not long ago, still worried because at Sharazad's house they had used the iron door knocker again and again but to no avail. Then they had come here. Ross, dozing on the sofa, had almost leaped out of sleep when the front door opened, kukri threateningly in his hand.

'Sorry,' he had said shakily, sheathing the weapon.

'That's all right,' Gavallan had pretended, not over his fright. 'I'm Andrew Gavallan. Hi, Charlie! Where's Azadeh?'

'She's still asleep in the spare bedroom,' Pettikin answered.

'Sorry to make you jump,' Gavallan had said. 'What happened, Captain, at Tabriz?'

So Ross had told them, disjointedly, jumping back and forth until he had finished. Exploding out of heavy sleep had creased him. His head ached, everything ached, but he was glad to be telling what had happened, reconstructing everything, gradually filling in the blank parts, putting the pieces into place. Except Azadeh. No, I can't put her in place yet.

This morning when he had come out of a malevolent wake-sleep dream he had been terrified, everything mixed up, jet engines and guns and stones and explosions and cold, and staring at his hands to make sure what was dream and what was real. Then he had seen a man peering at him and had cried out, 'Where's Azadeh?'

'She's still asleep, Captain Ross, she's in the spare room down the hall,' Pettikin had told him, calming him. 'Remember me? Charlie Pettikin – Doshan Tappeh?'

Searching his memory. Things coming back slowly, hideous things. Big blanks, very big. Doshan Tappeh? What about Doshan Tappeh? Going there to hitch a chopper ride and . . . 'Ah yes, Captain, how are you? Good to . . . to see you. She's asleep?'

'Yes, like a baby.'

'Best thing, best thing for her to sleep,' he had said, his brain still not working easily.

'First a cuppa. Then a bath and shave and I'll fix you up with some clothes and shaving gear. You're about my size. You hungry? We've eggs and some bread, the bread's a bit stale.'

'Oh, thanks, no, no I'm not hungry – you're very kind.'

'I owe you one – no, at least ten. I'm damned pleased to see you. Listen, much as I'd like to know what happened. . . well, McIver's gone to the airport to pick up our boss, Andy Gavallan. They'll be back shortly, you'll have to tell them so I can find out then – so no questions till then, you must be exhausted.'

'Thanks, yes it's . . . it's still all a bit . . . I can remember leaving Azadeh on the hill, then almost nothing, just flashes, dreamlike, until I woke a moment ago. How long have I been asleep?'

'You've been out for about sixteen hours. We, that's Nogger and our two mecs, half-carried you both in here and then you both passed out. We put you and Azadeh to bed like babies – Mac and I. We undressed you, washed part of the muck off, carried you to bed – not too gently by the way – but you never woke up, either of you.'

'She's all right? Azadeh?'

'Oh, yes. I checked her a couple of times but she's still flat out. What did . . . sorry, no questions! First a shave and bath. 'Fraid the water's barely warm but I've put the electric heater in the bathroom, it's not too bad . . .'

Now Ross was watching Pettikin who was handing the whisky to McIver and to Gavallan. 'Sure you won't, Captain?'

'No, no thanks.' Without noticing it he felt his right wrist and rubbed it. His energy level was ebbing fast. Gavallan saw the man's tiredness and knew there was not much time. 'About Erikki. You can't remember anything else to give us an idea where he might be?'

'Not any more than I've told you. Azadeh may be able to help – the Soviet's name was something like Certaga, the man Erikki was forced to work with up by the border – as I said they were using her as a threat and there was some complication about her father and a trip they were going to make together – sorry, I can't remember exactly. The other man, the one who was friends with Abdollah Khan was called Mzytryk, Petr Oleg.' That reminded Ross about Vien Rosemont's code message for the Khan, but he decided that was none of Gavallan's business, nor about all the killing, nor about shoving the old man in front of the truck on the hill, nor that one day he would go back to the village and hack off the head of the butcher and the kalandar who, but for the grace of God or the spirits of the High Land, would have stoned her and mutilated him. He would do that after the debriefing when he saw Talbot, or the American colonel, but before that he would ask them who had betrayed the operation at Mecca. Someone had. For a moment the thought of Rosemont and Tenzing and Gueng blinded him. When the mist cleared, he saw the clock on the mantelpiece. 'I have to go to a building near the British embassy. Is that far from here?'

'No, we could take you if you like.' Gavallan glanced at McIver. 'Mac, let's go now . . . perhaps I can catch Talbot. We'll still have time to come back to see Azadeh, and Nogger if he's here.'

'Good idea.'

'Could that be now? Sorry, but I'm afraid I'll pass out again if I don't get with it.'

Gavallan got up and put on his heavy coat.

Pettikin said to Ross, 'I'll lend you a coat and some gloves.' He saw his eyes stray down the corridor. 'Would you like me to wake Azadeh?'

'No, thanks. I'll . . . I'll just look in.'

'It's the second door on the left.'

They watched him go along the corridor, his walk noiseless and catlike, open the door silently and stand there a moment and close it again. He collected his assault rifle and the two kukris, his and Gueng's. He thought a moment, then put his on the mantelpiece.

'In case I don't get back,' he said, 'tell her this's a gift, a gift for Erikki. For Erikki and her.'

At the Palace of the Khan: 5:19 P.M. The kalandar of Abu Mard was on his knees and petrified. 'No, no, Highness, I swear it was the mullah Mahmud who told us – '

'He's not a real mullah, you son of a dog, everyone knows that! By God, you . . . you were going to stone my daughter?' the Khan shrieked, his face mottled, his breath coming in great pants. '*You* decided? *You* decided you were going to stone *my* daughter?'

'It was him, Highness,' the kalandar whispered, 'it was the mullah who decided after questioning her and her admitting adultery with the saboteur . . .'

'You son of a dog! You aided and abetted that false mullah . . . Liar! Ahmed told me what happened!' The Khan propped himself on his bed pillows, a guard behind him, Ahmed and other guards close to the kalandar in front of him, Najoud, his eldest daughter, and Aysha, his young wife, seated to one side trying to hide their terror at his rage and petrified that he would turn on them. Kneeling beside the door still in his travel-stained clothes and filled with dread was Hakim, Azadeh's brother, who had just arrived, rushed here under guard in response to the Khan's summons, and who had listened with equal rage to Ahmed relating what had happened at the village.

'You son of a dog,' the Khan shouted again, his mouth salivating. 'You let . . . you let the dog of a saboteur escape . . . you let him drag my daughter off with him . . . you harbour the saboteur and then . . . then you dare to judge one of my – MY – family and would stone . . . without seeking my – MY – approval?'

'It was the mullah . . .' the kalandar cried out, repeating it again and again.

'*Shut him up!*'

Ahmed hit him hard on one of his ears, momentarily stunning him. Then dragged him roughly back on to his knees and hissed, 'Say one more word and I'll cut your tongue out.'

The Khan was trying to catch his breath. 'Aysha, give me . . . give me one of those. . . those pills . . .' She scurried over, still on her knees, opened the bottle and put a pill into his mouth and wiped it for him. The Khan kept the pill under his tongue as the doctor had told him and in a moment the spasm passed, the thundering in his ears lessened and the room stopped weaving.

His bloodshot eyes went back on to the old man who was whimpering and shaking uncontrollably. 'You son of a dog! So you dare to bite the hand that owns you – you, your butcher and your festering village? Ibrim,' the Khan said to one of the guards, 'take him back to Abu Mard and stone him, have the villagers stone him, *stone him*, then cut off the hands of the butcher.'

Ibrim and another guard pulled the howling man to his feet, smashed him into silence and opened the door, stopped as Hakim said harshly, 'Then burn the village!'

The Khan looked at him, his eyes narrowed. 'Yes, then burn the village,' he echoed and kept his eyes on Hakim who looked back at him, trying to be brave. The door closed and now the quiet heightened, broken only by Abdollah's breathing. 'Najoud, Aysha, leave!' he said.

Najoud hesitated, wanting to stay, wanting to hear sentence pronounced on Hakim, gloating that Azadeh had been caught in her adultery and was therefore due punishment whenever she was recaptured. Good, good, good. With Azadeh they both perish, Hakim and the Redhead of the Knife. 'I will be within instant call, Highness,' she said.

'You can go back to your quarters. Aysha – you wait at the end of the corridor.' Both women left. Ahmed closed the door contentedly, everything going as planned. The other two guards waited in silence.

The Khan shifted painfully, motioning to them. 'Wait outside. Ahmed, you stay.' When they had gone and there were just the three of them in the big, cold room he changed his gaze back to Hakim. 'Burn the village, you said. A good idea. But that doesn't excuse your treachery, or your sister's.'

'Nothing excuses treachery against a father, Highness. But neither Azadeh or I have betrayed you or plotted against you.'

'Liar! You heard Ahmed! She admitted fornicating with the saboteur, she admitted it.'

'She admitted "loving" him, Highness, years and years ago. She swore before God she had never committed adultery or betrayed her husband. Never! In front of those dogs and sons of dogs and worse, that mullah of the Left Hand, what should the daughter of a Khan say? Didn't she try to protect your name in front of that godless mob of shit?'

'Still twisting words, still protecting the whore she became?'

Hakim's face went ashen. 'Azadeh fell in love as Mother fell in love. If she's a whore, then you whored my mother!'

Blood surged back into the Khan's face. '*How dare you say such a thing!*'

'It's true. You lay with her before you were married. Because she loved you she let you secretly into her bedroom and so risked death. She risked death because she loved you and you begged her. Didn't our *mother* persuade her father to accept you, and persuade your father to allow *you* to marry her, instead of your older brother who wanted her as a second wife for himself?' Hakim's voice broke, remembering her in her dying, him seven, Azadeh six, not understanding very much, only that she was in terrible pain from something called 'tumour' and outside, in the courtyard, their father Abdollah beset with grief. 'Didn't she always stand up for you against your father and your older brother and then, when your brother was killed and you became heir, didn't she heal the breach with your father?'

'You can't, can't know such things, you were . . . you were too young!'

'Old Nanny Fatemeh told us, she told us before she died, she told us everything she could remember . . .'

The Khan was hardly listening, remembering too, remembering his brother's hunting accident he had so deftly engineered – old Nanny might have known about that too and if she did then Hakim knows and Azadeh knows, all the more reason to silence them. Remembering, too, all the magic times he had had with Napthala the Fair, before and after marriage and during all the days until the beginning of the pain. They had been married not even one year when Hakim was born, two when Azadeh appeared, Napthala just sixteen then, tiny, physically a pattern of Aysha but a thousand times more beautiful, her long hair like spun gold. Five more heavenly years, no more children but that never mattered, hadn't he a son at long last, strong and upright – where his three sons from his first wife had all been born sickly, soon to die, his four daughters ugly and squabbling. Wasn't his wife still only twenty-two, in good health, as strong and as wonderful as the two children she had already birthed? Plenty of time for more sons.

Then the pain beginning. And the agony. No help from all the doctors in Tehran.

Insha'Allah, they said.

No relief except drugs, ever more strong as she wasted away. God grant her the peace of Paradise and let me find her there. He was watching Hakim, seeing the pattern of Azadeh who was a pattern of the mother, listening to him running on. 'Azadeh only fell in love, Highness. If she loved that man, can't you forgive her? Wasn't she only sixteen and banished to school in Switzerland as later I was banished to Khvoy?'

'Because you were both treacherous, ungrateful, and poisonous!' the Khan shouted, his ears beginning to thunder again. 'Get out! You're to . . . to stay away from all others, under guard, until I send for you. Ahmed, see to it, then come back here.'

Hakim got up, near tears, knowing what was going to happen and powerless to prevent it. He stumbled out. Ahmed gave the necessary orders to the guards and came back into the room. Now the Khan's eyes were closed, his face very grey, his breathing more laboured than before. Please God do not let him die yet, Ahmed prayed.

The Khan opened his eyes and focused. 'I have to decide about him, Ahmed. Quickly.'

'Yes, Highness,' his counsellor began, choosing his words carefully, 'you have but two sons, Hakim and the babe. If Hakim were to die or,' he smiled strangely, 'happened to become sightless and crippled, then Mahmud, husband of her Highness Najoud will be regent unt – '

'That fool? Our lands and power would be lost within a year!' Patches of redness flared in the Khan's face and he was finding it increasingly difficult to think clearly. 'Give me another pill.'

Ahmed obeyed and gave him water to drink, gentling him. 'You're in God's hands, you will recover, don't worry.'

'Don't worry,' the Khan muttered, pain in his chest. 'The Will of God the mullah died in time . . . strange. Petr Oleg kept his bargain . . . though he . . . the mullah died too fast . . . too fast.'

'Yes, Highness.'

In time the spasm again passed. 'Wh . . . what's your advice . . . about Hakim?'

Ahmed pretended to think a moment. 'Your son Hakim is a good Muslim, he could be trained, he has managed your affairs in Khvoy well and has not fled as perhaps he could have done. He is not a violent man – except to protect his sister, eh? But that's very important, for therein lies his key.' He came closer and said softly, 'Decree him your heir, High – '

'Never!'

'Providing he swears by God to guard his young brother as he would his sister, providing further his sister returns at once of her own will to Tabriz. In truth, Highness, you have no real evidence against them, only hearsay. Entrust me to find out the truth of him and of her – and to report secretly to you.'

The Khan was concentrating, listening carefully though the effort was taxing him. 'Ah, the brother's the bait to snare the sister – as she was the bait to snare the husband?'

'As they're both bait for the other! Yes, Highness, of course you thought of it before me. In return for giving the brother your favour, she must swear before God to stay here to help him.'

'She'll do that, oh, yes, she'll do that!'

'Then they'll both be within your reach and you can toy with them at your pleasure, giving and withholding at your whim, whether they're guilty or not.'

'They're guilty.'

'If they're guilty, and I will know quickly if you give me complete authority to investigate, then it's God's will that they will die slowly, that you decree Fazulia's husband to be Khan after you, not much better than Mahmud. If they're not guilty, then let Hakim remain heir, providing she stays. And if it were to happen, again at God's will, that she is a widow, she'd even betroth him whom you choose, Highness, to keep Hakim your heir.'

Abdollah Khan sighed, lost in his thoughts. Tiredness swamped him. 'I'll sleep now. Send my guard back and after I've eaten tonight, assemble my "devoted" family here and we will do as you suggest.' His smile was cynical. 'It's wise to have no illusions.'

'Yes, Highness.' Ahmed got to his feet. The Khan envied him his lithe and powerful body.

'Wait, there was something . . . something else.' The Khan thought a moment, the process strangely tiring. 'Ah yes, where's Redhead of the Knife?'

'With Cimtarga, up near the border, Highness. Cimtarga said they might be away for a few days. They left Tuesday night.'

'Tuesday? What's today?'

'Saturday, Highness,' Ahmed replied, hiding his concern.

'Ah yes, Saturday.' Another wave of tiredness. His face felt strange and he lifted his hand to rub it but found the effort too much. 'Ahmed, find out where he is. If anything happens . . . if I have another attack and I'm . . . well, see that . . . that I'm taken to Tehran, to the International Hospital, at once. At once. Understand?'

'Yes, Highness.'

'Find out where he is and. . . and for the next few days keep him close by . . . overrule Cimtarga. Keep He of the Knife close by.'

'Yes, Highness.'

When the guard came back into the room, the Khan closed his eyes and felt himself sinking into the depths. 'There is no other God but God . . .' he muttered, very afraid.

Near the North Border, East of Julfa: 6:05 P.M. It was near sunset and Erikki's 212 was under a crude, hastily constructed lean-to, the roof already a foot deep in snow from the storm last night, and he knew much more exposure in sub zero weather would ruin her. 'Can't you give me blankets or straw or something to keep her warm?' he had asked Sheik Bayazid the moment they had arrived back from Rezaiyeh with the body of the old woman, the Chieftain, two days ago. 'The chopper needs warmth.'

'We do not have enough for the living.'

'If she freezes she won't work,' he had said, fretting that the Sheik would not allow him to leave at once for Tabriz, barely sixty miles away – worried sick about Azadeh and wondering what had happened to Ross and Gueng. 'If she won't work, how are we going to get out of these mountains?'

Grudgingly, the Sheik had ordered his people to construct the lean-to and had given him some goat and sheep skins that he had used where he thought they would do the most good. Just after dawn yesterday he had tried to leave. To his total dismay Bayazid had told him that he and the 212 were to be ransomed.

'You can be patient, Captain, free to walk our village with a calm guard, to tinker with your airplane,' Bayazid had said curtly, 'or you can be impatient and angry and you will be bound up and tethered as a wild beast. I seek no trouble, Captain, want none, or argument. We seek ransom from Abdollah Khan.'

'But I've told you he hates me and won't help me to be rans – '

'If he says no, we seek ransom elsewhere. From your company in Tehran, or your government – perhaps your Soviet employers. Meanwhile, you stay here as guest, eating as we eat, sleeping as we sleep, sharing equally. Or bound and tethered and hungry. Either way you stay until ransom is paid.'

'But that might take months an – '

'Insha'Allah!'

All day yesterday and half the night Erikki had tried to think of a way out of the trap. They had taken his grenade but left him his knife. But his guards were watchful and constant. In these deep snows, it would be almost impossible for him in flying boots and without winter gear to get down to the valley below, and even then he was in hostile country. Tabriz was barely thirty minutes away by 212, but by foot?

'More snow tonight, Captain.'

Erikki looked around. Bayazid was a pace away and he had not heard him approach. 'Yes, and a few more days in this weather and my bird, my airplane, won't fly – the battery'll be dead and most of the instruments wrecked. I have to start her up to charge the battery and warm her pots, have to. Who's going to ransom a wrecked 212 out of these hills?'

Bayazid thought a moment. 'For how long must engines turn?'

'Ten minutes a day – absolute minimum.'

'All right. Just after full dark, each day you may do it but first you ask me. We help you drag her – why is it "she", not an "it" or a "he"?'

Erikki frowned. 'I don't know. Ships are always "she" – this is a ship of the sky.' He shrugged.

'Very well. We help you drag her into open and you start her up and while her engines running there will be five guns within five feet should you be tempted.'

Erikki laughed. 'Then I won't be tempted.'

'Good.' Bayazid smiled. He was a handsome man though his teeth were bad.

'When do you send word to the Khan?'

'It already gone. In these snows it takes a day to get down to road, even on horseback, but not long to reach Tabriz. If the Khan replies favourably, at once, perhaps we hear tomorrow, perhaps day after, depending on the snows.'

'Perhaps never. How long will you wait?'

'Are all people from Far North so impatient?'

Erikki's chin jutted. 'The ancient gods were very impatient when they were held against their will – they passed it on to us. It's bad to be held against your will, very bad.'

'We are a poor people, at war. We must take what the One God gives us. To be ransomed is an ancient custom.' He smiled thinly. 'We learned from Saladin to be chivalrous with our captives, unlike many Christians. Christians are not known for their chivalry. We are treat – ' His ears were sharper than Erikki's and so were his eyes. 'There, down in the valley!'

Now Erikki heard the engine also. It took him a moment to pick out the low-flying, camouflaged helicopter approaching from the north. 'A Kajychokiv 16. Close-support Soviet army gunship . . . what's she doing?'

'Heading for Julfa.' The Sheik spat on the ground. 'Those sons of dogs come and go as they please.'

'Do many sneak in now?'

'Not many – but one is too many.'

Sunday

Chapter 16

In the Northern Suburbs: 9:14 P.M. Azadeh drove the small, badly dented car fast along the street that was lined with fine houses and apartment buildings – most of them dark, a few vandalised – headlights carelessly on full, dazzling the oncoming traffic, her horn blaring. She braked, skidded as she cut dangerously across the traffic, narrowly avoiding an accident, and headed into the garage of one of the buildings with a screech of rubber.

The garage was dark. In the side pocket was a flash. She turned it on, got out, and locked the car. Her coat was well cut and warm, skirt and boots and fur mitts and hat, her hair flowing. On the other side of the garage was a staircase and a switch for the lights. When she tried it, the nearest bulb sparked and died. She went up the stairs heavily. Four apartments on each landing. The apartment that her father had loaned to her and Erikki was on the third landing, facing the street. 'It's not risky, Mac,' she had said when she announced she was going and he had tried to persuade her to remain in his apartment, 'but if my father orders me back in Tabriz, staying here with you won't help me at all. In the apartment I've a phone, I'm only half a mile away and can walk it easily, I've clothes there and a servant. I'll check every day and come into the office, and wait, that's all I can do.'

She had not said that she preferred to be away from him and Charlie Pettikin. I like them both dearly, she thought, but they're nothing like Erikki. Or Johnny. Ah, Johnny, you were wise to leave Mac's, so wise, yet still so close, your embassy, so close. What to do about you, dare I see you again?

The third landing was dark but she had the flash and found her key, put it in the lock, felt eyes on her and whirled in fright. The swarthy, unshaven lout had his pants open and he waved his stiff penis at her. 'I've been waiting for you, princess of all whores, and God curse me if it's not ready for you front or back or sideways . . .' He came forward mouthing obscenities and she backed against the door in momentary terror, grabbed the key, turned it and flung the door open.

The Doberman guard dog was there. The man froze. An ominous growl, then the dog charged. In panic the man screamed and tried to beat the dog off, then took to his heels down the steps, the dog growling and snarling and ripping at his legs and back, tearing his clothes, and Azadeh shouted after him, 'Now show it to me!'

'Oh, Highness, I didn't hear you knock, what's going on?' the old man-servant called out, rushing from the kitchen area.

Angrily she wiped the perspiration off her face and told him. 'God curse you, Ali, I've told you twenty times to meet me downstairs with the dog. I'm on time, I'm always on time. Have you no brains?'

The old man apologised but a rough voice behind her cut him short. 'Go and get the dog!' She looked around. Her stomach twisted.

'Good evening, Highness.' It was Ahmed Dursak, tall, bearded, chilling, standing in the doorway of the living-room. Insha'Allah, she thought. The waiting is over and now it begins again. 'Good evening, Ahmed.'

'Highness, please excuse me, I didn't realise about people in Tehran or I would have waited downstairs myself. Ali, get the dog!'

Afraid and still mumbling apologies, the servant scuttled down the stairs. Ahmed closed the door and watched Azadeh use the heel fork to take off her boots, slip her small feet into curved Turkish slippers. She went past him into the comfortable, Western-style living room and sat down, her heart thumping. A fire flickered in the grate. Priceless carpets, others used as wall hangings. Beside her was a small table. On the table was the kukri that Ross had left her. 'You have news of my father and my husband?'

'His Highness the Khan is ill, very ill an – '

'What illness?' Azadeh asked, at once genuinely concerned.

'A heart attack.'

'God protect him – when did this happen?'

'On Thursday last.' He read her thought. 'That was the day you and . . . and the saboteur were in the village of Abu Mard. Wasn't it?'

'I suppose so. The last few days have been very confused,' she said icily. 'How is my father?'

'The attack on Thursday was mild, thanks be to God. Just before midnight Saturday he had another. Much worse.' He watched her.

'How much worse? Please don't play with me! Tell me everything at once!'

'Ah so sorry, Highness, I did not meant to toy with you.' He kept his voice polite and his eyes off her legs, admiring her fire and pride and wanting to toy with her very much. 'The doctor called it a stroke and now the left side of His Highness is partially paralysed; he can still talk – with some difficulty – but his mind is as strong as ever. The doctor said he would recover much quicker in Tehran but the journey is not possible yet.'

'He will recover?' she asked.

'I don't know, Highness. As God wants. To me he seems very sick. The doctor, I don't think much of him, all he said was His Highness's chances would be better if he was here in Tehran.'

'Then bring him here as soon as possible.'

'I will, Highness, never fear. Meanwhile I have a message for you. The Khan, your father, says, "I wish to see you. At once. I do not know how long I will live but certain arrangements must be made and confirmed. Your brother Hakim is with me now and – "'

'God protect him,' Azadeh burst out. 'Is my father reconciled with Hakim?'

'His Highness has made him his heir. But pl – '

'Oh that's wonderful, wonderful, God be praised! But h – '

'Please be patient and let me finish his message: "Your brother Hakim is with me now and I have made him my heir, subject to certain conditions, from you and from him."' Ahmed hesitated and Azadeh wanted to rush into the gap, her happiness brimming and her caution brimming. Her pride stopped her.

'"It is therefore necessary that you return with Ahmed at once." That is the end of the message, Highness.'

The front door opened. Ali relocked it and unleashed the dog. At once the dog loped into the living room and put his head in Azadeh's lap. 'Well done, Reza,' she said petting him, welcoming the moment to collect her wits. 'Sit. Go on, sit! Sit!' Happily the dog obeyed, then lay at her feet, watching the door and watching Ahmed who stood near the other sofa. Absently her hand played with the hilt of the kukri, its touch giving her reassurance. Obliquely Ahmed was conscious of it and its implications. 'Before God you have told me the truth?'

'Yes, Highness. Before God.'

'Then we will go at once.' She got up. 'You came by car?'

'Yes, Highness. I brought a limousine and chauffeur. But there's a little more news – good and bad. A ransom note came to His Highness on Sunday. His Excellency your husband is in the hands of bandits, tribesmen . . .' She tried to maintain her composure, her knees suddenly weak. '. . . somewhere near the Soviet border. Both him and his helicopter. It seems that these . . . these bandits claim to be Kurds but the Khan doubts it. They surprised the Soviet Cimtarga and his men and killed them all, capturing His Excellency and the helicopter, early Thursday they claimed. Then they flew to Rezaiyeh where he was seen and appeared unharmed before flying off again.'

'Praise be to God,' was all her pride allowed herself. 'Is my husband ransomed?'

'The ransom note arrived late on Saturday, through intermediaries. As soon as His Highness regained consciousness yesterday he gave me the message for you and sent me here to fetch you.'

She heard the 'fetch' and knew its seriousness but Ahmed made nothing of it openly and reached into his pocket. 'His Highness Hakim gave me this for you.' He handed her the sealed envelope. She ripped it open, startling the dog. The note was in Hakim's handwriting: 'My darling, His Highness has made me his heir and reinstated both of us, subject to conditions, wonderful conditions easy to agree. Hurry back, he's very ill and he will not deal with the ransom until he sees you. Salaam.'

Swamped with happiness she hurried out, packed a bag in almost no time, scribbled a note for McIver, telling Ali to deliver it tomorrow. As an after-thought she picked up the kukri and walked out, cradling it. Ahmed said nothing, just followed her.

Tuesday

Chapter 17

Tabriz – at the Khan's Palace: 10:50 A.M. Azadeh followed Ahmed into the Western-style room and over to the fourposter bed, and now that she was again within the walls she felt her skin crawling with fear. Sitting near the bed was a nurse in a starched white uniform, a book half open in her lap, watching them curiously through her glasses. Musty brocade curtains covered the windows against draughts. Lights were dimmed. And the stench of an old man hung in the air.

The Khan's eyes were closed, his face pasty and breathing strangled, his arm connected to a saline drip that stood beside the bed. Half asleep in a chair nearby was Aysha, curled up and tiny, her hair dishevelled and her face tear-stained. Azadeh smiled at her tentatively, sorry for her, then said to the nurse in a voice not her own, 'How is His Highness, please?'

'Fair. But he mustn't have an excitement, or be disturbed,' the nurse said softly in hesitant Turkish. Azadeh looked at her and saw that she was European, in her fifties, dyed brown hair, a red cross on her sleeve.

'Oh, you're English, or French?'

'Scots,' the woman replied in English with obvious relief, her accent slight. She kept her voice down, watching the Khan. 'I'm Sister Bain from the Tabriz Hospital and the patient is doing as well as can be expected – considering he will no' do as he's told. And who might you be, please?'

'I'm his daughter, Azadeh. I've just arrived from Tehran – he sent for me. We've . . . we travelled all night.'

'Ah, yes,' she said, surprised that someone so beautiful could have been created by a man so ugly. 'If I might suggest, lassie, it would be better to leave him sleeping. As soon as he wakes I'll tell him you're here and send for you. Better he sleeps.'

Ahmed said irritably, 'Please, where's His Highness's guard?'

'There's no need for armed men in a sickroom. I sent him away.'

'There will always be a guard here unless the Khan orders him out or I order him out.' Angrily Ahmed turned and left.

Azadeh said, 'It's just a custom, Sister.'

'Aye, very well. But that's another custom we can do without.'

Azadeh looked back at her father, hardly recognising him, trying to stop the terror that possessed her. Even like that, she thought, even like that he can still destroy us, Hakim and me – he still has his running dog Ahmed. 'Please, really, how is he?'

The lines on the nurse's face creased even more. 'We're doing all we can.'

'Would it be better for him to be in Tehran?'

'Aye, if he has another stroke, yes it would.' Sister Bain took his pulse as she talked. 'But I wouldna' recommend moving him, not at all, not yet.' She made a notation on a chart and then glanced at Aysha. 'You could tell the lady there's no need to stay, she should get some proper rest too, poor child.'

'Sorry, I may not interfere. Sorry, but that's a custom too. Is . . . is it likely he'll have another stroke?'

'You never know, lassie, that's up to God. We hope for the best.' They looked around as the door opened. Hakim stood there beaming. Azadeh's eyes lit up and she said to the nurse, 'Please call me the instant His Highness awakes,' then hurried across the room, out into the corridor, closed the door, and hugged him. 'Oh, Hakim, my darling, it's been such a long time,' she said breathlessly. 'Oh, is it really true?'

'Yes, yes, it is but how did . . .' Hakim stopped, hearing footsteps. Ahmed and a guard turned into the corridor and came up to them. 'I'm glad you're back, Ahmed,' he said politely. 'His Highness will be happy too.'

'Thank you, Highness. Has anything happened in my absence?'

'No, except that Police Colonel Fazir came this morning to see Father.'

Ahmed was chilled. 'Was he allowed in?'

'No. You left instructions no one was to be admitted without His Highness's personal permission, he was asleep at the time and he's been asleep most of the day – I check every hour and the nurse says he's unchanged.'

'Good. Thank you. Did the colonel leave a message?'

'No. We'll be in the Blue Salon, please summon us the moment my father awakens.'

Ahmed watched them go arm in arm down the corridor, the young man tall and handsome, the sister willowy and desirable. Traitors? Not much time to get the proof, he thought. He went back into the sickroom and saw the pallor of the Khan, his nostrils rebelling against the smell. He squatted on his haunches, careless of the disapproving nurse and began his vigil.

What did that son of a dog Fazir want? he asked himself. Saturday evening a secret courier from Petr Mzytryk had arrived.

'I have a private message for His Highness,' the Soviet had said.

In the sickroom the man said, 'Highness, I'm to give it to you when you're alone.'

'Give it to me now. Ahmed is my most trusted counsellor. Give it to me!' Reluctantly the man obeyed and Ahmed remembered the sudden flush that had rushed into the Khan's face the moment he began to read it.

'There is an answer?' the Soviet had said truculently.

Choked with rage the Khan had shaken his head and dismissed the man and had handed Ahmed the letter. It read: 'My friend, I was shocked to hear about your illness and would be with you now but I have to stay here on urgent matters. I have bad news for you: it may be that you and your spy ring are betrayed to Inner Intelligence or SAVAMA – did you know that turncoat Abrim Pahmudi now heads this new version of SAVAK? If you're betrayed to Pahmudi, be prepared to defect at once or you'll quickly see the inside of a torture chamber. I have alerted our people to help you if necessary. If it appears safe, I will arrive Tuesday at dusk. Good luck.'

Almost at the same time police chief Fazir had arrived to arrest the man he had betrayed. The Khan had had no option but to show him the message. 'Is it true? About Pahmudi?'

'Yes. He's an old friend of yours, isn't he?' Fazir had said, taunting him.

'No . . . no he is not. Get out!'

'Certainly. Highness. Meanwhile this palace is under surveillance. There's no need to defect. Please do nothing to interfere with Mzytryk's arrival on Tuesday, do nothing to encourage any more revolt in Azerbaijan. As to Pahmudi and SAVAMA, they can do nothing here without my approval. I'm the law in Tabriz now. Obey and I'll protect you, disobey and you'll be his pishkesh.'

He had left, and the Khan had exploded with rage, more angry than Ahmed had ever seen him. The paroxysm became worse and worse then suddenly it ceased, the Khan was lying on the floor and he was looking down on him, expecting to see him dead but he was not. Just a waxen pallor and twitching, breathing choked.

'As God wants,' Ahmed muttered, not wanting to relive that night.

In the Blue Salon: 11.15 A.M. When they were quite alone, Hakim swung Azadeh off her feet. 'Oh, it's wonderful wonderful wonderful to see you again . . .' she began but he whispered, 'Keep your voice down, Azadeh, there are ears everywhere and someone's sure to misinterpret everything and lie again.'

'Najoud? May she be cursed for ever an – '

'Shushhhh, darling, she can't hurt us now. I'm the heir, officially.'

'Oh, tell me what happened, tell me everything!'

They sat on the long cushion sofa and Hakim could hardly get the words out fast enough. 'First about Erikki: the ransom is ten million rials, for him and the 212 an – '

'Father can bargain that down and pay, he can certainly pay, then find them and have them torn apart.'

'Yes, yes of course he can and he told me in front of Ahmed as soon as you're back he'll start and it's true he's made me his heir provided I swear by God to cherish little Hassan as I would cherish you – of course I did that happily at once – and said that you would also swear by God to do the same, that we would both swear to remain in Tabriz, me to learn how to follow him and you to be here to help me and oh we're going to be so happy!'

'That's all we have to do?' she asked incredulously.

'Yes, yes, that's all – he made me his heir in front of all the family – they looked as though they would die but that doesn't matter, Father named the conditions in front of them, I agreed at once, of course, as you will – why shouldn't we?'

'Of course, of course – anything! God is watching over us!' Again she embraced him, burying her face into his shoulder so that the tears of joy would be dried away. All the way back from Tehran, the journey rotten and Ahmed uncommunicative, she had been terrified what the 'conditions' would be. But now? 'It's unbelievable, Hakim, it's like magic! Of course we'll cherish little Hassan and you'll pass the Khanate on to him if that's Father's wish. God protect us and protect him and Erikki, and Erikki can fly as much as he likes – why shouldn't he? Oh it's going to be wonderful.' She dried her eyes. 'Oh I must look awful.'

'You look wonderful. Now tell me what happened to you – I know only that you were caught in the village with . . . with the British saboteur and then somehow escaped.'

'It was another miracle, only with the help of God, Hakim, but at the time terrible, that vile mullah – I can't remember how we got out only what Johnny . . . what Johnny told me. My Johnny Brighteyes, Hakim.'

His eyes widened. 'Johnny from Switzerland?'

'Yes. Yes it was him. He was the British officer.'

'But how . . . It seems impossible.'

'He saved my life, Hakim, and oh, there's so much to tell.'

'When Father heard about the village he . . . you know the mullah was shot by Green Bands, don't you?'

'I don't remember it but Johnny told me.'

'When Father heard about the village he had Ahmed drag the kalandar here, questioned him, then sent him back, had him stoned, the hands of the butcher cut off and then the village burned. Burning the village was my idea – those dogs!'

Azadeh was greatly shocked. The whole village was too terrible a vengeance.

But Hakim allowed nothing to interrupt his euphoria. 'Azadeh, Father's taken off the guard and I can go where I like – I even took a car and went into Tabriz today alone. Everyone treats me as heir, all the family, even Najoud though I know she's gnashing her teeth and has to be guarded against. It's . . . it's not what I expected.' He told her how he had been almost dragged from Khvoy, expecting to be killed, or mutilated. 'Don't you remember when I was banished, he cursed me and swore Shah Abbas knew how to deal with traitorous sons?'

She trembled, recollecting that nightmare, the curses and rage and so unfair, both of them innocent. 'What made him change? Why should he change towards you, towards us?'

'The Will of God. God's opened his eyes. He has to know he's near death and must make provisions . . . he's, he's the Khan. Perhaps he's frightened and wants to make amends. We were guilty of nothing against him. What does the reason matter? I don't care. We're free of the yoke at long last, free.'

In the Sickroom: 11:16 P.M. The Khan's eyes opened. Without moving his head he looked to his limits. Ahmed, Aysha and the guard. No nurse. Then he centred on Ahmed who was sitting on the floor. 'You brought her?' He stammered the words with difficulty.

'Yes, Highness. A few minutes ago.'

The nurse came into his field of vision. 'How do you feel, Excellency?' she said in English as he had ordered her, telling her her Turkish was vile.

'S'ame.'

'Let me make you more comfortable.' With great tenderness and care – and strength – she lifted him and straightened the pillows and bed. 'Do you need a bottle, Excellency?'

The Khan thought about that. 'Yes.'

She administered it and he felt befouled that it was done by an Infidel woman but since she had arrived he had learned she was tremendously efficient, very wise and very good, the best in Tabriz, Ahmed had seen to that – so superior to Aysha who had proved to be totally useless. He saw Aysha smile at him tentatively, big eyes, frightened eyes. I wonder if I'll ever thrust it in again, up to its hilt, stiff as bone, like the first time, her tears and writhing improving the act, momentarily.

'Excellency?'

He accepted the pill and the sip of water and was glad for the cool of her hands that guided the glass. Then he saw Ahmed again and he smiled at him, glad his confidant was back. 'Good jour'ney?'

'Yes, Highness.'

'Will'ingly? Or with for'ce?'

Ahmed smiled. 'It was as you planned, Highness. Willingly. Just as you planned.'

'I dinna think you should talk so much, Excellency,' the nurse said.

'Go aw'ay.'

She patted his shoulder kindly. 'Would you like some food, perhaps a little horisht?'

'Halvah.'

'The doctor said sweets were not good for you.'

'Halvah!'

Sister Bain sighed. The doctor had forbidden them and then added, 'But if he insists you can give him them, as many as he wants, what does it matter now? Insha'Allah.' She found them and popped one into his mouth and wiped the saliva away, and he chewed it with relish, nutty but smooth and oh so sweet.

'Your daughter's arrived from Tehran, Excellency,' she said. 'She asked me to tell her the moment you awoke.'

Abdollah Khan was finding talking very strange. He would try and say the sentences, but his mouth did not open when it was supposed to open and the words stayed in his mind for a long time and then, when a simple form of what he wanted to say came out, the words were not well formed though they should have been. But why? I'm not doing anything differently than before. Before what? I don't remember, only a massive blackness and blood roaring and possessed by red-hot needles and not being able to breathe.

I can breathe now and hear perfectly and see perfectly and my mind's working perfectly and filled with plans as good as ever. It's just getting it all out. 'Ho'w?'

'What, Excellency?'

Again the waiting. 'How ta'lk bett'r?'

'Ah,' she said, understanding at once, her experience of strokes great. 'Dinna worry, you'll find it just a wee bit difficult at first. As you get better, you'll regain all your control. You must rest as much as you can, that's very important. Rest and medicine, and patience, and you'll be as good as ever. All right?'

'Yes.'

'Would you like me to send for your daughter? She was very anxious to see you, such a pretty girl.'

Waiting. 'Late'r. See late'r. Go'way, everyone . . . not Ahm'd.'

Sister Bain hesitated, then again patted his hand kindly. 'I'll give you ten minutes – if you promise to rest afterwards. All right?'

'Yes.'

When they were alone Ahmed went closer to the bed. 'Yes, Highness?'

'Wh'at time?'

Ahmed glanced at his wristwatch. It was gold and ornate and he admired it very much. 'It's almost one thirty on Tuesday.'

'Pe'tr?'

'I don't know, Highness.' Ahmed told him what Hakim had related. 'If Petr comes today to Julfa, Fazir will be waiting for him.'

'Insh'Allah. Az'deh?'

'She was genuinely worried about your health and agreed to come here at once. A moment ago I saw her together with your son. I'm sure she will agree to anything to protect him – as he will to protect her.' Ahmed was trying to say everything clearly and concisely, not wanting to tire him. 'What do you want me to do?'

'Ev'thing.' Everything I've discussed with you and a little more, the Khan thought with relish, his excitement picking up: now that Azadeh's back cut the throat of the ransom messenger so the tribesmen in fury will do the same to the pilot; find out if those whelps are traitors by whatever means you want, and if they are take out Hakim's eyes and send her north to Petr. If they're not, cut up Najoud slowly and keep them close confined here, until the pilot's dead by whatever means, then send her north. And Pahmudi! Now I'm putting a price on his head that would tempt even Satan. Ahmed, offer it first to Fazir and tell him I want vengeance, I want Pahmudi racked, poisoned, cut up, mutilated, castrated . . .

His heart began creaking, palpitating, and he lifted his hand to rub his chest but his hand did not move. Not an inch. Even now as he looked down at it lying on the counterpane, willing it to move, there was no motion. Nothing. Nor feeling. Neither in his hand nor in his arm. Fear gushed through him.

Don't be afraid, the nurse said, he reminded himself desperately, sound of waves roaring in his ears. You've had a stroke, that's all, not a bad one, the doctor said and he said many people have strokes. Old Komargi had one a year or so ago and he's still alive and active and claims he can still bed his young wife. With modern treatment . . . you're a good Muslim and you'll go to Paradise so there's nothing to fear, nothing to fear, nothing to fear . . . nothing to fear if I die I go to Paradise . . .

I don't want to die, he shrieked. I don't want to die, he shrieked again but it was only in his head and no sound came out.

'What is it, Highness?'

He saw Ahmed's anxiety and that calmed him a little. God be thanked for Ahmed, I can trust Ahmed, he thought, sweat pouring out of him. Now what do I want him to do? 'Family, all he're later. First Aza'deh, H'kim Naj'oud – under's'd?'

'Yes Highness. To confirm the succession?'

'Y'es.'

'I have your permission to question Her Highness?'

He nodded, his eyelids leaden, waiting for the pain in his chest to lessen. While he waited he moved his legs, feeling pins and needles in his feet. But nothing moved, not the first time, only the second and only then with an effort. Terror rushed back into him. In panic he changed his mind: 'Pay ran'som quick'ly, get pil'ot here, Erikki here, me to Teh'ran. Under'stand?' He saw Ahmed nod. 'Quickly!' he mouthed and motioned him to go but his left hand still did not move. Terrified he tried his right hand and it worked, not easily, but it moved. Part of his panic subsided. 'Pay ran'som no'w – kee'p secr't. Get nur'se.'

Near the Iran-Soviet Border: 11:05 P.M. Erikki was pretending to sleep in the small, crude hut, his chin stubbled. A wick, floating in oil in an old chipped clay cup, was guttering and cast strange shadows. Embers in the rough stone fireplace glowed in the draughts. His eyes opened and he looked around. No one else was in the hut. Noiselessly he slid from under the blankets and animal skins. He was fully dressed. He put on his boots, made sure his knife was under his belt and went to the door, opened it softly.

For a moment he stood there, listening, head slightly on one side. Layers of high clouds misted the moon and the wind moved the lightest of the pine branches. The village was quiet under its coverlet of snow. No guards that he could see. No movement near the lean-to where the 212 was parked. Moving as a hunter would move, he skirted the huts and headed for the lean-to.

The 212 was bedded down, skins and blankets where they were most needed, all the doors closed. Through a side window of the cabin he could see two tribesmen rolled up in blankets sprawled full length on the seats snoring. Rifles beside them. He eased forward slightly. The guard in the cockpit was cradling his gun, wide awake. He had not yet seen Erikki. Quiet footsteps approaching, the smell of goat and sheep and stale tobacco preceding them.

'What is it, pilot?' the young Sheik Bayazid asked softly.

'I don't know.'

Now the guard heard them and he peered out of the cockpit window, greeted his leader and asked what was the matter. Bayazid replied, 'Nothing,' waved him back on guard and searched the night thoughtfully. In the few days the stranger had been in the village he had come to like him and respect him, as a man and as a hunter. Today he had taken him into the forest, to test him, and then as a further test and for his own pleasure he had given him a rifle. Erikki's first shot killed a distant, difficult mountain goat as cleanly as he could have done. Giving the rifle was exciting, wondering what the stranger would do, if he would, foolishly, try to turn it on him or even more foolishly take off into the trees when they could hunt him with great enjoyment. But the Redhead of the Knife had just hunted and kept his thoughts to himself, though they could all sense the violence simmering.

'You felt something – danger?' he asked.

'I don't know.' Erikki looked out at the night and all around. No sounds other than the wind, a few night animals hunting, nothing untoward. Even so he was unsettled. 'Still no news?'

'No, nothing more.' This afternoon one of the messengers had returned. 'The Khan is very sick, near death,' the man had said. 'But he promises an answer soon.'

Bayazid had reported all this faithfully to Erikki. 'Pilot, be patient,' he said, not wanting trouble.

'What's the Khan sick with?'

'Sick – the messenger said they'd been told he was sick, very sick. Sick!'

'If he dies, what then?'

'His heir will pay – or not pay. Insha'Allah.' The Sheik eased the weight of his assault rifle on his shoulder. 'Come into the lee, it's cold.' From the edge of the hut now they could see down into the valley. Calm and quiet, a few specks of headlamps from time to time on the road far, far below.

Barely thirty minutes from the palace and Azadeh, Erikki was thinking, and no way to escape.

Every time he started engines to recharge his batteries and circulate the oil, five guns were pointing at him. At odd times he would stroll to the edge of the village or, like tonight, he would get up, ready to run and chance it on foot but never an opportunity, guards too alert. During the hunting today he had been sorely tempted to try to break out, useless of course, knowing they were just playing with him.

'It's nothing, pilot, go back to sleep,' Bayazid said. 'Perhaps there'll be good news tomorrow. As God wants.'

Erikki said nothing, his eyes raking the darkness, unable to be rid of his foreboding. Perhaps Azadeh's in danger or perhaps. . . or perhaps it's nothing and I'm just going mad with the waiting and the worry and what's going on? Did Ross and the soldier make a break for it and what about Petr *matyeryebyets* Mzytryk and Abdollah? 'As God wants, yes, I agree, but I want to leave. The time has come.'

The younger man smiled, showing his broken teeth. 'Then I will have to tie you up.'

Erikki smiled back, as mirthlessly. 'I'll wait tomorrow and tomorrow night, then the next dawn I leave.'

'No.'

'It will be better for you and better for me. We can go to the palace with your tribesman, I can lan – '

'No. We wait.'

'I can land in the courtyard, and I'll talk to him and you'll get the ransom and th – '

'No. We wait. We wait here. It's not safe there.'

'Either we leave together or I leave alone.'

The Sheik shrugged. 'You have been warned, Pilot.'

At the Palace of the Khan: 11:38 P.M. Ahmed drove Najoud and her husband Mahmud down the corridor before him like cattle. Both were tousled and still in their nightclothes, both petrified, Najoud in tears, two guards behind them. Ahmed still had his knife out. Half an hour ago he had rushed into their quarters with the guards, dragged them out of their carpet beds, saying the Khan at long last knew they'd lied about Hakim and Azadeh plotting against him, because tonight one of the servants admitted he had overheard the same conversation and nothing wrong had been said.

'Lies,' Najoud gasped, pressed against the carpet bed, half blinded by the flashlight that one of the guards directed at her face, the other guard holding a gun at Mahmud's head, 'all lies . . .'

Ahmed slid out his knife, needle sharp, and poised it under her left eye. 'Not lies, Highness! You perjured yourself to the Khan, *before God*, so I am here at the Khan's orders to take out your sight.' He touched her skin with the point and she cried out, 'No please I beg you I beg you please don't . . . wait wait . . .'

'You admit lying?'

'No. I never lied. Let me see my father he'd never order this without seeing me fir – '

'You'll never *see* him again! Why should he *see* you? You lied before and you'll lie again!'

'I . . . I never lied never lied . . .'

His lips twisted into a smile. For all these years he had known she had lied. It had mattered nothing to him. But now it did. 'You lied, *in the Name of God*.' The point pricked the skin. The panic-stricken woman tried to scream but he held his other hand over her mouth and he was tempted to press the extra half inch, then out and in again the other side and out and all finished, finished for ever. 'Liar!'

'Mercy,' she croaked, 'mercy, in the Name of God . . .'

He relaxed his grip but not the point of the knife. 'I cannot grant you mercy. Beg the mercy of God, the Khan has sentenced you!'

'Wait . . . wait,' she said frantically, sensing his muscles tensing for the probe, 'please . . . let me go to the Khan . . . let me ask his mercy I'm his daugh – '

'You admit you lied?'

She hesitated, eyes fluttering with panic along with her heart. At once the knife point went in a fraction and she gasped out, 'I admit . . . I admit I exagg – '

'In God's Name did you lie or didn't you?' Ahmed snarled.

'Yes . . . yes . . . yes I did . . . please let me see my father . . . please.' The tears were pouring out and he hesitated, pretending to be unsure of himself, then glared at her husband who lay on the carpet nearby quivering with terror. 'You're guilty too!'

'I knew nothing about this, nothing,' Mahmud stuttered, 'nothing at all, I've never lied to the Khan never never I knew nothing . . .'

Ahmed shoved them both ahead of him. Guards opened the door of the sickroom. Azadeh and Hakim and Aysha were there, summoned at a moment's notice, in nightclothes, all frightened, the nurse equally, the Khan awake and brooding, his eyes bloodshot. Najoud went down on her knees and blurted out that she had exaggerated about Hakim and Azadeh and when Ahmed came closer she suddenly broke, 'I lied I lied I lied please forgive me Father please forgive me . . . forgive me . . . mercy . . . mercy . . .' in a mumbling gibberish. Mahmud was moaning and crying, saying he knew nothing about this or he would have spoken up, of course he would have, before God, of course he would, both of them begging for mercy – everyone knowing there would be none.

The Khan cleared his throat noisily. Silence. All eyes on him. His mouth worked but no sound came out. Both the nurse and Ahmed came closer. 'Ah'med stay an'd Hakim, Aza'deh . . . res't go – *them* un'der gu'ard.'

'Highness,' the nurse said gently, 'can it no' wait until tomorrow? You've tired yourself very much. Please, please make it tomorrow.'

The Khan just shook his head. 'N'ow.'

The nurse was very tired. 'I dinna accept any responsibility, Excellency Ahmed. Please make it as short as possible.' Exasperated, she walked out. Two guards pulled Najoud and Mahmud to their feet and dragged them away. Aysha followed shakily. For a moment the Khan closed his eyes, gathering his strength. Now only his heavy, throttled breathing broke the silence. Ahmed and Hakim and Azadeh waited. Twenty minutes passed. The Khan opened his eyes. For him the time had been only seconds. 'My so'n, trus't Ahmed as fir'st confid'ant.'

'Yes, Father.'

'Swea'r by G'd, bo'th of you.'

He listened carefully as they both chorused, 'I swear by God I will trust Ahmed as first confidant.' Earlier they had both sworn before all the family the same thing and everything else he required of them: to cherish and guard little Hassan; for Hakim to make Hassan his heir; for the two of them to stay in Tabriz, Azadeh to stay at least two years in Iran without leaving: 'This way, Highness,' Ahmed had explained earlier, 'no alien outside influence, like that of her husband, could spirit her away before she's sent north, whether guilty or innocent.'

That's wise, the Khan thought, disgusted with Hakim – and Azadeh – that they had allowed Najoud's perjury to be buried for so many years and to let it go unpunished for so many years – loathing Najoud and Mahmud for being so weak. No courage, no strength. Well, Hakim'll learn and she'll learn. If only I had more time . . .

'Aza'deh.'

'Yes, Father?'

'Naj'oud. Wh'at punish'ment?'

She hesitated, frightened again, knowing how his mind worked, feeling the trap close on her. 'Banishment. Banish her and her husband and family.'

Fool, you'll never breed a Khan of the Gorgons, he thought but he was too tired to say it so he just nodded and motioned her to leave. Before she left, Azadeh went to the bed and bent and kissed her father's hand. 'Be merciful, please be merciful, Father.' She forced a smile, touched him again, and then she left.

He watched her close the door. 'Hak'im?'

Hakim also had detected the trap and was petrified of displeasing his father, wanting vengeance but not the malevolent sentence the Khan would pronounce. 'Internal banishment for ever, penniless,' he said. 'Let them earn their own bread in future and expel them from the tribe.'

A little better, thought Abdollah. Normally that would be a terrible punishment. But not if you're a Khan and them a perpetual hazard. Again he moved his hand in dismissal. Like Azadeh, Hakim kissed his father's hand and wished a good night's sleep.

When they were alone, Abdollah said, 'Ah'med, what punis'h?'

'Tomorrow banish them to the wastelands north of Meshed, penniless, with guards. In a year and a day when they're sure they've escaped with their lives, when they've got some business going or house or hut, burn it and put them to death – and their three children.'

He smiled. 'G'ood, do i't.'

'Yes, Highness.' Ahmed smiled back at him, very satisfied.

'Now sl'eep.'

'Sleep well, Highness.' Ahmed saw the eyelids close and the face fall apart. In seconds the sick man was snoring badly.

Ahmed knew he had to be most careful now. Quietly he opened the door. Hakim and Azadeh were waiting in the corridor with the nurse. Worriedly, the nurse went past him, took the Khan's pulse, peering at him closely.

'Is he all right?' Azadeh asked from the doorway.

'Who can say, lassie? He's tired himself, tired himself badly. Best you all leave now.'

Nervously, Hakim turned to Ahmed, 'What did he decide?'

'Banished to the lands north of Meshed at first light tomorrow, penniless and expelled from the tribe. He will tell you himself tomorrow, Highness.'

'As God wants.' Azadeh was greatly relieved that worse had not been ordered. Hakim was glowing that his advice had been taken. 'My sister and I, we, er, we don't know how to thank you for helping us, Ahmed, and, well, for bringing the truth out at long last.'

'Thank you, Highness, but I only obeyed the Khan. When the time comes I will serve you as I serve His Highness, he made me swear it. Good night.' Ahmed smiled to himself and closed the door and went back to the bed. 'How is he?'

'No' so good, agha.' Her back was aching and she was sick with tiredness. 'I must have a replacement tomorrow. We should have two nurses and a sister in charge. Sorry, but I canna continue alone.'

'Whatever you want you will have, provided you stay. His Highness appreciates your care of him. If you like I will watch him for an hour or two. There's a sofa in the next room and I can call you in case anything happens.'

'Oh, that's very kind of you, I'm sure. Thank you, I could use a wee rest, but call me if he wakes, and anyway in two hours.'

He saw her into the next room, told the guard to relieve him in three hours and dismissed him, then began a vigil. Half an hour later he quietly peered in at her. She was deeply asleep. He came back into the sickroom and locked the door, took a deep breath, tousled his hair and rushed for the bed, shaking the Khan roughly. 'Highness,' he hissed as though in panic, 'wake up, wake up!'

The Khan clawed his way out of leaden sleep, not knowing where he was or what had happened or if he was nightmaring again. 'Wh'at . . . wh'at . . .' Then his eyes focused and he saw Ahmed, seemingly terrified which was unheard of. His spirit shuddered. 'Wh'a – '

'Quick, you've got to get up, Pahmudi's downstairs, Abrim Pahmudi with SAVAMA torturers, they've come for you,' Ahmed panted; 'someone opened the door to them, you're betrayed, a traitor betrayed you to him, Hashemi Fazir's given you to Pahmudi and SAVAMA as a pishkesh, quick, get up, they've overpowered all the guards and they're coming to take you away. . .' He saw the Khan's gaping horror, the bulging eyes, and he rushed on. 'There're too many to stop. Quick, you've got to escape . . .'

Deftly he unclipped the saline drip and tore the bedclothes back, started to help the mouthing, frantic man to get up, abruptly shoved him back and stared at the door. 'Too late,' he gasped, 'listen, here they come, here they come, Pahmudi at the head, here they come!'

Chest heaving, the Khan thought he could hear their footsteps, could see Pahmudi, could see his thin gloating face and the instruments of torture in the corridor outside, knowing there would be no mercy and they would keep him alive to howl his life away. Demented he shouted at Ahmed, Quick, help me. I can get to the window, we can climb down if you help me! In the Name of God, Ahmeddddddd . . . but he could not make the words come out. Again he tried but still his mouth did not coordinate with his brain, his neck muscles stretched with effort, the veins overloaded.

It seemed for ever he was screaming and shouting at Ahmed who just stood watching the door, not helping him, footsteps coming closer and closer. 'He'lp,' he managed to gasp, fighting to get out of bed, the sheets and coverlet weighing him down, restricting him, drowning him, chest pains growing and growing, monstrous now like the noise.

'There's no escape, they're here, I've got to let them in!'

At the limit of his terror he saw Ahmed start for the door. With the remains of his strength he shouted at him to stop but all that happened was a strangled croak. Then he felt something twist in his brain and something else snap. A spark leaped across the wires of his mind and chain-reacted the core. Pain ceased, sound ceased. He saw Ahmed's smile. His ears heard the quiet of the corridor and silence of the palace and he knew that he was truly betrayed. With a last, all-embracing effort, he lunged for Ahmed, the fires in his head lighting his way down into the funnel, red and warm and liquid, and there, at the nadir, he blew out all the fire and possessed the darkness.

Ahmed made sure the Khan was dead, glad that he had not had to use the pillow to smother him. Hastily he reconnected the saline drip, checked that there were no telltale leaks, partially straightened the bed, and then, with great care examined the room. Nothing to give him away that he could see. His breathing was heavy, his head throbbing, and his exhilaration immense. A second check, then he walked over to the door, quietly unlocked it, noiselessly returned to the bed. The Khan was lying sightlessly against the pillows, blood haemorrhaged from his nose and mouth.

'Highness!' he bellowed. 'Highness . . .' then leaned forward and grabbed him for a moment, released him and rushed across the room, tore open the door. 'Nurse!' he shouted and rushed into the next room, grabbed the woman out of her deep sleep and half carried, half dragged her back to the Khan.

'Oh my God,' she muttered, weak with relief that it had not happened while she was alone, perhaps to be blamed by this knife-wielding, violent bodyguard or these mad people, screaming and raving. Sickly awake now, she wiped her brow and pushed her hair into shape, feeling naked without her headdress. Quickly she did what she had to and closed his eyes, her ears hearing Ahmed moaning and grief-stricken. 'Nothing anyone could do, agha,' she was saying. 'It could have happened any time. He was in a great deal of pain, his time had come, better this way, better than living as a vegetable.'

'Yes . . . yes, I suppose so.' Ahmed's tears were real. Tears of relief. 'Insha'Allah, Insha'Allah.'

'What happened?'

'I . . . I was dozing and he just . . . just gasped and started to bleed from his nose and mouth.' Ahmed wiped some of the tears away, letting his voice break. 'I grabbed him as he was falling out of bed and then . . .

then I don't know I . . . he just collapsed and . . . and I came running for you.'

'Dinna worry, agha, nothing anyone could do. Sometimes it's sudden and quick, sometimes not. Better to be quick, that's a blessing.' She sighed and straightened her uniform, glad it was over and now she could leave this place. 'He, er, he should be cleaned before the others are summoned.'

'Yes. Please let me help, I wish to help.'

Ahmed helped her sponge away the blood and make him presentable and all the time he was planning: Najoud and Mahmud to be banished before noon, the rest of their punishment a year and a day from now; find out if Fazir caught Petr Oleg; make sure the ransom messenger's throat was cut this afternoon as he had ordered in the Khan's name.

Fool, he said to the corpse, fool to think I'd arrange to pay ransom to bring back the pilot to fly you to Tehran to save your life. Why save a life for a few more days or a month? Dangerous to be sick and helpless with your sickness, minds become deranged, oh, yes, the doctor told me what to expect, losing more of your mind, more vindictive than ever, more dangerous than ever, dangerous enough to perhaps turn on me! But now, now the succession is safe, I can dominate the whelp and with the help of God marry Azadeh. Or send her north – her hole's like any other.

The nurse watched Ahmed from time to time, his deft strong hands and their gentleness, for the first time glad of his presence and not afraid of him, now watching him combing the beard. People are so strange, she thought. He must have loved this evil old man very much.

Wednesday

Chapter 18

Tehran: 6:55 A.M. McIver continued sorting through the files and papers he had taken from the big office safe, putting only those that were vital into his briefcase. He had been at it since 5:30 this morning and now his head ached, his back ached, and the briefcase was almost full. So much more I should be taking, he thought, working as fast as he could. In an hour, perhaps less, his Iranian staff would arrive and he would have to stop.

Bloody people, he thought irritably, never here when we wanted them but now for the last few days, can't get rid of them, like bloody limpets: 'Oh, no, Excellency, please allow me to lock up for you, I beg you for the privilege . . .' or 'Oh no, Excellency, I'll open the office for you, I insist that is not the job for your Excellency.' Maybe I'm getting paranoid but it's just as though they're spies, ordered in to watch us, the partners more nosy than ever. Almost as though someone's on to us.

And yet, so far – touch wood – everything's working like a well-tuned jet: us out by noon today or a little after; already Rudi's poised for Friday with all of his extra bods and a whole load of spares already out of Bandar-e Delam by road to Abadan where a BA Trident snuck in to evacuate British oilers; at Kowiss, by now Starke should have cached the extra fuel, all his lads still cleared to leave tomorrow on the 125 – touch more wood – already three truck loads of spares out to Bushire for trans-shipment to Al Shargaz; at Lengeh Scrag'll be having no problems, plenty of coastal ships available for his spares and nothing more to do but wait for D – no, not D-day – W-day.

Only bad spot, Azadeh. And Erikki. Why the devil didn't she tell me before leaving on a wild-goose chase after poor old Erikki? Never expected her to rush off like that! I could have told her about Whirlwind! My God, she escapes Tabriz with the skin of her skin and then goes and puts her pretty little head back in it. Women! They're all crazy. Ransom? Balls! I'll bet it's another trap set by her father, the rotten old bastard.

His stomach began churning. How the hell can we get them to safety? Must come up with something. We've two more days, perhaps . . .

He whirled, startled, not having heard the door open. His chief clerk, Gorani, stood in the doorway, tall and balding, a devout Shi'ite, a good man who had been with them for many years. 'Salaam, agha.'

'Salaam. You're early.' McIver saw the man's open surprise at all the mess

– normally McIver was meticulously tidy – and felt as though he'd been caught
with his hand in the chocolate box.

'As God wants, agha. The Imam's ordered normality and everyone to work
hard for the success of the revolution. Can I help?'

'Well, er, no, no, thank you. I, er, I'm just in a hurry. I've lots to do today,
I'm off to the embassy.' McIver knew his voice was running away from him
but he was unable to stop it. 'I've, er, appointments all day and must be at
the airport by noon. I have to do some homework for the Doshan Tappeh
komiteh. I won't come back to the office from the airport so you can close
early, take the afternoon off – in fact you can take the day off.'

'Oh, thank you, agha, but the office should remain open until the us – '

'No, we'll close for the day when I leave. I'll go straight home and be there if
I'm needed. Please come back in ten minutes, I want to send some telexes.'

'Yes, agha, certainly, agha.' The man left.

McIver hated the twistings of the truth. What's going to happen to Gorani?
he asked himself again, to him and all the rest of our people all over Iran, some
of them fine, them and their families?

Unsettled, he finished as best he could. There were a hundred thousand rials
in the cashbox. He left notes, relocked the safe, and sent some inconsequential
telexes. The main one he had sent at 5:30 this morning to Al Shargaz: '*Air
freighting the five crates of parts to Al Shargaz for repairs as planned.*' Translated,
the code meant that Nogger, Pettikin and he, and the last two mechanics he
had not been able to get out of Tehran, were readying to board the 125 today,
as planned, and it was still all systems go.

'Which crates are these, agha?' Somehow Gorani had found the copies of
the telex.

'They're from Kowiss, they'll go on the 125 next week.'

'Oh very well. I'll check it for you. Before you go, could you please tell me
when does our 212 return? The one we loaned to Kowiss.'

'Next week, why?'

'Excellency Minister and Board Director Ali Kia wanted to know, agha.'
McIver was instantly chilled. 'Oh? Why?'

'He probably has a charter for it, agha. His assistant came here last night,
after you had left, and he asked me. Minister Kia also wanted a progress report
today of our three 212s sent out for repairs. I, er, I said I would have it today –
he is coming this morning, so I can't close the office.'

They had never discussed the three aircraft, or the peculiarly great
number of spares they had been sending out by truck, car, or as personal baggage – no aircraft space for freight. It was more than possible that Gorani would know the 212s did not need repair. He shrugged
and hoped for the best. 'They'll be ready as planned. Leave a note on
the door.'

'Oh, but that would be very impolite. I will relay that message. He said he
would return before noon prayer and particularly asked for an appointment
with you. He has a very private message from Minister Kia.'

'Well, I'm going to the embassy.' McIver debated a moment. 'I'll be back as soon as I can.' Irritably he picked up the briefcase and hurried down the stairs, cursing Ali Kia and then adding a curse for Ali Baba too.

Ali Baba – so named because he reminded McIver of the Forty Thieves – was the wheedling half of their live-in couple who had been with them for two years but had vanished at the beginning of the troubles. Yesterday at dawn Ali Baba came back, beaming and acting as though he had just been away for the weekend instead of almost five months, happily insisting he take his old room back: 'Oh, most definitely, agha, the home has to be most clean and prepared for the return of Her Highness; next week my wife will be here to do that but meanwhile I bring you tea-toast in a most instant as you ever liked. May I be sacrificed for you but I bargained mightily today for fresh bread and milk from the market at the oh so reasonable best price for me only, but the robbers charge five times last year's, so sad, but please give me the money now, and as most soon as the Bank is opened you can pay me my mucroscupic back salary . . .'

Bloody Ali Baba, the revolution hasn't changed him a bit. 'Mucroscupic?' It's still one loaf for us and five for him, but never mind, it was fine to have tea and toast in bed – but not the day before we sneak out. How the hell are Charlie and I going to get our luggage out without him smelling the proverbial rat?

In the garage he unlocked his car. 'Lulu, old girl,' he said, 'sorry, there's bugger all I can do about it, it's time for the Big Parting. Don't quite know how I'm going to do it, but I'm not leaving you as a burnt offering or for some bloody Iranian to rape.'

At the British Embassy: 0930 A.M. Talbot was waiting for him in a spacious, elegant office. 'My dear Mr. McIver, you're bright and early, I heard all the adventures of young Ross – my word we were all very lucky, don't you think?'

'Yes, yes we were. How is he?'

'Getting over it. Good man, did a hell of a good job. I'm seeing him for lunch and we're getting him out on today's BA flight – just in case he's been spotted, can't be too careful. Any news of Erikki? We've had some inquiries from the Finnish embassy asking for help.'

McIver told him about Azadeh's note. 'Bloody ridiculous.'

Talbot steepled his fingers. 'Ransom doesn't sound too good. There's, er, there's a rumour the Khan's very sick indeed. Stroke.'

McIver frowned. 'Would that help or hurt Azadeh and Erikki?'

'I don't know. If he does pop off, well, it'll certainly change the balance of power in Azerbaijan for a while, which will certainly encourage our misguided friends north of the border to agitate more than usual, which'll cause Carter and his powers-that-be to fart more dust.'

'What the devil's he doing now?'

'Nothing, old boy, sweet Fanny Adams – that's the trouble. He scattered his peanuts and scarpered.'

'Anything more on us being nationalise?'

'It might well be you'll lose positive control of your aircraft imminently,'

Talbot said with studied care and McIver's attention zeroed. 'It, er, might be more of a personal acquisition by interested parties.'

'You mean Ali Kia and the partners?'

Talbot shrugged. 'Ours not to reason why, eh?'

'This is official?'

'My dear chap, good Lord, no!' Talbot was quite shocked. 'Just a personal observation, off the record. What can I do for you?'

'Off the record, on Andy Gavallan's instructions, all right?'

'Let's have it on the record.'

McIver saw the slightly pink humourless face and got up, relieved. 'No way, Mr. Talbot. It was Andy's idea to keep you in the picture, not mine.'

Talbot sighed with practised eloquence. 'Very well, off the record.'

McIver sat. 'We're, er, we're transferring our HQ to Al Shargaz today.'

'Very wise. So?'

'We're going today. All remaining expat personnel. On our 125.'

'Very wise. So?'

'We're er, we're closing down all operations in Iran. *On Friday.*'

Talbot sighed wearily. 'Without personnel I'd say that's axiomatic. So?'

McIver was finding it very hard to say what he wanted to say. 'We, er, we're taking our aircraft out on Friday – this Friday.'

'Bless my soul,' Talbot said in open admiration. 'Congratulations! How on earth did you twist that rotter Kia's arm to get the permits? You must've promised him a life membership at the Royal Box at Ascot!'

'Er, no, no, we didn't. We decided not to apply for exit permits, waste of time.' McIver got up. 'Well, see you soo – '

Talbot's smile almost fell off his face. 'No permits?'

'No. You know yourself our birds're going to be nicked, nationalised, taken over. Whatever you want to call it, there's no way we could get exit permits so we're just going.' McIver added airily, 'Friday we flit the coop.'

'Oh, my word!' Talbot was shaking his head vigorously, his fingers toying with a file on his desk. 'Bless my soul, very very un-bloody-wise.'

'There isn't any alternative. Well, Mr. Talbot, that's all, have a nice day. Andy wanted to forewarn you so you could. . . so you could do whatever you want to do.'

'What the hell is that?' Talbot exploded.

'How the hell do I know?' McIver was equally exasperated. 'You're supposed to protect your nationals.'

'But y – '

'I'm just not going to be put out of business and that's the end of it!'

Talbot's fingers drummed nervously. 'I think I need a cup of tea.' He clicked on the intercom. 'Celia, two cups of the best and I think you better insert a modest amount of Nelson's Blood into the brew.'

'Yes, Mr. Talbot,' the adenoidal voice said and sneezed.

'Bless you,' Talbot said automatically. His fingers stopped drumming and he smiled sweetly at McIver. 'I'm awfully glad you didn't tell me anything about anything, old boy.'

'So'm I. Could you use your radio link to ask your man in Tabriz to get Erikki a message? All phone lines are down.'

'How the hell can he do that?'

'I don't know,' McIver said patiently. 'But he could get one to Azadeh and she might be able to pass it on. Please, it's important.'

'All right. Our radio link's out but it's promised for tomorrow or the next day. I'll signal him – depending on the message.'

'Ask him to tell Erikki, or tell Azadeh to tell him I said to *Take a powder*.'

'That's apt,' Talbot said witheringly. 'Rest assured, should I ever hear you're in pokey doing – what's the expression? Ah, yes, "doing porridge" – I shall be glad to visit you on behalf of Her Majesty's Government and attempt to extricate you from the errors of your ways.' His eyebrows went off his forehead. 'Grand larceny! Bless my soul, but jolly good luck, old boy, and don't worry about Erikki. I'll get the message through to him somehow.'

At McIver's Apartment: 11:50 A.M. Pettikin came into the living room carrying a suitcase and was surprised to see the servant, Ali Baba, tentatively polishing the sideboard. 'I didn't hear you come back. I thought I'd given you the day off,' he said irritably, putting down the suitcase.

'Oh, yes, agha, but there is most much to do, the place she is filth-filled and the kitchen . . .' His lush brown eyebrows rose to heaven.

'Yes, yes, that's true but you can start in tomorrow.' Pettikin saw him looking at the suitcase and swore. Directly after breakfast he had sent Ali Baba off for the day with instructions to be back at midnight, which normally would mean that he would not come back until the next morning. 'Now off you go.'

'Yes, agha, you are going on holiday or on the leaves?'

'No, I'm, er, I'm going to stay with one of the pilots for a few days, so make sure my room's cleaned tomorrow. Oh, yes, and you better give me your key, I've misplaced mine.' Pettikin held out his hand, cursing himself for not thinking of it before. With curious reluctance, Ali Baba gave it to him. 'Captain McIver wants the place to himself, he has work to do and doesn't want to be disturbed. See you soon, good-bye.'

'But agha . . .'

'Good-bye!' He made sure Ali Baba had his coat, opened the door, half shoved him out, and closed it again. Nervously he glanced again at his watch. Almost noon and still no McIver and they were supposed to be at the airport by now. He went into the bedroom, reached into the cupboard for the other suitcase, also packed, then came back and put it beside the other one, near the front door.

Two small cases and a carryall, he thought. Not much to show for all the years in Iran. Never mind, I prefer to travel light and perhaps this time I can get lucky and make more money or start a business on the side and then there's Paula. How in the hell can I afford to get married again? Married? Are you mad? An affair's about all you could manage. Yes, but Goddam, I'd like to marry her an –

The phone rang and he almost jumped out of himself, so unused to its ringing. He picked it up, his heart pounding. 'Hello?'

'Charlie? It's me, Mac, thank God the bloody thing's working, tried it on the off chance. I've been delayed.'

'You've a problem?'

'Don't know, Charlie, but I've got to go and see Ali Kia – bastard's sent his bloody assistant and a Green Band to fetch me.'

'What the hell does Kia want?' Outside, all over the city, muezzins began calling the Faithful to noon prayer, distracting him.

'Don't know. The appointment's in half an hour. You'd better go on out to the airport and I'll get there as soon as I can. Get Johnny Hogg to delay.'

'Okay, Mac. What about your gear, is it in the office?'

'I snuck it out early this morning while Ali Baba was snoring and it's in Lulu's boot. Charlie, there's one of Genny's needlepoints in the kitchen, "Down with cornbeef pie". Stick it in your suitcase for me, will you? She'd have my guts for garters if I forgot that. If I've time I'll come back and make sure everything's okay.'

'Do I shut the gas off, or electricity?'

'Christ, I don't know. Leave it, okay?'

'All right. You sure you don't want me to wait?' he asked, the metallic, loudspeaker voices of muezzins adding to his disquiet. 'I don't mind waiting. Might be better, Mac.'

'No, you go on out. I'll be there right smartly. 'Bye.'

' 'Bye.' Pettikin frowned, then, having a dialling tone, he dialled their office at the airport. To his astonishment the connection went through.

'Iran Helicopters, hello?'

He recognised the voice of their freight manager. 'Morning, Adwani, this's Captain Pettikin. Has the 125 come in yet?'

'Ah, Captain, yes it's in the pattern and should be landing any minute.'

'Is Captain Lane there?'

'Yes, just a moment please . . .'

Pettikin waited, wondering about Kia.

'Hello, Charlie, Nogger here – you've friends in high places?'

'No, the phone just started working. Can you talk privately?'

'No. Not possible. What's cooking?'

'I'm still at the flat. Mac's been delayed – he's got to go and see Ali Kia. I'm on my way to the airport now and he'll come directly from Kia's office. Are you ready to load?'

'Yes, Charlie, we're sending the engines for repair and reconditioning as Captain McIver ordered. Everything as ordered.'

'Good, are the two mecs there?'

'Yes. But those spares are also ready for shipping.'

'Good. No problem that you can see?'

'Not yet, old chum.'

'See you.' Pettikin hung up. He looked around the apartment a last time, now curiously saddened. Good times and bad times but the best when Paula was staying. Out of the window he noticed distant smoke over Jaleh and now as the muezzins' voices died away, the usual sporadic gunfire. 'The hell with all of them,' he muttered. He got up and went out with his luggage and locked the door carefully. As he drove out of the garage he saw Ali Baba duck back into a doorway across the road. With him were two other men he had never seen before. What the hell's that bugger up to, he thought uneasily.

At the Ministry of Transport: 1:07 P.M. The huge room was freezing in spite of a log fire, and Minister Ali Kia wore a heavy, expensive Astrakhan overcoat with a hat to match, and he was angry. 'I repeat, I need transport to Kowiss tomorrow and I require you to accompany me.'

'Can't tomorrow, sorry,' McIver said, keeping his nervousness off his face with difficulty. 'I'd be glad to join you next week. Say Monday an – '

'I'm astonished that after all the "co-operation" I've given you it's necessary even to argue! Tomorrow, Captain, or . . . or I shall cancel all clearances for our 125 – in fact, I'll hold it on the ground today, impound it today pending investigations!'

McIver was standing in front of the vast desk, Kia sitting behind it in a big carved chair that dwarfed him. 'Could you make it today, Excellency? We've an Alouette to ferry to Kowiss. Captain Lochart's leav – '

'Tomorrow. Not today.' Kia flushed even more. 'As ranking board director you are ordered: you *will* come with me, we *will* leave at ten o'clock. Do you understand?'

McIver nodded bleakly, trying to figure a way out of the trap. The pieces of a tentative plan fell into place. 'Where do you want to meet?'

'Where's the helicopter?'

'Doshan Tappeh. We'll need a clearance. Unfortunately there's a Major Delami there, along with a mullah, and both're rather difficult, so I don't see how we can do it.'

Kia's face darkened even more. 'The PM's given new orders about mullahs and interference with the legal government and the Imam agrees wholeheartedly. They both better behave. I will see you at 10 tomorrow an – '

At that moment there was a large explosion outside. They rushed to the window but could see only a cloud of smoke billowing into the cold sky from around the bend in the road. 'Sounded like another car bomb,' McIver said queasily. Over the last few days there had been a number of assassination attempts and car bomb attacks by left-wing extremists, mostly on high-ranking ayatollahs in the government.

'Filthy terrorists, may God burn their fathers, and them!' Kia was clearly frightened, which pleased McIver.

'The price of fame, Minister,' he said, his voice heavy with concern. 'Those in high places, important people like you, are obvious targets.'

'Yes . . . yes . . . we know, we know. Filthy terrorists . . .'

McIver smiled all the way back to his car. So Kia wants to go to

Kowiss. I'll see he bloody gets to Kowiss and Whirlwind continues as planned.

Around the corner, the main road ahead was partially blocked with debris, a car still on fire, others smouldering, and a hole in the roadbed where the parked car bomb had exploded, blowing out the front of a restaurant and the shuttered foreign bank beside it, glass from them and other shop windows scattered everywhere. Many injured, dead or dying. Agony and panic and the stink of burning rubber.

Traffic was jammed both ways. There was nothing to do but wait. After half an hour an ambulance arrived, some Green Bands and a mullah began directing traffic. In time McIver was waved forward, cursed forward. Easing past the wreckage, all traffic enraged and blaring, he did not notice the headless body of Talbot half buried under the restaurant debris, nor recognise Ross dressed in civvies, lying half against the wall, his coat ripped, blood seeping from his nose and ears.

At Tehran Airport: 6:05 P.M. Johnny Hogg, Pettikin and Nogger stared at McIver blankly. 'You're staying – you're not leaving with us?' Pettikin stuttered.

'No. I told you,' McIver said briskly. 'I've got to accompany Kia to Kowiss tomorrow.' They were beside his car in their car park, away from alien ears, the 125 on the apron, labourers loading the last few crates, the inevitable group of Green Band guards watching. And a mullah.

'The mullah's one we've never seen before,' Nogger said nervously, like all of them trying to hide it.

'Good. Is everyone else ready to board?'

'Yes, Mac, except Jean-Luc.' Pettikin was very unsettled. 'Don't you think you'd better chance leaving Kia?'

'That'd really be crazy, Charlie. Nothing to worry about. You can set up everything at Al Shargaz Airport with Andy. I'll be there tomorrow. I'll get on the 125 tomorrow at Kowiss with the rest of the lads.'

'But for God's sake they're all cleared, you're not,' Nogger said.

'For God's sake, Nogger, none of us're cleared from here, for God's sake.' McIver added with a laugh, 'How the hell will we be sure of our Kowiss lads until they're airborne and out of Iran airspace? Nothing to worry about. First things first, we've got to get this part of the show in the air.' He glanced at the taxi skidding to a stop. Jean-Luc got out, gave the driver the other half of the note and strolled over carrying a suitcase.

'*Alors, mes amis,*' he said with a contented smile. '*Ça marche?*'

McIver sighed. 'Jolly sporting of you to advertise you're going on a holiday, Jean-Luc.'

'What?'

'Never mind.' McIver liked Jean-Luc, for his ability, his cooking, and single-mindedness. When Gavallan had told Jean-Luc about Whirlwind, Jean-Luc had said at once, 'Me, I will certainly fly out one of the Kowiss

212s – providing I can be on the Wednesday flight to Tehran and go into Tehran for a couple of hours.'

'To do what?'

'*Mon Dieu*, you *Anglais*! To say *adieu* to the Imam perhaps?'

McIver grinned at the Frenchman. 'How was Tehran?'

'*Magnifique!*' Jean-Luc grinned back, and thought, I haven't seen Mac so young in years. Who's the lady? '*Et toi, mon vieux?*'

'Good.' Behind him, McIver saw Jones, the co-pilot, come down the steps two at a time, heading for them. Now there were no more crates left on the tarmac and their Iranian ground crew were all strolling back to the office. 'You all set aboard?'

'All set, Captain, except for passengers,' Jones said, matter of fact. 'ATC's getting itchy and says we're overdue. Quick as you can, all right?'

'You're still cleared for a stop at Kowiss?'

'Yes, no problem.'

McIver took a deep breath. 'All right, here we go, just as we planned, except I'll take the papers, Johnny.' Johnny Hogg handed them to him and the three of them, McIver, Hogg and Jones, went ahead, straight to the mullah, hoping to distract him. By prearrangement the two mechanics were already aboard, ostensibly loaders. 'Good day, agha,' McIver said, and ostentatiously handed the mullah the manifest, their position blocking a direct view of the steps. Nogger, Pettikin and Jean-Luc went up them nimbly to vanish inside.

The mullah leafed through the manifest, clearly not accustomed to it. 'Good. Now inspect,' he said, his accent thick.

'No need for that, agha, ev – ' McIver stopped. The mullah and the two guards were already going for the steps. 'Soon as you're aboard, start engines, Johnny,' he said softly and followed.

The cabin was piled with crates, the passengers already seated, seat belts fastened. All eyes studiously avoided the mullah. The mullah stared at them. 'Who men?'

McIver said brightly, 'Crews for replacements, agha.' His excitement picked up as the engines began to howl. He motioned haphazardly at Jean-Luc. 'Pilot for Kowiss replacement, agha,' then more hurriedly, 'Tower komiteh wants the aircraft to leave now. Hurry, all right?'

'What in crates?' The mullah looked at the cockpit as Johnny Hogg called out in perfect Farsi, 'Sorry to interrupt, Excellency, as God wants, but the tower orders us to take off at once. With your permission, please?'

'Yes, yes, of course, Excellency pilot.' The mullah smiled. 'Your Farsi is very good, Excellency.'

'Thank you, Excellency, God keep you, and His blessings on the Imam.'

'Thank you, Excellency pilot, God keep you.' The mullah left.

On his way out McIver leaned into the cockpit. 'What was that all about, Johnny? I didn't know you spoke Farsi.'

'I don't,' Hogg told him dryly – and what he had said to the mullah. 'I just learned that phrase, thought it might come in handy.'

McIver smiled. 'Go to the top of the class!' Then he dropped his voice.

'When you get to Kowiss get Starke to arrange with Hotshot, however he can, to pull the lads' ferry forward, early as possible in the morning. I don't want Kia there when they take off – get 'em out early, however he can. Okay?'

'Yes, of course, I'd forgotten that. Very wise.'

'Have a safe flight – see you in Al Shargaz.' From the tarmac he gave them a beaming thumbs up as they taxied away.

The second they were airborne Nogger exploded, with a cheer, 'We did it!' that everyone echoed, except Jean-Luc who crossed himself superstitiously and Pettikin touched wood. '*Merde,*' he called out. 'Save your cheers, Nogger, you may be grounded in Kowiss. Save your cheers for Friday, too much dust to blow across the Gulf between now and then!'

'Right you are, Jean-Luc,' Pettikin said, sitting in the window seat beside him, watching the airport receding. 'Mac was in good humour. Haven't seen him that happy for months and he was pissed off this morning. Curious how people can change.'

'Yes, curious. Me, I would be very pissed off indeed to have such a change of plan.' Jean-Luc was getting himself comfortable and sat back, his mind on Sayada and their parting that had been significant and sweet sorrow. He glanced at Pettikin and saw the heavy frown. 'What?'

'I suddenly wondered how Mac's getting to Kowiss.'

'By chopper, of course. There're two 206s and an Alouette left.'

'Tom ferried the Alouette to Kowiss today, and there aren't any pilots left.'

'So he is going by car, of course. Why?'

'You don't think he'd be crazy enough to fly Kia himself, do you?'

'Are you mad? Of course not, he's not that cr – ' Jean-Luc's eyebrows soared. '*Merde,* he's that crazy.'

Thursday

Chapter 19

In the Village Near the North Border: 5:30 A.M. In the light of false dawn Erikki pulled on his boots. Now on with his flight jacket, the soft, well-worn leather rustling, knife out of the scabbard and into his sleeve. He eased the hut door open. The village was sleeping under its snow coverlet. No guards that he could see. The chopper's lean-to was also quiet but he knew she would still be too well guarded to try. Various times during the day and night he had experimented. Each time the cabin and cockpit guards had just smiled at him, alert and polite. No way he could fight through the three of them and take off. His only chance by foot and he had been planning it ever since he had had the confrontation with Sheik Bayazid the day before yesterday.

His senses reached out into the darkness. The stars were hidden by thin clouds. Now! Surefooted he slid out of the door and along the line of huts, making for the trees, and then he was enmeshed in the net that seemed to appear out of the sky and he was fighting for his life.

Four tribesmen were on the ends of the net used for trapping and for curbing wild goats. Skilfully they wound it around him, tighter and tighter, and though he bellowed with rage and his immense strength ripped some of the ropes asunder, soon he was helplessly thrashing in the snow. For a moment he lay there panting, then again tried to break his bonds, the feeling of impotence making him howl. But the more he fought the ropes, the more they seemed to knot tighter. Finally he stopped fighting and lay back, trying to catch his breath, and looked around. He was surrounded. All the village was awake, dressed and armed. Obviously they had been waiting for him. Never had he seen or felt so much hatred.

It took five men to lift him and half carry, half drag him into the meeting hut and throw him roughly on the dirt floor in front of Sheik Bayazid who sat cross-legged on skins in his place of honour near the fire. The hut was large, smoke-blackened and filled with tribesmen.

'So,' the Sheik said. 'So you dare to disobey me?'

Erikki lay still, gathering his strength. What was there to say?

'In the night one of my men came back from the Khan.' Bayazid was shaking with fury. 'Yesterday afternoon, on Khan's orders, my messenger's throat was cut against all the laws of chivalry! What do you say to that? His throat cut like a dog! Like a dog!'

'I . . . I can't believe the Khan would do that,' Erikki said helplessly. 'I can't believe it.'

'In all the Names of God, his throat was cut. He's dead and we're dishonoured. All of us, me! Disgraced, because of you!'

'The Khan's a devil. I'm sorry but I'm no – '

'We treated with the Khan honourably, and you honourably, you were spoils of war won from Khan's enemies and ours, you married to his daughter, and he's rich with more bags of gold than a goat has hairs. What's ten million rials to him? A piece of goat's shit. Worse, he's taken away our honour. God's death on him!'

A murmur went through those who watched and waited, not understanding the English but hearing the jagged barbs of anger.

Again the hissing venom: 'Insha'Allah! Now we release you as you want, on foot, and then we will hunt you. We will not kill you with bullets, nor will you see the sunset and your head will be a Khan's gift.' The Sheik recalled the punishment in his own tongue and waved his hand. Men surged forward.

'Wait, wait!' Erikki shouted as his fear thrust an idea at him.

'You wish to beg for mercy?' Bayazid said contemptuously. 'I thought you were a man – that's why I didn't order your throat cut while you sleep.'

'Not mercy, vengeance!' Then Erikki roared, 'Vengeance!' There was an astonished silence. 'For you and for me! Don't you deserve vengeance for such dishonour?'

The younger man hesitated. 'What trickery is this?'

'I can help you regain your honour – I alone. Let us sack the palace of the Khan and both be revenged on him.' Erikki prayed to his ancient gods to make his tongue golden.

'Are you mad?'

'The Khan is my enemy more than yours, why else would he disgrace both of us if not to infuriate you against me? I know the palace. I can get you and fifteen armed men into the forecourt in a split second an – '

'Madness,' the Sheik scoffed. 'Should we throw our lives away like hashish-infected fools? The Khan has too many guards.'

'Fifty-three on call within the walls, no more than four or five on duty at any one time. Are your fighters so weak they can't deal with fifty-three? We have surprise on our side. A sudden commando attack from the sky, a relentless charge to avenge your honour – I could get you in and out the same way in minutes. Abdollah Khan's sick, very sick, guards won't be prepared, nor the household. I know the way in, where he sleeps, everything . . .'

Erikki heard his voice pick up excitement, knowing it could be done: the violent flare over the walls and sudden touchdown, jumping out, leading the way up the steps and in, up the staircase on to the landing, down the corridor, knocking aside Ahmed and whoever stood in the way, into the Khan's room, then stepping aside for Bayazid and his men to do what they wanted, somehow getting to the north wing and Azadeh and saving her, and if she was not there or hurt, then killing and killing, the Khan, guards, these men, everyone.

His plan possessed him now. 'Wouldn't your name last a thousand years because of your daring? Sheik Bayazid, he who dared to humble, to challenge the Khan of all the Gorgons inside his lair for a matter of honour? Wouldn't minstrels sing songs about you for ever at the campfires of all the Kurds? Isn't that what Saladin the Kurd would do?'

He saw the eyes in the firelight glowing differently now, saw Bayazid hesitate, the silence growing, heard him talk softly to his people – then one man laughed and called out something that others echoed and then, with one voice, they roared approval.

Willing hands cut him loose. Men fought viciously for the privilege of being on the raid. Erikki's fingers trembled as he pressed Engine Start. The first of the jets exploded into life.

In the Palace of the Khan: 6:35 A.M. Hakim came out of sleep violently. His bodyguard near the door was startled. 'What is it, Highness?'

'Nothing, nothing, Ishtar, I was . . . I was just dreaming.' Now that he was wide awake, Hakim lay back and stretched luxuriously, eager for the new day. 'Bring me coffee. After my bath, breakfast here – and ask my sister to join me.'

'Yes, Highness, at once.'

His bodyguard left him. Again he stretched his taut body. Dawn was murky. The room ornate and vast and draughty and chilly but the bedroom of the Khan. In the huge fireplace a fire burned brightly, fed by the guard through the night, no one else allowed in, the guard chosen by him personally from the fifty-three within the palace, pending a decision about their future. Where to find those to be trusted, he asked himself, then got out of bed, wrapping the warm brocade dressing gown tighter – one of a half a hundred that he had found in the wardrobe – faced Mecca and the open Koran in the ornately tiled niche, knelt and said the first prayer of the day. When he had finished he stayed there, his eyes on the ancient Koran, immense, bejewelled, hand calligraphed and without price, the Gorgon Khan's Koran – *his* Koran. So much to thank God for, he thought, so much still to learn, so much still to do – but a wonderful beginning already made.

Not long after midnight yesterday, before all the assembled family in the house, he had taken the carved emerald and gold ring – symbol of the ancient Khanate – from the index finger of his father's right hand and put it on his own. He had had to fight the ring over a roll of fat and close his nostrils to the stink of death that hung in the room. His excitement had overcome his revulsion, and now he was truly Khan. Then all the family present knelt and kissed his ringed hand, swearing allegiance, Azadeh proudly first, next Aysha trembling and frightened, then the others, Najoud and Mahmud outwardly abject, secretly blessing God for the reprieve.

Then downstairs in the Great Room with Azadeh standing behind him, Ahmed and the bodyguards also swore allegiance – the rest of the far-flung family would come later, along with other tribal leaders, personal and household staff and servants. At once he had given orders for the funeral and then he allowed his eyes to see Najoud. 'So.'

'Highness,' Najoud said unctuously, 'with all our hearts, before God, we congratulate you, and swear to serve you to the limits of our power.'

'Thank you, Najoud,' he had said. 'Thank you. Ahmed, what was the Khan's sentence decreed on my sister and her family before he died?' Tension in the Great Room was sudden.

'Banishment, penniless to the wastelands north of Meshed, Highness, under guard – at once.'

'I regret, Najoud, you and all your family will leave at dawn as decreed.'

He remembered how her face had gone ashen and Mahmud's ashen and she had stammered, 'But, Highness, now you are Khan, your word is our law. I did not expect . . . you're Khan now.'

'But the Khan, our father, gave the order when he was the law, Najoud. It is not correct to overrule him.'

'But you're the law now,' Najoud had said with a sickly smile. 'You do what's right.'

'With God's help I will certainly try, Najoud. I can't overrule my father on his deathbed.'

'But, Highness . . .' Najoud had come closer. 'Please, may . . . may we discuss this in private?'

'Better here before the family, Najoud. What did you want to say?'

She had hesitated and come even closer and he felt Ahmed tense and saw his knife hand ready, and the hair on his neck stiffened. 'Just because Ahmed *says* that the Khan gave such an order doesn't mean that it. . . does it?' Najoud had tried to whisper but her words echoed off the walls.

Breath sighed out of Ahmed's lips. 'May God burn me for ever if I lied.'

'I know you didn't, Ahmed,' Hakim had said sadly. 'Wasn't I there when the Khan decided? I was there, Najoud, so was Her Highness, my sister, I regret th – '

'But you can be merciful!' Najoud had cried out. 'Please, please be merciful!'

'Oh but I am, Najoud. I forgive you. But the punishment was for lying in the Name of God,' he had said gravely, 'not punishment for lying about my sister and me, causing us years of grief, losing us our father's love. Of course we forgive you that, don't we, Azadeh?'

'Yes, yes, that is forgiven.'

'That is forgiven openly. But lying in the Name of God? The Khan made a decree. I cannot go against it.'

Mahmud burst out over her pleadings, 'I knew nothing about this, Highness, nothing, I swear before God, I believed her lies. I divorce her formally for being a traitor to you, I never knew anything about her lies!'

In the Great Room everyone watched them both grovel, some loathing them, some despising them for failing when they had had the power. 'At dawn, Mahmud, you are banished, you and your family,' he had said so sadly, 'penniless, under guard. . . pending my pleasure. As to divorce it is forbidden in my house. If you wish to do that north of Meshed . . . Insha'Allah. You are still banished there, pending my pleasure . . .'

Oh you were perfect, Hakim, he told himself delightedly, for of course everyone knew this was your first test. You were perfect! Never once did you gloat openly or reveal your true purpose, never once did you raise your voice, keeping calm and gentle and grave as though you really were sad with your father's sentence but, rightly, unable to overrule it. And the benign, sweet promise of 'pending my pleasure'? My pleasure's that you're all banished for ever and if I hear one tiny threat of a plot, I will snuff you all out as quickly as an old candle. By God and the Prophet, on whose Name be Praise, I'll make the ghost of my father proud of this Khan of all the Gorgons – may he be in hell for believing such wanton lies of an evil old hag.

So much to thank God for, he thought, mesmerised by the firelight flickering in the Koran's jewels. Didn't all the years of banishment teach you secretiveness, deception and patience? Now you've your power to cement, Azerbaijan to defend, a world to conquer, wives to find, sons to breed and a lineage to begin. May Najoud and her whelps rot!

At dawn he had 'regretfully' gone with Ahmed to witness their departure. Wistfully he had insisted that none of the rest of the family see them off. 'Why increase their sorrow and mine?' There, on his exact instructions, he had watched Ahmed and guards tear through their mountains of bags, removing anything of value until there was but one suitcase each for them and their three children who watched, petrified.

'Your jewellery, woman,' Ahmed had said.

'You've taken everything, everything . . . please, Hakim . . . Highness, please . . .' Najoud sobbed. Her special jewel satchel, secreted in a pocket of her suitcase, had already been added to the pile of valuables. Abruptly Ahmed reached out and ripped off her pendant and tore the neck of her dress open. A dozen necklaces weighed her down, diamonds, rubies, emeralds and sapphires.

'Where did you get these?' Hakim had said, astonished.

'They're . . . they're my . . . my mother's and mine I bought over the ye – ' Najoud stopped as Ahmed's knife came out. 'All right . . . all right . . .' Frantically she pulled the necklaces over her head, unfastened the rest and gave them to him. 'Now you have everyth – '

'Your rings!'

'But Highness leave me someth – ' She screamed as Ahmed impatiently grabbed a finger to cut it off with the ring still on it, but she pulled away, tore the rings off and also the bracelets secreted up her sleeve, howling with grief, and threw them on the floor. 'Now you've everything. . . .'

'Now pick them up and hand them to His Highness, on your knees!' Ahmed hissed and when she did not obey instantly, he grabbed her by the hair and shoved her face on the floor, and now she was grovelling and obeying.

Ah, that was a feast, Hakim thought, reliving every second of their humiliation. After they're dead, God will burn them.

He made another obeisance, put God away until next prayer at noon and jumped up, brimming with energy. A maid was on her knees pouring the coffee, and he saw the fear in her eyes and was very pleased. The moment he became Khan, he had known it was vital to work quickly to take over the reins of power. Yesterday morning he had inspected the palace. The kitchen was not clean enough for him, so he had had the chef beaten senseless and put outside the walls, then promoted the second chef in his place with dire warnings. Four guards were banished for oversleeping, two maids whipped for slovenliness. 'But, Hakim, my darling,' Azadeh had said when they were alone, 'surely there was no need to beat them?'

'In a day or two there won't be,' he had told her. 'Meanwhile the palace *will* change to the way I want it.'

'Of course you know best, my darling. What about the ransom?'

'Ah yes, at once.' He had sent for Ahmed.

'I regret, Highness, the Khan your father ordered the messenger's throat cut yesterday afternoon.'

Both he and Azadeh had been appalled. 'But that's terrible! What can be done now?' she had cried out.

Ahmed said, 'I will try to contact the tribesmen – perhaps, because now the Khan your father is dead they will . . . they will treat with you newly. I will try.'

Sitting there in the Khan's place, Hakim had seen Ahmed's suave confidence and realised the trap he was in. Fear swept up from his bowels. His fingers were toying with the emerald ring on his finger. 'Azadeh, come back in half an hour, please.'

'Of course,' she said obediently and when he was alone with Ahmed, he said, 'What arms do you carry?'

'A knife and an automatic, Highness.'

'Give them to me.' He remembered how his heart had throbbed and there was an unusual dryness in his mouth but this had had to be done and done alone. Ahmed had hesitated then obeyed, clearly not pleased to be disarmed. But Hakim had pretended not to notice, just examined the action of the gun and cocked it thoughtfully. 'Now listen carefully, Counsellor: you won't *try* to contact the tribesmen, you will do it very quickly and you will make arrangements to have my sister's husband returned safely – on your head, by God and the Prophet of God!'

'I – of course, Highness.' Ahmed tried to keep the anger off his face.

Lazily Hakim pointed the gun at his head, sighting down it. 'I swore by God to treat you as first counsellor and I will – while you live.' His smile twisted. 'Even if you happen to be crippled, perhaps emasculated, even blinded by your enemies. Do you have enemies, Ahmed Dursak the Turkoman?'

Ahmed laughed, at ease now, pleased with the *man* who had become Khan and not the whelp that he had imagined – so much easier to deal with a man, he thought, his confidence returning. 'Many, Highness, many. Isn't it custom to measure the quality of a man by the importance of his enemies? Insha'Allah! I didn't know you knew how to handle guns.'

'There are many things you don't know about me, Ahmed,' he had said with grim satisfaction, an important victory gained. He had handed him back the knife, but not the automatic. 'I'll keep this as pishkesh. For a year and a day don't come into my presence armed.'

'Then how can I protect you, Highness?'

'With wisdom.' He had allowed a small measure of the violence he had kept pent up for years to show. 'You have to prove yourself. To me. To me alone. What pleased my father won't necessarily please me. This is a new era, with new opportunities, new dangers. Remember, by God, the blood of my father rests easily in my veins.'

The remainder of the day and well into the evening he had received men of importance from Tabriz and Azerbaijan and asked questions of them, about the insurrection and the leftists, the mujhadin and fedayeen and other factions. Bazaaris had arrived and mullahs and two ayatollahs, local army commanders and his cousin, the chief of police, and he had confirmed the man's appointment. All of them had brought suitable pishkesh.

And so they should, he thought, very satisfied, remembering their contempt in the past when his fortune had been zero and his banishment to Khvoy common knowledge. Their contempt will be very costly to every last one.

'Your bath is ready, Highness, and Ahmed's waiting outside.'

'Bring him in, Ishtar. You stay.' He watched the door open. Ahmed was tired and crumpled.

'Salaam, Highness.'

'What about the ransom?'

'Late last night I found the tribesmen. There were two of them. I explained that Abdollah Khan was dead and the new Khan had ordered me to give them half the ransom asked at once as a measure of faith, promising them the remainder when the pilot is safely back. I sent them north in one of our cars with a trusted driver and another car to follow secretly.'

'Do you know who they are, where their village is?'

'They told me they were Kurds, one named Ishmud, the other Alilah, their chief al-Drah and their village was called Broken Tree in the mountains north of Khvoy – I'm sure all lies, Highness, and they're not Kurds though they claim to be. I'd say they were just tribesmen, bandits mostly.'

'Good. Where did you get the money to pay them?'

'The Khan, your father, put twenty million rials into my safekeeping against emergencies.'

'Bring the balance to me before sunset.'

'Yes, Highness.'

'Are you armed?'

Ahmed was startled. 'Only with my knife, Highness.'

'Give it to me,' he said, hiding his pleasure that Ahmed had fallen into the trap he had set for him, accepting the knife, hilt first. 'Didn't I tell you not to come into my presence armed for a year and a day?'

'But as . . . you gave my knife back to me I thought . . . I thought the knife. . .' Ahmed stopped, seeing Hakim standing in front of him, knife held correctly, eyes dark and hard and the pattern of the father. Behind him, the guard Ishtar watched open-mouthed. The hackles on Ahmed's neck twisted. 'Please excuse me, Highness, I thought I had your permission,' he said in real fear.

For a moment Hakim Khan just stared at Ahmed, the knife poised in his hand, then he slashed upwards. With great skill only the point of the blade went through Ahmed's coat, touched the skin but only enough to score it then came out again in perfect position for the final blow. But Hakim did not make it, though he wanted to see blood flow and this a good time, but not the perfect time. He still had need of Ahmed.

'I give you back your . . . your body.' He chose the word and all it implied with great deliberation. 'Intact, just this once.'

'Yes, Highness, thank you, Highness,' Ahmed muttered, astonished that he was still alive, and went down on his knees. 'I . . . it will never happen again.'

'No, it won't. Stay there. Wait outside, Ishtar.' Hakim Khan sat back on the cushions and toyed with the knife, waiting for the adrenalin to subside, remembering that vengeance was a dish best eaten cold. 'Tell me everything you know about the Soviet, this man called Mzytryk: what holds he had over my father, my father over him.'

Ahmed obeyed. He told him all the Khan had told him in secret over the years, about the dacha near Tbilisi that he too had visited, how the Khan contacted Mzytryk, their code words, what Hashemi Fazir had said and threatened, what was in Mzytryk's letter, what he had overheard and what he had witnessed a few days ago.

The air hissed out of Hakim's mouth. 'My father was going to take my sister to . . . he was going to take her to this dacha and give her to Mzytryk?'

'Yes, Highness, he even ordered me to send her north if . . . if he had to leave for hospital in Tehran.'

'Send for Mzytryk. Urgently. Ahmed, do it now. At once.'

'Yes Highness,' Ahmed said and trembled at the contained violence. 'Best, at the same time, best to remind him of his promises to Abdollah Khan, that you expect them fulfilled.'

'Good, very good. You've told me everything?'

'Everything I can remember now,' Ahmed told him sincerely. 'There must be other things – in time I can tell you all manner of secrets, Khan of all the Gorgons, and I swear again before God to serve you faithfully.' I'll tell you everything, he thought fervently, except the manner of the Khan's death and that now, more than ever, I want Azadeh as wife. Some way I will make you agree – she'll be my only real protection against you, spawn of Satan!

Just Outside Tabriz: 7:20 A.M. Erikki's 212 came over the rise of the forest, inbound at max revs. All the way Erikki had been at treetop level, avoiding roads and airfields and towns and villages, his mind riveted on Azadeh and vengeance against Abdollah Khan, all else forgotten. Now, suddenly ahead, the city was rushing towards them. As suddenly a vast unease washed over him.

'Where's the palace, pilot?' Sheik Bayazid shouted gleefully, 'where is it?'

'Over the ridge, agha,' he said into the boom mike, part of him wanting to add, We'd better rethink this, decide if the attack's wise, the other part shouting This's the only chance you've got, Erikki, you can't change plans, but how in the hell're you going escape with Azadeh from the palace and from this bunch of maniacs? 'Tell your men to fasten their seat belts, to wait until the skids touch down, not to take off their safety catches until they're on the ground and spread out, tell two of them to guard the chopper and protect it with their lives. I'll count down from "ten" for the landing and . . . and I'll lead.'

'Where's the palace, I can't see it.'

'Over the ridge, a minute away – tell them!' The trees were blurring as he went closer to them, his eyes on the col in the mountain ridge, horizon twisting. 'I want a gun,' he said, sick with anticipation.

Bayazid bared his teeth. 'No gun until we possess the palace.'

'Then I won't need one,' he said with a curse. 'I've got to ha – '

'You can trust me, you have to. Where's this palace of the Gorgons?'

'There!' Erikki pointed to the ridge just above them, 'Ten . . . nine . . . eight . . .'

He had decided to come in from the east, partially covered by the forests, city well to his right, the col protecting him. Fifty yards to go. His stomach tightened.

The rocks hurtled at them. He felt more than saw Bayazid cry out and hold up his hands to protect himself against the inevitable crash, then Erikki slid through the col and swung down, straight for the walls. At the exact last moment he cut all power, hauled the chopper up over the wall with inches to spare, flaring into an emergency stop procedure, banked slightly for the forecourt and let her fall out of the air, cushioned the fall perfectly and set down on the tiles to skid forward a few yards with a screech, then stop. His right hand jerked the circuit breakers out, his left unsnapped the seat belt and shoved the door open and he was still easily first on the ground and rushing for the front steps. Behind him Bayazid was now following, the cabin doors open and men pouring out, falling over one another in their excitement, the rotor still turning but the engines dying.

As he reached the front door and swung it open, servants and an astonished guard came running up to see what all the commotion was about. Erikki tore the assault rifle out of his hands, knocked him unconscious. The servants scattered and fled, a few recognising him. For the moment the corridor ahead was clear. 'Come on!' he shouted, then as Bayazid and some of the others joined him, rushed down the hallway and up the staircase towards the landing. A guard poked his head over the banister, levelled his gun but tribesmen peppered him. Erikki jumped over the body and rushed the corridor.

A door opened ahead. Another guard came out, gun blazing. Erikki felt bullets slice through his parka but he was untouched, Bayazid blew the man against the doorjamb, and together they charged past towards the Khan's room. Once there Erikki kicked the door open. Sustained gunfire came at him, missed him and the Sheik but caught the man next to him and spun the man around. The others scattered for cover and the badly hurt tribesman went forward towards the tormentor, taking more bullets and more but firing back even after he was dead.

For a second or two there was a respite, then to Erikki's shock Bayazid pulled the pin out of a grenade and tossed it through the doorway. The explosion was huge. Smoke billowed out into the corridor. At once Bayazid leaped through the opening, gun levelled, Erikki beside him.

The room was wrecked, windows blown out, curtains ripped, the carpet bed torn apart, the remains of the guard crumpled against a wall. In the alcove at the far end of the huge room, half-covered from the main bedroom, the table was upended, a serving-maid moaning, and two inert bodies half buried under tablecloth and smashed dishes. Erikki's heart stopped as he recognised Azadeh. In panic he rushed over and shoved the debris off her – in passing noticed the other person was Hakim – lifted her into his arms, her hair flowing, and carried her into the light. His breathing did not start again until he was sure she was still alive – unconscious, only God knew how damaged, but alive. She wore a long blue cashmere peignoir that hid all of her, but promised everything. The tribesmen pouring into the room were swept by her beauty. Erikki took off his flight jacket and wrapped it around her, oblivious of them. 'Azadeh . . . Azadeh . . .'

'Who this, Pilot?'

Through his fog Erikki saw Bayazid was beside the wreckage. "That's Hakim, my wife's brother. Is he dead?'

'No.' Bayazid looked around furiously. Nowhere else for the Khan to hide. His men were crowding through the doorway and he cursed them, ordering them to take up defensive positions at either end of the corridor and for others to go outside on to the wide patio and to guard that too. Then he scrambled over to Erikki and Azadeh and looked at her bloodless face and breasts and legs pressing against the cashmere, 'Your wife?'

'Yes.'

'She's not dead, good.'

'Yes, but only God knows if she's hurt. I've got to get a doctor . . .'

'Later, first we ha – '

'Now! She may die!'

'As God wants, Pilot,' Bayazid said, then shouted angrily, 'You said you knew everything, where the Khan would be, in the Name of God where is he?'

'These . . . these were his private quarters, agha, private, I've never seen anyone else here, heard of anyone else here, even his wife could only come here by invitation an – ' A burst of firing outside stopped Erikki. 'He's got to be here if Azadeh and Hakim are here!'

'Where? Where can he hide?'

In turmoil Erikki looked around, settled Azadeh as best he could then rushed for the windows – they were barred, the Khan could not have escaped this way. From here, a defensible corner abutment of the palace, he could not see the forecourt or the chopper, only the best view of the gardens and orchards southward, past the walls to the city a mile or so distant below. No other guards threatening them yet. As he turned, his peripheral vision caught a movement from the alcove, he saw the automatic, shoved Bayazid out of the way of the bullet that would have killed him and lunged for Hakim who lay in the debris. Before other tribesmen could react he had the young man pinioned, the automatic out of his hand and was shouting at him, trying to get him to understand, 'You're safe, Hakim, it's me, Erikki, we're friends, we came to rescue you and Azadeh from the Khan . . . we came to rescue you!'

'Rescue me . . . rescue me from what?' Hakim was staring at him blankly, still numb, still dazed, blood seeping from a small wound in his head. 'Rescue?'

'From the Khan an – ' Erikki saw terror come into the eyes, whirled and caught the butt of Bayazid's assault rifle just in time. 'Wait, agha, wait, it's not his fault, he's dazed . . . wait, he was . . . he was aiming at me not you, he'll help us. Wait!'

'Where's Abdollah Khan?' Bayazid shouted, his men beside him now, guns cocked and ready to kill. 'Hurry and tell me or you're both dead men!'

And when Hakim didn't answer at once, Erikki snarled, 'For God's sake, Hakim, tell him where he is or we're all dead.'

'Abdollah Khan's dead, he's dead . . . he died last night, no . . . the night before last. He died the night before last, near midnight . . .' Hakim said weakly and they stared at him with disbelief, his mind coming back slowly and he still could not understand why he was lying here, head pounding, legs numb, Erikki holding him when Erikki was kidnapped by tribesmen, when he was having breakfast with Azadeh, then guns exploding and diving for cover, guards firing and then the explosion and half the ransom's already been paid.

Abruptly his mind cleared. 'In God's Name,' he gasped. He tried to get up and failed. 'Erikki, in God's Name why did you fight in here, half your ransom's been paid . . . why?'

Erikki got up angrily. 'There's no ransom, the messenger's throat was cut, Abdollah Khan had the man's throat cut!'

'But the ransom – half was paid, Ahmed did it last night!'

'Paid, paid to whom?' Bayazid snarled. 'What lies are these?'

'Not lies, half was paid last night, half paid by the new Khan as . . . as an act of faith for the . . . the mistake about the messenger. Before God, I swear it. Half's paid!'

'Lies,' Bayazid scoffed, and aimed the gun at him. 'Where's the Khan?'

'Not lies! Should I lie before God? I tell you before God! Before God! Send for Ahmed, send for the man Ahmed, he paid them.'

One of the tribesmen shouted something, Hakim blanched and repeated in Turkish: 'In the Name of God, half the ransom's already paid! Abdollah

Khan's dead! He's dead and half the ransom was paid.' A murmur of astonishment went through the room. 'Send for Ahmed, he'll tell you the truth. Why are you fighting here, there's no reason to fight!'

Erikki rushed in: 'If Abdollah Khan's dead and half's been paid, agha, the other half promised, your honour's vindicated. Agha, please do as Hakim asks, send for Ahmed – he'll tell you who he paid and how.'

Fear in the room was very high now, Bayazid and his men hating the closeness here, wanting to be in the open, in the mountains, away from these evil people and place, feeling betrayed. But if Abdollah's dead and half's paid . . . 'Pilot, go and get his man Ahmed,' Bayazid said, 'and remember, if you cheat me, you will find your wife noseless.' He ripped the automatic out of Erikki's hand. 'Go and get him!'

'Yes, yes of course.'

'Erikki . . . first help me up,' Hakim said, his voice throaty and weak. Erikki was helplessly trying to make sense of all this as he lifted him easily and pushed through the men crowding near, and settled him on the sofa cushions beside Azadeh. Both saw her pallid face, but both also noticed her regular breathing. 'God be thanked,' Hakim muttered.

Then once more Erikki was half in nightmare, walking out of the room unarmed to the head of the stairs, shouting for Ahmed not to shoot, 'Ahmed, Ahmed, I've got to talk to you, I'm alone . . .'

Now he was downstairs and still alone, still no firing. Again he shouted for Ahmed but his words just echoed off the walls and he wandered into rooms, no one around, everyone vanished and then a gun was in his face, another in his back. Ahmed and a guard, both nervous.

'Ahmed, quick,' he burst out, 'is it true that Abdollah's dead and there's a new Khan and that half the ransom's paid?'

Ahmed just gaped at him.

'For Christ sake is it true?' he snarled.

'Yes, yes that's true. But th – '

'Quick, you've got to tell them!' Relief flooding over him for he had only half believed Hakim. 'Quick, they'll kill him and kill Azadeh – come on!'

'Then the . . . they're not dead?'

'No, of course not, come on!'

'Wait! What exactly did th . . . did His Highness say?'

'What the hell difference do – '

The gun jammed into Erikki's face. *'What did he say exactly?'*

Erikki searched his memory and told him as best he could, then added, 'Now for the love of God, come on!'

For Ahmed time stopped. If he went with the Infidel he would probably die, Hakim Khan would die, his sister would die and the Infidel who was responsible for all this trouble would probably escape with his devil tribesmen. But then, he thought, if I could persuade them to let the Khan live and his sister live, persuade them to leave the palace, I would have proved myself beyond all doubt, both to the Khan and to *her* and I can kill the pilot later. Or I can kill him now and escape easily and live –

but only as a fugitive despised by all as one who betrayed his Khan. Insha'Allah!

His face creased into a smile. 'As God wants!' He took out his knife and gave it and his gun to the white-faced guard and walked around Erikki. 'Wait,' Erikki said. 'Tell the guard to send for a doctor. Urgently. Hakim and my wife . . . they may be hurt.'

Ahmed told the man to do it and went along the corridor and into the hall and up the staircase. On the landing tribesmen searched him roughly for arms then escorted him into the Khan's room, crowding after him, shoving him into the vast, empty space – Erikki they held at the door, a knife at his throat – and when Ahmed saw his Khan was truly alive, sitting bleakly on the cushions near Azadeh who was still unconscious, he muttered, 'Praised be to God,' and smiled at him. 'Highness,' he said calmly, 'I've sent for a doctor.' Then he picked out Bayazid.

'I am Ahmed Dursak the Turkoman,' he said proudly, speaking Turkish with great formality. 'In the Name of God: it's true that Abdollah Khan is dead, true that I paid half the ransom – five million rials – last night on the new Khan's behalf to two messengers of the chief al-Drah of the village of Broken Tree as an act of faith because of the unwarranted dishonour to your messenger ordered by the dead Abdollah Khan. Their names were Ishmud and Alilah and I hurried them north in a fine car.' A murmur of astonishment went through the room. There could be no mistake for all knew these false names, code names, given to protect the village and the tribe. 'I told them, on behalf of the new Khan, the second half would be paid the moment the pilot and his air machine were released safely.'

'Where is this new Khan, if he exists?' Bayazid scoffed. 'Let him talk for himself.'

'I am Khan of all the Gorgons,' Hakim said and there was a sudden silence. 'Hakim Khan, eldest son of Abdollah Khan.'

All eyes left him and went to Bayazid who noticed the blank astonishment on Erikki's face. He scowled, unsure. 'Just because you say it doesn't mean th – '

'You call me a liar in my own house?'

'I only say to this man,' Bayazid jerked a thumb at Ahmed, 'just because he says he paid the ransom, half of it, does not mean he paid it and did not then have them ambushed and killed – like my other messenger, by God!'

Ahmed said venomously, 'I told you the truth before God, and say again before God that I sent them north, safely with the money. Give me a knife, you take a knife, and I will show you what a Turkoman does to a man who calls him liar!' The tribesmen were horrified that their leader had put himself into such a bad position. 'You call me a liar and my Khan liar?'

In the silence Azadeh stirred and moaned, distracting them. At once Erikki began to go to her but the knife never wavered, the tribesman muttered a curse and he stopped. Another little moaning sigh that almost drove him mad, then he saw Hakim awkwardly move closer to his sister and hold her hand and this helped him a little.

Hakim was afraid, aching everywhere, knowing he was as defenceless as she was defenceless and needing a doctor urgently, that Ahmed was under siege, Erikki impotent, his own life threatened and his Khanate in ruins. Nonetheless he gathered his courage back. I didn't outfox Abdollah Khan and Najoud and Ahmed to concede victory to these dogs! Implacably he looked up at Bayazid. 'Well? Do you call Ahmed a liar – yes or no?' he said harshly in Turkish so all could understand him and Ahmed loved him for his courage. All eyes now on Bayazid. 'A *man* must answer that question. Do you call him a liar?'

'No,' Bayazid muttered. 'He spoke the truth, I accept it as truth.' Someone said, 'Insha'Allah,' fingers loosened off triggers but nervousness did not leave the room.

'As God wants,' Hakim said, his relief hidden, and rushed onward, every moment more in command. 'More fighting will achieve nothing. So, half the ransom is already paid and the other half promised when the pilot is released safely. The . . .' He stopped as nausea threatened to overwhelm him but dominated it, easier this time than before. 'The pilot's there and safe and so is his machine. Therefore I will pay the rest at once!'

He saw the greed and promised himself vengeance on all of them. 'Ahmed, over by the table, Najoud's satchel's somewhere there.' He watched Ahmed shove through the tribesmen arrogantly, to begin searching the debris for the soft leather purse he had been showing to Azadeh just before the attack began, happily telling her the jewels were family heirlooms that Najoud had admitted stealing and, in complete contrition, had given him before she left. 'I'm glad you didn't relent, Hakim, very glad,' Azadeh had said. 'You'd never be safe with her and her brood close to you.'

I'll never be safe again, he thought without fear, concentrating on Ahmed. I'm glad I left Ahmed whole, he thought, and glad we had the sense, Azadeh and I, to stay in the alcove under cover of the wall at the first sound of firing. If we'd been here in the room . . . Insha'Allah. His fingers gripped her wrist and the warmth pleased him, her breathing still regular. 'God be praised,' he murmured then noticed the men threatening Erikki. 'You,' he pointed imperiously at them, 'let the pilot go!' Nonplussed the rough, bearded men looked at Bayazid who nodded. At once Erikki went through them to Azadeh, eased his heavy sweater away to give him readier access to the knife in the centre of his back, then knelt, holding her hand, and faced Bayazid, his bulk protecting her and Hakim.

'Highness!' Ahmed gave Hakim Khan the purse. Leisurely he opened it, spilling the jewels into his hands. Emeralds and diamonds and sapphires, necklaces, encrusted golden bracelets, pendants. A great sigh went through the room. Judiciously Hakim chose a ruby necklace worth ten to fifteen million rials, pretending not to notice how all eyes were concentrated and the almost physical smell of greed that permeated the room. Abruptly he discarded the rubies and chose a pendant worth twice as much, three times as much.

'Here,' he said still speaking Turkish, 'here is full payment.' He held up the diamond pendant and offered it to Bayazid who, mesmerised by the fire glittering from the single stone, came forward, his hand out. But before Bayazid could take it, Hakim closed his fist. 'Before God you accept it as full payment?'

'Yes . . . yes, as full payment, before God,' Bayazid muttered, never believing that God would grant him so much wealth – enough to buy herds and guns and grenades and silks and warm clothes. He held out his hand, 'I swear it before God!'

'And you will leave here at once, in peace, before God?'

Bayazid pulled his brain off his riches. 'First we have to get to our village, agha, we need the airplane and the pilot.'

'No, by God, the ransom's for the safe return of the airplane and the pilot, nothing more.' Hakim opened his hand, never taking his eyes off Bayazid who now only saw the stone. 'Before God?'

Bayazid and his men stared at the liquid fire in the rock steady hand. 'What's . . . what's to prevent me taking all of them, everything,' he said sullenly, 'what's to prevent me killing you – killing you and burning the palace and taking her hostage to force the pilot, eh?'

'Nothing. Except honour. Are Kurds without honour?' Hakim's voice rasped and he was thinking, how exciting this is, life the prize and death for failure. 'This is more than full payment.'

'I . . . I accept it before God as payment in full, for the pilot and the . . . and the airplane.' Bayazid tore his eyes off the gem. 'For the pilot and the airplane. But for you, you and the woman . . .' The sweat was trickling down his face. So much wealth there, his mind was shouting, so much, so easy to take, so easy but there is honour in this, oh yes, very much. 'For you and the woman there should be a fair ransom too.'

Outside a car gunned its engine. Men rushed to the broken window. The car was racing for the main gate and as they watched, it hurtled through, heading for the city below.

'Quick,' Bayazid said to Hakim, 'make up your mind.'

'The woman is worthless,' Hakim said, afraid of the lie, aware that he had to bargain or they were still lost. His fingers chose a ruby bracelet and offered it. 'Agreed?'

'To you the woman may be worthless – not to the pilot. The bracelet and the necklace, that one, together with the bracelet with the green stones.'

'Before God that's too much,' Hakim exploded, 'this bracelet's more than enough – that's more than the value of the pilot and the airplane!'

'Son of a burnt father! This one, the necklace and that other bracelet, the one with the green stones!'

They haggled back and forth, angrier and angrier, everyone listening intently except Erikki who was still locked in his own private hell, only concerned with Azadeh and where was the doctor and how he could help her and help Hakim. His hand was stroking her hair, his nerves pushed near the breaking point by the enraged voices of the two men as they reached the crescendo, the insults even more violent. Then Hakim judged the moment right and let out a wail that was also part of the game of bargaining. 'You're too good a negotiator for me, by God! You'll beggar me! Here, my final offer!' He put the diamond bracelet and the smaller of the emerald necklaces and the heavy gold bracelet on to the carpet. 'Do we agree?'

It was a fair price now, not as much as Bayazid wanted but far more than he had expected. 'Yes,' he said and scooped up his prize and contentment filled the room. 'You swear by God not to pursue us? Not to attack us?'

'Yes, yes, before God.'

'Good. Pilot, I need you to take us home . . .' Bayazid said in English now and saw the rage soar into Hakim's face and added hastily, 'I ask, not order, agha. Here,' he offered Erikki the gold bracelet, 'I wish to hire your services, this's paym – ' He stopped and looked up as one of his men guarding the patio, called out urgently, 'There's a car coming up from the city!'

Bayazid was sweating more now. 'Pilot, I swear by God I'll not harm you.'

'There's not enough gasoline.'

'Then not all the way, halfway, just halfw – '

'There's not enough gasoline.'

'Then take us and drop us in the mountains – just a little way. I ask you – not order,' Bayazid said, then added curiously, 'By the Prophet I treated you fairly and him fairly and . . . have not molested her. I ask you.'

They had all heard the threat under the voice, perhaps a threat, perhaps not, but Erikki knew beyond any doubt that the fragile bubble of 'honour' or 'before God' would vanish with the first bullet, that it was up to him now to try to correct the disaster that the attack had become, chasing a Khan already dead, the ransom already half paid, and now Azadeh lying there, hurt as only God knows, and Hakim almost killed. Set-faced he touched her a last time, glanced at the Khan, nodded, half to himself, then got up, abruptly jerked the Sten gun out of the nearest tribesman's hands. 'I'll accept your word before God and I'll kill you if you cheat. I'll drop you north of the city, in the mountains. Everyone in the chopper. Tell them!'

Bayazid hated the idea of the gun in the hands of this brooding, revenge-seeking monster. Neither of us has forgotten I threw the grenade that perhaps has killed this Houri, he thought. 'Insha'Allah!' Quickly he ordered the retreat. Taking the body of their dead comrade with them, they obeyed. 'Pilot, we will leave together. Thank you, Agha Hakim Khan. God be with you,' he said and backed to the door, weapon held loosely, but ready. 'Come on!'

Erikki raised his hand in farewell to Hakim, consumed with anguish at what he has precipitated. 'Sorry . . .'

'God be with you, Erikki, and come back safely,' Hakim called out and Erikki felt better for that. 'Ahmed, go with him, he can't fly and use a gun at the same time. See that he gets back safely.' Yes, he thought, icily, I've still a score to settle with him for the attack on *my* palace!

'Yes, Highness. Thank you, Pilot.' Ahmed took the gun from Erikki, checked the action and magazine, then smiled crookedly at Bayazid. 'By God and the Prophet, on whose Name be Praise, let no man cheat.' Politely he motioned Erikki to leave, then followed him. Bayazid went last.

At the Foothills to the Palace: 11:05 A.M. The police car was racing up the winding road towards the gates, other cars and an army lorry filled with troops following. Hashemi Fazir in the back of the lead car which skidded through the gate into the forecourt where an ambulance and other cars were already parked. Hakim Khan was waiting for him in his place of honour, pale and drawn but regal, guards around him, this part of the palace undamaged.

'Highness, God be praised you were not hurt – we've just heard about the attack. May I introduce myself? I'm Colonel Hashemi Fazir of Inner Intelligence. Would you please tell me what happened?' Hakim Khan related his version of the attack.

'Highness, how long ago did the pilot leave?'

Hakim glanced at his watch. 'About two and a half hours ago.'

'Did he say how much fuel he had with him?'

'No, only that he would take them a little way and drop them.'

Hashemi was standing in front of the raised platform with its rich carpets and cushions, Hakim Khan dressed formally in warm brocades, a string of pearls around his neck with a diamond pendant four times the size of the one he had bartered their lives for. 'They weren't Kurds though they claimed to be, just bandits, and they'd kidnapped Erikki and forced him to lead them against the Khan, my father.' The young Khan frowned then said firmly, 'The Khan my father should not have had their messenger killed. He should have bartered the ransom down then paid it – and then had them killed for their impertinence.'

'I will see they are all hunted down.'

'And all my property recovered.'

'Of course. Is there anything, anything at all, I or my department can do for you?' He was watching the young man closely and saw, or thought he saw, a flash of sardonic amusement and it rattled him. At that moment the door opened and Azadeh came in.

She was dressed in Western clothes, grey green that set off her green-flecked eyes, stockings and soft shoes – her face very pale and made up just enough. Her walk was slow and somewhat painful, but she bowed to her brother with a sweet smile, 'Sorry to interrupt you, Highness, but the doctor asked me to remind you to rest. He's about to leave, would you like to see him again?'

'No, no thank you. You're all right?'

'Oh, yes,' she said and forced a smile. 'He says I'm fine.'

'May I present Colonel Hashemi Fazir – Her Highness, my sister, Azadeh.'

'I was so relieved that neither you or the Khan were hurt.'

'Thank you,' she said, her ears and head still aching badly and her back giving her problems. The doctor had said, 'We'll have to wait for a few days, Highness, although we will X-ray you both as soon as possible. Best you go to Tehran, both of you, they have better equipment. With an explosion like that . . . you never know, Highness, best to go, I wouldn't like to be responsible . . .'

Azadeh sighed, 'Please excuse me for interrup – ' She stopped abruptly, listening, head slightly on its side. They listened too. Just the wind picking up and a distant car.

'Not yet,' Hakim said kindly.

She tried to smile and murmured, 'As God wants,' then went away.

Hashemi broke the small silence. 'We should leave you too, Highness,' he said deferentially, in Farsi again. 'Perhaps we could come back tomorrow?' He saw the young Khan take his eyes off the door and look at him under his dark eyebrows, the handsome face in repose, fingers toying with the jewelled ornamental dagger at his belt. He must be made of ice, he thought, politely waiting to be dismissed.

But instead Hakim Khan dismissed all his guards, except one he stationed at the door, well out of listening range. 'Now we will speak English. What is it you really want to ask me?' he said softly.

Hashemi sighed, sure that Hakim Khan already knew, and more than sure now that here he had a worthy adversary, or ally. 'Help on two matters, Highness: your influence in Azerbaijan could immeasurably help us to put down hostile elements in rebellion against the state.'

'What's the second?'

He had heard the touch of impatience and it amused him. 'Second is somewhat delicate. It concerns a Soviet called Oleg Petr Mzytryk, an acquaintance of your father, who for some years, from time to time, visited here – as Abdollah Khan visited his dacha in Tbilisi. Whilst Mzytryk posed as a friend of Abdollah Khan and Azerbaijan, in reality he's a very senior KGB officer and very hostile.'

'Ninety-eight out of every hundred Soviets who come to Iran are KGB, therefore enemy, and the other two GRU, therefore enemy. As Khan, my father would have to deal with all manner of enemies' – again a fleeting sardonic smile that Hashemi noted – 'all manner of friends and all those in between. So?'

'We would very much like to interview him.' Hashemi waited for some reaction but there was none and his admiration for the young man increased. 'Before Abdollah Khan died he had agreed to help us. Through him we heard the man intended secretly to come over the border last Saturday and again on Tuesday, but both times he did not appear.'

'How was he entering?'

Hashemi told him, not sure how much Hakim Khan knew, feeling his way with greater caution. 'We believe the man may contact you – if so, would you please let us know? Privately.'

Hakim Khan decided it was time to put this Tehrani enemy in place. Son

of a burnt father, am I so naive I don't know what's going on? 'In return for
what?' he said bluntly.

Hashemi was equally blunt. 'What do you want?'

'First: all senior SAVAK and police officers in Azerbaijan put on suspension at once, pending review – by me – and all future appointments to be
subject to my prior approval.'

Hashemi flushed. Not even Abdollah Khan had ever had this. 'What's
second?' he asked dryly.

Hakim Khan laughed. 'Good, very good, agha. Second will wait until
tomorrow or the next day, so will third and perhaps fourth. But about
your first point, at 10 a.m. tomorrow bring me specific requests how I
could help stop all fighting in Azerbaijan – and how you, personally, if you
had the power, how you would . . .' he thought for a moment, then added,
'how you would make us safe against enemies from without, and safe from
enemies from within.' He frowned. 'How would I have access to the Mzytryk
information?'

'However you want, Highness,' Hashemi said, 'however you want.'

Another small silence. 'I'll consider what y – ' Hakim Khan stopped,
listening. Now they all heard the approaching putt-putt of rotors and the
sound of the jets. Both men started for the tall windows. 'Wait,' Hakim said.
'Please give me a hand.'

Astonished, they helped him stand. 'Thank you,' he said, painfully. 'That's
better. It's my back. In the explosion I must have twisted it.' Hashemi took
some of his weight and between them he hobbled to the tall windows that
overlooked the forecourt.

The 212 was coming in slowly, drifting down to her landing. As she got
closer they recognised Erikki and Ahmed in the front seats but Ahmed was
slumped down, clearly hurt. A few bullet holes in the airframe, a great chunk
of plastic out of a side window. Their concern increased. She settled into a
perfect landing. At once the engines began to die. Now they saw the blood
staining Erikki's white collar and sleeve.

'Christ . . .' Armstrong muttered.

'Agha,' Hakim Khan said urgently to Hashemi, 'see if you can stop the
doctor leaving.' Instantly Hashemi rushed off.

From where they were they could see the front steps. The huge door opened
and Azadeh ran out and stood there a moment, a statue, others gathering
beside her now, guards and servants and some of the family. Erikki opened
his side door and got out awkwardly. Tiredly he went towards her. But his
walk was firm and tall and then she was in his arms.

BOOK THREE

Friday

Chapter 20

Al Shargaz – The Oasis Hotel: 5:37 A.M. Gavallan stood at his window, already dressed, night still heavy except to the east, dawn due soon now. Threads of mist came in from the coast, half a mile away, to vanish quickly in the desert reaches. Sky eerily cloudless to the east, gradually building to thick cover overall. From where he was he could see most of the airfield. Runway lights were on, a small jet already taxiing out, and the smell of kerosene was on the wind that had veered more southerly. A knock on the door. 'Come in! Ah, 'morning, Jean-Luc, 'morning, Charlie.'

''Morning, Andy. If we're to catch our flight it's time to leave,' Pettikin said, his nervousness running the words together. He was due to go to Kuwait, Jean-Luc to Bahrain.

'Yes, best be on your way,' Gavallan was pleased that his voice sounded calm. Pettikin beamed, Jean-Luc muttered *Merde*. 'With your approval, Charlie, I propose pushing the button at 7 a.m. as planned – provided none of the bases pull the plug beforehand. If they do we'll try again tomorrow. Agreed?'

'Agreed. No calls yet?'

'Not yet.'

Pettikin could hardly contain his excitement. 'Well, off we go into the wild blue yonder! Come on, Jean-Luc!'

Jean-Luc's eyebrows soared. '*Mon Dieu*, it's Boy Scouts time!' 'Erikki, Andy. He still doesn't know about "Whirlwind?"'

'No, not actually. But Mac sent him and Azadeh a code message to Tabriz to get out at once, he sent it through Talbot at the embassy a few days ago. They should be well over the border by now into Turkey – Talbot wouldn't fail us. I'm seeing Newbury at the consulate first thing to alert our folk there that Erikki and Azadeh should be expected and to ease things for them. You two had better get going. Call me the moment you land. I'll be in the office from 6 a.m.'

He closed the bedroom door after them. Now it was done. Unless one of the bases aborted.

At Al Shargaz Headquarters: 0659 A.M. Gavallan, his son, Scot, Nogger Lane and Genny were watching the clock. Outside the weather was cheerless, the wind blustering. A British Airways jet took off enhancing their silence. 0700.

'Well, here we go,' Gavallan said and picked up the mike, clicked the transmit button and gave the code: 'This is Sierra One, you read?'

'Check, Sierra One,' came over the loudspeaker as the bases across the Gulf acknowledged in turn.

'This is Sierra One. Our forecast is settled. We expect improving weather but watch out for small whirlwinds. Do you copy?'

"We copy, Sierra One and will watch for whirlwinds,' came the confirm reports, hetrodyning badly.

Now there was only radio static. Gavallan bit his lower lip. It's done, he thought, heart grinding. Nine 212s and their crews are launched, shit or bust.

Silence in the office. Genny put a reassuring hand on his shoulder that he did not notice. They began the long wait.

Later the phone rang and Scot grabbed it. 'S-G Helicopters? Oh hello, Charlie, hang on . . .' He passed the phone to his father. 'From Kuwait . . .'

'Hello, Charlie. All's well?'

'Yes, thanks. I'm at Kuwait airport, phoning from Patrick's office at Guerneys'.' Though the two companies were rivals worldwide, they had very friendly relations. 'What's new?'

'Delta Four, nothing else yet. I'll phone the moment Jean-Luc's checked in from Bahrain – he's with Delarne at Gulf Air de France if you want him. Is Genny with you?'

'No, she went back to the hotel but I'm all set the moment Mac and the others arrive. Funny thing, Andy, the BA rep here, a couple of other guys and Patrick have this crazy idea we're up to something – like pulling all our birds out. Can you imagine?'

Gavallan sighed. 'Don't jump the gun, Charlie, keep to the plan.' This was to keep quiet until the Kowiss choppers were in the Kuwait system, then to trust Patrick. 'I'll phone when I have anything. 'Bye – oh hang on, I almost forgot. You remember Ross, John Ross?'

'Could I ever forget? Why?'

'I heard he's in Kuwait International Hospital. The Consul said he was hurt in Tehran and they evacuated him there. Check on him when you've squared away, will you?'

'Of course, right away, Andy. What's the matter with him?'

'Don't know. Call me if you have any news. 'Bye.' He replaced the phone. Another deep breath. 'The word's out in Kuwait.'

'Christ, if it's out th – ' Scot was interrupted by the phone ringing. 'Hello? Just a moment. It's Mr. Newbury from the Consulate, Dad.'

Gavallan took it. ''Morning, Roger, how're tricks?'

'Oh. Well, I, er, wanted to ask you that. How are things going? Off the record of course.'

'Fine, fine,' Gavallan said noncommittally. 'Will you be in your office all day? I'll drop by, but I'll call before I leave here.'

'Yes, please do, I'll be here until noon. It's a long weekend you know.

Please phone me the moment you, er, hear anything – off the record. The moment. We're rather concerned and, well, we can discuss it when you arrive. 'Bye.'

'Hang on a moment. Did you get word about young Ross?'

'Yes, yes I did. Sorry but we understand he was badly hurt. Damn shame but there you are. See you before noon. 'Bye.'

Gavallan put the phone down. They all watched him. 'Apparently . . . it seems young Ross is badly hurt.'

Nogger muttered, 'What a bugger! My God, not fair . . .' He had told them all about Ross, how he had saved their lives, and Azadeh's.

'Dad, did Newbury tell you what happened?'

Gavallan shook his head, hardly hearing him. He was thinking about Ross, of an age with Scot, more tough and rugged and indestructible than Scot and now . . . Poor laddie! Maybe he'll pull through . . . oh God, I hope so! What to do? Continue, that's all you can do. Azadeh'll be rocked, poor lassie. Erikki'll be as rocked as Azadeh, he owes her life to him. 'I'll be back in a second,' he said and walked out, heading for their other office where he could phone Newbury in private.

Nogger was standing at the window, looking out at the day and the airfield, not seeing any of it. He was seeing the wild-eyed, maniac killer at Tabriz One holding the severed head aloft, baying like a wolf to the sky, the angel of sudden death who became the giver of life – to him, to Arberry, to Dibble, and most of all to Azadeh. God, if you are God, save him like he saved us . . .

'Tehran, this is Bandar-e Delam, do you read?'

'Five minutes on the dot,' Scot muttered. 'Jahan doesn't miss a bloody second. Didn't Siamaki say he'd be in the office from 0900 onwards?'

'Yes, yes he did.' All their eyes went to the clock. It read 8.54.

Chapter 21

At Bahrain Airport: 11:28 A.M. Jean-Luc and Mathias Delarne were standing beside a station wagon near the helipad, watching the incoming 212, shading their eyes against the sun, still unable to recognise the pilot. Mathias was a short, thickset man, with dark wavy hair, half a face, the other half badly burn-scarred when he had bailed out on fire not far from Algiers.

'It's Dubois,' he said.

'No, you're wrong, it's Sandor.' Jean-Luc waved, motioning him to land crosswind. The moment the skids touched, Mathias rushed under the rotors for the left cockpit door – paying no attention to Sandor who was shouting across at him. He carried a large paintbrush and a can of quick drying airplane paint and he slapped the white paint over the Iran registration letters just below the door's window. Jean-Luc used the stencil they had prepared and black paint and his brush, then carefully peeled the stencil off. Now she was G-HXXI and legal.

Meanwhile Mathias had gone to the tail boom and painted out IHC, ducked under the boom to do the same the other side. Sandor just had time to move his arm out of the way of the door as, enthusiastically, Jean-Luc stencilled the second G-HXXI.

'*Voilà!*' Jean-Luc gave his material back to Mathias who went to the station wagon to stash it under a tarpaulin, while Jean-Luc wrung Sandor's hand and told him about Rudi and Kelly and asked about Dubois.

'Don' know, old buddy,' Sandor said. 'I've been on empty, warning lights on, for maybe ten goddam minutes and crapping for twenty. What about the others?'

'Rudi and Kelly landed on Abu Sabh beach – Rod Rodrigues's looking after them – nothing yet on Scrag, Willi, or Vossi, but Mac's still at Kowiss.'

'Jesusss!'

'*Oui*, along with Freddy and Tom Lochart, at least they were, ten or fifteen minutes ago.' Jean-Luc turned to Mathias who came up to them. 'Are you tuned into the tower?'

'Yes, no problem.'

'Mathias Delarne, Sandor – Johnson, our mec.'

They greeted each other and shook hands. 'How was your trip – *merde*, best you don't tell me,' Mathias added, then saw the approaching car. 'Trouble,' he warned.

'Stay in the cockpit, Sandor,' Jean-Luc ordered. 'Johnson, back in the cabin.'

The car was marked 'official' and it stopped broadside to the 212 twenty yards away. Two Bahraini men got out, a uniformed Immigration captain and an officer from the tower, the latter wearing a long-flowing white dishdash and headcloth with a twisted black coil holding it in place. Mathias went to meet them. ''Morning, Sayyid Yusuf, Sayyid Bin Ahmed. This is Captain Sessonne.'

''Morning,' both said politely and continued to study the 212. 'And the pilot?'

'Captain Petrofi. Mr. Johnson, a mechanic, is in the cabin.' Jean-Luc felt sick. The sun was glistening off the new paint but not the old, and the bottom of the 'I' had a dribble of black from each corner. He waited for the inevitable remark and then the inevitable question, 'What was her last point of departure?' and then his airy, 'Basra, Iraq' as the nearest possible. But so simple to check there and no need to check, just walk forward five yards and draw a finger through the new paint to find the permanent letters below. Mathias was equally perturbed. Easy for Jean-Luc, he thought, he doesn't live here, doesn't have to work here.

'How long will G-HXXI be staying, Captain?' the Immigration officer asked. He was a clean-shaven man with sad eyes.

Jean-Luc and Mathias groaned inwardly at the accent on the letters. 'She's due to leave for Al Shargaz at once, Sayyid,' Mathias said, 'for Al Shargaz, at once – the very moment she's refuelled. Also the others who, er, ran out of fuel.'

Bin Ahmed, the tower officer, sighed. 'Very bad planning to run out of fuel. I wonder what happened to the legal 30 minutes of reserve.'

'The, er, the headwind I expect, Sayyid.'

'It is strong today, that's certain.' Bin Ahmed looked out into the Gulf, visibility about a mile. 'One 212 here, two on our beach and the fourth . . . the fourth out there.' The dark eyes came back on to Jean-Luc. 'Perhaps he turned back for . . . for his departure point.'

Jean-Luc gave him his best smile. 'I don't know, Sayyid Bin Ahmed,' he answered carefully.

Once more the two men looked at the chopper. Now the rotor stopped. The blades trembled a little in the wind. Casually Bin Ahmed took out a telex. 'We've just received this from Tehran, Mathias, about some missing helicopters,' he said politely. 'From Iran's Air Traffic Control. It says, *"Urgent Urgent Urgent. To all Gulf States: Please be on the lookout for some of our helicopters that have been exported illegally. Please impound them, arrest those aboard, inform our nearest embassy who will arrange for immediate deportation of the criminals and repatriation of our equipment."'* He smiled again and handed it to him. 'Curious, eh?'

'Very,' Mathias said. He read it, glazed, then handed it back.

'Captain Sessonne, have you been to Iran?'

'Yes, yes I have.'

'Terrible, all those deaths, all the unrest, all the killings, Muslim killing Muslim. Persia's always been different, troublesome to others who live in the Gulf. Claiming our Gulf, the Persian Gulf, as though we, this side, did not exist,' Bin Ahmed said, matter-of-fact. 'Didn't the Shah even claim our island was Iranian just because three centuries ago Persians conquered us for a few years, we who have always been independent?'

'Yes, but he, er, he renounced the claim.'

'Ah, yes, yes, that is true – and occupied the oil islands of Tums and Abu Musa. Very hegemonistic are Persian rulers, very strange, whoever they are, wherever they come from. Sacrilege to plant mullahs and ayatollahs between man and God. Eh?'

'They, er, they have their way of life,' Jean-Luc agreed, 'others have theirs.'

Bin Ahmed glanced into the back of the station wagon. Jean-Luc saw part of the handle of a paintbrush sticking out from under the tarpaulin. 'Dangerous times we're having in the Gulf. Very dangerous. Anti-God Soviets, closer every day from the north, more anti-God Marxists south in Yemen arming every day, all eyes on us and our wealth – and Islam. Only Islam stands between them and world dominance.'

Mathias wanted to say, What about France and of course America? Instead he said, 'Islam'll never fail. Nor will the Gulf States if they're vigilant.'

'With the help of God, I agree.' Bin Ahmed nodded and smiled at Jean-Luc. 'Here on our island we must be very vigilant against all those who wish to cause us trouble. Eh?'

Jean-Luc nodded. He was finding it hard not to look at the telex in the man's hand; if Bahrain had one, the same would have gone to every tower this side of the Gulf.

'With the help of God we will succeed.'

The Immigration officer nodded agreeably. 'Captain, I would like to see the pilot's papers, and the mechanic's. And them. Please.'

'Of course, at once.' Jean-Luc walked over to Sandor. 'Tehran's telexed them to be on the lookout for Iran registereds,' he whispered hastily and Sandor went pasty. 'No need for panic, *mon vieux*, volunteer nothing, you too Johnson, and don't forget you're G-HXXI out of Basra.'

'But Jesus,' Sandor croaked, 'we'd have to've been stamped outta Iraq, and I got Iranian stamps over most every page.'

The Immigration officer took the American passport. Punctiliously he studied the photograph, compared it to Sandor who weakly took off his sunglasses, then handed it back without leafing through the other pages. 'Thank you,' he said and accepted Johnson's British passport. Again the studious look at the photograph only. Bin Ahmed went a pace nearer the chopper. Johnson had left the cabin door open.

'What's aboard?'

'Spares,' Sandor, Johnson and Jean-Luc said together.

'You'll have to clear customs.'

Mathias said politely, 'Of course he *is* in transit, Sayyid Yusuf, and will take off the moment he's refuelled. Perhaps it would be possible to allow him to sign the transit form, guaranteeing he lands nothing and carries no arms or drugs or ammunition.' He hesitated. 'I would guarantee it too, if it was of value.'

'Your presence is always of value, Sayyid Mathias,' Yusuf said. 'I suppose for a British plane in transit, it would be all right, even for the other two on the beach. Eh?'

The tower man turned his back on the chopper. 'Why not? We'll clear them for Al Shargaz as soon as they're refuelled.' Again he looked out to sea and his dark eyes showed his concern. 'And the fourth, when she arrives? What about her – I presume she's also British registered?'

'Yes, yes she is,' Jean-Luc heard himself say, giving him the new registration, saluting the two men with Gallic charm as they left, hardly able to grasp the miracle of the reprieve.

Is it because their eyes were blinded or because they did not wish to see? I don't know, I don't know but blessed be the Madonna for looking after us again.

'Jean-Luc, you'd better phone Gavallan about the telex,' Mathias said.

At Kuwait Airport: 2:56 P.M. Genny and Charlie Pettikin were sitting in the open-air restaurant on the upper level of the sparkling, newly opened terminal. It was a grand, sunny day, sheltered from the wind. Bright yellow tablecloths and umbrellas, everyone eating and drinking with enjoyment and gusto. Except for them. Genny had hardly touched her salad, Pettikin had picked at his rice and curry.

'Charlie,' Genny said abruptly, 'I think I'll have a vodka martini after all.'

'Good idea.' Pettikin waved for a waiter and ordered for her. He would have liked to join her but he was expecting to replace or spell either Lochart or Ayre on the next leg down the coast to Jellet Island – at least one refuelling stop, perhaps two, before reaching Al Shargaz – God curse this sodding wind. 'Won't be long now, Genny.'

Oh, for Christ's sake, how many times do you have to say it, Genny wanted to scream, sick of waiting. Stoically she kept up her pretence of calm. 'Not long, Charlie. Any moment now.' Their eyes went seawards. The distant seascape was hazed, visibility poor, but they would know the instant the choppers came into Kuwait radar range. The Imperial Air rep was waiting in the tower.

How long is long? she asked herself, trying to pierce the heat haze, all her energy pouring out, seeking Duncan, sending prayers and hopes and strengths that he might need. The word that Gavallan had passed on this morning had not helped: 'What on earth's he flying Kia for, Andy? What does that mean?'

'Don't know, Genny. I'm telling you as he said it. Our interpretation is that Freddy was sent to the fuel rendezvous first. Mac took off with Kia – he's either taking him to the rendezvous or he'll put him off en route. Tom's holding the fort for a time to give the others a breathing space, then he'll head for the RV. We got Mac's initial call at ten-forty-two. Give him till eleven a.m. for him and Freddy to take off. Give them another hour to get to the RV and refuel, add two hours thirty flight time, they should arrive Kuwait around two-thirty at the earliest. Depending on how long they wait at the RV it could be anytime, from two-thirty onwards . . .'

She saw the waiter bringing her drink. On the tray was a mobile phone. 'Phone call for you, Captain Pettikin,' the waiter said as he put the glass in front of her. Pettikin pulled out the antenna, held the phone to his ear. 'Hello? Oh, hello, Andy.' She watched his face, 'No . . . no, not yet . . . Oh? . . .' He listened intently for a long time, just an occasional grunt and nod, nothing showing outwardly, and she wondered what Gavallan was saying that she was not supposed to hear. '. . . Yes, sure . . . no . . . yes, everything's covered as far as we can . . . Yes, yes, she is . . . all right, hang on.' He passed the phone over. 'He wants to say hello.'

'Hello, Andy, what's new?'

'Just reporting in, Genny. Not to worry about Mac and the others – no telling how long they had to wait at the RV.'

'I'm fine, Andy. Don't worry about me. What about the others?'

'Rudi, Pop Kelly and Sandor are en route from Bahrain – they refuelled at Abu Dhabi and we're in contact with them – John Hogg's our relay station – their ETA here's in twenty minutes. Johnny Hogg'll be in your area about now and he'll be listening too. We'll keep in touch. Can I speak to Charlie again, please.'

'Of course, but what about Marc Dubois and Fowler?'

A pause. 'Nothing yet. We're hoping they've been picked up – Rudi, Sandor and Pop backtracked and searched as long as they could. No wreckage, there're lots of ships in those waters and platforms. We're sweating them out.'

'Now tell me what Charlie's supposed to know but I'm not.' She scowled into the dead silence on the phone, then heard Gavallan sigh.

'You're one for the book, Genny. All right. I asked Charlie if any telex had arrived from Iran yet, like the one we got here, in Dubai and Bahrain. I'm trying to pull all the strings I can through Newbury and our Kuwaiti embassy in case of a foul-up, though Newbury says not to expect much, Kuwait being so close to Iran and not wanting to offend Khomeini and petrified he'll send or allow a few export fundamentalists to stir up the Kuwaiti Shi'as. I've no contact with Erikki yet.'

'He and Azadeh are sitting ducks to be arrested and held as hostages.'

'Yes. One step at a time. I told Charlie that I'm trying to get word to Ross's parents in Nepal and to his regiment. That's the lot.' In a more kindly voice, 'I didn't want to upset you more than necessary. Okay?'

'Yes, thanks. Yes, I'm . . . I'm fine. Thanks, Andy.' She passed the phone back and looked at her glass. Beads of moisture had formed. Some were trickling. Like the tears on my cheeks, she thought and got up. 'Back in a sec.'

Sadly Pettikin watched her go. He listened to Gavallan's final instructions. 'Yes, yes, of course,' he said. 'Don't worry, Andy I'll take care of . . . I'll take care of Ross, and I'll call the very moment we have them on the screen. Bloody awful about Dubois and Fowler, we'll just have to think good thoughts and hope. Great about the others. 'Bye.'

Finding Ross had shattered him. The moment he had got Gavallan's call this morning he had rushed to the hospital. Today being Friday, with minimum staff, there was just one receptionist on duty and he spoke only Arabic. The man smiled and shrugged and said, '*Bokrah*' – tomorrow. But Pettikin had persisted and eventually the man had understood what he wanted and had made a phone call. At length a male nurse arrived and beckoned him. They went along corridors and then through a door and there was Ross naked on a slab.

It was the suddenness, the totality of nakedness, of seeming defilement, and the obliteration of any shred of dignity that had torn Pettikin apart, not the fact of death. This man who had been so fine in life had been left like a carcass. On another slab were sheets. He took one and covered him and that seemed to make it better.

It had taken Pettikin more than an hour to find the ward where Ross had been, to track down an English-speaking nurse and to find his doctor.

'So very sorry, so very sorry, sir,' the doctor, a Lebanese, had said in halting English. 'The young man arrived yesterday in a coma. He had a fractured skull and we suspected brain damage; it was from a terrorist bomb we were told. Both eardrums were broken and he had a number of minor cuts and bruises. We X-rayed him, of course, but apart from binding his skull there was little we could do but wait. He had no internal damage or haemorrhage. He died this morning with the dawn. The dawn was beautiful today, wasn't it? I signed the death certificate – would you like a copy? We've given one to the English embassy – together with his effects.'

'Did he . . . did he recover consciousness before he died?'

'I do not know. He was in intensive care and his nurse . . . let me see.' Laboriously the doctor had consulted his lists and found her name. 'Sivin Tahollah. Ah, yes. Because he was English we assigned her to him.'

She was an old woman, part of the flotsam of the Middle East, knowing no forebears, part of many nations. Her face was ugly and pockmarked but she was not, her voice gentle and calming, her hands warm. 'He was never conscious, Effendi,' she said in English, 'not truly.'

'Did he say anything particularly, anything you could understand, anything at all?'

'Much that I understood, Effendi, and nothing.' The old woman thought a moment. 'Most of what he said was just mind wanderings, the spirit fearing what should not be feared, wanting that which could not be had. He would murmur "azadeh" – azadeh means "born free" in Farsi though it is also a woman's name. Sometimes he would mutter a name like "Erri" or "Ekki" or "Kukri" and then again "azadeh". His spirit was at peace but not quite though he never wept like some do, or cry out, nearing the threshold.'

'Was there anything more – anything?'

She toyed with the watch she wore on her lapel. 'From time to time his wrists seemed to bother him and when I stroked them he became calm again. In the night he spoke a tongue I have never heard before. I speak English, a little French, and many dialects of Arabic, many. But this tongue I have never heard before. He spoke it in a lilting way, mixed with wanderings and "azadeh", sometimes words like . . .' She searched her memory. 'Like "regiment" and "edelweiss" and "highlands" or "high land", and sometimes, ah, yes, words like "gueng" and "tens'ng", sometimes a name like "Roses" or "Rose mountain" – perhaps it was not a name but just a place but it seemed to sadden him.' Her old eyes were rheumy. 'I've seen much of death, Effendi, very much, always different, always the same. But his passing was peaceful and his going over the threshold without hurt. The last moment was just a great sigh – I think he went to Paradise, if Christians go to Paradise, and found his Azadeh . . .'

Chapter 22

Tabriz – At the Khan's Palace: 3:40 P.M. Azadeh walked slowly along the corridor towards the Great Room where she was meeting her brother, her back still troubling her from the grenade explosion yesterday. God in heaven, was it only yesterday that the tribesmen and Erikki almost killed us? she thought. It seems more like a thousand days, and a light-year since Father died.

It was another lifetime. Nothing good in that lifetime except Mother and Erikki and Hakim, Erikki and . . . and Johnny. A lifetime of hatreds and killings and terrors and madness, madness living like pariahs, Hakim and I, surrounded by evil, madness at the Qazvin roadblock and that vile, fat-faced mujhadin squashed against the car, oozing like a swatted fly, madness of our rescue by Charlie and the KGB man – what was his name, ah yes, Rakoczy – Rakoczy almost killing all of us, madness at Abu Mard that has changed my life for ever, madness at the base where we'd had so many fine times, Erikki and I, but where Johnny killed so many so fast and so cruelly.

She had told Erikki everything last night – almost everything. 'At the base he . . . he became a killing animal. I don't remember much, just flashes, giving him the grenade in the village, watching him rush the base . . . grenades and machine guns, one of the men wearing a kukri, then Johnny holding up his severed head and howling like a banshee . . . I know now the kukri was Gueng's. Johnny told me in Tehran.'

'Don't say any more now, leave the rest until tomorrow, my darling. Go to sleep, you're safe now.'

'No. I'm afraid to sleep, even now in your arms, even with all the glorious news about Hakim, when I sleep I'm back in the village, back at Abu Mard and the mullah's there, cursed of God, the kalandar's there and the butcher's got his carving knife on.'

'There's no more village or mullah, I've been there. No more kalandar nor butcher. Ahmed told me about the village, part of what had happened there.'

'You went to the village?'

'Yes, this afternoon, when you were resting. I took a car and went there. It's a heap of burned rubble. Just as well,' Erikki had said ominously.

In the corridor Azadeh stopped a moment and held on to the wall until the fit of trembling passed. So much death and killing and horror. Yesterday when she had come out on to the steps of the palace and had seen Erikki in the cockpit, blood streaming down his face and into his stubbled beard, more dripping from his sleeve, Ahmed crumpled beside him, she had died and then, seeing him get out and stand tall and walk to her, her own legs useless, and catch her up into his arms, she had come to life again, all her terrors had poured out with her tears. 'Oh, Erikki, oh, Erikki, I've been so afraid, so afraid . . .'

He had carried her into the Great Room and the doctor was there with Hakim, Robert Armstrong and Colonel Hashemi Fazir. A bullet had torn away part of Erikki's left ear, another had scored his forearm. The doctor had cauterised the wounds and bound them up, injecting him with antitetanus serum and penicillin, more afraid of infection than of loss of blood: 'Insha'Allah, but there's not much I can do, Captain, you're strong, your pulse is good, a plastic surgeon can make your ear look better, your hearing's not touched, praised be to God! Just beware of infection . . .'

'What happened, Erikki?' Hakim had asked.

'I flew them north into the mountains and Ahmed was careless – it wasn't his fault, he got airsick – and before we knew what was happening Bayazid had a gun to his head, another tribesman had one to mine and Bayazid said, "Fly to the village, then you can leave."

'"You swore a holy oath you wouldn't harm me!" I said.

'"I swore I wouldn't harm you and I won't, but my oath was mine, not of my men," Bayazid said, and the man with a gun to my head laughed and shouted, "Obey our Sheik or by God you will be so filled with pain you will beg for death."'

'I should have thought of that,' Hakim said with a curse. 'I should have bound them all with the oath. I should have thought of that.'

'It wouldn't have made any difference. Anyway it was all my fault; I'd brought them here and almost ruined everything. I can't tell you how sorry I am but it was the only way to get back and I thought I'd find Abdollah Khan. I never thought that *matyeryebyets* would use a grenade.'

'We're not hurt, through God's will, Azadeh and I. How could you know Abdollah Khan was dead, or that half your ransom was paid? Go on with what happened,' Hakim had said and Azadeh noticed a strangeness under the voice. Hakim's changed, she thought. I can't understand what's in his mind like I used to. Before he became Khan, really Khan, I could but not now. He's still my darling brother but a stranger. So much has changed, so fast. I've changed. So has Erikki, my God how much! Johnny hasn't changed . . .

In the Great Room, Erikki had continued: 'Flying them away was the only way to get them out of the palace without further trouble or killing. If Bayazid hadn't insisted, I would have offered – no other way'd've been safe for you and Azadeh. I had to gamble that somehow they'd obey the oath. But whatever happened, it was them or me, I knew it and so did they, for of course I was the only one who knew who they were and where they lived and a Khan's vengeance is serious. Whatever I did, drop them off halfway or go to the village, they'd never let me go. How could they – it was the village or me and their One God would vote for their village along with them, whatever they'd agreed or sworn!'

'That's a question only God could answer.'

'My gods, the ancient gods, don't like to be used as an excuse, and they don't like this swearing in their name. They disapprove of it greatly, in fact they forbid it.' Azadeh heard the bitterness and touched him gently. He had held her hand. 'I'm fine now, Azadeh.'

'What happened next, Erikki?' Hakim asked.

'I told Bayazid there wasn't enough gasoline and tried to reason with him and he just said, "As God wants," stuck the gun into Ahmed's shoulder and pulled the trigger. "Go to the village! The next bullet goes into his stomach." Ahmed passed out and Bayazid reached over him for the Sten gun that had slipped to the floor of the cockpit, half under the seat, but he couldn't quite get it. I was strapped in, so was Ahmed, they weren't, so I shifted her around the skies in ways I didn't think a chopper could stand, then let her drop out and made a landing. It was a bad one; I thought I'd broken a skid but later I found it was only bent. As soon as we'd stopped I used the Sten and my knife and killed those who were conscious and hostile, disarmed the unconscious ones, and dumped them out of the cabin. Then, after a time, I came back.'

'Just like that, fourteen men.'

'Five, and Bayazid. The others . . .' Azadeh had her arm on his shoulder and she felt the shrug and the following tremor. 'I left them.'

'Where?' Hashemi Fazir had said. 'Could you describe where, Captain?' Erikki had done so, accurately, and the colonel had sent men to find them.

Erikki put his good hand into his pocket and brought out the ransom jewels and gave them to Hakim Khan. 'Now I think I would like to talk to my wife, if it pleases you. I'll tell you the rest later.' Then she and he had gone to their own rooms and he said nothing more, just held her gently in his great embrace. Her presence soothed away his anguish. Soon to sleep. She slept barely at all, at once back in the village to tear herself in panic from its suffocating grasp. She had stayed quiet for a time in his arms, then moved to a chair and half dozed, content to be with him. He had slept dreamlessly until it was dark, then awoke.

'First a bath and then a shave and then some vodka and then we will talk,' he had said, 'I've never seen you more beautiful nor loved you more and I'm sorry, sorry I was jealous – no, Azadeh, don't say anything yet. Then I want to know everything.'

In the dawn she had finished telling all there was to tell – as much as she would ever tell – and he his story. He had hidden nothing, not his jealousy, or the killing rage and the joy of battle or the tears he had shed on the mountainside, seeing the savagery of the mayhem he had dealt to the tribesmen. 'They . . . they did treat me fairly in their village and ransom is an ancient custom. If it hadn't been for Abdollah murdering their messenger. . . that might have made the difference, perhaps, perhaps not. But that doesn't forgive the killings. I feel I'm a monster, you married a madman, Azadeh. I'm dangerous.'

'No, no, you're not, of course you're not.'

'By all my gods, I've killed twenty or more men in half that number of days and yet I've never killed before except those assassins, those men who charged in here to murder your father before we were married. Outside of Iran I've never killed anyone, never hurt anyone – I've had plenty of fights with or without pukoh but never serious. Never. If that kalandar and the village had existed, I would have burned him and them without a second thought. I can understand your Johnny at the base; I thank all gods for bringing him to us to protect you and curse him for taking away my peace though I know I'm in his immortal debt. I can't deal with the killings and I can't deal with him. I can't, I can't, not yet.'

'It doesn't matter, not now, Erikki. Now we've time. Now we're safe, you're safe and I'm safe and Hakim's safe, we're safe, my darling. Look at the dawn, isn't it beautiful? Look, Erikki, it's a new day now, so beautiful, a new life. We're safe, Erikki.'

In the Great Room: 3:45 P.M. Hakim Khan was alone except for Hashemi Fazir. Half an hour ago Hashemi had arrived unbidden. He had apologised for the intrusion, handing him a telex. 'I thought you'd better see this at once, Highness.'

The telex read: 'URGENT. To Colonel Fazir, Inner Intelligence, Tabriz: Arrest Erikki Yokkonen, husband of Her Highness, Azadeh Gorgon, for crimes committed against the State, for complicity in air piracy, hijacking, and high treason. Put him in chains and send him at once to my Headquarters here. Director, SAVAMA, Tehran.'

Hakim Khan dismissed his guards. 'I don't understand, Colonel. Please explain.'

'The moment I'd decoded it, I phoned for further details, Highness. It seems last year S-G Helicopters sold a number of helicopters to IHC an – '

'I don't understand.'

'Sorry, to Iran Helicopters Company, an Iranian company, Captain Yokkonen's present employer. Amongst them were – are – ten 212s including his. Today the other nine, valued at nine million dollars, were stolen and illegally flown out of Iran by IHC pilots – SAVAMA presumes to one of the Gulf states.'

Hakim Khan said coldly, 'Even if they have, this doesn't affect Erikki. He's done nothing wrong.'

'We don't know that for certain, Highness. SAVAMA says perhaps he knew of the conspiracy – it certainly had to have been planned for some time because three bases are involved – Lengeh, Bandar-e Delam, and Kowiss – as well as their Tehran Head Office. SAVAMA are very, very agitated because it's also been reported that vast quantities of valuable Iranian spares have been whisked away. Even mo – '

'Reported by whom?'

'The IHC managing director, Siamaki. Even more serious, all IHC foreign personnel, pilots and mechanics and office staff, have vanished as well.

Everyone, so of course it was a conspiracy. It seems that yesterday there were perhaps twenty of them all over Iran, last week forty, today none. There are no S-G, or more correctly IHC foreigners left in all Iran. Except Captain Yokkonen.'

At once the implication of Erikki's importance leaped into Hakim's mind and he cursed himself for allowing his face to give him away when Hashemi said blithely, 'Ah, yes, of course you see it too! SAVAMA told me that even if the captain is innocent of complicity in the conspiracy, he's the essential means to persuade the ringleaders and criminals, Gavallan and McIver – and certainly the British government must have been party to the treason – to return our airplanes, our spares, to pay an indemnity of very serious proportions, to return to Iran and stand trial for crimes against Islam.'

Hakim Khan shifted uneasily on his cushions, the pain in his back surfacing, and he wanted to shout with rage because all the pain and anguish was unnecessary, and now, hardly able to stand without pain, he might be permanently injured. Put that aside for later, he told himself grimly, and deal with this dangerous son of a dog who sits there patiently like an accomplished salesman of precious carpets who has laid out his wares and now waits for the negotiation to begin. If I want to buy.

To buy Erikki out of the trap I shall have to give this dog a personal pishkesh, of value to him not SAVAMA, God curse them by any name. What? Petr Oleg Mzytryk at least. I could pass him over to Hashemi without a belch if he comes, when he comes. He'll come. Yesterday Ahmed sent for him in my name – I wonder how Ahmed is, did his operation go well? I hope the fool doesn't die; I could use his knowledge for a while more. Fool to be caught off guard, fool! Yes he's a fool but this dog isn't. With the gift of Mzytryk and more help in Azerbaijan, and a promise of future friendship, I can buy Erikki out of the trap. Why should I?

Because Azadeh loves him? Unfortunately she is sister to the Khan of all the Gorgons and this is a khan's problem, not a brother's problem.

Erikki's a hazard to me and to her. He's a dangerous man with blood on his hands. The tribesmen, be they Kurds or not, will seek vengeance – probably. He's always been a bad match though he brought her great joy, still brings her happiness – but no children – and now he cannot stay in Iran. Impossible. No way for him to stay. I couldn't buy him two years of protection and Azadeh's sworn by God to stay here at least two years – how cunning my father was to give me power over her. If I buy Erikki out of the trap she can't go with him. In two years many estrangements could happen by themselves. But if he's no good for her, why buy him out? Why not let them take Erikki to checkmate a treason? It's treason to steal our property.

'This is too serious a matter to answer at once,' he said.

'There is nothing for you to answer, Highness. Only Captain Yokkonen. I understand he's still here.'

'The doctor ordered him to rest.'

'Perhaps you would send for him, Highness.'

'Of course. But a man of your importance and learning would understand there are rules of honour and hospitality in Azerbaijan, and in my tribe. He is my brother-in-law and even SAVAMA understands family honour.' Both men knew this was just an opening gambit in a delicate negotiation – delicate because neither wanted SAVAMA's wrath on their heads, neither knew yet how far to go, or even if a private deal was wanted. 'I presume many know of this . . . this treason?'

'Only me, here in Tabriz, Highness. At the moment,' Hashemi said at once. He could see Hakim Khan's disquiet and was sure he had him trapped. 'I'm sure you'll understand, Highness, but I have to answer this telex quickly.'

Hakim Khan decided on a partial offer. 'Treason and conspiracy should not go unpunished. Anywhere it is to be found. I've sent for the traitor you wanted. Urgently.'

Hashemi saw the young Khan shift painfully and tried to decide whether to delay or to press home his advantage, sure the pain was genuine. The doctor had given him a detailed diagnosis of the Khan's possible injuries and those of his sister. To cover every eventuality he had ordered the doctor to give Erikki some heavy sedation tonight, just in case the man tried to escape. 'There is so much to do in Tabriz, Highness, following your advice of this morning, that I doubt if I could deal with the telex before then.'

'You destroy the leftist mujhadin headquarters tonight?'

'Yes, Highness, now that we have your permission, and your guarantee of no repercussions from the Tudeh. It would be unfortunate if the captain was not available for . . . for questioning this evening.'

Hakim Khan's eyes narrowed at the unnecessary threat. As if I didn't understand, you rude son of a dog. 'I agree.' There was a knock on the door. 'Come in.'

Azadeh opened it. 'Sorry to interrupt, Highness, but you told me to remind you half an hour before it was time to go to the hospital for X-rays. Greetings, peace be with you, Colonel.'

'And God's peace be with you, Highness.' I'm glad such beauty will be forced into chador soon, Hashemi was thinking. She'd tempt Satan, let alone the unwashed illiterate scum of Iran. He looked back at the Khan. 'I should be going, Highness.'

'Please come back at seven, Colonel. If I've any news before then I'll send for you.'

'Thank you, Highness.'

She closed the door after him. 'How're you feeling, Hakim, darling?'

'Tired. Lots of pain.'

'Me too. Do you have to see the colonel later?'

'Yes. It doesn't matter. How's Erikki?'

'Asleep.' She was joyous. 'We're so lucky, the three of us.'

Chapter 23

Tabriz – At the International Hospital: 6:24 P.M. Hakim Khan walked painfully into the private room, the doctor and a guard following him. He was using crutches now and they made his walking easier, but when he bent or tried to sit, they did not relieve the pain. Only pain killers did that. Azadeh was waiting downstairs, her X-ray better than his, her pain less than his.

'So, Ahmed, how do you feel?'

Ahmed lay in bed, awake, his chest and stomach bandaged. The operation to remove the bullet lodged in his chest had been successful. The one in his stomach had done much damage, he had lost a great deal of blood, and internal bleeding had started again. But the moment he saw Hakim Khan he tried to raise himself.

'Don't move, Ahmed,' Hakim Khan said, his voice kind. 'The doctor says you're mending well.'

'The doctor's a liar, Highness.'

The doctor began to speak but stopped as Hakim said, 'Liar or not, get well, Ahmed.'

'Yes, Highness. With the Help of God. But you, you are all right?'

'If the X-ray doesn't lie, I've just torn ligaments.' He shrugged, 'With the Help of God.'

'Thank you . . . thank you for the private room, Highness. Never have I had . . . such luxury.'

'It's merely a token of my esteem for such loyalty.' Imperiously he dismissed the doctor and the guard. When the door was shut, he went closer. 'You asked to see me, Ahmed?'

'Yes, Highness, please excuse me that I could not . . . could not come to you.' Ahmed's voice was phlegmy, and he spoke with difficulty. 'The Tbilisi man you want . . . *The Soviet* . . . he sent a message for you. It's . . . it's under the drawer . . . he taped it under the drawer there.' With an effort he pointed to the small bureau.

Hakim's excitement picked up. Awkwardly he felt underneath the drawer. The adhesive bandages strapping him made bending difficult. He found the small square of folded paper and it came away easily. 'Who brought it and when?'

'It was today . . . some time today . . . I'm not sure, I think it was this afternoon. I don't know. The man wore a doctor's coat and glasses but he wasn't a doctor. An Azerbaijani, perhaps a Turk, I've never seen him before. He spoke Turkish – all he said was, "This is for Hakim Khan, from a friend in Tbilisi. Understand?" I told him yes and he left as quickly as he arrived. For a long time I thought he was a dream. . . .'

The message was scrawled in writing Hakim did not recognise: 'Many, many congratulations on your inheritance, may you live as long and be as productive as your predecessor. Yes, I would like to meet urgently too. But here, not there. Sorry. Whenever you're ready I would be honoured to receive you, with pomp or in privacy, whatever you want. We should be friends, there's much to accomplish and we have many interests in common. Please tell Hashemi Fazir that Yazernov is buried in the Russian Cemetery at Jaleh and he looks forward to seeing him when convenient.' There was no signature.

Greatly disappointed, he went back to the bed and offered the paper to Ahmed. 'What do you make of that?'

Ahmed did not have the strength to take it. 'Sorry, Highness, please hold it so I can read it.' After reading it, he said, 'It's not Mzytryk's writing. I'd . . . I'd recognise his writing but it . . . I believe it genuine. He would have transmitted it to . . . to underlings to bring here.'

'Who's Yazernov and what does it mean?'

'I don't know. It's a code . . . it's a code they'd understand.'

'It is an invitation to a meeting, or a threat. Which?'

'I don't know, Highness. I would guess a meet – ' A spasm of pain went through him. He cursed in his own language.

'Is Mzytryk aware that both the last times they were in ambush? Aware that Abdollah Khan had betrayed him?'

'I . . . I don't know, Highness. I told you he was cunning and the Khan your father very . . . very careful in his dealings.' The effort of talking and concentrating was taking much of Ahmed's strength. 'That Mzytryk knows they are in contact with you . . . that both of them are here now means nothing, his spies abound. You're Khan and of course . . . of course you know you're . . . you're spied on by all kinds of men, most of them evil, who report to their superiors – most of them even more evil.' A smile went over his face and Hakim pondered its meaning. 'But then, you know all about hiding your true purpose, Highness. Not once . . . not once did Abdollah Khan suspect how brilliant you are, not once. If . . . if he'd known one hundredth part of who you really are . . . really are, he would have never banished you but made you . . . made you heir and chief counsellor.'

'He would have had me strangled.' Not for a millionth of a second was Hakim Khan tempted to tell Ahmed that he had sent the assassins whom Erikki had killed, or about the poison attempt that had also failed. 'A week ago he would have ordered me mutilated and you would have done it happily.'

Ahmed looked up at him, eyes deep set and filled with death. 'How do you know so much?'

'The Will of God.'

The ebb had begun. Both men knew it. Hakim said, 'Colonel Fazir showed me a telex about Erikki.' He told Ahmed the contents. 'Now I have no Mzytryk to barter with, not immediately. I can give Erikki to Fazir or help him escape. Either way my sister is committed to stay here and cannot go with him. What is your advice?'

'For you it is safer to give the Infidel to the colonel as a pishkesh and pretend to her there's nothing you can do to prevent the . . . the arrest. In truth there isn't if the colonel wants it that way. He of the Knife . . . he will resist and so he will be killed. Then you can promise her secretly to the Tbilisi . . . But never give her to him, then you will control . . . then you may control him . . . but I doubt it.'

'And if He of the Knife "happens" to escape?'

'If the colonel allowed it . . . he will require payment.'

'Which is?'

'Mzytryk. Now or sometime . . . sometime in the future. While He of the Knife lives, Highness, she will never divorce him – forget the saboteur, he was another lifetime – and when the two years are . . . are over she will go to him, that is if . . . if he allows her to . . . to stay here. I doubt if even Your Highness . . .' Ahmed's eyes closed and a tremor went through him.

'What happened with Bayazid and the bandits? Ahmed . . .'

Ahmed did not hear him. He was seeing the steppes now, the vast plains of his homelands and ancestors, the seas of grass from whence his forebears came forth to ride near the cloak of Genghis Khan, and then that of the grandson Kubla Khan and *his* brother Hulagu Khan who came down into Persia to erect mountains of skulls of those who opposed him. Here in the golden lands since ancient times, Ahmed thought, lands of wine and warmth and wealth and women of great doe-eyed beauty and sensuality, prized since ancient times like Azadeh . . . ah, now I will never take her like she should be taken, dragged off by the hair as spoils of war, shoved across a saddle to be bedded and tamed on the skins of wolves . . .

From a long way off he heard himself say, 'Please, Highness, I would beg a favour, I would like to be buried in my own land and in our own fashion . . .' Then I can live for ever with the spirits of my fathers, he thought, the lovely space beckoning him.

'Ahmed, what happened with Bayazid and the bandits when you landed?'

With an effort Ahmed came back. 'They weren't Kurds, just tribesmen pretending to be Kurds and He of the Knife killed them all, Highness, with very great brutality,' he said with strange formality. 'In his madness he killed them all – with knife and gun and hands and feet and teeth, all except Bayazid who, because of his oath to you, would not come against him.'

'He left him alive?' Hakim was incredulous.

'Yes, God give him peace. He . . . put a gun in my hand and held the Bayazid near the gun and I . . .' The voice trailed away, waves of grass beckoning as far as eyes could see . . .

'You killed him?'

'Oh yes, looking . . . looking into his eyes.' Anger came into Ahmed's voice. 'The son of a . . . dog shot me in the back, twice, without honour, the son of a dog, so he died without honour and without . . . without manhood, the son of a dog.' The bloodless lips smiled and he closed his eyes. He was dying fast now, his words imperceptible. 'I took vengeance.'

Hakim said quickly, 'Ahmed, what haven't you told me that I need to know?'

'Nothing . . .' In a little while his eyes opened and Hakim saw into the pit. 'There is no . . . no other God but God and . . .' A little blood seeped out of the side of his mouth. '. . . I made you Kh . . .' The last of the word died with him.

Hakim was uncomfortable under the frozen stare.

'Doctor!' he called out.

At once the man came in, and the guard. The doctor closed his eyes. 'As God wills. What should we do with the body, Highness?'

'What do you usually do with bodies?' Hakim moved his crutches and walked away, the guard followed. So, Ahmed, he was thinking, so now you're dead and I'm alone, cut from the past and obliged to no one. Made me Khan? Is that what you were going to say? Did you know there were spy holes in that room too?

A smile touched him. Then hardened. Now for Colonel Fazir and Erikki, He of the Knife as you called him.

At the Palace: 6:48 P.M. In the failing light Erikki was carefully repairing one of the bullet holes in the plastic windshield of the 212 with clear tape. It was difficult with his arm in a sling but his hand was strong and the forearm wound shallow – no sign of infection. His ear was heavily taped, part of his hair shaved away for cleanliness, and he was mending fast. The hours of talk that he had had with Azadeh had given him a measure of peace.

That's all it is, he thought, it's only a measure, not enough to forgive the killings or the danger that I am. So be it. That's what gods made me and that's what I am. Yes, but what about Ross and what about Azadeh? And why does she keep the kukri so close by her: 'It was his gift to you, Erikki, to you and to me.'

'It's unlucky to give a man a knife without taking money, at once, just a token, in return. When I see him I will give him money and accept his gift.'

Once again he pressed Engine Start. Once again the engine caught, choked and died. What about Ross and Azadeh?

He sat back on the edge of the cockpit and looked at the sky. The sky did not answer him. Nor the sunset. The overcast had broken up in the west, the sun was down and the clouds menacing. Calls of the muezzins began. Guards on the gate faced Mecca and prostrated themselves; so did those inside the palace and those working in the fields and carpet factory and sheep pens.

Unconsciously his hand went to his knife. Without wishing to, his eyes checked that the Sten gun was still beside his pilot's seat and armed with a full clip. Hidden in the cabin were other weapons, weapons from the tribesmen.

AK47s and M16s. He could not remember taking them or hiding them, had discovered them this morning when he made his inspection for damage and was cleaning the interior.

With the tape over his ear he did not hear the approaching car as soon as he would have done normally, and was startled when it appeared at the gate. The Khan's guards there recognised the occupants and waved the car through to stop in the huge forecourt near the fountain. Again he pressed Engine Start, again the engine caught for a moment, then shuddered the whole airframe as it died.

''Evening, Captain,' Hashemi Fazir said. 'How are you feeling today?'

'With luck, in a week or so I'll be better than ever,' Erikki said pleasantly but his caution was complete.

'The guards say that Their Highnesses are not back yet – the Khan expects us, we're here at his invitation.'

'They're at the hospital being X-rayed. They left while I was asleep, they shouldn't be long.' Erikki watched them. 'Would you care for a drink? There's vodka, whisky and tea, of course coffee.'

'Thank you, whatever you have,' Hashemi said. 'How's your helicopter?'

'Sick,' he said disgustedly. 'I've been trying to start her for an hour. She's had a miserable week.' Erikki led the way up the marble steps. 'The avionics are messed. I need a mechanic badly. Our base's closed as you know and I tried to phone Tehran but the phones are out again.'

'Perhaps I can get you a mechanic, tomorrow or the next day, from the air base.'

'You could, Colonel?' His smile was sudden and appreciative. 'That'd help a lot. And I could use fuel, a full load. Would that be possible?'

'Could you fly down to the airfield?'

'I wouldn't risk it, even if I could start her – too dangerous. No I wouldn't risk that.' Erikki shook his head. 'The mechanic must come here.' He led the way along a corridor, opened the door to the small salon on the ground floor that Abdollah Khan had set aside for non-Islamic guests. It was called the European Room. The bar was well stocked. By custom, there were always full ice trays in the refrigerator, the ice made from bottled water, with club soda and soft drinks of many kinds – and chocolates and the halvah he had adored. 'I'm having vodka,' Erikki said.

Hashemi asked for a soft drink, 'I'll have a vodka too, when the sun's down.' Faintly the muezzins were still calling. '*Prosit!*' Erikki clinked glasses and drank the tot in one swallow. He poured himself another. Hearing a car they all glanced out of the window. It was the Rolls.

'Excuse me a minute, I'll tell Hakim Khan you're here.' Erikki walked out and greeted Azadeh and her brother on the steps. 'What did the X-rays show?'

'No sign of bone damage for either of us.' Azadeh was happy, her face carefree. 'How are you, my darling?'

'Wonderful!' His smile at Hakim was genuine. 'I'm so pleased. You've a

guest – I put him in the European Room.' Erikki saw Hakim's tiredness.
'Shall I tell him to come back tomorrow?'

'No, no thank you. Azadeh, would you tell him I'll be fifteen minutes but
to make himself at home. I'll see you later, at dinner.' Hakim watched her
touch Erikki and smile and walk off. How lucky they are to love each other
so much, and how sad for them. 'Erikki, Ahmed's dead, I didn't want to tell
her yet.'

Erikki was filled with sadness. 'My fault he's dead – Bayazid – he never
gave him a chance. *Matyeryebyets.*'

'God's will. Let's go and talk a moment.' Hakim went down the corridor
into the Great Room, leaning more and more on the crutches. The guards
stayed at the door, out of listening range. Hakim went to a niche, put aside
his crutches, faced Mecca, gasped with pain as he knelt and tried to make
obeisance. Even forcing himself, he failed again and had to be content with
intoning the Shahada. 'Erikki, give me a hand, will you, please?'

Erikki lifted him easily. 'You'd better give that a miss for a few days.'

'Not pray?' Hakim gaped at him.

'I meant . . . perhaps the One God will understand if you say it and don't
kneel. You'll make your back worse. Did the doctor say what it was?'

'He thinks it's torn ligaments – I'll go to Tehran as soon as I can with
Azadeh and see a specialist.' Hakim accepted his crutches. 'Thanks.' After
a moment's consideration he chose a chair instead of his usual lounging
cushions and eased himself into it, then ordered tea.

Erikki's mind was on Azadeh. So little time. 'The best back specialist in
the world's Guy Beauchamp, in London. He fixed me up in five minutes after
doctors said I'd have to lie in traction for three months or have two joints
fused. Don't believe an ordinary doctor about your back, Hakim. The best
they can do is pain killers.'

The door opened. A servant brought in the tea. Hakim dismissed him and
the guards. 'See that I'm not disturbed.' The tea was hot, mint-flavoured,
sweet and drunk from tiny silver cups. 'Now, we must settle what you're to
do. You can't stay here.'

'I agree,' Erikki said, glad that the waiting was over. 'I know I'm . . . I'm
an embarrassment to you as Khan.'

'Part of Azadeh's agreement and mine with my father, for us to be redeemed
and me to be made heir, were the oaths we swore to remain in Tabriz, in Iran,
for two years. So, though you must leave, she may not.'

'She told me about the oaths.'

'Clearly you're in danger, even here. I can't protect you against police or
the government. You should leave at once, fly out of the country. After two
years when Azadeh can leave, she will leave.'

'I can't fly. Fazir said he could give me a mechanic tomorrow, maybe.
And fuel. If I could get hold of McIver in Tehran he could fly someone
up here.'

'Did you try?'

'Yes, but the phones are still out. I would have used the HF at our base but the office's totally wrecked – I flew over the base coming back here, it's a mess, no transport, no fuel drums. When I get to Tehran McIver can send a mechanic here to repair the 212. Until she can fly, can she stay where she is?'

'Yes. Of course.' Hakim poured himself some more tea, convinced now that Erikki knew nothing about the escape of the other pilots and helicopters. But that changes nothing, he told himself. 'There aren't any airlines serving Tabriz or I'd arrange one of those for you. Still, I think you should leave at once; you are in very great danger, immediate danger.'

Erikki's eyes narrowed. 'You're sure?'

'Yes.'

'What danger?'

'I can't tell you. But it's not in my control, it's serious, immediate, does not concern Azadeh at the moment but could, if we're not careful. For her protection this must remain just between us. I'll give you a car, any one you want from the garage. There're about twenty, I believe. What happened to your Range Rover?'

Erikki shrugged, his mind working. 'That's another problem, killing that *matyeryebyets* mujhadin who took my papers, and Azadeh's, then blasting the others.'

Hakim pressed onward. 'There's not much time.'

Erikki moved his head around to ease the tension in his muscles and take away the ache. 'How immediate a danger, Hakim?'

Hakim's eyes were level. 'Immediate enough to suggest you wait till dark, then take the car and go – and get out of Iran as quickly as you can,' he added deliberately. 'Immediate enough to know that if you don't, Azadeh will have greater anguish. Immediate enough to know you should not tell her before you leave.'

'You swear it?'

'Before God I swear that is what I believe.'

He saw Erikki frown and he waited patiently. He liked his honesty and simplicity but that meant nothing in the balance. 'Can you leave without telling her?'

'If it's in the night, nearer to dawn so long as she's sleeping. If I leave tonight, pretending to go out, say to go to the base, she'll wait for me and if I don't come back it will be very difficult – for her and for you. The village preys on her. She'll have hysterics. A secret departure would be wiser, just before dawn. She'll be sleeping then – the doctor gave her sedatives. She'll be sleeping and I could leave a note.'

Hakim nodded, satisfied. 'Then it's settled.' He wanted no hurt or trouble for or from Azadeh either.

Erikki had heard the finality and he knew beyond any doubt, now, that if he left her he would lose her for ever.

In the Bathhouse: 7:15 P.M. Azadeh lowered herself into the hot water up to her neck. The bath was beautifully tiled and fifteen yards square and many tiered, shallow at one end with lounging platforms, the hot water piped from the furnace room adjoining. The room was warm and large, a happy place with kind mirrors. Her hair was tied up in a towel and she rested against one of the tilted backrests, her legs stretched out, the water easing her. 'Oh, that's so good, Mina,' she murmured.

Mina was a strong good-looking woman, one of Azadeh's three maid-servants. She stood over her in the water, wearing just a loincloth, gently massaging her neck and shoulders. The bathhouse was empty but for Azadeh and the maidservant – Hakim had sent the rest of the family to other houses in Tabriz: 'to prepare for a fitting Mourning Day for Abdollah Khan,' had been the excuse, but all were aware that the forty days of waiting was to give him time to inspect the palace at his leisure and reapportion suites as it pleased him. Only the old Khananum was undisturbed, and Aysha and her two infants.

Without disturbing Azadeh's tranquillity, Mina eased her into shallower water and on to another platform where Azadeh lay full length, her head propped comfortably on a pillow, so that she could work on her chest and loins and thighs and legs, preparing for the real oil massage that would come later when the water's heat had become deep-seated.

'Oh, that's so good,' Azadeh said again. She was thinking how much nicer this was than their own sauna – that raw strong heat and then the frightful plunge into the snow, the aftershock tingling and life-giving but not as good as this, the sensuality of the perfumed water and quiet leisure and no aftershocks and oh that is so good . . . but why is the bathhouse a village square and now it's so cold and there's the butcher and the false mullah's shouting, 'First his right hand . . . stone the harlottttt!' She screamed soundlessly and leapt away.

'Oh, did I hurt you, Highness, I'm so sorry!'

'No, no, it wasn't you, Mina, it was nothing, nothing, please go on.' Again the soothing fingers. Her heart slowed. I hope soon I'll be able to sleep without . . . without the village. Last night with Erikki it was already a little better, in his arms it was better, just being near him. Perhaps tonight it will be better still. I wonder how Johnny is. He should be on his way home now, home to Nepal on leave. Now that Erikki's back I'm safe again, just so long as I'm with him, near him. By myself I'm not . . . not safe even with Hakim. I don't feel safe anymore. I just don't feel safe anymore.

The door opened and Aysha came in. Her face was lined with grief, her eyes filled with fear, the black chador making her appear even more emaciated. 'Hello, Aysha dear, what's the matter?'

'I don't know. The world is strange and I've no . . . I'm centreless.'

'Come into the bath,' Azadeh said, sorry for her, she looked so thin and old and frail and defenceless. Difficult to believe she's my father's widow with a son and daughter, and only seventeen. 'Get in, it's so good.'

'No, no, thank you I . . . I just wanted to talk to you.' Aysha looked at Mina then dropped her eyes and waited. Two days ago she would have just sent for Azadeh who would have come at once and bowed and knelt and waited for orders, as now she knelt as petitioner. As God wills, she thought; except for my terror for the future of my children I would shout with happiness – no more of the foul stench and sleep-shattering snores, no more of the crushing weight and moans and rage and biting and desperation to achieve that which he could but rarely. 'It's your fault, your fault your fault . . .' How could it be my fault? How many times did I beg him to show me what to do to help, and I tried and tried and tried and yet it was only so rarely and then at once the weight was gone, the snoring would begin, and I was left awake to lie in the sweat and in the stink. Oh, how many times I wanted to die.

'Mina, leave us alone until I call you,' Azadeh said. She was obeyed instantly. 'What's the matter, Aysha dear?'

The girl trembled. 'I'm afraid. I'm afraid for my son, and I came to beg you to protect him.'

Azadeh said gently, 'You've nothing to fear from Hakim Khan and me, nothing. We've sworn by God to cherish you, your son and daughter, you heard us, we did it in front of . . . of your husband, our father, and then again, after his death. You've nothing to fear. Nothing.'

'I've everything to fear,' the girl stammered. 'I'm not safe anymore, nor is my son. Please, Azadeh, couldn't . . . couldn't Hakim Khan . . . I'd sign any paper giving up any rights for him, any paper, I only want to live in peace and for him to grow up and live in peace.'

'Your life is with us, Aysha. Soon you will see how happy we'll all be together,' Azadeh said. The girl's right to be afraid, she thought. Hakim will never surrender the Khanate out of his line if he has sons of his own – he must marry now, I must help find him a fine wife. 'Don't worry, Aysha.'

'Worry? You're safe now, Azadeh, you who just a few days ago lived in terror. Now I'm not safe and I'm in terror.'

Azadeh watched her. There was nothing she could do for her. Aysha's life was settled. She was the widow of a Khan. She would stay in the palace, watched and guarded, living as best she could. Hakim would not dare to let her remarry, could not possibly allow her to give up a son's rights granted by the public will of the dying husband. 'Don't worry,' she said.

'Here.' Aysha pulled out a bulky manila envelope from under her chador. 'This is yours.'

'What is it?' Azadeh's hands were wet and she didn't want to touch it.

The girl opened the envelope and showed her the contents. Azadeh's eyes widened. Her passport, ID, and other papers, Erikki's also, all the things that had been stolen from them by the mujhadin at the roadblock. This was a pishkesh indeed. 'Where did you get them?'

The girl was sure there was no one listening, but still lowered her voice. 'The leftist mullah, the same mullah of the village, he gave them to His Highness, the Khan, to Abdollah Khan two weeks ago, when you were in Tehran . . . the same mullah as at the village.'

Incredulously Azadeh watched her. 'How did he get them?'

Nervously the girl shrugged her thin shoulders. 'The mullah knew all about the roadblock and what happened there. He came here to try to take possession of the . . . of your husband. His Highness . . .' She hesitated, then continued in her halting whispers. 'His Highness told him no, not until he approved it, sent him away, and kept the papers.'

'Do you have other papers, Aysha? Private papers?'

'Not of yours or your husband's.' Again the girl trembled. 'His Highness hated you all so much. He wanted your husband destroyed, then he was going to give you to the Soviet, and your brother was to be . . . neutered. There's so much I know that could help you and him, and so much I don't understand. Ahmed . . . beware of him, Azadeh.'

'Yes,' Azadeh said slowly. 'Did Father send the mullah to the village?'

'I don't know. I think he did. I heard him ask the Soviet to dispose of Mahmud, ah, yes, that was that false mullah's name. Perhaps His Highness sent him there to torment you and the saboteur, and also sent him to his own death – but God intervened. I heard the Soviet agree to send men after this Mahmud.'

Azadeh said casually, 'How did you hear that?'

Aysha nervously gathered the chador closer around her and knelt on the edge of the bath. 'The palace is a honeycomb of listening holes and spy holes, Azadeh. He . . . His Highness trusted no one, spied on everyone, even me. I think we should be friends, allies, you and I, we're defenceless – even you, perhaps you more than any of us and unless we help each other we're all lost. I can help you, protect you.' Beads of sweat were on her forehead. 'I only ask you to protect my son, please. I can protect you.'

'Of course we should be friends,' Azadeh said, not believing that she was under any threat, but intrigued to know the secrets of the palace. 'You will show me these secret places and share your knowledge?'

'Oh, yes, yes, I will.' The girl's face lit up. 'I'll show you everything and the two years will pass quickly. Oh, yes, we'll be friends.'

'What two years?'

'While your husband is away, Azadeh.'

Azadeh jerked upright, filled with alarm. 'He's going away?'

Aysha stared at her. 'Of course. What else can he do?'

In the European Room: Hashemi was reading the scrawled message from Mzytryk that Hakim had just given him.

'Colonel, what's this about Yazernov and Jaleh Cemetery?'

Hashenu said, smoothly, 'It's an invitation, Highness. Yazernov's an intermediary Mzytryk uses from time to time, acceptable to both sides, when something of importance to both sides has to be discussed. As soon as convenient to meet Yazernov!' Hashemi said, 'I think, Highness, we'd better return to Tehran tomorrow.'

'Yes,' Hakim said. Coming back in the car from the hospital with Azadeh, Hakim had decided the only way to deal with Mzytryk's message was head-on. 'When will you come back to Tabriz?'

'If it pleases you, next week. Then we could discuss how to tempt Mzytryk here. With your help there's much to do in Azerbaijan. We've just had a report that the Kurds are in open rebellion nearer to Rezaiyeh, now heavily provisioned with money and guns by the Iraqis – may God consume them. Khomeini has ordered the army to put them down, once and for all time.'

'The Kurds?' Hakim smiled. 'Even he, God keep him safe, even he won't do that – not once and for all.'

'This time he might, Highness. He has fanatics to send against fanatics.'

'Green Bands can obey orders and die but they do not inhabit those mountains, they do not have Kurdish stamina nor their lust for earthly freedom en route to Paradise.'

'With your permission I will pass on your advice, Highness.'

Hakim said sharply, 'Will it be given any more credence than my father's – or my grandfather's – whose advice was the same?'

'I would hope so, Highness. I would hope . . .' His words were drowned as the 212 fired up, coughed, held for a moment, then died again. Out of the window they saw Erikki unclip one of the engine covers and stare at the complexity inside with a flashlight. Hashemi turned back to the Khan who sat on a chair, stiffly upright. The silence became complicated, the two men's minds racing, each as strong as the other, each bent on violence of some kind.

Hakim Khan said carefully, 'He cannot be arrested in my house or my domain. Even though he knows nothing of the telex, he knows he cannot stay in Tabriz, even Iran, nor may my sister go with him, even leave Iran for two years. He knows he must leave at once. His machine cannot fly. I hope he avoids arrest.'

'My hands are tied, Highness.' Hashemi's voice was apologetic and patently sincere. 'It is my duty to obey the law of the land.' Absently he noticed a piece of fluff on his sleeve and brushed it away with the perfect amount of sadness. 'It's our duty to obey the law.'

'I'm certain, quite certain, he was not part of any conspiracy, knows nothing about the flight of the others, and I would like him left alone to leave in peace.'

'I would be glad to inform SAVAMA of your wishes.'

'I would be glad if you would do what I suggest.'

'I will, Highness. If others intercept him . . .' Hashemi shrugged. 'As God wants.'

Chapter 24

Tabriz – At the Palace: 10:05 P.M. The three of them were sitting in front of the wood fire drinking after-dinner coffee and watching the flames, the room small and richly brocaded, warm and intimate, one of Hakim's guards beside the door. But there was no peace between them, though all pretended otherwise, now and during the evening. The flames held their attention, each seeing different pictures therein. Erikki was watching the fork in the road, always the fork, one way the flames leading to loneliness, the other to fulfilment – perhaps and perhaps not. Azadeh watched the future, trying not to watch it.

Hakim Khan took his eyes off the fire and threw down the gauntlet. 'You've been distracted all evening, Azadeh,' he said.

'Yes. I think we all are.' Her smile was not real. 'Do you think we could talk in private, the three of us?'

'Of course.' Hakim motioned to the guard. 'I'll call if I need you.' The man obeyed and closed the door after him. Instantly the mood of the room changed. Now all three were adversaries, all aware of it, all on guard and all ready. 'Yes, Azadeh?'

'Is it true that Erikki must leave at once?'

'Yes.'

'There must be a solution. I cannot endure two years without my husband.'

'With the Help of God the time will pass quickly.' Hakim Khan sat stiffly upright, the pain eased by the codeine.

'I cannot endure two years,' she said again.

'Your oath cannot be broken.'

Erikki said, 'He's right, Azadeh. You gave the oath freely, Hakim is Khan and the price . . . fair. But all the killings – I must leave, the fault's mine, not yours or Hakim's.'

'You did nothing wrong, nothing, you were forced into protecting me and yourself, they were carrion bent on murdering us, and as to the raid . . . you did what you thought best, you had no way of knowing the ransom was part paid or Father was dead . . . he should not have ordered the messenger killed.'

'That changes nothing. I have to go tonight. We can accept it, and leave it at that,' Erikki said, watching Hakim. 'Two years will pass quickly.'

'If you live, my darling.' Azadeh turned to her brother who looked back at her, his smile still the same, eyes the same.

Erikki glanced from brother to sister, so different and yet so similar. What's changed her, why has she precipitated that which should not have been precipitated?

'Of course if I live,' he said, outwardly calm.

An ember fell into the hearth and he reached forward and moved it to safety. He saw that Azadeh had not taken her gaze off Hakim, nor he off her. The same calm, same polite smile, same inflexibility.

'Yes, Azadeh?' Hakim said.

'A mullah could absolve me from my oath.'

'Not possible. Neither a mullah nor I could do that, not even the Imam would agree.'

'I can absolve myself. This is between me and God, I can ab – '

'You cannot, Azadeh. You cannot and live at peace with yourself.'

'I can. I can and be at peace.'

'Not and remain Muslim.'

'Yes,' she said simply, 'I agree.'

Hakim gasped. 'You don't know what you say.'

'Oh, but I do, I've considered even that.' Her voice was toneless. 'I've considered that solution and found it bearable. I will not endure two years of separation, nor will I endure any attempt on my husband's life, or forgive it.' She sat back and left the lists for the moment, nauseous but glad she had brought the matter into the open but frightened all the same. Once more she blessed Aysha for forewarning her.

'I will not allow you to renounce Islam under any circumstances.'

She just looked back at the flames.

The minefield was all around them, all mines triggered, and though Hakim was concentrating on her, his senses probed Erikki, He of the Knife, knowing the man was waiting too, playing a different game now that the problem was before them. Should I have dismissed the guard, he asked himself, outraged by her threat, the smell of danger filling his nostrils. 'Whatever you say, Azadeh, whatever you try, for the sake of your soul I would be forced to prevent an apostasy – in any way I could. That's unthinkable.'

'Then please help me. You're very wise. You're Khan and we have been through much together. I beg you, remove the threat to my soul and to my husband.'

'I don't threaten your soul or your husband.' Hakim looked at Erikki directly. 'I don't.'

Erikki said, 'What were those dangers you mentioned?'

'I can't tell you, Erikki,' Hakim said.

'Would you excuse us, Highness? We must get ready to leave.' Azadeh got up. So did Erikki.

'You must stay where you are!' Hakim was furious. 'Erikki, you'd allow her to forswear Islam, her heritage, and her chance of life everlasting?'

'No, that's not part of my plan,' he said. Both of them stared at him, bewildered. 'Please tell me what dangers, Hakim.'

'What plan? You have a plan? To do what?'

'The dangers, first tell me what dangers. Azadeh's Islam is safe with me, by my own gods I swear it. What dangers?'

It had never been part of Hakim's strategy to tell them, but now he was rocked by her intractability, aghast that she would consider committing the ultimate heresy, and further disoriented by this strange man's sincerity. So he told them about the telex and the pilots and airplanes fleeing, and his conversation with Hashemi, noticing that though Azadeh was as aghast as Erikki, her surprise did not seem real. It's almost as though she already knew, had been present, both times, but how could she possibly know? He rushed on: 'I told him you could not be taken in my house or domain or in Tabriz, that I would give you a car, that I hoped you'd escape arrest, and that you would leave just before dawn.'

Erikki was shattered. The telex's changed everything, he thought. 'So they'll be waiting for me.'

'Yes. But I did not tell Hashemi I had another plan, that I've already sent a car into Tabriz, that the moment Azadeh was asleep I wo – '

'You'd've left me, Erikki?' Azadeh was appalled. 'You'd've left me without telling me, without asking me?'

'Perhaps. What were you saying, Hakim; please finish what you were saying.'

'The moment Azadeh was asleep I planned to smuggle you out of the palace into Tabriz where the car is and point you towards the border, the Turkish border. I have friends in Khvoy and they would help you across it, with the Help of God,' Hakim added automatically, enormously relieved that he had had the foresight to arrange this alternative plan – just in case it was needed. And now it's happened, he thought. 'You have a plan?'

'Yes.'

'What is it?'

'If you don't like it, Hakim Khan, what then?'

'In that case I would refuse to allow it and try to stop it.'

'I would prefer not to risk your displeasure.'

'Without my help, you cannot leave.'

'I'd like your help, that's true.' Erikki was no longer confident. With Mac and Charlie and the rest gone – how in hell could they do it so fast? Why the hell didn't it happen while we were in Tehran but thank all gods Hakim's Khan now and can protect Azadeh – it's clear what SAVAK'll do to me if they catch me, when they catch me. 'You were right about the danger. You think I could sneak out as you said?'

'Hashemi left two policemen on the gate. I think you could be smuggled out – somehow it should be possible to distract them – I don't know if there're others on the road down to the city but there may be, more than likely there would be. If they're vigilant and you're intercepted . . . that's God's will.'

Azadeh said, 'Erikki, they're expecting you to go alone, and the colonel agreed not to touch you inside Tabriz. If we were hidden in the back of an old truck – we only need a little luck to avoid them.'

'You cannot leave,' Hakim said impatiently, but she did not hear him. Her mind had leaped to Ross and Gueng and the previous escape, and how difficult those two had found it even though they were trained saboteurs and fighters. Poor Gueng. A chill went through her. The road north's as difficult as the one south, so easy to ambush us, so easy to put up roadblocks. Not so far in miles to Khvoy, and past Khvoy to the frontier, but a million miles in time and with my bad back . . . I doubt if I could walk even one of them.

'Never mind,' she muttered. 'We'll get there all right. With the Help of God we'll escape.'

Hakim flared, 'By God and the Prophet, what about your oath, Azadeh?'

Her face was very pale now and she held on to her fingers to stop the tremble. 'Please forgive me, Hakim, I've told you. And if I'm prevented from leaving with Erikki now, or if Erikki won't take me with him, I'll escape somehow, I will, I swear it, I swear it.' She glanced at Erikki.

'If Mac and all the others have fled, you could be used as a hostage.' 'I know. I have to get out as fast as I can. But you have to stay. You can't give up your religion just because of the two years, much as I loathe leaving you,' Erikki said carefully. 'You're the sister of a Khan and you swore to stay.'

'That's between me and God,' Azadeh said stubbornly.

'Erikki, I must know your plan.' Hakim interrupted coldly.

'Sorry, I trust no one in this.'

The Khan's eyes narrowed to slits, and it took all of his will not to call the guard. 'So there's an impasse. Azadeh, pour me some coffee, please.' At once she obeyed. He looked at the huge man who stood with his back to the fire. 'Isn't there?'

'Please solve it, Hakim Khan,' Erikki said. 'I know you to be a wise man and I would do you no harm, or Azadeh harm.'

Hakim accepted the coffee and thanked her, watched the fire, weighing and sifting, needing to know what Erikki had in his mind, wanting an end to all this and Erikki gone and Azadeh here and as she always was before, wise and gentle and loving and obedient – and Muslim. But he knew her too well to be sure she would not do as she threatened, and he loved her too much to allow her to carry out the threat.

'Perhaps this would satisfy you, Erikki: I swear by God I will assist you, providing your plan does not negate my sister's oath, does not force her to apostatise, does not put her in spiritual danger or political danger . . .' He thought a moment, '. . . does not harm her or harm me – and has a chance of success.'

Azadeh bridled angrily, 'That's no help, how can Erikki possib – '

'Azadeh!' Erikki said curtly. 'Where are your manners? Keep quiet. The Khan was talking to me, not you. It's my plan he wants to know, not yours.'

'Sorry, please excuse me,' she said at once, meaning it. 'Yes, you're right. I apologise to both of you, please excuse me.'

'When we were married, you swore to obey me. Does that still apply?' he asked harshly, furious that she had almost ruined his plan, for he had seen Hakim's eyes cross with rage and he needed him calm, not agitated.

'Yes, Erikki,' she told him immediately, still shocked by what Hakim had said, for that closed every path except the one she had chosen – and that choice petrified her. 'Yes, without reservation, provided you don't leave me.'

'Without reservation – yes or no?'

Pictures of Erikki flashed through her mind, his gentleness and love and laughter and all the good things, along with the brooding violence that had never touched her but would touch anyone who threatened her or stood in his way, Abdollah, Johnny, even Hakim – particularly Hakim.

Without reservation, yes, she wanted to say, except against Hakim, except if you leave me. His eyes were boring into her. For the first time she was afraid of him. She muttered, 'Yes, without any reservation. I beg you not to leave me.'

Erikki turned his attention to Hakim: 'I accept what you said, thank you.' He sat down again. Azadeh hesitated, then knelt beside him, resting her arm on his knees, wanting the contact, hoping it would help to push away her fear and anger with herself for losing her temper. I must be going mad, she thought. God help me . . .

'I accept the rules you've set, Hakim Khan,' Erikki was saying quietly. 'Even so I'm still not going to tell you my pl – Wait, wait, wait! You swore you'd help if I didn't put you at risk, and I won't. Instead,' he said carefully, 'instead I'll give you a hypothetical approach to a plan that might satisfy all your conditions.' Unconsciously his hand began stroking her hair and her neck. She felt the tension leaving her. Erikki watched Hakim, both men ready to explode. 'All right so far?'

'Go on.'

'Say hypothetically my chopper was in perfect shape, that I'd been pretending I couldn't start her properly to throw everyone off, and to get everyone used to the idea of the engines starting and stopping, say I'd lied about the fuel and there was enough for an hour's flight, easily enough to get to the border and – '

'Is there?' Hakim said involuntarily, the idea opening a new avenue.

'For the sake of this hypothetical story, yes.' Erikki felt Azadeh's grip tighten on his knee but pretended not to notice. 'Say in a minute or two, before we all went to bed, I told you I wanted to start her again. Say I did just that, the engines caught and held enough to warm her and then died, no one'd worry – the Will of God. Everyone'd think the madman won't leave well alone, why doesn't he quit and let us sleep in peace? Then say I started her, pushed on all power and pulled her into the sky. Hypothetically I could be away in seconds – provided the guards didn't fire on me, and provided there were no hostiles, Green Bands, or police with guns on the gate or outside the walls.'

The breath escaped from Hakim's lips. Azadeh shifted a little. The silk of her dress rustled. 'I pray that such a make-believe could come to pass,' she said.

Hakim said, 'It would be a thousand times better than a car, ten thousand times better. You could fly all the way by night?'

'I could, providing I had a map. Most pilots who've spent time in an area keep a good map in their heads – of course, this is all make-believe.'

'Yes, yes it is. Well, then, so far so good with your make-believe plan. You could escape this way, if you could neutralise the hostiles in the forecourt. Now, hypothetically, what about my sister?'

'My wife isn't in on any escape, real or hypothetical. Azadeh has no choice: she must stay of her own accord and wait the two years,' Erikki saw Hakim's astonishment and felt Azadeh's instant rebellion under his fingers. But he did not allow his fingers to cease their rhythm on her hair and neck, soothing her, coaxing her, and he continued smoothly, 'She is committed to stay in obedience to her oath. She cannot leave. No one who loves her, most of all me, would allow her to give up Islam because of two years. In fact, Azadeh, make-believe or not, *it is forbidden*. Understand?'

'I hear what you say, husband,' she said through her teeth, so angry she could hardly speak and cursing herself for falling into his trap.

'You are bound by your oath for two years, then you can leave freely. It's ordered!'

She looked up at him, and said darkly, 'Perhaps after two years I might not wish to leave.'

Erikki rested his great hand on her shoulder, his fingers lightly around her neck. 'Then, woman, I shall come back and drag you out by your hair.' He said it so quietly with such venom that it froze her. In a moment she dropped her eyes and looked at the fire, still leaning against his legs. He kept his hand on her shoulder. She made no move to remove it. But he knew she was seething, hating him. Still he knew it was necessary to say what he had said.

'Please excuse me a moment,' she said, her voice like ice.

The two men watched her leave.

When they were alone, Hakim said, 'Will she obey?'

'No,' Erikki said. 'Not unless you lock her up and even then . . . No. Her mind's made up.'

'I will never, never allow her to break her oath and renounce Islam, you must understand that, even . . . even if I have to kill her.'

Erikki looked at him. 'If you harm her, you're a dead man – if I'm alive.'

At the Palace: 11:04 P.M. Silently the phosphorescent, red night-flying lights of the massed instrument panel came to life. Erikki's finger pressed Engine Start. The jets caught, coughed, caught, hesitated as he eased the circuit breakers carefully in and out. Then he shoved them home. The engines began a true warm-up.

Floodlights at half power were on in the forecourt. Azadeh and Hakim Khan, heavy-coated against the night cold, stood just clear of the turning blades, watching him. At the front gate a hundred yards or so away two guards and Hashemi's two police also watched but idly. Their cigarettes glowed. The two policemen shouldered their Kalashnikovs and strolled nearer.

Once more the engines spluttered and Hakim Khan called out over the noise, 'Erikki, forget it for tonight!' But Erikki did not hear him. Hakim moved away from the noise, nearer to the gate, Azadeh following him reluctantly. His walk was ponderous and awkward, and he cursed, unused to his crutches.

'Greetings, Highness,' the policemen said politely.

'Greetings. Azadeh,' Hakim said irritably, 'your husband's got no patience, he's losing his senses. What's the matter with him? It's ridiculous to keep trying the engines. What good would it do even if he could start them?'

'I don't know, Highness.' Azadeh's face was white in the pale light and she was very uneasy. 'He's . . . since the raid he's been very strange, very difficult, difficult to understand – he frightens me.'

'I don't wonder! He's enough to frighten the Devil.'

'Please excuse me, Highness,' Azadeh said apologetically, 'but in normal times he's . . . he's not frightening.'

Politely the two policemen turned away, but Hakim stopped them. 'Have you noticed any difference in the pilot?'

'He's very angry, Highness. He's been angry for hours. Once I saw him kick the machine – but different or not is difficult to say. I've never been near to him before.' The corporal was in his forties and wanted no trouble. The other man was younger and even more afraid. Their orders were to watch and wait until the pilot left by car, or any car left, not to hinder its leaving but to report to HQ at once by their car radio. Both of them realised the danger of their position – the arm of the Gorgon Khan had a very long reach. Both knew of the servants and guards of the late Khan accused by him of treason still rotting in police dungeons. But both also knew the reach of Inner Intelligence was more certain.

'Tell him to stop it, Azadeh, to stop the engines.'

'He's never before been so . . . so angry with me, and tonight . . .' Her eyes almost crossed in her rage. 'I don't think I can obey him.'

'You will!'

After a pause she muttered, 'When he's even a little angry, I can do nothing with him.'

The policemen saw her paleness and were sorry for her but more sorry for themselves – they had heard what had happened on the mountainside. God protect us from He of the Knife! What must it be like to marry such a barbarian who everyone knows drank the blood of the tribesmen he slaughtered, worships forest spirits against the law of God, and rolls naked in the snow, forcing her to do the same.

The engines spluttered and began to die and they saw Erikki bellow with rage and smash his great fist on the side of the cockpit, denting the aluminum with the force of his blow.

'Highness, with your permission I will go to bed – I think I will take a sleeping pill and hope that tomorrow is a better . . .' Her words trailed off.

'Yes. A sleeping pill is a good idea. Very good. I'm afraid I'll have to take two, my back hurts terribly and now I can't sleep without them.' Hakim added angrily, 'It's his fault! If it wasn't for him I wouldn't be in pain.' He turned to his bodyguard, 'Fetch my guards on the gate, I want to give them instructions. Come along, Azadeh.'

Painfully he walked off, Azadeh obediently and sullenly at his side. The engines started shrieking again. Irritably Hakim Khan turned and snapped at the policemen, 'If he doesn't stop in five minutes, order him to stop in my name! Five minutes, by God!'

Uneasily the two men watched them leave, the bodyguard with the two gate guards hurrying after them up the steps. 'If Her Highness can't deal with him, what can we do?' the older policeman said.

The lights in the forecourt went out. After six minutes the engines were still starting and stopping. 'We'd better obey.' The young policeman was very nervous. 'The Khan said five. We're late.'

'Be prepared to run and don't irritate him unnecessarily. Take your safety catch off.' Nervously they went closer. 'Pilot!' But the pilot still had his back to them and was half inside the cockpit. Son of a dog! Closer, now up to the whirling blades. 'Pilot!' the corporal said loudly.

'He can't hear you, who can hear anything? You go forward, I'll cover you.'

The corporal nodded, commended his soul to God, and ducked into the wash of air. 'Pilot!' He had to go very close, and touch him. 'Pilot!' Now the pilot turned, his face grim, said something in barbarian that he did not understand. With a forced smile and forced politeness, he said, 'Please, Pilot Excellency, we would consider it an honour if you would stop the engines, His Highness the Khan has ordered it.' He saw the blank look, remembered that He of the Knife could not speak any civilised language, so he repeated what he had said, speaking louder and slower and using signs. To his enormous relief, the pilot nodded apologetically, turned some switches, and now the engines were slowing and the blades were slowing.

Praise be to God! Well done, how clever you are, the corporal thought, gratified. 'Thank you, Excellency Pilot. Thank you.' Very pleased with himself he imperiously peered into the cockpit. Now he saw the pilot making signs to him, clearly wishing to please him – as so he should, by God – inviting him to get into the pilot's seat. Puffed with pride, he watched the barbarian politely lean into the cockpit and move the controls and point at instruments.

Not able to contain his curiosity the younger policeman came under the blades that were circling slower and slower, up to the cockpit door. He leaned in to see better, fascinated by the banks of switches and dials that glowed in the darkness.

'By God, Corporal, have you ever seen so many dials and switches? You look as though you belong in that seat!'

'I wish I was a pilot,' the corporal said. 'I th – ' He stopped, astonished, as his words were swallowed by a blinding red fog that sucked the breath out of his lungs and made the darkness complete.

Erikki had rammed the younger man's head against the corporal's, stunning both of them. Above him the rotors stopped. He looked around. No movement in the darkness, just a few lights on in the palace. No alien eyes or presence that he could sense. Quickly he stowed their guns behind the pilot's seat. It took only seconds to carry the two men to the cabin and lay them inside, force their mouths open, put in the sleeping pills that he had stolen from Azadeh's cabinet, and gag them. A moment to collect his breath, before he went forward and checked that all was ready for instant departure. Then he came back to the cabin. The two men had not moved. He leaned against the doorway ready to silence them again if need be. His throat was dry. Sweat beaded him. Waiting. Then he heard dogs and the sound of chain leashes. Quietly he readied the Sten gun. The wandering patrol of two armed guards and the Doberman pinschers passed around the palace but did not come near him. He watched the palace, his arm no longer in the sling.

In the Palace Forecourt: 12:03 A.M. Erikki was leaning against the 212 when he saw the lights in the Khan's quarters on the second floor go out. A careful check on the two drugged policemen fast asleep in the cabin reassured him. Quietly he slid the cabin door closed, eased his knife under his belt and picked up the Sten. With the skill of a night hunter he moved noiselessly towards the palace. The Khan's guards on the gate did not notice him go – why should they bother to watch him? The Khan had given them clear orders to leave the pilot alone and not agitate him, that surely he would soon tire of playing with the machine. 'If he takes a car, let him. If the police want trouble, that's their problem.'

'Yes, Highness,' they had both told him, glad they were not responsible for He of the Knife.

Erikki slipped through the front door and along the dimly lit corridor to the stairs leading to the north wing, well away from the Khan's area. Noiselessly up the stairs and along another corridor. He saw a shaft of light under the door of their suite. Without hesitation he went into the anteroom, closing the door silently after him. Across the room to their bedroom door and swung it open. To his shock Mina, Azadeh's maid, was there too. She was kneeling on the bed where she had been massaging Azadeh who was fast asleep.

'Oh, your pardon,' she stuttered, terrified of him like all the servants. 'I didn't hear Your Excellency. Her Highness asked. . . asked me to continue as long as I could with . . . with the massage, then to sleep here.'

Erikki face was a mask, the oil streaks on his cheeks and on the taped bandage over his ear making him appear more dangerous. 'Azadeh!'

'Oh you won't wake her, Excellency, she took a . . . she took two sleeping pills and asked me to apologise for her if you c – '

'Dress her!' he hissed.

Mina blanched. 'But, Excellency!' Her heart almost stopped as she saw a knife appear in his hand.

'Dress her quickly and if you make a sound I'll gut you. *Do it!*' He saw her grab the dressing gown. 'Not that, Mina! Warm clothes, ski clothes – by all the gods, it doesn't matter which but be quick!' He watched her, positioning himself between her and the door so she couldn't bolt. On the bedside table was the sheathed kukri. A twinge went through him and he tore his eyes away, and when he was sure Mina was obeying he took Azadeh's purse from the dressing table. All her papers were in it, ID, passport, driver's licence, birth certificate, everything. Good, he thought, and blessed Aysha for the gift that Azadeh had told him about before dinner and thanked his ancient gods for giving him the plan this morning. Ah, my darling, did you think I'd really leave you?

Also in the purse was her soft silk jewellery bag which seemed heavier than normal. His eyes widened at the emeralds and diamonds and pearl necklaces and pendants that it now contained. The rest of Najoud's, he thought, the same that Hakim had used to barter with the tribesmen and that I retrieved from Bayazid. In the mirror he saw Mina gaping at the wealth he held in his hand, Azadeh inert and almost dressed. 'Hurry up!' he grated at her reflection.

At the Ambush Roadblock below the Palace: 12:17 A.M. Both the sergeant of police and his driver in the car waiting beside the road were staring up at the palace four hundred yards away, the sergeant using binoculars. Just the dim lights on the outside of the vast gatehouse, no sign of any guards, or of his own two men. 'Drive up there,' the sergeant said uneasily. 'Something's wrong, by God! They're either asleep or dead. Go slowly and quietly.' He reached into the scabbard beside him and put a shell into the breech of the M16. The driver gunned the engine and eased out into the empty roadway.

At the Main Gate: Babak, the guard, was leaning against a pillar inside the massive iron gate that was closed and bolted. The other guard was curled up nearby on some sacking, fast asleep. Through the bars of the gate could be seen the snowbanked road that wound down to the city. Beyond the empty fountain in the forecourt, a hundred yards away, was the helicopter. The icy wind moved the blades slightly.

He yawned and stamped his feet against the cold, then began to relieve himself through the bars, absently waving the stream this way and that. Earlier when they had been dismissed by the Khan and had come back to their post, they had found that the two policemen had gone. 'They're off to scrounge some food, or to have a sleep,' he had said. 'God curse all police.'

Babak yawned, looking forward to the dawn when he would be off duty for a few hours. Only the pilot's car to usher through just before dawn, then relock the gate, and soon he would be in bed with a warm body. Automatically he scratched his genitals, feeling himself stir and harden. Idly he leaned back, playing with himself, his eyes checking that the gate's heavy bolt was in place and the small side gate also locked. Then the edge of his eyes caught a movement. He centered it. The pilot was slinking out of a side door of the palace with a large bundle over his shoulder, his arm no longer in the sling and carrying a gun. Hastily Babak buttoned up, slipped his rifle off his shoulder, moved farther out of view. Cautiously he kicked the other guard who awoke soundlessly. 'Look,' he whispered, 'I thought the pilot was still in the cabin of the helicopter.'

Wide-eyed, they watched Erikki keep to the shadows, then silently dart across the open space to the far side of the helicopter. 'What's he carrying? What's the bundle?'

'It looked like a carpet, a rolled-up carpet,' the other whispered. Sound of the far cockpit door opening.

'But why? In all the Names of God, what's he doing?'

There was barely enough light but their vision was good and hearing good. They heard an approaching car but were at once distracted by the sound of the far cabin door sliding open. They waited, hardly breathing, then saw him dump what appeared to be two similar bundles under the belly of the helicopter, then duck under the tail boom and reappear on their side. For a moment he stood there, looking towards them but not seeing them, then eased the cockpit door open, and got in with the gun, the carpet bundle now propped on the opposite seat.

Abruptly the jets began and both guards jumped. 'God protect us, what do we do?'

Nervously Babak said, 'Nothing. The Khan told us exactly: "Leave the pilot alone, whatever he does, he's dangerous," that's what he told us, didn't he? "When the pilot takes the car near dawn let the pilot leave."' Now he had to talk loudly over the rising scream. 'We do nothing.'

'But we weren't told he would start his engines again, the Khan didn't say that, or sneak out with bundles of carpets.'

'You're right. As God wants, but you're right.' Their nervousness increased. They had not forgotten the guards jailed and flogged by the old Khan for disobedience or failure, or those banished by the new one. 'The engines sound good now, don't you think?' They both looked up as lights came on at the second floor, the Khan's floor, then they jerked around as the police car came swirling to a stop outside the gate. The sergeant jumped out, a flashlight in his hand. 'What's going on, by God?' the sergeant shouted. 'Open the gate, by God! Where're my men?'

Babak rushed for the side gate and pulled the bolt back. In the cockpit Erikki's hands were moving as quickly as possible, the wound in his arm inhibiting him. The sweat ran down his face and mixed with a trickle of blood from his ear where the taped bandages had become displaced. His breath came in great pants from the long run from the north wing with Azadeh bundled in the carpet, drugged and helpless, and he was cursing the needles to rise quicker. He had seen the lights go on in Hakim's apartments and now heads were peering out. Before he had left their suite he had carefully knocked Mina unconscious, hoping he had not hurt her, to protect her as well as himself so she would not sound an alarm or be accused of collusion, had wrapped Azadeh in the carpet and attached the kukri to his belt.

'Come on,' he snarled at the needles, then glimpsed two men at the main gate in police uniforms. Suddenly the helicopter was bathed in a shaft of light from the flashlight and his stomach turned over. Without thinking, he grabbed his Sten, shoved the nose through the pilot's window, and pulled the trigger, aiming high.

The four men scattered for cover as bullets ricocheted off the gate masonry. In his panic the sergeant dropped the flash, but not before all had seen two crumpled, inert bodies of the corporal and the other policeman sprawled on the ground and presumed them dead. As the burst stopped, the sergeant scrambled for the side gate and his car and his M16.

'Fire, by God,' the driver policeman shouted. Whipped by the excitement, Babak squeezed the trigger, the shots going wild. Incautiously, the driver moved into the open to retrieve the flash. Another burst from the helicopter and he leaped backward, 'Son of a burnt father. . . .' The three of them cowered in safety. Another burst at the flashlight danced it, then smashed it.

Erikki saw his escape plan in ruins, the 212 a helpless target on the ground. Time had run out for him. For a split second he considered closing down. The needles were far too low. Then he emptied his Sten at the gate with a howling battle-cry, slammed the throttles forward, and let out another primeval scream that chilled those who heard it. The jets went to full power, shrieked under the strain as he put the stick forward and dragged her airborne a few inches and now, tail high, she lurched ahead, skids screeching on the forecourt as she bounced and rose and fell back and bounced again and now was airborne but lumbering badly. At the main gate the driver tore the gun from a guard and went to the pillar, peered around it to see the helicopter escaping, and pulled the trigger.

On the second floor of the palace Hakim was blearily leaning out of his bedroom window, grasped from drugged sleep by the noise. His bodyguard, Margol, was beside him. They saw the 212 almost collide with a small wooden outhouse, her skids ripping away part of the roof, then struggle onward in a drunken climb. Outside the walls was the police car, the sergeant silhouetted in the beam of its headlights. Hakim watched him aim and willed the bullets to miss.

Erikki heard bullets zinging off metal, prayed they had touched nothing vital, and banked dangerously away from the exposed outer wall towards some space where he could slip behind the safety of the palace. In the wild turn the bundled carpet containing Azadeh toppled over and tangled with the controls. For a moment he was lost, then he used his massive strength to shove her away. The wound in his forearm split open.

Now he swerved behind the north wing, the chopper still only a few feet high and heading towards the other perimeter wall near the hut where Ross and Gueng had been hidden. Still only a few feet high, a stray bullet punctured his door, hacked into the instrument panel, exploding glass.

When the helicopter had disappeared from Hakim's view, he had hobbled across the huge bedroom, past the wood fire that blazed merrily, out into the corridor to the windows there. 'Can you see him?' he asked, panting from the exertion.

'Yes, Highness,' Margol said, and pointed excitedly. 'There!'

The 212 was just a black shape against more blackness, then the perimeter floodlights came on and Hakim saw her stagger over the wall with only inches to spare and dip down. A few seconds later she had reappeared, gaining speed and altitude. At that moment Aysha came running along the corridor, crying out hysterically, 'Highness, Highness. . . . Azadeh's gone, she's gone . . . that devil's kidnapped her and Mina's been knocked unconscious. . . .'

It was hard for Hakim to concentrate against the pills, his eyelids never so heavy. 'What are you talking about?'

'Azadeh's gone, your sister's gone, he wrapped her in a carpet and he's kidnapped her, taken her with him . . .' She stopped, afraid, seeing the look on Hakim's face, ashen in this bleak light, eyes drooping – not knowing about the sleeping pills. 'He's kidnapped her!'

'But that . . . that's not possible . . . not poss – '

'Oh, but it is, she's kidnapped and Mina's unconscious!'

Hakim blinked at her, then stuttered, 'Sound the alarm, Aysha! If she's kidnapped . . . by God, sound . . . sound the alarm! I've taken sleeping pills and they . . . I'll deal with that devil tomorrow, by God, I can't now, not now, but send someone . . . to the police . . . to the Green Bands . . . spread the alarm, there's a Khan's ransom on his head! Margol, help me back to my room.'

Frightened servants and guards were collecting at the end of the corridor and Aysha ran tearfully back to them, telling them what had happened and what the Khan had ordered.

Hakim groped for his bed and lay back, exhausted. 'Margol, tell the . . . tell guards to arrest those fools on the gate. How could they have let that happen?'

'They can't have been vigilant, Highness.' Margol was sure they would be blamed – someone had to be blamed – even though he had been present when the Khan had told them not to interfere with the pilot. He gave the order and came back. 'Are you all right, Highness?'

'Yes, thank you. Don't leave the room . . . wake me at dawn. Keep the fire going and wake me at dawn.'

Gratefully Hakim let himself go into the sleep that beckoned so seductively, his back no longer paining him, his mind focused on Azadeh and on Erikki. When she had walked out of the small room and left him alone with Erikki, he had allowed his grief to show: 'There's no way out of the trap, Erikki. We're trapped, all of us, you, Azadeh, and me. I still can't believe she'd renounce Islam, at the same time I'm convinced she won't obey me or you. I've no wish to hurt her but I've no alternative, her immortal soul is more important than her temporary life.'

'I could save her soul, Hakim. With your help.'

'How?' He had seen the tension in Erikki, his face tight, eyes strange.

'Remove her need to destroy it.'

'How?'

'Say, hypothetically, this madman of a pilot was not Muslim but barbarian and so much in love with his wife that he goes a little more mad and instead of just escaping by himself, he suddenly knocks her out, kidnaps her, flies her out of her own country against her will, and refuses to allow her to return. In most countries a husband can . . . can take extreme measures to hold on to his wife, even to force her obedience and curb her. This way she won't have broken her oath, she'll never need to give up Islam, you'll never need to harm her, and I'll keep my woman.'

'It's a cheat,' Hakim had said, bewildered. 'It's a cheat.'

'It's not, it's make-believe, hypothetical, all of it, only make-believe, but hypothetically it fulfils the rules you swore to abide by, and no one'd ever believe the sister of the Gorgon Khan would willingly break her oath and renounce Islam over a barbarian. No one. Even now you don't know for certain she would, do you?'

Hakim had tried to find the flaws. There's none, he had thought, astonished. And it would solve most of . . . wouldn't it solve everything if it came to pass? If Erikki was to do this without her knowledge and help . . . Kidnap her! It's true, no one'd ever believe she'd willingly break her oath. Kidnapped! I could deplore it publicly and rejoice for her in secret, if I want her to leave, and him to live. But I have to, it's the only way: to save her soul I have to save him.

In the peace of the bedroom he opened his eyes briefly. Flame shadows danced on the ceiling. Erikki and Azadeh were there. God will forgive me, he thought, swooping into sleep. I wonder if I'll ever see her again?

Saturday

Chapter 25

Near the Iran-Turkish Border: 7:59 A.M. Azadeh shielded her eyes against the rising sun. She had seen something glint in the valley below. Was that light reflected off a gun, or harness? She readied the M16, picked up the binoculars. Behind her Erikki lay sprawled on some blankets in the 212's open cabin, heavily asleep. His face was pale and he had lost a lot of blood but she thought he was all right. Through the lenses she saw nothing move. Down there the countryside was snow-locked and sparsely treed. Desolate. No villages and no smoke. The day was good but very cold. No clouds and the wind had dropped in the night. Slowly she searched the valley. A few miles away was a village she had not noticed before.

The 212 was parked in rough mountainous country on a rocky plateau. Last night after the escape from the palace, because a bullet had smashed some instrumentation, Erikki had lost his way. Afraid to exhaust all his fuel, and unable to fly and at the same time staunch the flow of blood from his arm, he had decided to risk landing and wait for dawn. Once on the ground, he had pulled the carpet out of the cockpit and unrolled it. Azadeh was still sleeping peacefully. He had tied up his wound as best he could, then rewrapped her in the carpet for warmth, brought out some of the guns and leaned against the skid on guard. But much as he tried he could not keep his eyes open.

He had awakened suddenly. False dawn was touching the sky. Azadeh was still huddled down in the carpet but now she was watching him. 'So. You've kidnapped me!' Then her pretended coldness vanished and she scrambled into his arms, kissing him and thanking him for solving the dilemma for all three of them with such wisdom, saying the speech she had rehearsed: 'I know a wife can do little against a husband, Erikki, hardly anything at all. Even in Iran where we're civilised, even here, a wife's almost a chattel and the Imam is very clear on wifely duties, and in the Koran,' she added, 'in the Koran and Sharia her duties are oh so clear. Also I know I'm married to a non-Believer, and I openly swear I will try to escape at least once a day to try to go back to fulfil my oath, and though I'll be petrified and know you'll catch me every time and will keep me without money or beat me and I have to obey whatever you order, I will do it.' Her eyes were brimming with happy tears. 'Thank you, my darling, I was so afraid . . .'

'Would you have done that? Given up your God?'

'Erikki, oh, how I prayed God would guide you.'

'Would you?'

'There's no need now even to think the unthinkable, is there, my love?'

'Ah,' he said, understanding. 'Then you knew, didn't you? You knew that this was what I had to do!'

'I only know I'm your wife, I love you, I must obey you, you took me away without my help and against my will. We need never discuss it again. Please?'

Blearily he peered at her, disoriented, and could not understand how she could seem to be strong and have come out of the drugged sleep so easily. Sleep! 'Azadeh, I've got to have an hour of proper sleep. Sorry, I can't go on. Without an hour or so, I can't. We should be safe enough here. You guard, we should be safe enough.'

'Where are we?'

'Still in Iran, somewhere near the border.' He gave her a loaded M16, knowing she could use it accurately. 'One of the bullets smashed my compass.' She saw him stagger as he went for the cabin, grope for some blankets, and lie down. Instantly he was asleep. While she waited for the daylight she thought about their future and about the past. Still Johnny to settle. Nothing else. How strange life is. I thought I would scream a thousand times closed up in that vile carpet, pretending to be drugged. As if I would be so stupid as to drug myself in case I would have to help defend us! So easy to dupe Mina and my darling Erikki and even Hakim, no longer my darling: 'Her everlasting spirit's more important than her temporary body!' He would have killed me. Me! His beloved sister! But I tricked him.

She was very pleased with herself and with Aysha who had whispered about the secret listening places so that when she had stormed out of the room in pretended rage and left Hakim and Erikki alone, she had scurried to overhear what they were saying. Oh, Erikki, I was petrified you and Hakim weren't going to believe that I'd really break my oath – and frantic in case the clues I'd placed before you all evening wouldn't add up to your perfect stratagem. But you went one better than me – you even arranged the helicopter. Oh, how clever you were, I was, we were together. I even made sure you brought my handbag and jewel bag with Najoud's loot that I wheedled out of Hakim so now we're rich as well as safe, if only we can get out of this God-lost country.

'It is God-lost, my darling,' Ross had said the last time she had seen him in Tehran, just before he had left her – she could not endure parting without saying goodbye so she had gone to Talbot to inquire after him and then, a few hours later, he had knocked on her door, the apartment empty but for them. 'It's best you leave Iran, Azadeh. Your beloved Iran is once again bereft. This revolution's the same as all of them: a new tyranny replaces the old. Your new rulers will implant their law, their version of God's law, as the Shah implanted his. Your ayatollahs will live and die as popes live and die, some good men, some bad and some evil. In God's time the world'll get a little better, the beast in men that needs to bite and hack and kill and torment and torture will become a little more human and a little more restrained. It's only people that bugger up the world, Azadeh. Men mostly. You know I love you?'

'Yes. You said it in the village. You know I love you?'

'Yes.'

So easy to swoop back into the womb of time as when they were young. 'But we're not young now and there's a great sadness on me, Azadeh.'

'It'll pass, Johnny,' she had said, wanting his happiness. 'It'll pass as Iran's troubles will pass. We've had terrible times for centuries but they've passed.' She remembered how they had sat together, not touching now, yet possessed, one with the other. Then later he had smiled and raised his hand in his devil-may-care salute and he had left silently.

Again the glint in the valley. Anxiety rushed back into her. Now a movement through the trees and she saw them. 'Erikki!' He was instantly awake. 'Down there. Two men on horseback. They look like tribesmen.' She handed him the binoculars.

'I see them.' The men were armed and cantering along the valley bed, dressed as hill people would dress, keeping to cover where there was cover. Erikki focused on them. From time to time he saw them look up in their direction. 'They can probably see the chopper but I doubt if they can see us.'

'They're heading up here?'

Through his aching and tiredness he had heard the fear in her voice. 'Perhaps. Probably yes. It'd take them half an hour to get up here, we've plenty of time.'

'They're looking for us.' Her face was white and she moved closer to Erikki. 'Hakim will have alerted everywhere.'

'He won't have done that. He helped me.'

'That was to escape.' Nervously she looked around the plateau and the tree line and the mountains, then back at the two men. 'Once you escaped he'd act like a Khan. You don't know Hakim, Erikki. He's my brother but before that he's Khan.'

Through the binoculars he saw the half-hidden village beside the road in the middle distance. Sun glinted off telephone lines. His own anxiety increased. 'Perhaps they're just villagers and curious about us. But we won't wait to find out.' Wearily he smiled at her. 'Hungry?'

'Yes, but I'm fine.' Hastily she began bundling the carpet that was ancient, priceless, and one of her favourites. 'I'm thirsty more than hungry.'

'Me too but I feel better now. The sleep helped.' His eyes ranged the mountains, setting what he saw against his remembrance of the map. A last look at the men still far below. No danger for a while, unless there are others around, he thought, then went for the cockpit. Azadeh shoved the carpet into the cabin and tugged the door closed. There were bullet holes in it that she had not noticed before. Another spark of sunlight off metal in the forest, much closer, that neither saw.

Erikki's head ached and he felt weak. For the first time in many a day he thought about McIver and the others, cursed McIver for not warning him and prayed he and all the others had escaped safely. Mac should have sent me, *Take a powder*, but then, how could he?

He concentrated, and pressed the starting button. Wind up, immediate and correct. A quick check of his instruments. Rev counter shattered, no compass, no ADF. No need for some instruments – the sound of the engines would tell him when the needles would be in the Green. But needles on the fuel gauges were stuck at a quarter full. No time to check on them or any other damage and if there was damage, what could he do? All gods great and small, old and new, living or dead or yet to be born, be on my side today, I'll need all the help you can give me. His eyes saw the kukri that he remembered vaguely shoving in the seat pocket. Without conscious effort his fingers reached out and touched it. The feel of it burned.

Azadeh hurried for the cockpit, turbulence from the rotors picking up speed clawing at her, chilling her even more. She climbed into the seat and locked the door, turning her eyes away from the mess of dried blood on the seat and floor. Her smile died, noticing his brooding concentration and the strangeness, his hand almost near the kukri but not quite. Again she wondered why he had brought it.

'Are you all right, Erikki?' she asked, but he did not appear to have heard her. Insha'Allah. It's God's will he is alive and I'm alive, that we're together and almost safe. But now it's up to me to carry the burden and to keep us safe. He's not my Erikki yet, neither in looks nor in spirit. I can almost hear the bad thoughts pounding in his head. Soon the bad will again overpower the good. God protect us. 'Thank you, Erikki,' she said, accepting the headset he handed her, mentally girding herself for battle.

He made sure she was strapped in and adjusted the volume for her. 'You can hear me, all right?'

'Oh, yes, my darling. Thank you.'

Part of his hearing was concentrated on the sound of the engines, a minute or two yet before they could take off. 'We've not enough fuel to get to Van which's the nearest airfield in Turkey – I could go south to the hospital in Rezaiyeh for fuel but that's too dangerous. I'm going north a little. I saw a village that way and a road. Perhaps that's the Khvoy-Van road.'

'Good, let's hurry, Erikki, I don't feel safe here. Are there any airfields near here? Hakim's bound to have alerted the police and they'll have alerted the air force. Can we take off?'

'Just a few more seconds, engines're almost ready.' He saw the anxiety and her beauty and once more the picture of her and John Ross together tumbled into his mind. He forced it away. 'I think there are airfields in the border sector. We'll go as far as we can. I think we've enough fuel to get over the border.' He made an effort to be light. 'Maybe we can find a gas station. Do you think they'd take a credit card?'

She laughed nervously and lifted up her bag, winding the strap around her wrist. 'No need for credit cards, Erikki. We're rich – you're rich. I can speak Turkish and if I can't beg, buy, or bribe our way through I'm not of the tribe Gorgon! But through to where? Istanbul? You're overdue a fabulous holiday, Erikki. We're safe only because of you, you did everything, thought of everything!'

'No, Azadeh, you did.' You and John Ross, he wanted to shout and looked back at his instruments to hide. But without Ross, Azadeh'd be dead and therefore I'd be dead and I can't live with the thought of you and him together. I'm sure you lov –

At that moment his disbelieving eyes saw the groups of riders break out of the forest a quarter of a mile away on both sides of him, police among them, and begin galloping across the rocky space to head them off. His ears told him the engines were in the Green. At once his hands shoved full throttle. Time slowing. Creeping off the ground, no way that the attackers could not shoot them down. A million years of time for them to rein in, aim and fire, any one of the dozen men. Look, the gendarme in the middle, the sergeant, he's pulling the M16 out of his saddle holster!

Abruptly time came back at full speed and Erikki swung away and fled from them, weaving this way and that, expecting every second to be the last, then they were over the side, roaring down into the ravine at treetop level.

'Hold your fire,' the sergeant shouted to the overexcited tribesmen who were at the lip, aiming and firing, their horses cavorting. 'In the Name of God I told you we were ordered to capture them, to save her and kill him, not kill her!' Reluctantly the others obeyed and when he came up to them he saw the 212 was well away down in the valley. He pulled out the walkie-talkie and switched on: 'HQ. This is Sergeant Zibri. The ambush failed. His engines were going before we got into position. But he's flushed out of his hiding place.'

'Which way is he heading?'

'He's turning north towards the Khvoy-Van road.'

'Did you see Her Highness?'

'Yes. She looked petrified. Tell the Khan we saw the kidnapper strap her into the seat and it looked as though the kidnapper also had a strap around her wrist. She . . .' The sergeant's voice picked up excitedly. 'Now the helicopter's turned eastward, it's keeping about two or three kilometres south of the road.'

'Good. Well done. We'll alert the air force . . .'

Chapter 26

At the Bahrain Hospital – Across the Gulf: 1:16 P.M. 'Good morning, Dr. Lanoire. Captain McIver, is it good or bad?' Jean-Luc asked.

The doctor steepled his fingers. He was a distinguished man in his late thirties, trained in Paris and London, trilingual, Arabic, French and English. 'We won't know with much accuracy for a few days: we still have to make several tests. We'll know the real good or bad when he has an angiogram a month from now, but in the meantime Captain McIver's responding to treatment and is not in pain.'

'But is he going to be all right?'

'Angina is quite ordinary, usually. I understand from his wife he's been under very great stress for the last few months, and even worse for the last few days on this Whirlwind exercise of yours – and no wonder. What courage! I salute him to fly all that way and make a safe landing, and I salute you and all those who took part. At the same time I'd strongly advise that all pilots and crews be given two or three months off.'

Jean-Luc beamed. 'May I have that in writing, please? Of course the three months sick leave should be with full pay – and allowances.'

'Of course. What a magnificent job all of you did for your company, risking your lives – you should all get a well-deserved bonus! I wonder why more of you don't have heart attacks. The two months is to recuperate, Jean-Luc – it's essential you have a careful checkup before you continue flying.'

Jean-Luc was perplexed. 'We can all expect heart attacks?'

'Oh, no, no, not at all.' Lanoire smiled. 'But it would be very wise to be checked thoroughly – just in case. It can happen anytime.'

'It can?' Jean-Luc's discomfort increased. Piece of shit! It'd just be my luck to have a heart attack. *Mon Dieu*, Jean-Luc thought squeamishly, bucket of shit. 'How long will Mac be in the hospital?'

'Four or five days. I would suggest you leave him today and visit tomorrow, but don't tax him. He must have a month's leave, then some further tests.'

'What are his chances?'

'That's up to God.'

On the veranda of a pleasant room overlooking the blue waters, Genny was dozing in a chair, today's London *Times* brought by BA's early flight open on her lap. McIver lay comfortably in the starched clean bed. The breeze came off the sea and touched him and he woke up. Wind's changed, he thought. It's back to the standard northeasterly. Good. He moved to see better out into the Gulf. The slight movement awakened her instantly. She folded the paper and got up.

'How're you feeling, luv?'

'Fine. I'm fine now. No pain. Just a bit tired. Vaguely heard you talking to the Doc, what did he say?'

'Everything seems fine. The attack wasn't bad. You'll have to take it easy for a few days, then a month off and then some more tests – he was very encouraging because you don't smoke, you're ever so fit, considering.' Genny stood over the bed, against the light, but he could see her face and read the truth thereon. 'You can't fly anymore – as a pilot,' she said and smiled.

'That's a bugger,' he said drily. 'Have you been in touch with Andy?'

'Yes. I called last night and this morning and will check again in an hour or so. Nothing yet on young Marc Dubois and Fowler, Erikki and Azadeh, Tom – Scrag was delayed but he's airborne now – still plenty of time. Our birds at Al Shargaz are being stripped for freighting out tomorrow. Andy was so proud of you. I talked to him this morning too.'

The shadow of a smile. 'You're okay?'

'Oh, yes.' She touched his shoulder. 'I'm ever so glad you're better – you did give me a turn.'

'I gave me a turn, Gen.' He smiled and held out his hand and said gruffly, 'Thanks, Mrs. McIver.'

She took it and put it to her cheek, then bent down and touched his lips with hers, warmed by the enormity of the affection in his face. 'You did give me such a turn,' she said again.

He noticed the newspaper. 'That today's, Gen?'

'Yes, dear.'

'Seems years since I saw one. What's new?'

'More of the usual.' She folded the paper and put it aside carelessly. 'Strikes, Callaghan's messing up poor old Britain more than ever. They say he might call a snap election this year, and if he does Maggie Thatcher's got a good chance. Wouldn't that be super? Be a change to have someone sensible in charge.'

'Because she's a woman?' He smiled wryly. 'That'd certainly set the cat among the chickens. Christ Almighty, a woman PM! Don't know how she ever wangled the leadership away from Heath in the first place . . . she must have iron-plated knickers! If only the bloody Liberals'd stayed out of the way . . .' His voice trailed off and she saw him look out to sea, some passing dhows beautiful, and knew he was willing the missing ones to land safely.

Quietly she sat down and waited, wanting to let him drift back to sleep, or talk a little, whatever pleased him. He must be getting better if he's already taking off after the Libs, she thought, bemused, letting herself drift, watching the sea. Her hair was moved by the breeze that smelled of sea salt. It was pleasant just sitting, knowing that he was all right now, 'responding to treatment. No need to worry, Mrs. McIver.' Easy to say, hard not to do.

There'll be a huge change in our lives, has to be, apart from losing Iran and all our stuff there, lot of old rubbish, most of it, that I won't miss. Now that Whirlwind's almost over – I must have been mad to suggest it – but already most of our lads are out safely – won't think about Marc or Fowler, Erikki and Azadeh, Sharazad and Lochart, and Scrag, though he's almost safe – God protect them all. There's still time for them. We've most of our equipment out, we've kept our face, and now we can stay in business. We won't be penniless and that's a blessing.

'Duncan, going back to England won't be bad, I promise.'

After a pause he nodded, half to himself. 'We'll wait and see, Gen. We won't make any decision yet. No need to decide what we'll do in a month or so. Don't worry, eh?'

'I'm not worried now.'

'Good, no need to worry.' Once more his attention strayed to the sea. Come on for God's sake, you lot out there, he was thinking, knowing she was sweating them in just as much as he was. For the love of God, you can do it, you can . . .

England? Retire? Christ, if I stop working I'll go mad and I'm damned if I'll spend the rest of our lives battling the bloody English weather . . . seven out of ten birds safe already and still time . . .

His eyes saw a tiny dot low on the sea, far out. His breathing stopped momentarily. But it was not a chopper, just a native boat. His anxiety came back and with it a twinge that increased his anxiety that brought a bigger twinge . . .

'What are you thinking, Duncan?'

'That it's a beautiful day.'

'Yes, yes, it is, and Whirlwind will have a happy ending,' she said, outwardly confident.

He took her hand and squeezed it and both hid their fear, of the future, for the others, for him and for her.

Chapter 27

Just Inside Turkey: 4:23 P.M. They had landed just outside the village this morning barely a mile inside Turkey. Erikki would have preferred to have gone farther into safety but his tanks were dry. He had been intercepted and ambushed again, this time by two fighters and two Huey gunships and had had to endure them for more than a quarter of an hour before he could duck across the line. The two Hueys had not ventured after him but remained circling in station just their side of the border.

'Forget them, Azadeh,' he said joyously. 'We're safe now.'

But they were not. The villagers surrounded them. Police arrived. Four men, a sergeant, and three others, all in uniform – crumpled and ill fitting – with holstered revolvers. The sergeant wore dark glasses against the glare of the sun off the snow. None of them spoke English. Azadeh greeted them according to the plan she and Erikki had concocted, explaining that Erikki, a Finnish citizen, had been employed by a British company under contract to Iran-Timber, that in the Azerbaijan riots and fighting near Tabriz his life had been threatened by leftists, that she, his wife, had been equally threatened, so they had fled.

'Ah, the Effendi is Finnish but you're Iranian?'

'Finnish by marriage, Sergeant Effendi, Iranian by birth. Here are our papers.' She gave him her Finnish passport which did not include references to her late father, Abdollah Khan. 'May we use the telephone, please? We can pay, of course. My husband would like to call our embassy, and also his employer in Al Shargaz.'

'Ah, Al Shargaz.' The sergeant nodded pleasantly. He was heavyset, close-shaven, even so the blue-black of his beard showed through his golden skin. 'Where's that?'

She told him, very conscious of the way she and Erikki looked. Erikki with the filthy, bloodstained bandage on his arm and the crude adhesive over his damaged ear, she with her hair matted and dirty clothes and face. Behind her the two Hueys circled. The sergeant watched them thoughtfully. 'Why would they dare to send fighters into our airspace and helicopters after you?'

'The Will of God, Sergeant Effendi. I'm afraid that on that side of the border many strange things are happening now.'

'How are things over the border?' He motioned the other policeman towards the 212 and began to listen attentively. The three policemen wandered

over, peered into the cockpit. Bullet holes and dried blood and smashed
instruments. One of them opened the cabin door. Many automatic weapons.
More bullet holes. 'Sergeant!'

The sergeant acknowledged but waited politely until Azadeh had finished.
Villagers listened wide-eyed, not a chador or veil among them. Then he
pointed to one of the crude village huts. 'Please wait over there in the shade.'
The day was cold, the land snowbound, the sun bright off the snow. Leisurely
the sergeant examined the cabin and the cockpit. He picked up the kukri, half
pulled it out of the scabbard, and shoved it home again. The he beckoned
Azadeh and Erikki with it. 'How do you explain the guns, Effendi?'

Uneasily Azadeh translated the question for Erikki.

'Tell him they were left in my plane by tribesmen who were attempting to
hijack her.'

'Ah, tribesmen,' the sergeant said. 'I'm astonished tribesmen would leave
such wealth for you to fly away with. Can you explain that?'

'Tell him they were all killed by loyalists, and I escaped in the mêlée.'

'Loyalists, Effendi? What loyalists?'

'Police. Tabrizi police,' Erikki said, uncomfortably aware that each question would pull them deeper into the quicksand. 'Ask him if I can use the
telephone, Azadeh.'

'Telephone? Certainly. In due time.' The sergeant studied the circling
Hueys for a moment. Then he turned his hard brown eyes back to Erikki.
'I'm glad the police were loyal. Police have a duty to the state, to the people,
and to uphold the law. Gunrunning is against the law. Fleeing from police
upholding the law is a crime. Isn't it?'

'Yes, but we're not gunrunners, Sergeant Effendi, nor fleeing from police
upholding the law,' Azadeh had said, even more afraid now. The border was
so close, too close. For her the last part of their escape had been terrifying.
Obviously Hakim had alerted the border area: no one but he had the power
to arrange such an intercept so fast, both on the ground and in the air.

'Are you armed?' the sergeant asked politely.

'Just a knife.'

'May I have it please?' The sergeant accepted it. 'Please follow me.'

They had gone to the police station, a small brick building with cells and a
few offices and telephones near the mosque in the little village square. 'Over
the last months we've had many refugees of all sorts passing along our road,
Iranians, British, Europeans, Americans, many Azerbaijanis, many – but no
Soviets.' He laughed at his own joke. 'Many refugees, rich, poor, good,
bad, many criminals among them. Some were sent back, some went on.
Insha'Allah, eh? Please wait there.'

'There' was not a cell but a room with a few chairs and a table and bars on
the windows, many flies and no way out. But it was warm and relatively clean.
'Could we have some food and drink and use the telephone, please?' Azadeh
asked. 'We can pay, Sergeant Effendi.'

'I will order some for you from the hotel here. The food is good and not
expensive.'

'My husband asks, can he use the telephone, please?'

'Certainly – in due course.'

That had been this morning, and now it was late afternoon. In the intervening time the food had arrived, rice and mutton stew and peasant bread and Turkish coffee. She had paid with rials and was not overcharged. The sergeant had allowed them to use the foul-smelling hole in the ground squatter, and water from a tank and an old basin to wash in. There were no medical supplies, just iodine. Erikki had cleaned his wounds as best he could, gritting his teeth at the sudden pain, still weak and exhausted. Then, with Azadeh close beside him, he had propped himself on a chair, his feet on another, and had drifted off. From time to time the door would open and one or other of the policemen would come in, then go out again. '*Matyeryebyets*,' Erikki muttered. 'Where can we run to?'

She had gentled him and stayed close and kept a steel gate on her own fear. I must carry him, she thought over and over. She was feeling better now with her hair combed and flowing, her face clean, her cashmere sweater tidy. Through the door she could hear muttered conversation, occasionally a telephone ringing, cars and trucks going past on the road from and to the border, flies droning. Her tiredness took her and she slept fitfully, her dreams bad: noise of engines and firing and Hakim mounted like a Cossack charging them, both she and Erikki buried up to their necks in the earth, hooves just missing them, then somehow free, rushing for the border that was acres of massed barbed wire, the false mullah Mahmud and the butcher suddenly between them and safety and th –

The door opened. Both of them awoke, startled. A major in immaculate uniform stood there, glowering, flanked by the sergeant and another policeman. He was a tall, hard-faced man. 'Your papers, please,' he said to Azadeh.

'I, I gave them to the sergeant, Major Effendi.'

'You gave him a Finnish passport. Your Iranian papers.' The major held out his hand. She was too slow. At once the sergeant went forward and grabbed her shoulder bag and spilled the contents on to the table. Simultaneously, the other policeman stalked over to Erikki, his hand on the revolver in his open holster, waved him into a corner against the wall. The major flicked some dirt off a chair and sat down, accepted her Iranian ID from the sergeant, read it carefully, then looked at the contents on the table. He opened the jewel bag. His eyes widened. 'Where did you get these?'

'They're mine. Inherited from my parents.' Azadeh was frightened, not knowing what he knew or how much, and she had seen the way his eyes covered her. So had Erikki. 'May my husband please use the telephone? He wish – '

'In due course! You have been told that many times. In due course is in due course.' The major zipped up the bag and put it on the table in front of him. His eyes strayed to her breasts. 'Your husband doesn't speak Turkish?'

'No, no he doesn't, Major Effendi.'

The officer turned on Erikki and said in good English, 'There's a warrant out for your arrest from Tabriz. For attempted murder and kidnapping.'

Azadeh blanched and Erikki held on to his panic as best he could. 'Kidnapping who, sir?'

A flash of irritability washed over the major. 'Don't try to play with me. This lady. Azadeh, sister to Hakim, the Gorgon Khan.'

'She's my wife. How can a hus – '

'I know she's your wife and you'd better tell me the truth, by God. The warrant says you took her against her will and flew off in an Iranian helicopter.' Azadeh started to answer but the major snapped, 'I asked him, not you. Well?'

'It was without her consent and the chopper is British not Iranian.'

The major stared at him, then turned to Azadeh. 'Well?'

'It . . . it was without my consent . . .' The words trailed off.

'But what?'

Azadeh felt sick. Her head ached and she was in despair. Turkish police were known for their inflexibility, their great personal power and toughness. 'Please, Major Effendi, perhaps we may talk in private, explain in private?'

'We're in private now, madam,' the major said curtly, then seeing her anguish and appreciating her beauty, added, 'English is more private than Turkish. Well?'

So, haltingly, choosing her words carefully, she told him about her oath to Abdollah Khan and about Hakim and the dilemma, unable to leave, unable to stay and how Erikki, of his own volition and wisdom, had cut through the Gordian knot. Tears streaked her cheeks. 'Yes, it was without my consent but in a way it was with the consent of my brother who helped Er – '

'If it was with Hakim Khan's consent then why has he put a huge reward on this man's head, alive or dead,' the major said, disbelieving her, 'and had the warrant issued in his name, demanding immediate extradition if necessary?'

She was so shocked she almost fainted. Without thinking Erikki moved towards her, but the revolver went into his stomach. 'I was only going to help her,' he gasped.

'Then stay where you are!' In Turkish the officer said, 'Don't kill him.' In English he said, 'Well, Lady Azadeh? Why?'

She could not answer. Her mouth moved but made no sound. Erikki said for her, 'What else could a Khan do, Major? A Khan's honour, his face is involved. Publicly he would have to do that, wouldn't he, whatever he approved in private?'

'Perhaps, but certainly not so quickly, no, not so quickly, not alerting fighters and helicopters – why should he do that if he wanted you to escape? It's a miracle you weren't forced down, didn't fall down with all those bullet holes. It sounds like a pack of lies – perhaps she's so frightened of you she'll say anything. Now, your so-called escape from the palace: exactly what happened?'

Helplessly Erikki told him. Nothing more to do, he thought. Tell him the truth and hope. Most of his concentration was on Azadeh, seeing the blank horror pervading her, yet of course Hakim would react the way he had – of course dead or alive – wasn't the blood of his father strong in his veins?

'And the guns?'

Once more Erikki told it exactly, about being forced to fly the KGB, about Sheik Bayazid and his kidnap and ransom and the attack on the palace, having to fly them off and then their breaking their oaths and so having to kill them somehow.

'How many men?'

'I don't remember exactly. Half a dozen, perhaps more.'

'You enjoy killing, eh?'

'No, Major, I hate it, but please believe us, we've been caught up in a web not of our seeking, all we want to do is be let go, please let me call my embassy . . . they can vouch for us . . . we're a threat to no one.'

The major just looked at him. 'I don't agree, your story's too far fetched. You're wanted for kidnapping and attempted murder. Please go with the sergeant,' he said and repeated it in Turkish. Erikki did not move, his fists bunched, and he was near exploding. At once the sergeant's gun was out, both police converged on him dangerously, and the major said harshly, 'It's a very serious offence to disobey police in this country. Go with the sergeant! Go with him.'

Azadeh tried to say something, couldn't. Erikki thrust off the sergeant's hand, contained his own impotent panic-rage, and tried to smile to encourage her. 'It's all right,' he muttered and followed the sergeant.

Azadeh's panic and terror had almost overwhelmed her. Now her fingers and knees were trembling, but she wanted so much to sit tall and be tall, knowing she was defenceless and the major was sitting there opposite her watching her, the room empty but for the two of them. Insha'Allah, she thought and looked at him, hating him.

'You have nothing to fear,' he said, his eyes curious. Then he reached over and picked up her jewel bag. 'For safekeeping,' he said thinly and stalked for the door, closed it after him, and went down the passageway.

The cell at the end was small and dirty, more like a cage than a room, with a cot, bars on the tiny window, chains attached to a huge bolt in one wall, a foul-smelling bucket in a corner. The sergeant slammed the door and locked it on Erikki. Through the bars the major said, 'Remember, the Lady Azadeh's . . . "comfort" depends on your docility.' He went away.

Now, alone, Erikki started prowling the cage, studying the door, lock, bars, floor, ceiling, walls, chains – seeking a way out.

At the Oasis Hotel: Al Shargaz: 11:52 P.M. In the darkness the telephone jangled discordantly, jerking Gavallan out of a deep sleep. He groped for it, switching on his sidetable light. 'Hello?'

'Hello, Andrew, this is Roger Newbury, sorry to call so late but th – '

'Oh, that's all right, I said to call up till midnight.'

'Good. How the hell you managed I don't know – and I hate to bring bad tidings along with the good but we've just had a telex from Henley in Tabriz.'

Sleep vanished from Gavallan. 'Trouble?'

'Afraid so. It sounds bizarre but this's what it says.' There was a rustle of paper, then, 'Henley says "We hear there was some sort of attack yesterday or last night on Hakim Khan's life, Captain Yokkonen is supposed to be implicated. Last night he fled for the Turkish border in his helicopter, taking his wife Azadeh with him, against her will. A warrant for attempted murder and kidnapping has been issued in Hakim Khan's name. A great deal of fighting between rival factions is presently going on in Tabriz which is making accurate reporting somewhat difficult. Further details will be sent immediately they are available." That's all there is. Astonishing, what?' Silence. 'Andrew? Are you there?'

'Yes . . . yes, I am. Just . . . just, er, trying to collect my wits. There's no chance there'd be a mistake?'

'I doubt that. I've sent an urgent signal for more details. We might get something tomorrow. I suggest you contact the Finnish ambassador in London, alert him. The embassy number is 01-766 8888. Sorry about all this.'

Gavallan thanked him and, dazed, replaced the phone.

Sunday

Chapter 28

At the Turkish Village: 10:20 A.M. Azadeh awoke with a start. For a moment she could not remember where she was, then the room came into focus – small, drab, two windows, the straw mattress of the bed hard, clean but coarse sheets and blankets – and she recalled that this was the village hotel and last night at sunset, in spite of her protests and not wanting to leave Erikki, she had been escorted here by the major and a policeman. The major had brushed aside her excuses and insisted on dining with her in the tiny restaurant that had emptied immediately they had arrived. 'Of course you must eat something to keep up your strength. Please sit down. I will order whatever you eat for your husband and have them send it to him. Would you like that?'

'Yes, please,' she said, also in Turkish, and sat down, understanding the implied threat, the hackles on her neck twisting. 'I can pay for it.'

The barest touch of a smile moved his full lips. 'As you wish.'

'Thank you, Major Effendi. When can my husband and I leave, please?'

'I will discuss that with you tomorrow, not tonight.' He motioned to the policeman to stand guard on the door. 'Now we will speak English,' he said, offering her his silver cigarette case.

'No, thank you. I don't smoke. When can I have my jewellery back, please, Major Effendi?'

He selected a cigarette and began tapping the end on the case, watching her. 'As soon as it is safe. My name is Abdul Ikail. I'm stationed at Van and responsible for this whole region, up to the border.' He used his lighter, exhaled smoke, his eyes never leaving her. 'Have you been to Van before?'

'No, no I haven't.'

'It's a sleepy little place. It was,' he corrected himself, 'before your revolution though it's always been difficult on the border.' Another deep intake of smoke. 'Undesirables on both sides wanting to cross or to flee. Smugglers, drug dealers, arms dealers, thieves, all the carrion you can think of.' He said it casually, wisps of smoke punctuating the words. The air was heavy in the little room and smelled of old cooking, humans, and stale tobacco. She was filled with foreboding. Her fingers began to toy with the strap of her shoulder bag.

'Have you been to Istanbul?' he asked.

'Yes. Yes, once for a few days when I was a little girl. I went with my father, he had business there and I, I was put on a plane for school in Switzerland.'

'I've never been to Switzerland. I went to Rome once on a holiday. And to Bonn on a police course, and another one in London, but never Switzerland.' He smoked a moment, lost in thought, then stubbed out the cigarette in a chipped ashtray and beckoned the hotel owner who stood abjectly by the door, waiting to take his order. The food was primitive but good and served with great, nervous humility that further unsettled her. Clearly the village was not used to such an august presence.

'No need to be afraid, Lady Azadeh, you're not in danger,' he told her as though reading her mind. 'On the contrary. I'm glad to have the opportunity to talk to you, it's rare a person of your . . . your quality passes this way.' Throughout dinner, patiently and politely, he questioned her about Azerbaijan and Hakim Khan, volunteering little, refusing to discuss Erikki or what was going to happen. 'What will happen will happen. Please tell me your story again.'

'I've . . . I've already told it to you, Major Effendi. It's the truth, it's not a story. I told you the truth, so did my husband.'

'Of course,' he said, eating hungrily. 'Please tell it to me again.'

So she had, afraid, reading his eyes and the desire therein though he was always punctilious and circumspect. 'It's the truth,' she said, hardly touching the food in front of her, her appetite vanished. 'We've committed no crime, my husband only defended himself and me – before God.'

'Unfortunately God cannot testify on your behalf. Of course, in your case, I accept what you say as what you believe. Fortunately here we're more of this world, we're not fundamentalist, there's a separation between Islam and state, no self-appointed men get between us and God, and we're only fanatic to keep our own way of life as we want it – and other people's beliefs or laws from being crammed down our throats.' He stopped, listening intently. Walking here in the falling light they had heard distant firing and some heavy mortars. Now, in the silence of the restaurant, they heard more. 'Probably Kurds defending their homes in the mountains.' His lips curled disgustedly. 'We hear Khomeini is sending your army, and Green Bands, against them.'

'Then it's another mistake,' she said. 'That's what my brother says.'

'I agree. My family is Kurd.' He got up. 'A policeman will be outside your door all night. For your protection,' he said with the same curious half smile that greatly perturbed her. 'For your protection. Please stay in your room until I . . . I come for you or send for you. Your compliance assists your husband. Sleep well.'

So she had gone to the room she had been given and then, seeing there was no lock or bolt on the door, had jammed a chair under the knob. The room was cold, the water in the jug icy. She washed and dried herself, then prayed, adding a special prayer for Erikki, and sat on the bed.

With great care she slipped out the six-inch, steel hatpin that was secreted in the binding of her shoulder bag, studied it for a second. The point was needle sharp, the head small but big enough to grip for a thrust. She slid it into the underside of the pillow as Ross had shown her: 'Then it's no danger to you,' he had said with a smile, 'a hostile wouldn't notice it, and you can get it easily. A beautiful young girl like you should always be armed, just in case.'

'Oh, but, Johnny, I'd never be able to . . . never.'

'You will when – if – the time ever comes, and you should be prepared to. So long as you're armed, know how to use the weapon whatever it is, and accept that you may have to kill to protect yourself, then you'll never, ever, need to be afraid.' Over those beautiful months in the High Lands he had shown her how to use it. 'Just an inch in the right place is more than enough, it's deadly enough . . .' She had carried it ever since, but never once had had to use it – not even in the village. The village. Leave the village to the night, not to the day.

Her fingers touched the head of the weapon. Perhaps tonight, she thought. Insha'Allah! What about Erikki? Insha'Allah! Then she was reminded of Erikki saying, ' "Insha'Allah's" fine, Azadeh, and a great excuse, but God by any name needs a helping earthly hand from time to time.'

Yes. I promise you I'm prepared, Erikki. Tomorrow is tomorrow and I will help, my darling. I'll get you out of this somehow.

Reassured she blew out the candle, curled up under the sheets and covers still dressed in sweater and ski pants. Moonlight came through the windows. Soon she was warm. Warmth and exhaustion and youth led her into sleep that was dreamless.

In the night she was suddenly awake. The doorknob was turning softly. Her hand went to the spike and she lay there, watching the door. The handle went to the limit, the door moved a fraction but did not budge, held tightly closed by the chair that now creaked under the strain. In a moment the knob turned quietly back to its resting place. Again silence. No footsteps or breathing. Nor did the knob move again. She smiled to herself. Johnny had also showed her how to place the chair. Ah, my darling, I hope you find the happiness you seek, she thought, and slept again, facing the door.

Now she was awake and rested and knew that she was much stronger than yesterday, more ready for the battle that would soon begin. Yes, by God, she told herself, wondering what had brought her out of sleep. Sounds of traffic and street vendors. No, not those. Then again a knock on the door.

'Who is it, please?'

'Major Ikail.'

'One moment, please.' She pulled on her boots, straightened her sweater and her hair. Deftly she disengaged the chair. 'Good morning, Major Effendi.'

He glanced at the chair, amused. 'You were wise to jam the door. Don't do it again – without permission.' Then he scrutinised her. 'You seem rested. Good. I've ordered coffee and fresh bread for you. What else would you like?'

'Just to be let go, my husband and I.'

'So?' He came into the room and closed the door and took the chair and sat down, his back to the sunlight that streamed in from the window. 'With your cooperation that might be arranged.'

When he had moved into the room, without being obvious she had retreated and now sat on the edge of the bed, her hand within inches of the pillow. 'What cooperation, Major Effendi?'

'It might be wise not to have a confrontation,' he said curiously. 'If you cooperate . . . and go back to Tabriz of your own free will this evening, your husband will remain in custody tonight and be sent to Istanbul tomorrow.'

She heard herself say, 'Sent where in Istanbul?'

'First to prison – for safekeeping – where his ambassador will be able to see him and, if it's God's will, to be released.'

'Why should he be sent to prison, he's done noth – '

'There's a reward on his head. Dead or alive.' The major smiled thinly. 'He needs protection – there are dozens of your nationals in the village and near here, all on the edge of starvation. Don't you need protection too? Wouldn't you be a perfect kidnap victim, wouldn't the Khan ransom his only sister at once and lavishly? Eh?'

'Gladly I'll go back if that will help my husband,' she said at once. 'But if I go back, what . . . what guarantee do I have that my husband will be protected and be sent to Istanbul, Major Effendi?'

'None.' He got up and stood over her. 'The alternative is if you don't cooperate of your own free will, you'll be sent to the border today and he . . . he will have to take his chances.'

She did not get up, nor take her hand away from the pillow. Nor look up at him. I'd do that gladly but once I'm gone Erikki's defenceless. Cooperate? Does that mean bed this man of my own free will? 'How must I cooperate? What do you want me to do?' she asked and was furious that her voice seemed smaller than before.

He half laughed and said sardonically, 'To do what all women have difficulty in doing: to be obedient, to do what they're told without argument, and to stop trying to be clever.' He turned on his heel. 'You will stay here in the hotel. I will return later. I hope by then you'll be prepared . . . to give me the correct answer.' He shut the door after him.

If he tries to force me, I will kill him, she thought. I cannot bed him as a barter – my husband would never forgive me, nor could I forgive myself, for we both know the act would not guarantee his freedom or mine, and even if it did he could not live with the knowledge and would seek revenge. Nor could I live with myself.

She got up and went to the window and looked out at the busy village, snow-covered mountains around it, the border over there, such a little way.

'The only chance Erikki has is for me to go back,' she muttered. 'But I can't, not without the major's approval. And even then . . .'

At the Police Station: 11:58 A.M. Gripped by Erikki's great fists, the lower end of the central iron bar in the window came free with a small shower of cement. Hastily he pushed it back into its hole, looked out of the cage door and down the corridor. No jailer appeared. Quickly he stuffed small pieces of cement and rubble back around the base camouflaging it – he had been working on this bar most of the night, worrying it as a dog would a bone. Now he had a weapon and a lever to bend the other bars out of shape.

It'll take me half an hour, no more, he thought, and sat back on his bunk, satisfied. After bringing the food last evening the police had left him alone, confident in the strength of their cage. This morning they had brought him coffee that had tasted vile and a hunk of rough bread and had stared at him without understanding when he asked for the major and for his wife. He did not know the Turkish for "major" nor had he the officer's name, but when he pointed to his lapel, miming the man's rank, they had understood him and had just shrugged, spoken more Turkish that he did not understand, and gone away again. The sergeant had not reappeared.

Each of us knows what to do, he thought, Azadeh and I, each of us is at risk, each will do the best we can. But if she's touched, or hurt, no god will help him who touched her while I live. I swear it.

The door at the end of the corridor opened. The major strode towards him. 'Good morning,' he said, his nostrils crinkling at the foul smell.

'Good morning, Major. Where's my wife, please, and when are you letting us go?'

'Your wife is in the village, quite safe, rested. I've seen her myself.' The major eyed him thoughtfully, noticed the dirt on his hands, glanced keenly at the lock on the cage, the window bars, the floor, and the ceiling. 'Her safety and treatment are dependent on you. You do understand?'

'Yes, yes, I do understand. And I hold you as the senior policeman here responsible for her.'

The major laughed. 'Good,' he said sardonically, then the smile vanished. 'It seems best to avoid a confrontation. If you cooperate you will stay here tonight, tomorrow I'll send you under guard to Istanbul – where your ambassador can see you if he wants – to stand trial for the crimes you're accused of, or to be extradited.'

Erikki dismissed his own problems. 'I brought my wife here against her will. She's done nothing wrong, she should go home. Can she be escorted?'

The major watched him. 'That depends on your cooperation.'

'I will ask her to go back. I'll insist, if that's what you mean.'

'She could be sent back,' the major said, taunting him. 'Oh, yes. But of course it's possible that on the way to the border or even from the hotel, she could be "kidnapped" again, this time by bandits, Iranian bandits, bad ones, to be held in the mountains for a month or two, eventually to be ransomed to the Khan.'

Erikki was ashen. 'What do you want me to do?'

'Not far away is the railway. Tonight you could be smuggled out of here and taken safely to Istanbul. The charges against you could be quashed. You could be given a good job, flying, training our fliers – for two years. In return you agree to become a secret agent for us, you supply us with information about Azerbaijan, particularly about this Soviet you mentioned, Mzytryk, information about Hakim Khan, where and how he lives, how to get into the palace – and anything else that is wanted.'

'What about my wife?'

'She stays in Van of her own free will, hostage to your behaviour . . . for a month or two. Then she can join you, wherever you are.'

'Provided she's escorted back to Hakim Khan today, safely, unharmed and it's proved to me she's safe and unharmed, I will do what you ask.'

'Either you agree or you don't,' the major said impatiently. 'I'm not here to bargain with you!'

'Please, she's nothing to do with any crimes of mine. Please let her go. Please.'

'You think we're fools? Do you agree or don't you?'

'Yes! But first I want her safe. First!'

'Perhaps first you'd like to watch her spoiled. First.'

Erikki lunged for him through the bars and the whole cage door shuddered under the impact. But the major stood there just out of range and laughed at the great hand clawing for him impotently. He had judged the distance accurately, far too practised to be caught unawares, far too experienced an investigator not to know how to taunt and threaten and tempt, how to jeer and exaggerate and use the prisoner's own fears and terrors, how to twist truths to break through the curtain of inevitable lies and half-truths – to get at the real truth.

His superiors had left it up to him to decide what to do about both of them. Now he had decided. Without hurrying he pulled out his revolver and pointed it at Erikki's face. And cocked the pistol. Erikki did not back off, just held the bars with his huge hands, his breath coming in great pants.

'Good,' the major said calmly, holstering the gun. 'You have been warned your behaviour gauges her treatment.' He walked away. When Erikki was alone again, he tried to tear the cage door off its hinges. The door groaned but held firm.

At the Police Station in the Turkish Village: 5:18 P.M. '. . . just as you say, Effendi. You will make the necessary arrangements?' the major said deferentially into the phone. He was sitting at the only desk in the small, scruffy office, the sergeant standing nearby, the kukri and Erikki's knife on the desktop. '. . . Good. Yes . . . yes, I agree. Salaam.' He replaced the phone, lit a cigarette, and got up. 'I'll be at the hotel.'

'Yes, Effendi.' The sergeant's eyes glinted with amusement but, carefully, he kept it off his face. He watched the major straighten his jacket and hair and put on his fez, envying him his rank and power. The phone rang. 'Police, yes? . . . oh, hello, Sergeant.' He listened with growing astonishment. 'But . . . yes . . . yes, very well.' Blankly he put the phone back on its hook. 'It . . . it was Sergeant Kurbel at the border, Major Effendi. There's an Iran Air Force truck with Green Bands and a mullah coming to take the helicopter and the prisoner and her back to Ir – '

The major exploded. 'In the Name of God who allowed hostiles over our border without authority? There're standing orders about mullahs and revolutionaries!'

'I don't know, Effendi,' the sergeant said, frightened by the sudden rage. 'Kurbel just said they were waving official papers and insisted – everyone knows about the Iranian helicopter so he just let them through.'

'Are they armed?'

'He didn't say, Effendi.'

'Get your men, all of them, with submachine guns.'

'But . . . but what about the prisoner?'

'Forget him!' the major said and stormed out cursing.

On the Outskirts of the Village: 5:32 P.M. The Iran Air Force truck was a four-wheel drive, part tanker and part truck and it turned off the side road that was little more than a track on to the snow, changed gears, and headed for the 212. Nearby, the police sentry went to meet it.

Half a dozen armed youths wearing green armbands jumped down, then three unarmed uniformed Iran Air Force personnel, and a mullah. The mullah slung his Kalashnikov. 'Salaam. We're here to take possession of our property in the name of the Imam and the people,' the mullah said importantly. 'Where is the kidnapper and the woman?'

'I . . . I don't know anything about this.' The policeman was flustered. His orders were clear: Stand guard and keep everyone away until you're told otherwise. 'You'd better go to the police station first and ask there.' He saw one of the air force personnel open the cockpit door and lean into the cockpit, the other two were reeling out refuelling hoses. 'Hey, you three, you're not allowed near the helicopter without permission!'

The mullah stood in his path. 'Here is our authority!' He waved papers in the policeman's face and that rattled him even more, for he could not read.

'You better go to the station first . . .' he stammered, then with vast relief saw the station police car hurtling along the little road towards them from the direction of the village. It swerved off into the snow, trundled a few yards and stopped. The major, sergeant and two policemen got out, riot guns in their hands. Surrounded by his Green Bands, the mullah went towards them, unafraid.

'Who're you?' the major said harshly.

'Mullah Ali Miandiry of the Khvoy komiteh. We have come to take possession of our property, the kidnapper and the woman, in the name of the Imam and the people.'

'Woman? You mean Her Highness, the sister of Hakim Khan?'

'Yes. Her.'

' "Imam"? Imam who?'

'Imam Khomeini, peace be on him.'

'Ah, Ayatollah Khomeini,' the major said, affronted by the title. 'What "people"?'

Just as toughly the mullah shoved some papers towards him. 'The People of Iran. Here is our authority.'

The major took the papers, scanned them rapidly. There were two of them, hastily scrawled in Farsi. The sergeant and his two men had spread out, surrounding the truck, submachine guns in their hands. The mullah and Green Bands watched them contemptuously.

'Why isn't it on the correct legal form?' the major said. 'Where's the police seal and the signature of the Khvoy police chief?'

'We don't need one. It's signed by the komiteh.'

'What komiteh? I know nothing about komitehs.'

'The revolutionary komiteh of Khvoy has authority over this area and the police.'

'This area? This area's Turkey!'

'I meant authority over the area up to the border.'

'By whose authority? Where is your authority? Show it to me!'

A current went through the youths. 'The mullah's shown it to you,' one of them said truculently. 'The komiteh signed the paper.'

'Who signed it? You?'

'I did,' the mullah said. 'It's legal. Perfectly legal. The komiteh is the authority.' He saw the air force personnel staring at him. 'What are you waiting for? Get the helicopter refuelled!'

Before the major could say anything, one of them said deferentially, 'Excuse me, Excellency, the panel's in a mess, some of the instruments are broken. We can't fly her until she's checked out. It'd be safer to g – '

'The Infidel flew it all the way from Tabriz safely by night and by day, landed it safely, why can't you fly it during the day?'

'It's just that it'd be safer to check before flying, Excellency.'

'Safer? Why safer?' one of the Green Bands said roughly, walking over to him. 'We're in God's hands doing God's work. Do you want to delay God's work and leave the helicopter here?'

'Of course not, of co – '

'Then obey our mullah and refuel it! Now!'

'Yes, yes, of course,' the pilot said lamely. 'As you wish.' Hastily the three of them hurried to comply – the major shocked to see that the pilot, a captain, allowed himself to be overridden so easily by the young thug who now stared back at him with flat, challenging eyes.

'The komiteh has jurisdiction over the police, agha,' the mullah was saying. 'Police served the Satan Shah and are suspect. Where is the kidnapper and the . . . the sister of the Khan?'

'Where's your authority to come over the border and ask for anything?' The major was coldly furious.

'In the Name of God, this is authority enough!' The mullah stabbed his finger at the papers. One of the youths cocked his gun.

'Don't,' the major warned him. 'If you pull a single trigger on our soil, our forces will come over your border and burn everything between here and Tabriz!'

'If it's the Will of God!' The mullah stared back, dark eyes and dark beard and just as resolved, despising the major and the loose regime the man and uniform represented to him. War now or later was all the same to him, he was in God's hands and doing God's work and the Word of the Imam would sweep them to victory – over all borders. But now was not the time for war, too much to do in Khvoy, leftists to overcome, revolts to put down, the Imam's enemies to destroy, and for that, in these mountains, every helicopter was priceless.

'I . . . I ask for possession of our property,' he said, more reasonably. He pointed at the markings. 'There are our registrations, that's proof that it is our property. It was stolen from Iran – you must know there was no permission to leave Iran, legally it is still our property. The warrant,' he pointed to the papers in the major's hand, 'the warrant is legal, the pilot kidnapped the woman, so we will take possession of them too. Please.'

The major was in an untenable situation. He could not possibly hand over the Finn and his wife to illegals because of an illegal piece of paper – that would be a gross dereliction of duty and would, correctly, cost him his head. If the mullah forced the issue he would have to resist and defend the police station, but obviously he had insufficient men to do so, obviously he would fail in the confrontation. Equally he was convinced that the mullah and Green Bands were prepared to die this very minute as he himself was not.

He decided to gamble. 'The kidnapper and the Lady Azadeh were sent to Van this morning. To extradite them you have to apply to Army HQ, not to me. The . . . the importance of the Khan's sister meant that the army took possession of both of them.'

The mullah's face froze. One of the Green Bands said sullenly, 'How do we know that's not a lie?' The major whirled on him, the youth jumped back a foot, Green Bands behind the truck aimed, the unarmed airmen dropped to the ground aghast, the major's hand went for his revolver.

'Stop!' the mullah said. He was obeyed, even by the major who was furious with himself for allowing pride and reflexes to overcome his self-discipline. The mullah thought a moment, considering possibilities. Then he said, 'We will apply to Van. Yes, we will do that. But not today. Today we will take our property and we will leave.' He stood there, legs slightly apart, assault rifle over his shoulder, supremely confident.

The major fought to hide his relief. The helicopter had no value to him or his superiors and was an extreme embarrassment. 'I agree they're your markings,' he said shortly. 'As to ownership, I don't know. If you sign a receipt leaving ownership open, you may take it and leave.'

'I will sign a receipt for our helicopter.'

On the back of the warrant the major scrawled what would satisfy him and perhaps satisfy the mullah. The mullah turned and scowled at the airmen who hurriedly began reeling in the fuel hoses, and the pilot stood beside the cockpit once more, brushing the snow off. 'Are you ready now, pilot?'

'Any moment, Excellency.'

'Here,' the major said to the mullah, handing him the paper.

With barely concealed derision the mullah signed it without reading it. 'Are you ready now, pilot?' he said.

'Yes, Excellency, yes.' The young captain looked at the major and the major saw – or thought he saw – the misery in his eyes and the unspoken plea for asylum that was impossible to grant. 'Can I start up?'

'Start up,' the mullah said imperiously. 'Of course start up.' In seconds the engines began winding up sweetly, rotors picking up speed. 'Ali and Abrim, you go with the truck back to the base.'

Obediently the two young men got in with the air force driver. The mullah motioned them to leave and the others to board the helicopter. The rotors were thrashing the air and he waited until everyone was in the cabin, then unslung his gun, sat beside the pilot and pulled the door closed.

Engines building, an awkward liftoff, the 212 started trundling away. Angrily the sergeant aimed his submachine gun. 'I can blow the motherless turds out of the sky, Major.'

'Yes, yes, we could.' The major took out his cigarette case. 'But we'll leave that to God. Perhaps God will do that for us.' He used the lighter shakily, inhaled, and watched the truck and the helicopter grinding away. 'Those dogs will have to be taught manners and a lesson.' He walked over to the car and got in. 'Drop me at the hotel.'

At the Hotel: Azadeh was leaning out of the window, searching the sky. She had heard the 212 start up and take off and was filled with impossible hope that Erikki had somehow escaped. 'Oh, God, let it be true . . .'

Villagers were also looking up at the sky and now she too saw the chopper well on its way back to the border. Her insides turned over. Has he bartered his freedom for mine? Oh, Erikki . . .

Then she saw the police car come into the square, stop outside the hotel, and the major get out, straighten his uniform. Her face drained. Resolutely she closed the window and sat on the chair facing the door, near the pillow. Waiting. Waiting. Now footsteps. The door opened. 'Follow me,' he said. 'Please.'

For a moment she did not understand. 'What?'

'Follow me. Please.'

'Why?' she asked suspiciously, expecting a trap and not wanting to leave the safety of the hidden spike. 'What's going on? Is my husband flying the helicopter? It's going back. Have you sent him back?' She felt her courage leaving her fast, her anxiety that Erikki had given himself up in return for her safety making her frantic. 'Is he flying it?'

'No, your husband's in the police station. Iranians came for the helicopter, for him and you.' Now that the crisis was over, the major felt very good. 'The airplane was Iran-registered, had no clearance to leave Iran, so therefore they still had a right to it. Now, follow me.'

'Where to, please?'

'I thought you might like to see your husband.' The major enjoyed looking at her, enjoyed the danger, wondering where her secret weapon was. These women always have a weapon or venom of some kind, death of some kind lurking for the unwary rapist. Easy to overcome if you're ready, if you watch their hands and don't sleep. 'Well?'

'There are . . . there are Iranians at the police station?'

'No. This is Turkey, not Iran, no alien is waiting for you. Come along, you've nothing to fear.'

'I'll . . . I'll be right down. At once.'

'Yes, you will – at once,' he said. 'You don't need a bag, just your jacket. Be quick before I change my mind.' He saw the flash of fury and it further amused him. But this time she obeyed, seething, put on her jacket and went down the stairs, hating her helplessness. Across the square beside him, eyes watching them. Into the station and the room, the same one as before. 'Please wait here.'

Then he closed the door and went into the office. The sergeant held out the phone for him. 'I have Captain Tanazak, Border Station duty officer for you, sir.'

'Captain? Major Ikail. The border's closed to all mullahs and Green Bands until further orders. Arrest the sergeant who let some through a couple of hours ago and send him to Van in great discomfort. An Iranian truck's coming back. Order it harassed for twenty hours, and the men in it. As for you, you're subject to court-martial for failing to ensure standing instructions about armed men!' He put the phone down, glanced at his watch. 'Is the car ready, Sergeant?'

'Yes, Effendi.'

'Good.' The major went through the door, down the corridor to the cage, the sergeant following him. Erikki did not get up. Only his eyes moved. 'Now, Mr. Pilot, if you're prepared to be calm, controlled, and no longer stupid, I'm going to bring your wife to see you.'

Erikki's voice grated. 'If you or anyone touches her I swear I'll kill you, I'll tear you to pieces.'

'I agree it must be difficult to have such a wife. Better to have an ugly one than one such as her – unless she's kept in purdah. Now do you want to see her or not?'

'What do I have to do?'

Irritably the major said, 'Be calm, controlled and no longer stupid.' To the sergeant he said in Turkish, 'Go and fetch her.'

Erikki's mind was expecting disaster or a trick. Then he saw her at the end of the corridor, and that she was whole, and he almost wept with relief, and so did she.

'Oh, Erikki . . .'

'Both of you listen to me,' the major said curtly. 'Even though you've both caused us a great deal of inconvenience and embarrassment, I've decided you were both telling the truth. You will be sent at once with a guard to Istanbul, discreetly, and handed over to your ambassador, discreetly – to be expelled, discreetly.'

They stared at him, dumbfounded. 'We're to be freed?' she said, holding on to the bars.

'At once. We expect your discretion – and that's part of the bargain. You will have to agree formally in writing. Discretion. That means no leaks, no public or private crowing about your escape or escapades. You agree?'

'Oh, yes, yes, of course,' Azadeh said. 'But there's, there's no trick?'

'No.'

'But . . . but why? Why after . . . why're you letting us go?' Erikki stumbled over the words, still not believing him.

'Because I tested both of you, you both passed the tests, you committed no crimes that we would judge crimes – your oaths are between you and God and not subject to any court – and, fortunately for you, the warrant was illegal and therefore unacceptable. Komiteh!' he muttered disgustedly, then noticed the way they were looking at each other. For a moment he was awed. And envious.

Curious that Hakim Khan allowed a komiteh to issue a warrant and sign it, not the police who would have made extradition legal. He motioned to the sergeant. 'Let him out. I'll wait for you both in the office. Don't forget I still have your jewellery to return to you. And the two knives.' He strode off.

The cage gate opened noisily. The sergeant hesitated, then left. Neither Erikki nor Azadeh noticed him go or the foulness of the cell, only each other, she just outside, still holding on to the bars, he just inside, holding on to the bars of the door. They did not move. Just smiled.

'Insha'Allah?' she said.

'Why not?' And then, still disoriented by their deliverance by an honest man whom Erikki would have torn apart as the epitome of evil a moment ago, Erikki remembered what the major had said about purdah, how desirable she was. In spite of his wish not to wreck the miracle of the good he blurted out, 'Azadeh, I'd like to leave all the bad here. Can we? What about John Ross?'

Her smile did not alter and she knew that they were at the abyss. With confidence she leaped into it, glad for the opportunity. 'Long ago in our beginning I told you that once upon a time I knew him when I was very young,' she said, her voice tender, belying her anxiety. 'In the village and at the base he saved my life. When I meet him again, if I meet him, I will smile at him and be happy. I beg you to do the same. The past is the past and should stay the past.'

Accept it and him, Erikki, now and for ever, she was willing him, or our marriage will end quickly, not of my volition but because you'll unman yourself, you'll make your life unbearable and you'll not want me near you. Then I'll go back to Tabriz and begin another life, sadly it's true, but that's what I've decided to do. I won't remind you of your promise to me before we were married, I don't want to humiliate you – but how rotten of you to forget; I forgive you only because I love you. Oh, God, men are so strange, so difficult to understand, please remind him of his oath at once!

'Erikki,' she murmured, 'let the past stay with the past. Please?' With her eyes she begged him as only a woman can beg.

But he avoided her look, devastated by his own stupidity and jealousy. Azadeh's right, he was shouting at himself. That's past. Azadeh told me about him honestly and I promised her freely that I could live with that and he did save her life. She's right, but even so I'm sure she loves him.

He looked down at her and into her eyes, a door slammed inside his head, he locked it and cast away the key. The old warmth pervaded him, cleansing him. 'You're right and I agree! You're right! I love you – and Finland for ever!' He lifted her off the ground and kissed her and she kissed him back, then held on to him as, more happy than he had ever been, he carried her effortlessly up the corridor. 'Do they have sauna in Istanbul, do you think he'll let us make a phone call, just one, do you think . . .'

But she was not listening. She was smiling to herself.